Folly Beach

Folly Beach

DOROTHEA BENTON FRANK

wm

WILLIAM MORROW
An Imprint of HarperCollins*Publishers*

FOLLY BEACH. Copyright © 2011 by Dorothea Benton Frank. All rights reserved. Printed in the United States of America. No part of this book may be used or reproduced in any manner whatsoever without written permission except in the case of brief quotations embodied in critical articles and reviews. For information, address HarperCollins Publishers, 195 Broadway, New York, NY 10007.

HarperCollins books may be purchased for educational, business, or sales promotional use. For information, please e-mail the Special Markets Department at SPsale@harpercollins.com.

A hardcover edition of this book was published in 2011 by William Morrow, an imprint of HarperCollins Publishers.

FIRST WILLIAM MORROW PAPERBACK EDITION PUBLISHED 2012.

Library of Congress Cataloging-in-Publication Data has been applied for.

ISBN 978-0-06-211173-9

17 18 19 OV/RRD 10 9 8 7

In memory of Dorothy Kuhns Heyward

DUSK

From *Carolina Chansons*

They tell me she is beautiful, my City,
That she is colorful and quaint, alone
Among the cities. But I, I who have known
Her tenderness, her courage, and her pity,
Have felt her forces mould me, mind and bone,
Life after life, up from her first beginning.
How can I think of her in wood and stone!
To others she has given of her beauty,
Her gardens, and her dim, old, faded ways,
Her laughter, and her happy, drifting hours,
Glad, spendthrift April, squandering her flowers,
The sharp, still wonder of her Autumn days;
Her chimes that shimmer from St. Michael's steeple
Across the deep maturity of June,
Like sunlight slanting over open water
Under a high, blue, listless afternoon.
But when the dusk is deep upon the harbor,

She finds *me* where her rivers meet and speak,

And while the constellations ride the silence

High overhead, her cheek is on *my* cheek.

I know her in the thrill behind the dark

When sleep brims all her silent thoroughfares.

She is the glamor in the quiet park

That kindles simple things like grass and trees.

Wistful and wanton as her sea-born airs,

Bringer of dim, rich, age-old memories.

Out on the gloom-deep water, when the nights

Are choked with fog, and perilous, and blind,

She is the faith that tends the calling lights.

Hers is the stifled voice of harbor bells

Muffled and broken by the mist and wind.

Hers are the eyes through which I look on life

And find it brave and splendid. And the stir

Of hidden music shaping all my songs,

And these my songs, my all, belong to her.

DuBose Heyward

CONTENTS

CHAPTER ONE

Folly Beach
A One-Woman Show with Images

By Cathryn Mahon Cooper

Setting: St. Philip's Cemetery in Charleston, South Carolina. Dorothy Kuhns Heyward rises from her grave and dusts herself off. She kisses her fingertips and touches the tombstone of DuBose Heyward, which is next to hers. She walks to center stage near the footlights and speaks.
Director's Note: Images to run on back wall scrim: photo of Folly Beach, the beach itself including the Morris Island Lighthouse, photo of Murray Boulevard with an enormous full moon, map of Ohio and Dorothy in evening dress, and DuBose in smoking jacket. Dorothy has a serious side but she's also very funny.

Act I
Scene I

Dorothy: I married an actual renaissance man. Yes, I really did! The story I have to tell you is about the deep and abiding love we shared. *Not* the carnal details, *please*, but some of its *other* aspects such as the sacrifices we were willing to make and the lengths to which we would go for each other. DuBose Heyward was the real and only true love of my life.

It was the summer of 1921 and when we met for the first time, we were both guests at the MacDowell Colony in New Hampshire. Mrs. MacDowell was a wonderful woman who had a very large estate but a very small family. But she *loved* the arts! So every summer she invited certain writers and artists of every genre and we packed our gear and took ourselves there to work. The minute I laid eyes on DuBose Heyward I knew he was going to be mine. We sized each other up and, without so much as a nod, we knew our feelings were mutual. When the summer had ended, he returned to Charleston and I returned to New York. We wrote to each other each week and sometimes more often and saw each other when we could. Finally, after our third summer together at Mac-Dowell we were married on September 23, 1923, at the Little Church Around the Corner in New York City.

DuBose returned to Charleston without me because my play *Nancy Ann* was about to open in New York. *That* set the Lowcountry jungle drums thumping like mad! *Where was his wife? And who was she anyway? From Ohio? She writes plays? A lady in the theater?* Well, I had to do the work I was being paid to do! But I knew enough about Charleston to know I'd better watch my step, so early on I adopted the *zippered lip* posture and took my lead from DuBose. It was his reputation we had to protect and he was so much smarter about those things than I was.

Oh! There is so much I want you to know. This was a crazy time in the world. The economy was going down and hemlines were going up. Women were bobbing their hair, throwing away their corsets, and kicking up their heels, doing the Charleston, especially in Charleston! And in the arts? In Charleston? Well, DuBose and his friends decided that big nasty misunderstanding with the Yankees was behind them and they had to look to the future. I mean, please! Charleston was spared a visit from Sherman but sentiments still ran so strong sixty years after the war ended? Honey, the way people whined and carried on, you'd think old Sherman barged into every lady's house on the Peninsula, broke all her china, stole her daughters, and punched her husband in the nose! Just ridiculous. I mean, people moaned and moaned about how much better things were before . . . wait, do you know the story about Oscar Wilde? No? Well then, listen to this. Oscar Wilde came to Charleston sometime around 1885, the exact year is a little fuzzy to me, but anyway, there's Oscar standing on the High Battery with a Charleston gentleman admiring the full moon. Oscar says, *My word, would you look at that extraordinary moon!* The Charleston gentleman says, *Ah, you should have seen it before the war!* So now you see, Charleston was reluctant to embrace the future if it meant deemphasizing the past one tiny iota. DuBose and his cohorts wanted to hold on to all the glories of the past but have their work reflect their observances of their present day *and* their hopes for the future.

God, I loved that man. We're not talking about moonlight and magnolias here. This is about the magic of a spectacular marriage and how it fueled our creative life and shaped our worldview.

There have been so many stories about DuBose and me and all of them are wrong. Not diabolically wrong, but just skewed at an off angle, enough to make our lives seem like something other than what they were. In public we were both extremely quiet, especially DuBose. In private we laughed about everything and argued loudly over every issue of the day. Well, maybe I was the one who provided the volume. The point is, very few people *really* knew us.

Maybe my words will be kind of a memoir of the Charleston Renaissance. I don't know. But someone has to paint the mood of the time and set the record straight. I guess that will have to be me, the spitfire from Ohio who was never afraid of the truth. Or passion. Not that DuBose was afraid of passion or of the truth. He was never a coward. It's just that his heart pumped the holy blood of old Charleston. Let me tell you this, old Charlestonians would just as soon be caught in their birthday suit walking down Murray Boulevard as reveal their hearts to outsiders. But in Canton, Ohio, we ladies were perhaps more inclined to gently speak our minds.

DuBose and I may not ever have earned a lot of money at one time, but ah well, such is a writer's lot in life. After he published *Porgy* with Doubleday in 1925, we had a few more cookies in our cookie jar and were able to acquire a little house in the wilds on Folly. We adored the island and every peculiarity about it. Yes, we did. In fact, the happiest days of my life all happened on Folly Beach. We were young then, our heads spinning with creativity, and we thought we had plenty, because we were rich in so many other ways. Who needed a telephone anyway?

And we had daily rituals that brought order and all the dignity of a Park Avenue parlor to our lives. For example, to celebrate civility, my darling DuBose and I enjoyed our own private happy hour every afternoon around dusk. Right before the sun turned deep red and began its slow descent into the horizon, we dressed for dinner. We both loved Hollywood glamour and sometimes referred to Folly Island as Follywood for the fun of it. And why not have a little glamour in our lives? No, I didn't put on a long satin frock and call for Jeeves to make highballs. Oh, no. Our life was substantially more modest! I simply re-applied my makeup and cologne, put on a fresh dress, and brushed my hair. DuBose slipped on his velvet smoking jacket and carefully slicked his hair back, so that in the rose-hued early evening he resembled a very dapper Fred Astaire, but younger and with more hair. And he always smelled like something delicious.

Fade to Darkness

CHAPTER TWO

At the Cemetery

Yea, though I walk through the valley of the shadow of death . . .

The minister's voice was a booming gothic drone. Pastor Edwin Anderson, our pastor with the movie-star looks, suffered from the unfortunate delusion that he was Richard Burton. He really did. Today of all days, it seemed he was brushing up to deliver the soliloquy from *Hamlet*. It was ridiculous. On any other occasion I would have been chewing on the insides of my cheeks until I tasted blood. I didn't dare look at my sister Patti or I'd surely blow my composure. What was the matter with that portion of my brain? Gallows humor? Wait! Did I really say *gallows humor*? Honey, that is the *last* term in the world I should use and that's for sure. But there it was. Some small twisted secret pocket of my mind, with no permission from me, plucked out the most insensitive detail of this somber and terrible event, made a joke of it, which would surely and extremely inappropriately reduce me to a snickering idiot if I didn't pay attention to myself. I cleared my throat, hoping it would send a signal to Pastor Anderson to bring it down a notch. He shot me a look and continued channeling Burton. God, he was unbelievably good-looking. Another inappropriate thought. It was true; I was verging on hysteria but who wouldn't?

The miserable weather just added icing to the unholy dramatic cake of a day. One minute, the skies above New Jersey were dumping snow and in the next, sleet fell like tiny ice picks. I was amazed that the governor had not closed the turnpike and the Garden State Parkway. Everything was a sheet of ice, the temperature around twenty. It was only by God's holy grace that we had all made it to the cemetery without flying off the highway and into a ditch. I was pretty sure the ditches were filled with mangled bodies.

There were probably only twenty of us huddled under the tent at the gravesite, standing, because the seats of the folding chairs were soaking-wet. We all attributed the sparse turnout to Mother Nature, but to tell you the truth I was in such a fog I barely knew what was going on around me. I could not have cared much less who showed up and who didn't. Over the last eighteen months, my life had become so isolated and my circle of friends had narrowed to almost no one. And now this.

We had skipped the traditional wake, deciding on a simple graveside service with the most accommodating pastor from our church. I didn't feel like talking to a lot of people, especially given the circumstances, and Addison was not particularly devout.

"Are you all right, Cate?"

Patti spoke in her normal tone for the hearing-impaired right over the minister, the sleet, the rain, and the wind. Considerations like when to say what and how loud did not occur to Patti. At all or ever. Sometimes that could be humorous, but other times it was unnerving. I was definitely startled by the pitch of her voice. Was I all right? Was I? No. I wasn't all right and we both knew it. Sisters can read each other's minds. I just looked at her. Answer this, Patti, I asked her telepathically, how could I *possibly* be all right? We were gathered in the most inclement conditions February in New Jersey could offer to bury Addison, my husband of way too many years.

"I'm okay," I lied, pushing aside my stupor and trying to gather my thoughts. I stepped forward and put my gloved hand on Addison's polished casket.

In the last two days, I had relived our entire twenty-six-year marriage, looking for clues for how Addison's zeal for life had deteriorated and how all the love we had shared over the years had completely and totally become unraveled. In the early days, we were *insane* over each other. I had never met a man like Addison. There I was, playing Cassie in a revival of *A Chorus Line,* when I caught his grin in the footlights. Sure, he was much older (twelve years) than I was, but he swept me right off my feet and then the stage forever, which, oddly enough, I never missed.

I was crazy about him. All I wanted to do was make him happy, and even now I believe that for a long time he had felt the same way. Our eyes were filled with each other and everything we did together seemed so perfect. A simple meal was a royal feast because we shared it. A country club waltz in a crowded room belonged only to us. He was ambitious, funny, charming, and so, so smart. The almost manic exuberance we felt was clear in every single photograph of us, and there were dozens of them from our early years all over our house. But as the children came along, demanding most of my time, he became consumed with business and slowly, slowly my diamond of a marriage began to lose its sparkle. I guess no honeymoon can last forever.

Oh Addison, I thought, how could you do it and *why* did you do it? Other men his age died from heart disease or cancer. But not my Addison. As he did most things, he leaped into projects full-strength and was a mad dog gnawing and growling until his battle was won. He leaped alright, but this time it was from the top of my piano with the extra-heavy-duty extension cord from our Christmas decorations tied around the rafters and his neck. I was the one who found him. I'd never get that vision of him out of my mind if I lived to be one hundred and ten years old.

I was white-hot furious with him for doing this to himself and to us. *Who's going to walk your daughter down the aisle, Addison?* I strummed my fingers on the top of the casket and began pulling flowers from the blanket of white roses until I had six or eight clenched in my fist. I just needed to pull something apart. I dropped them on the ground and began pounding the casket with my fist. That was when I felt the strong hand of Mark, Patti's husband, on my arm.

"Come on now, Cate. Come stand by me."

I backed away from the remains of my husband and let Mark put his arm around my shoulder. Mark was a great human being, even though he could be very cheap, which to my way of thinking was a really terrible and unattractive trait. Still, I considered myself lucky to have him as a brother-in-law, because he was the one who would step forward in a situation like this and take any potential problems in hand. Following his uncle's lead, my beautiful son Russ moved away from his contentious wife, Alice, and took my hand.

"It's gonna be okay, Mom. You'll see."

"I know," I said and thought I should be the one reassuring him.

But I *had* reassured him and Sara, my daughter. I had told them at least one hundred times in the last forty-eight hours that we would get through this together and everything would be all right. Talk about self-delusion? I didn't believe that any more than they did. Together was over. We would get through the *funeral* together. But then they would go back to their lives and resume them, maimed a bit, sad for a while, but they had lives and careers that waited for them. Well, to be honest, Russ had a satisfying job teaching and coaching high school basketball. But my daughter, Sara, did not. Sara was my soufflé, soft in the center but always in danger of falling if the temperature wasn't perfect. Even though we resembled each other—petite, dark-haired, blue-eyed—I was much stronger than she was. Still, she was on her own in California and reasonably solvent.

Anyway, at that moment, I had lost my rudder, because life without Addison wasn't a life I could simply pick up and navigate without missing a beat. You see, I lived in a world of *his* making, not mine. Everything, every single material thing we owned was a product of Addison's image of himself, how he thought he should live and how he wanted to be perceived by the outside world. The wine cellar, the cars, the art collection, the antiques—he had scoured auction houses and galleries, collecting and amassing that which was worthy of a financial czar. And the house? It was one of the largest homes in Alpine, located in the fourth most expensive zip code in America, roughly ten times the house that would have satisfied me but Addison wanted it all. He wanted just a mere glimpse of our home to make his investors, partners, and his enemies weak in the knees. And it did.

Every now and then I would moan a little with him in private, that I'd surely prefer a simpler life, one that (until I found Albertina, that is) was not so burdened with bickering staff who chipped your crystal, cleaned your silver with steel wool, and used *Shout!* on your vegetable-dyed antique rugs from Agra. Never mind the unending stream of workmen that came with the constant repairs and upkeep a large home required. Too often my days were defined by waiting for someone to show up to do something the right way, because Addison held me responsible for every last detail of our life outside of his business. Sometimes, no, a lot of the time, I felt more like a building superintendent than the beloved wife of a successful man. There were times—often, in fact—when I was merely the director and producer for the domestic theater of his life, and I knew it with certainty when he would rate my performance after a holiday or a dinner party for clients.

"The centerpieces looked cheap, Cate," he might say. Or, "The meat was overcooked. Shoe leather." Or, "Your staff didn't show well tonight, Cate. Service stunk. I thought you knew how important this dinner was to me."

It was never, "Gosh, honey, you went to so much trouble! I'm a lucky man! Thanks so much!"

He was so self-absorbed and pressured with work that days would pass without him saying anything particularly personal or pleasant to me, or without even making eye contact. I knew he was preoccupied because he was extremely worried about his investments, but still, his freezing-cold attitude chipped away at whatever affection I felt for him and I felt more and more detached from him. But I was grateful to God to have my children and I gave them everything there was in my heart. I had Patti. And Mark.

It didn't pay to moan about life in the gilded cage. Not a single member of the human race would have felt sorry for me for one second. Especially Addison. His familiar bark went like this: "Look, Cate. I work like an eff-ing *animal,* putting in *crazy* hours, dealing with more stress than the GD eff-ing president himself. So? When I come home I want to look around and believe, somehow believe, even if it's just for five minutes, that it was all worth the sacrifice! Why is that so eff-ing hard for you to understand?"

Nice, right? My neck got hot even then, remembering how terrible he made me feel. How low. How insignificant. The belittling, the judging, and then the terrible silences that followed.

Addison became possessed by the decadent spirits of his own desire. If he wanted to get in his Lamborghini and run it, he did. If he wanted to open a five-hundred-dollar bottle of wine and drink it with microwave popcorn, he did. Many afternoons I would find him downing an old Bordeaux while he watched the Golf Channel ad nauseam on our home theater screen that rivaled an IMAX. Once he paid to play with Tiger Woods to raise money for some charitable cause he could not have cared less about just so he could tell that story over and over as though he was Tiger's best friend. He stored a set of custom Majestic golf clubs in ten different locations from St. Andrews to Pebble Beach so he didn't have to say, "Gee, I wish I'd brought my clubs." He kept his G 550 at the ready, in case he wanted to fly to Vegas with a few of his partners or friends and hear Barry Manilow sing or watch Siegfried and Roy play with their big cats. Sick.

I hated all his toys because they represented just how horribly shallow he could be. We could've done so much good with all that money. If I wanted to support something like the library or the children's schools, he refused, saying he only wanted to give money to things that would thrill *him*. And he also never missed an opportunity to remind me that he earned the money, not me. He could and would do as he wanted.

He wanted, he wanted, he wanted . . . well, the wanting was at an end because the greedy, covetous, acquisitive son of a bitch was dead. Did he run around? Probably, but I never really knew for sure. That didn't mean I didn't have some very real suspicions.

In the last few years, it came to a point where Addison barely resembled the wonderful extraordinary man I had married. How, I wondered, had I managed all those years to keep my mountain of frustrations and deep disappointments out of the conversation with my children? It was either a miraculous accomplishment of mine or massive denial on their part that they merely viewed him as a well-meaning, very distracted man who was sometimes a difficult and demanding grump. I mean, they had their criticisms of him. When Russ was a teenager, he thought he worked way too much and would shrug his shoulders in disappointment when his father missed a basketball game. Russ was the captain of his team and had gone to the College of Charleston on a full ride, which was a point of pride for him to say he didn't owe that part of his education to his father. And Sara? She didn't fare as well. Sara suffered horribly from Addison's lack of attention and spent her high school years dating the wrong boys, getting her heart broken all the time. College had not been a lot better for her socially and so she turned to acting in theater, where she could express herself.

But when they heard the news about their father's death, they both swore that they adored him and they were honestly devastated to learn that he was dead.

The only person who knew the truth about how I really felt about my marriage was Patti, and she would never betray my confidence.

Never in a million years. We both figured we may as well bury the old bastard on a high note.

In some bizarre way, I still cared about Addison and always would. He had given me two wonderful children, a luxurious life, and a long list of things for which I would always be in his debt. After all, we had traveled the world as a family, the children had been sent to good schools, and he gave them incredible opportunities to learn, see, go, and do. If I had ever really felt our lifestyle was that unacceptably vulgar or that his cruelty was too much, could I have left? Of course I could have but we were a family, with all the good and bad, and I wasn't tearing my family apart over something so stupid as Addison's conspicuous consumption or because he became more unsatisfied with his entire personal life when the markets declined. It would only have made a bad situation worse. And living with Addison was generally a tolerable situation. Not a joyous one, but tolerable. But let me tell you, markets may rebound but chasing great wealth is a delusional trap.

Two years ago, Patti and Mark began to notice a marked difference in Addison, too, as he slid even further into a new hell. Mark would offer to talk to him all the time but I knew that would probably complicate things so we just held our breath and hoped that whatever problems he was dealing with would be resolved and the old Addison would soon reappear. He never did. And besides, Addison held Mark at a polite arm's length, because in his mind, he had no peer. He had liked Mark well enough but he probably believed his issues with declining global markets, international currencies, and what other troubles a Jedi like him had to endure and solve were far too complicated for someone like Mark, a mere podiatrist, to comprehend.

It was after Russ married Alice and Sara moved to Los Angeles that the most dangerous aspects of Addison's transformation began to materialize. He stopped sleeping regular hours and his normal voracious appetite seemed to disappear. He lost a staggering amount of weight. And he was frequently out of the house until late at night. And the outbursts began. I heard him raging for hours on the telephone with his partners. Like a lot of men, Addison didn't hesitate to raise his voice if he felt like it, especially in business, but this rage was something different, frightening. It was as though he had developed some kind of an evil personality disorder. I began to suspect he was using cocaine or something like cocaine. He had to have been. Or some kind of pills? But when he left for the office and I searched his office at home, his bathroom, and his drawers, I could find nothing. I looked under the mattress, in the toes of his shoes, and behind the books in his study. I read the labels of everything in his medicine cabinet and looked them up on the Internet. Not a speck of anything untoward. If he was abusing drugs, I couldn't prove it.

So what then was the source? I had seen him pitch tirades before but they had always blown over pretty quickly. Not lately. This anger was smoldering, always right under the surface, ready to explode. Anger became his new way of dealing with his life. Sure the economy was terrible, but the recession couldn't last forever, could it? I worried deeply and constantly. Sure he had always had a quick temper but never like this. I was afraid he was going to have a stroke or a heart attack.

As fate would have it, about a year ago, he became fanatical about his health, complaining of every ailment in the Merck manual. Good, I thought, now he'll get some help. And he did. Not a week went by that he didn't visit a doctor of one sort or another to medicate everything from his ears (tinnitus) to his big toe on his right foot (gout). He swore he'd clean up his diet but Addison following any of these doctors' orders didn't last long. The gastrointestinal specialist told him to give up lunchtime martinis and hard liquor of every kind, that his liver and esophagus were turning on him. For a short period he was sober but then I heard him say to someone laughingly that he didn't give a rip—not exactly the language he used—that he would send someone over to a Chinese prison and just buy a liver from some coolie on death row if he needed it. He thought it was a riot to look upon the horrified faces of his politically correct listeners. He bellowed with laughter, recounting his outrageous conversation with his doctor. I was mortified over and over again by his behavior and even his partners' wives, some of the most calcified, impervious women on earth, even *they* began to regard me with sympathy. I was so glad our children were out of the house by then so they didn't have to witness their father's slide into madness.

It just went on and on. His pulmonary physician told him he had to give up cigars, that his blood pressure was dangerously high, and I wouldn't even want to tell you what he said about that. Addison's humidors were bulging with imported Cohibas that he fully intended to smoke. Needless to say, his cholesterol was out of control, too, just like every other aspect of his life. Addison continued to drink what he wanted, eat what he wanted, and to smoke whenever the mood struck. No one could make Addison listen. No one could tell him what to do. In the end, still in charge, he died on a day of his own choosing. Ironically, all of these terrible habits had not killed him. Addison had the final word. He always did. If he had listened to his doctors' advice, maybe he could have dealt with his stress in a healthy way and he'd still be alive.

I looked around at the small crowd of people, shivering from the cold. Suddenly, it seemed that their jaws were tight and their faces unsympathetic. Was I imagining this? No. If that's how they felt, why had they come?

Amen.

The service was abruptly over, Pastor Anderson stepped over and shook my hand, and everyone stared at me. I had my arm around Sara then. My poor daughter had wept an ocean of tears. *Look what you've done, Addison. Look what you've done.* I just wanted to scream. I invited Pastor Anderson back to the house but he begged off. The weather, he said. I knew he was rushing back to that hot young thing he had married recently. Judi was her name and there wasn't a woman in our church who didn't want to be her. I thanked him for everything and thought, Gosh, everyone has a purpose in their life except me.

As Pastor Anderson turned and walked away, Addison's blond twenty-two-year-old secretary was the first one to approach us.

"Lauren, thank you for coming," I said. "You've met our daughter, Sara?"

"Yeah. I can't believe he's dead, and what he did, you know? I mean, he was so great back when we were together . . ."

"When who was together?" I said.

"Uh, *you* know," Lauren said and then paused, her eyes growing wide. "You mean, you *didn't* know?"

"Know what?" I said, the sordid truth dawning.

"Jesus, Mrs. Cooper, don't look at me like that! I thought everybody in New Jersey knew it! It was all over Twitter last year! He hooked up with like every girl who ever worked in the office!"

"What?" I felt all the air rush out of my chest and I thought I was going to faint. Did she mean that Addison had sex with all of them? Little Lauren read my mind.

"Like we had a choice? If Addison Cooper wanted something, he got it and you know it! A bunch of us were gonna file suit for sexual harassment but now that he's gone . . ."

"Mom!" Sara said. "Do something!"

"Lauren?" I was at a loss for words. "I think it's time for you to leave. Now." It was all I knew to say. If I had been in possession of my mind, I might have given her the back of my hand right across her face. Who was this horrible young woman? The Lauren I had known over the phone was polite and kind. True or not, how mean and unforgivably rude to say such a thing at Addison's funeral.

I turned away from her and nearly knocked down Shirley Hackett, the wife of Addison's most senior partner.

"I just wanted to say that, well, I feel for you, Cate."

"Thanks, Shirley. This was such a terrible shock."

"I'm sure. Between you and me, there are probably more shocks to come."

"What do you mean? And where's Alan?"

"Humph. Cate? I mean this in the nicest possible way, but if Addison had not died, Alan would've killed him. I came out of respect for you and the children but believe me, there's no love lost with Alan."

"Why? What in the world are you talking about? We've been friends for years!"

Shirley stood there and stared at me for what seemed like an eternity until finally she spoke again.

"We're broke, Cate. Addison lost all our money and most of the firm's clients. It's going down the tubes. Chapter Eleven."

"You've got to be wrong. You're exaggerating."

"Oh, my God," Sara said.

"No, I'm not. Remember that gorgeous house we had in Upper Saddle River? Well, now instead of taking a Citation X to San Francisco for dinner I'm driving a used Kia. I'm shopping at the Pathmark and cooking ramen in a studio apartment in Tenafly."

"What on *earth* are you talking about? When did all this happen?"

"Am I to believe that you don't know *anything* about this?"

"Absolutely! I mean, I heard Addison wasn't himself for the last year or so, and I knew things weren't great at the firm but I had no idea!"

"Well, then, darling? You'd better brace yourself."

She couldn't have been more like the Oracle of Delphi if she'd shown up in robes and looked into a pool of water. As I turned to see who was tapping me on the shoulder, I got another slap in the face from my new reality.

"You're Ms. Cooper, right?"

"Yes. Did you know my husband?"

"I sure did but believe me, I didn't know he had a wife. Good thing I read the obituaries." She reached in her purse and pulled out a small album of photographs. "Have a look."

I flipped through them and there was Addison, with the woman before me and a baby boy of about two years old. The boy was the spitting image of Addison.

"Mom! What is this?" Sara said. "I'm gonna throw up!"

"Oh, my God," I said. My head began to spin. How could all of this be happening?

"So, what I'm wondering is who has the mortgage on my condo? And who has the lease on my BMW? I mean, I'm sure he provided for us in his will . . ."

Sara, who had stood by completely dumbfounded, doubled over and began gagging. That was the last thing I remembered before the ground came up to get me.

CHAPTER THREE

Setting: The Porgy House downstairs drawing room. There is a bar cart, a penguin cocktail shaker, cocktail glasses, assorted liquors, and an ice bucket. In the corner stands an upright piano made by Cunningham Piano Co. and two comfortable armchairs.

Director's Note: When DuBose speaks, a head shot of him should cover the downstage scrim and a man's voice is heard from offstage. Use a shot of the downstairs drawing room. Dorothy is now wearing a pretty silk dress.

Act I
Scene 2

Dorothy: At five in the afternoon, in perfect synchronicity, we would meet in the downstairs drawing room. Out came our silver-toned penguin martini shaker and our cut-glass ice bucket. And, as this was our greatest daily indulgence in the name of pleasure (at least one that may be spoken of in polite company), the time was reserved for reminiscing and grandiose daydreams. Dreams didn't cost you a dime and what would life be without them?

The year was 1934 or 1935. It had been about ten years since DuBose left his insurance business and yes, I was the one who made him give it up. Our Jenifer was just a little girl then, I know that much. It doesn't matter which year but I remember clearly it was one particularly bone-chilling February evening. Lord! It got cold on that beach! We were downstairs and DuBose was shaking the penguin like mad. He was mixing up Albert Farmer's special recipe for mint juleps to cheer me up. I was feeling a little out of sorts. (Don't worry; the recipe is in the back of your program.)

Where was I? Oh, yes. Mint juleps coming up! To be completely honest, I knew a good drink would also ease the pain of his arthritis. His arthritis was so terrible and had twisted the bones of his hands so badly that on the worst days they resembled claws. Please don't say I told you—I wouldn't offend DuBose for the world! To be honest, neither of us was blessed with the best of health but we were so attuned to each other that we practically felt each other's aches and that seemed to help us endure.

I was usually a chipper soul, sometimes a little too chatty but almost always good-natured. But not that night. The combination of freezing damp weather and the dreary gloom of the fog, which blanketed the island? Well, it was as though the whole mess had leaked through the rattling old window frames and crept in under the uneven doorjambs like tear gas. I felt like indulging in a good cry. I sat at the piano and pushed back the cover over the keyboard.

DuBose knew I was really in the dumps when I sat down to play the piano. He began to shake the penguin in earnest. Although I had studied piano for years, I would surely never solo at Carnegie Hall. The music just wouldn't come out of my fingers the way I heard it in my head! And let's face it, I knew that the sound of me plunking out a tune was downright depressing to *everyone* within earshot. The neighborhood cats and dogs literally howled along with my music, which should tell you a lot.

I watched as DuBose hurried to pour two teaspoons of brandy on top of Farmer's concoction that was, frankly, as close to a regulation julep as a monkey was to a snake. He dropped in a paper straw, which was a good idea, and handed me the frosty glass.

We touched the sides of our glasses, and, as always, muttered *cheers* and took simultaneous sips.

"Golly, that's swell, DuBose. Thank you." The man sure had a way with a cocktail.

"You're welcome. Albert says we should repeat this exercise as often as our system demands."

"Really? Not if you want your dinner tonight." My husband was sure full of beans that night.

"Right you are." DuBose looked into my eyes and smiled warmly. "Darling? Do you remember the days when we used to live in Mark Twain's old house on Fifth and Twelfth in New York?"

"Of course I do. Why?"

"Do you think that someday, someone will live here and say that this is *our* old house? I mean, will they marvel to be *here*? Where *we* once were? With Gershwin? Writing grand music and having cocktails?"

He was too much! I burst into giggles then and now, just remembering. I gave him the devil, too. But good!

"Edwin DuBose Heyward! Of all the ridiculously arrogant things to suggest! Are you insane? In this modest little cottage? DuBose! Who cares about us? It's *Gershwin* they'll remember."

It was the awful truth. George Gershwin would even be carved on our tombstones. But it had been *nine years* since he first contacted DuBose about turning *Porgy* into an opera. Gershwin stayed up all night and read the book. Woo hoo! Then he wrote DuBose to see if the operatic rights were free. They were, and for the next *nine years* we waited for Gershwin to fit us into his busy schedule! We'd already had the book *Porgy* staged as a play in 1927! (It didn't make a fortune but it did make money and it got fabulous reviews and ran for 367 performances!)

"Yes, I imagine so but . . ."

"Any man who goes around saying things like *I write the greatest music in America* won't be forgotten so easily. I've never known someone in all my days with such ridiculous self-assurance." He actually said that. Gershwin was an arrogant windbag. Sorry, but there it is.

But DuBose, never one to criticize, came to Gershwin's defense.

"Now, now, little Dorothy. Isn't that a trifle harsh? We both know that he actually *does* write the greatest music in America. We should speak of our benefactor with kindness."

"Benefactor indeed. He's been waltzing us around the barn forever, driving us to the point of near poverty. I'm tired of soup! And, oh, now! *Now* he wants to write the music for *Porgy*? When the wolf is practically at our door? He's the Great Menace, DuBose."

"Ah! My dearest little Dorothy, drink up. History will decide that question, will it not?"

"I think that greatly depends on who writes the history, DuBose. I really do. I just hope the right person writes our history."

"May I freshen up your drink?"

I remember that I took a deep breath to calm myself. Ply me with bourbon, I thought. He was right. History would decide. But Gershwin had made us wait for so long! If we didn't poke and prod him into getting on with the musical score for *Porgy and Bess*, we'd be living on beans and pump water soon. I would broach the subject so many times until DuBose got after him, but on that night I didn't.

I simply said, "By all means. Thank you, DuBose, I feel better already. You are such a dear heart and truly, you are such a gentleman."

"And you, little Dorothy, you are my sun, my moon, and my stars!"

"And you are mine," I said and meant it.

In fact, I loved DuBose with a passion I have never felt before in my entire life. I had become the living embodiment of the woman who went whither he went, forsaking all, tolerating not just Gershwin but the clucking suspicions of the long-tongued matrons of Charleston, who said I would never be quite the ideal wife for this handsome descendant of South Carolina's, no, *America's* true aristocrats. *But!* they said, *she was so tiny and adorable and he was a diminutive and adorable man as well and oh my heavens, they could almost pass for twins!*

Well, tut tut tut. I was smart enough to recognize that sort of talk for what it was—silly. I aspired to my own goals and, to be fair, in those days Charleston's staid gentry *did* embrace their artists (to the extent they were ever overtly enthusiastic about anything), even if they did not and never would consider them to be peers. All their starch held little appeal for me in the first place. I never said one word about it, but they knew I didn't want to be one of them. My attitude rendered me *interesting. A curiosity.*

Don't forget, DuBose and I weren't the only writers in town. We shared the scene with other Lowcountry writers of aristocratic origins— Julia Peterkin and Josephine Pinckney in particular. They had broken rank with the ruling class and lived to tell the tales. And to write them, too. Didn't Julia Peterkin win a Pulitzer for *Scarlet Sister Mary*? And Jo Pinckney, whose great-great-great-grandfather signed the Declaration of Independence with DuBose's, broke convention by entertaining artists who visited Charleston from all over the country. In her home and *without* what some would have considered sufficient chaperone. Oh ho!

We were different, DuBose and I, from many other writers of the day. I much preferred the company of other forward-thinking writers and artists, which was why I liked Jo Pinckney so much. And it was that very frame of mind that led Jo and DuBose to get together with some others and form the Poetry Society of South Carolina way back in 1920. Now a poetry society may sound stuffy and boring to you but let me assure you, the Poetry Society brought every wild hare of the day to Charleston and we had a ball with them all!

But back to Mr. Gershwin. I was insightful enough to recognize George Gershwin for all he was—a monstrously talented man with a very healthy ego, who could or might, as though he was a big dry sponge, absorb all the credit for *Porgy and Bess* just by being so unforgivably comfortable in the glare of the limelight. The theatrical world shoveled critical praise at his feet, and he took bow after swooping bow. I didn't blame him for that but I knew doing business with someone as successful as Gershwin could be a slippery slope. DuBose and I might be swallowed up into history and forgotten altogether.

I didn't mind so much if the world didn't give me credit as the playwright for *Porgy*. In those days it was still downright unthinkable that a woman from elsewhere, meaning anywhere north or west of the Lowcountry, could possibly understand the complicated relationships, the unusual customs, the issues of faith, the Creole language, and the deep passions of the Gullah people. But I did. Yes, by golly, I surely did. And I swore I would live out my days working for the credit that was due, if not for myself, for my husband. We had bills to pay like everyone else. I remember thinking, *Look out George Gershwin, I've got my eye on you. And please, let's get this show on the road!*

Fade to Darkness

CHAPTER FOUR

Needs a Plan

The windshield wipers scraped and strummed across the glass in an irregular rhythm, back and forth, back and forth. It was driving me crazy. I barely remember the trip back to the funeral parlor to pick up our car, or the ride back to my house, but I would be haunted by the sound of windshield wipers shaving away ice for the rest of my life. My brother-in-law, sweet Mark, just herded us like a small flock of weary sheep from the limo to our SUV. He and Patti did the driving from that point on. What I do remember is that we were nearly silent for the duration. What were my children thinking? First, we were numb with shock and grief and now we were numb with another load of shock. Affairs left and right? A mistress with a condo? A baby? What other secrets did Addison have? What had Shirley Hackett meant? What else on God's green earth could possibly happen? All I wanted to do was go home and have this day push itself into the past.

I was never so happy to have an enclosed garage as I was that horrible day. Little blessings. Little blessings. What a dreadful, horrible day it had been. Surreal. The garage doors tumbled down behind us and clunked with a kind of finality not unlike a guillotine. The underside of the cars were encrusted with salt and sand from the roads. I don't know why I thought about that except it had to be from habit. If Addison ever saw anything like that, he would have a panic attack and rush his cars to the drive-through brushless car wash to rinse the offending mess all off to the last spec of grit. His precious vehicles could not be exposed to corrosion. I looked at the wet tire marks on the floor of the garage and the thick mud, sprayed and spattered all along the fenders, and thought, screw it. Let them all rot and see if I care.

I went up the few steps to the door and stepped into the mudroom and then into the kitchen. Suddenly, I felt sweaty and achy. My coat was too hot, my feet ached from the damp cold, and I was feeling thoroughly miserable. All I wanted to do was lie down and sleep for a thousand years.

My old friend, Richard Millman, who owned a catering company called Contemporary Foods, was waiting. He had promised to deliver sustenance and, true to his word, he was there himself with a couple of his longtime waiters. Immediately, he helped me with my muddy coat, folded it over his arm, and then he hugged me. It was out of character for Richard to be that familiar, even though we knew each other well. We had planned dozens of parties and special events together over the years for one organization or another and had suffered plenty of disasters together. One May years ago, the night before a benefit for the New Jersey Symphony, a storm came up carrying unpredicted, uninvited, and very unwelcome sixty-miles-per-hour winds that blew down the tent we had set up for 480 people. Chairs were broken, sound equipment destroyed, racks and racks of glasses smashed to smithereens . . . He just called me and said with all the serenity of the Buddha, "We have a little issue with the tent, Cate. You got a minute?"

Richard was always the consummate pro, completely calm and collected. But today was not like any other day, and I could sense from the shaky and hesitant sound of his voice that he was feeling unusually emotional. Natural disasters were one thing, death was bad enough, but suicide? Suicide destabilized everyone in ways that are difficult to understand, because for all the survivors, it is often impossible to comprehend why someone would do something so rash, so final, for *any* reason whatsoever. And was any part of their decision to end their life your fault?

"God, Cate, I'm so sorry. If there's anything I can do . . ."

"Thanks, Richard. I'm so glad you're here. Especially in this terrible weather, I had thought that maybe you wouldn't be able . . ."

"A blizzard couldn't stop me from coming." He shook my son's hand, *sorry, Russ,* and then took my daughter's hand in his and when he looked at her wretched face, he added, "Oh, Sara, I'm so sorry." This was a man who clearly knew heartbreak, something about him that I had never before considered. I wondered what had happened in his life and then I thought that he might just have been born with empathy. Empathy was often an underrated quality—especially by the kinds of sharks with whom Addison did business. They thought empathy made you soft and soft made you less commercial and less commercial made you a big fat stupid loser with a capital L. Nice.

"Thanks, Mr. Millman," she said, slipping off her coat with Mark's help.

"There are a few visitors in the living room," Richard said and quickly gathered all our wet coats. He then excused himself to hang them up somewhere to dry.

"He's such a sweetheart," Patti said. "Come on, Mark."

Patti and Mark went in to see who was there.

"Oh, Mrs. Cooper! I'm feeling so terrible. I can't imagine how you're coping with all this. Are you all right? Can I make you a cup of tea?"

It was Albertina, my housekeeper/friend/confidante/savior of the last five years. To my surprise, she was wearing a dark, wine-colored, wool knitted dress, heels, and makeup, instead of her usual gray cotton shirtwaist dress and white apron. I had never seen her wear lipstick, and I was taken by how very pretty she was. And young. Or maybe it was that on that day I felt particularly ancient.

"Oh, Albertina, thanks but I'm all right, I guess. I'm so glad you're here," I said and gave her a hug, the kind of hug that girls give each other to demonstrate camaraderie and compassion.

"And just where else would I be at a time like this? I put my things in the bedroom on the third floor and I plan to stay the night. My sister is with my kids. She sends her condolences and she made you a flan."

"She did? Gosh, thanks. That's so nice. Well, I'm glad you brought your things. I sure don't want you on the road in this weather."

"No. The roads are too slippery. Too slippery for my old car anyway."

"Yes," I said and for some reason I felt like weeping all over again. Did my Albertina, the woman who changed my sheets and did my laundry, the woman who sat with me in the kitchen so often and listened while I worried about my children and their futures, the woman who knew almost every intimate detail of my household, did she know the truth about Addison and his many indiscretions? But I didn't ask her to tell me what she knew and I knew then that for all the rugged terrain we had traveled in the past, this was one topic I would never discuss. Dignity had to be restored between us. It was enough that when she heard my hysterical screaming, she burst through the door of the family room and saw Addison's lifeless body hanging there as well. She started yelling in Portuguese and literally almost dragged me away and into the kitchen where she called 911. She also called a piano repair company to come right away and collect my old piano to be completely cleaned and sanitized as Addison had left behind some, well, bodily fluids in the lower register of ivory and ebony keys along with a note that said, "I'm sorry."

Instead of offering her my big SUV for the night, I just said, "Absolutely. Please stay." I was thinking, *We've had enough tragedy. Please don't take a risk.*

She nodded and said something about going to make herself useful by checking the fireplaces, to see if they were still burning, to add a log if it was needed, to throw some more salt on the walkway, and to check the powder room for hand towels, to be sure any arriving guests didn't track that salt into my rugs. It was unusual for Albertina to babble to me about her intentions, but it made me think she must have been very rattled by the whole catastrophe. I couldn't even remember if she had been at the cemetery, but assumed then that she had to have been, because of the way she was dressed. I wasn't thinking straight. Obviously.

My fingertips were numb and I rubbed my hands together to get the blood circulating and searched Russ and Sara's faces. And Alice's.

"Okay, are we ready to see who's here?"

"I just want to get this nightmare over with," Sara said.

"Understandable," I said and took a deep breath. "Me too."

"It's much *healthier* to let yourself grieve," said Alice, my shrink daughter-in-law, who is the world's authority on what there is to know about any kind of emotional malady and what to do to fix it. "Just let it all *go!*"

I heard Sara groan. "And just what makes you think we're *not* grieving?" Sara said, ready to take her on. Sara kept her jalapeño-tempered inner pit bull on a short leash, but when it came to Alice, she showed some tooth.

"All right, girls," I said. "That's enough. Let's go see our guests."

"Look, *excuse* me but this is my area of expertise and as a *professional* . . ."

"Alice? *Stop,* okay?" Russ said and Alice's furious mouth slammed shut but her face was in flames. She squinted with her unfortunately beady eyes in my son's direction and I thought it would not bother me a bit to reach over and give the sanctimonious inside of her upper arm a good and solid twisting pinch. I took a deep breath instead. After all, who was I to have an opinion about whom my son should love and marry? I only carried him for nine long months, brought him into this world after twenty hours of horrific labor, and took care of his every single solitary need for more than twenty years. What did I know?

Finally, we walked out together, swinging the door that led to the long butler's pantry, across the dining room and across our large foyer, our heels clicking like the tiny hammers of a silversmith plinking against the cream-colored marble. The long distance from the kitchen to the living room was not lost on me. All those shelves stacked with dishes, goblets, serving pieces, vases, and every kind of serving accessory down to six different sets of knife rests and forty-eight old Sheffield fish forks and knives, all made of silver with mother-of-pearl handles. Forty-eight. When was the last time I'd had forty-eight people over for fish? I could not remember that we ever had. Suddenly I wondered how long I would stay in that house, because all at once the excess seemed completely ludicrous. I was a widow now. A widow who had just buried her husband today and had no idea what to do tomorrow. Becoming a widow had never occurred to me. But that simpler life had. I had a lot of thinking to do but not then. For the next few hours, I would play hostess to whomever braved the elements to stop over and offer their sympathy. And then I would plan.

The eight or ten people in the living room were old high school friends of Russ and Sara. Naturally, they offered their polite condolences to me and to all of us. I made all the small talk I could and then drifted into the dining room alone. I noticed that the rye bread on the turkey sandwiches was beginning to curl on the edges. Going stale, hard crust, inedible . . . like so many things. Everything had an end, unpredictable maybe, but certain.

Where were Addison's colleagues? The only other people who rang the bell and stayed for a while were Addison and Mark's tennis partners, Mel his lawyer, and Dallas his accountant. I should have asked them what was going on with Addison's finances and if there was a will, but I couldn't bring myself to do it. No, that was business for another day. It was remarkable enough that I was still standing.

No one else came, no one from the neighborhood, not Joanne who did my hair or the women who sold me my clothes at Neiman Marcus. Where was my landscaper, my plumber, my electrician, or the guy who ordered all our wine for us? Maybe they didn't get the news. Maybe their bills never got paid? Maybe it was the weather?

It was almost four o'clock in the afternoon, the skies were growing darker by the minute and the weather was deteriorating still further. The wind howled around the house, the trees bending in fury. I was still standing in the dining room and heard the door close again. The house seemed quiet and I thought, well, the last visitor has left.

Patti came and stood by the table, inspecting the food.

"Look at all this stuff," she said.

"Yeah," I said. "What a waste." But then *waste* was the name of the game in Addison Land.

"I couldn't eat a thing. Not a thing! Well, maybe a bite. You want me to fix you a plate?"

"No thanks. I don't think I can swallow food right now."

"Gotcha. Well, how about a glass of wine?"

"No. I don't think . . . wait a minute. You know what? I will definitely have a glass of wine if you'll have one with me."

"You got it, sister!" Patti lifted the bottle from the cooler and wrinkled her nose. "Party wine. This might be the time to crack open some of Addison's Chateau Wawawa, instead of this swill. What do you think?"

"You're right but I don't feel like going down to that musty cellar and digging around."

"Then swill it is. Ice will improve it." She filled about a third of a goblet and handed it to me. Then she poured some for herself and held up the glass to toast. "What shall we drink to? Old Addison?"

"Sure, why not? The gates of hell are open today. Hope you had a nice trip!"

Patti giggled and told me I was horrible. We clinked the bowls of our glasses and I said, "Oh, fine. Here's to you, Addison Cooper, wherever you are, long may you wave!"

"Yep. Long may you wave—whatever that means. Let's call the kids. All this food is just sitting here. It's a *sin*. Russ? Sara?"

"Don't forget Alice."

"Like anyone could? Humph. Alice?"

"Don't talk to me about sin today. Shirley Hackett was probably right. It's a good thing he's gone or *I* might have helped her husband plot Addison's demise myself."

I picked up a small roll and examined its contents—smoked salmon with chive cream cheese. Platters of beautiful sandwiches—lobster salad on croissants, turkey on a combination of pumpernickel and rye bread, Black Forest ham and brie on sourdough, and others I had yet to discover—were placed on one side of the table and platters of bite-size pastries on the other. The coffee samovar stood on the far end with cups, saucers, cream, and sugar, and the tea service was on the other. Almost all of it was untouched.

"And no jury in the world would convict you either. Where are the kids? Russ!"

"I'm right here, Aunt Patti."

"Get something to eat, sweetheart," I said. "This is dinner."

"Yeah, sure," Russ said. "Gotta wonder what my little half-brother is eating tonight, right?"

Although Russ was usually my quiet child, it never meant the wheels of his clock weren't turning. The woman with those baby pictures had clearly upset him.

"You listen to me right now. There's no proof of anything," I said. "That child could be the mailman's for all we know."

"Your mother's right," Alice said and I smiled the incredulous smile of the mother-in-law who would be happy with only the merest crumb, the tiniest bit of support, and then is so very pleasantly surprised when the daughter-in-law throws her a whole baguette. "Won't you ask for DNA tests? I mean, she might be a complete fraud. I've heard of people like that, you know, showing up at weddings and funerals and making claims?"

I almost liked her then.

Mark, who was standing by taking large bites of a lobster salad sandwich, said, "Alice might be right but I think we ought to wait for her to rattle *our* cage. In the meanwhile, I asked Mel if there was a wills and estate guy in his firm."

Alice beamed with pride, vindicated for a brief moment from her unchallenged position as the family's royal pain in the ass.

"He's with Smythe and Lincoln," Patti said. "They probably have a *hundred* people who can take care of this."

I knew Smythe and Lincoln. They were an old, white-shoe law firm with a pristine reputation that dated back to the Revolution, one of the few left in the world you might actually trust to represent you with dignity and integrity. However, I also knew their historic dignity and integrity would probably cost four hundred dollars an hour. Or more. Ah, lawyers. Everyone knows the minute lawyers get involved, they turn their meters on like a taxi on a wild goose chase and that having a paralegal merely Xerox a document and send it across the street could cost you an outrageous amount of money. Before you know it, your wallet was hemorrhaging and you could have bought ocean-front property in Costa Rica for what it would cost to probate a will. I always exercised caution when I called a lawyer.

"Yeah, well, that sounds like a good plan to me," I said. "If I hear from her . . . what was her name?"

"I don't even remember," Mark said. "Did she say . . . ?"

"Jezzy LaBelle," Patti said over Mark.

"She never said her name," Sara said. "I was standing right there. All she did was flash the pictures of her bouncing little bastard and then Mom hit the dirt."

"Nice way to phrase it," Alice said, with her mouth twisted in disapproval.

"Who asked your opinion?" Sara said. "Do you have to have an opinion about everything?"

Alice shrugged her shoulders and looked away.

The doorbell rang and Albertina, who had been picking up glasses in the living room, hurried across the foyer to answer it. I put my arm around Sara to give her a little maternal support. My tiny Sara, dark-haired and moody, had never found her groove with her blond, lanky sister-in-law. Simply stated, the problems between Sara and Alice were that Alice had a boatload of advanced degrees, had stolen her precious brother, and had doomed him to a lifetime of prescribed boredom. Sara, who had a degree in musical theater from Northwestern and was a glamour puss if I ever saw one, felt inferior to Alice, which was completely ridiculous. I kept telling Sara that one day she would have a leading role in a film or on Broadway and she would show them all. So far, she had been in a television commercial for a feminine hygiene product and another one for garbage bags. But before I could pull her to the side, I looked up to see the county sheriff standing in the vaulted anteroom between the Corinthian columns that led from the entrance hall to my dining room. Something was wrong.

"Can I help you?" I didn't know if I was supposed to call him officer or sheriff or what. I mean, it wasn't like I welcomed the law into my home every day of the week.

"Are you Mrs. Cooper?"

"Why, yes. Is something wrong?" A rhetorical question if ever there was one.

"Ma'am, I understand from your housekeeper here that your husband's funeral was this afternoon and I know this probably seems like terrible timing, but I'm here to serve you with papers. The bank is foreclosing on your house for nonpayment of the mortgage."

"What?"

"Yes, ma'am. You are almost a year in arrears. And there's three big trucks outside from the D&D Building in New York? Your decorator sent them. Nonpayment of bills. Seems they want all your furniture, too. Except your mattresses—the bedbug thing, you know. And basically they're gonna take anything else they might be able to sell at auction to recoup their losses. Except for the chandeliers and the appliances. An electrician's coming tomorrow for that stuff."

"What are you saying?"

"Except your clothes. You can keep your clothes and linens, too. Did I mention that?"

"No."

"I'm real sorry about this. You've got forty-eight hours left to vacate the premises yourself."

"Forty-eight hours? Are you *serious*? Mark? He can't be serious, right? There must be some *mistake*! This is a horrible mistake!"

Mark took the papers from the sheriff and started looking them over.

"Son of a bitch," he said, "apparently this is your third notice. Addison must have known. He must have known about *all* of this!"

"He did know," Dallas, Addison's accountant, said. "I've been trying to hold them off for a while. I mean, I told them . . ."

We all stopped and stared at Dallas. I always thought he was a lightweight, now I knew why.

"Which is why he left first," Patti said. "Asshole. He might have said something besides *I'm sorry*."

"Why didn't Addison *tell* me?"

"Because he was a coward?" Patti said.

Mark said, "Officer, have a heart here. There has to be some way to do this another day, given the circumstances and the weather . . . ?"

"Believe me, sir, I'm not happy about this, either. I'm really sorry, I mean, the lady here just lost her husband and all. Makes me feel like a monster."

"You sort of are," Alice said.

"Shut up, Alice," Russ said.

"Oh, my God," I said and sank into a chair. "Oh my God! I'm broke! I'm ruined!"

"No, you're not," Patti said. "We'll figure this out, Cate."

"Mom!" Sara almost screamed. "What are we gonna do?"

"You might try getting a real job," Alice mumbled, not too quietly.

"Alice!" Russ said and gave her his most fearsome look.

The next few hours were completely unbelievable. After these burly men wrapped my dining-room chairs in plastic wrap and paraded them out, I couldn't stand anymore. I felt sick, physically sick. It was too much. I mean, I had said about a zillion times that I wanted a simpler life, sure, but surely there was an easier and more dignified way to get that, wasn't there? Holy shit, holy hopping hell, holy hell. Be careful what you wish for! And it wasn't like I hated *everything* in the house. Was this really happening? There were many things—rugs, paintings, lamps—that I completely adored and the thought of losing those things was wrenching. And losing *everything* and especially like *this* was so unbelievably shocking, I was reeling, just reeling, still not understanding what was really happening.

Patti said, as she took me by the arm, "Come on, let's get you out of here. We can go in the kitchen or something. You don't need to watch this."

"Okay. I think I might throw up. I'm not kidding."

"You're not going to throw up. Ever since you were five years old, I've seen you twist yourself like a freaking Cirque de Soleil acrobat so you wouldn't throw up."

"True."

"And let me tell you something, sister, if Old Aunt Daisy's string bean casserole didn't make you puke till you were purple, this won't either."

"I missed her today. She's always been our pillar of strength."

"Look, she sent gorgeous flowers and she's got a broken foot."

"True. Ah, Jesus, wait until she hears this part of the story."

"Yeah, her hair's gonna stand straight up on end."

"I never liked the dining-room table anyway," I said.

"Me either. Too Baroque."

"Baroque is when you're out of Monet," I said and Patti looked at me like I was crazy. "I have a T-shirt that says that."

"If you wear it in public I'm never speaking to you again," Patti said, deadpan.

"It used to be funny. Not so funny now."

"No. Not so funny now. Maybe I need a good shot of vodka."

"Maybe I need a martini."

The door from the butler's pantry whooshed to a close behind us and I suddenly realized that Richard and his team, and most especially Albertina, all of them had to be horrified by what was going on all around them. It had all happened so fast, I hadn't even thought of what to say to them. Repo men in the middle of a storm like this, on a day like this, at Cate Cooper's? No way.

Richard and his team had packed all the food up in aluminum containers and put them in the refrigerator and they were all standing by the back door, already bundled up in their coats and scarves, hats and gloves, ready to leave. I was going to tell him to take the food but he had already gone to the trouble of putting it away.

He came over to me, took both of my hands in his, and said, "I've gotta get them out of here before the roads freeze."

"Richard, thanks. I mean it."

"Listen, this is on the house today. When better days return? I'll charge you double."

That made me smile a little and I just shook my head with gratitude. Then I put my arms around his neck and hugged him.

"I'm so sorry," he whispered.

"Me too," I said. I wanted to add *thanks,* but the word got caught in my throat and I thought I might begin to cry again.

Albertina was wiping down the counters with a spray bottle of some mixture specifically designated for granite in one hand and a soft cloth in the other.

"It's none of my business," Albertina said to no one in particular. "I'm not asking any questions."

I put my hand over hers to stop her from giving the counters another single motion of polish, and I could see her eyes well up with tears.

"It's okay, Tina," I said, using her nickname. I wanted to show her I was feeling terrible for her unexpected loss, too.

"No, it's not okay," she said, and some pretty big tears bubbled over and rolled down her cheeks. She pulled a tissue from her sleeve with her free hand and wiped them away. "How can they *do* this to you?"

"I don't know. I guess I'll find out everything sooner or later but I'm sorry, Tina, I mean about your job here. I guess this is the end of the road for us."

"Oh shoot, Ms. Cooper, I can get a job tomorrow. That's no problem. Don't worry about me. But Mr. Cooper left you like *this*? I can't believe it. It's so wrong."

"Yeah, it's not great, is it? But I have my health. I have good children. I have . . ."

"Aw, jeez, Cate," Patti piped in. "All that's true enough but we've got to make a plan, sister. We've got to make a plan."

CHAPTER FIVE

Setting: Porgy House, upstairs, side porch. Old table with cloth, flowered china tea set, newspaper, two chairs.

Director's Note: Show photographs on scrim of side porch with table set for breakfast and the picture of Jenifer. When she talks about her story "The Young Ghost," show a cover of *McCall's* magazine. Voice of DuBose Heyward comes from off-stage.

Act I
Scene 3

Dorothy: There are some events in your life that are indelibly imprinted in your mind—funerals, childbirth, your wedding, the day the curtain goes up on your first play that made it to Broadway and on and on. You just don't forget anything about these things. It absolutely *was* in late February of 1934 that the haunting, or whatever you want to call it, began. I am going to be very careful in how I recount this story because otherwise you might think I was exaggerating. Writers are notorious for their expansive imaginations, you know. But, on my word, here is what I remember with certainty.

DuBose and I were comfortably settled at the old weather-beaten table on our side porch, enjoying our morning coffee and reading the newspaper. Jenifer was in school, fully ensconced in a kindergarten on James Island just a few miles away. It was a gorgeous day, crisp and clear, and although it was chilly, the sun warmed us as it danced on the countless ripples of the Atlantic Ocean right across the street. The world was alive and open for business. I brought up the previous night to DuBose in what I hoped was a nonchalant manner.

"DuBose? Did you hear all that crying last night?"

"Crying? No. I didn't. You know, darling, I sleep like the proverbial stone. It was probably some feral thing—a bobcat or a stray."

"Well, I don't think it was an animal. Golly, I was up half the night! Would you like an egg or some toast? Maybe food will wake me up."

"No, no breakfast for me thanks. Don't trouble yourself. You've *always* suffered so terribly with insomnia. Maybe we should stop the madness and just ask the doctor to give you something?"

"Maybe. I'll think about that. But DuBose? This is serious. I'm sure I heard a woman crying all night long, weeping! It was absolutely pitiful. She sounded just like that woman in my short story, 'The Young Ghost.' Remember her?"

DuBose folded his section of the newspaper back neatly to scan the obituaries.

"My, my. Look at this, will you? Old August Busch, the beer magnate, is gone to Glory! Looks like it was a suicide, it says here. Now why would someone with all that *money* do himself in?"

"DuBose! Have you heard a word I've said?"

"Yes, yes, of course I have. 'The Young Ghost'! That's the one about the accidental death or the suicide—another suicide!—of that young woman, isn't it?"

"Yes! Remember? Suzo, the very young bride, dies in the bathtub and Bobbel, her husband . . ."

"What kind of quirky names are those, dear? Russian?"

"They had nicknames for each other like we do. Well, like *you* do."

"Little Dorothy."

"Precious." I was not always so fond of being called *little Dorothy*. Dorothy wasn't really my name. "But remember how her husband struggles so hard? He's tortured really, trying to understand how and why his wife died. Was it an accident or not?"

"Right! And then the cad of the story . . . what was his name?"

"Keene Everett."

"Yes! Ah, Everett the Scoundrel, Connoisseur of the Wives of Others! As I recall, Everett let it slip that he and Suzo were an item and he implies that our little Suzo kills herself because her husband, *Bobbel*, the widower with the unfortunate name, said they had to stop riding around the town in his car with each other. Or some such nonsense."

"Nonsense? That story ran in *McCall's* magazine!"

"There, there! I meant no offense. It's just that . . ."

Too late. I was indeed offended, reminded for the umpteenth time that DuBose considered my writing to run along popular veins and that he was a more literary writer, more serious. After all, he was a founding member of the Poetry Society of South Carolina. And a celebrated poet. Descended from la-dee-da aristocracy. And I? I was only the Belmont Prize winner of Professor Baker's playwriting class from Harvard, thank you, which had been performed on Broadway, but I was from, alas, Ohio. In the world my husband grew up in, you were either a Charlestonian or you were not. You were literary or you were not. I pouted and waited for him to speak again but he was buried in that past Sunday's edition of the *New York Times*, which usually took us the whole week to finish.

"DuBose? I thought that story had a delicious air of mystery to it."

Not anxious to take on the task of self-defense first thing in the morning, DuBose avoided my eyes, put the newspaper down, and poured himself another cup of coffee from the pink-and-green flowered breakfast set that I treasured so. It had been a birthday gift from his formidable mother, which is the nicest way to describe her personality.

"Mysteries are fine for those who can abide them, I suppose. More coffee?"

Again, DuBose had stepped on my pride.

"What? No. Thank you." I took a deep breath and sighed hard, exasperated. "You know, DuBose, sometimes you are an insufferable snob. Many highly educated people happen to adore mysteries, myself among them. I'm just asking you this. What do you think? Why did she haunt the tenant with all that weeping?" What I really wanted to know was why was a weeping woman haunting *us*? Well, *me*, actually. And who was she?

He knew I was growing touchy and quickly working myself into a foul humor. DuBose, who obviously could not recall the finer points of "The Young Ghost," decided to take a benign position and let me talk it out.

"I have no idea, sweetheart. My memory isn't as sharp as yours. You tell me." *There, that's better,* I could see him thinking, *compliment her a little without seeming disingenuous.*

"Very well, I will! It was an accident. But here's the rub. People were blabbing all over town that she was having an affair with that simp Keene Everett when she most definitely was not. The rumors were terrible! So now that she was dead, how could she ever make her husband know that she loved only him?"

"Right, I remember now."

"She was robbed of her reputation and of her very life by an accident. But the crying? She was very worried that she would become nothing more than a bad memory. So she haunted their tenant, hoping he would help her straighten things out with Bobbel. Don't you remember she says, 'I'd rather be forgotten than be something you try to forget and can't.' She didn't want her husband to spend the rest of his life thinking she was unfaithful. And I'm telling you that all last night I heard a woman crying her heart out just like Suzo. Not some silly cat down the street. That's all."

At that point, DuBose had stopped and stared across the table at me. I could read his mind. Did *I* feel robbed? Had I ever thought of loving someone else? He dismissed the thought almost immediately with a shudder. No, if DuBose Heyward was certain of anything in his life it was my devoted love. Women were such complicated creatures, he thought loudly enough to be heard, but deliciously so.

"Perhaps I will have that egg," he said. "And maybe a slice of toast?"

"I'm ravenous this morning," I had said, "I am going to the kitchen. I'll be right back in two shakes."

I came around to his side of the table, smiled wide, kissed my fingertips, and touched his cheek with them. Harmony was restored. I knew that man and every cell of his brain. For the life of him, he could not even begin to comprehend why asking for an egg and a slice of toast would shake me from my truculent mood, but it seemed as though it had. At least I let him think so. I had made my point, and if I gave him a thousand dollars and all the tea in China, he couldn't tell me what that point was. Men.

Still, I had company the night before and I knew it.

Fade to Darkness

CHAPTER SIX

Packing

The sun was slowly rising like a fireball, searing the entire horizon in bands of blistering scarlet. Without so much as reaching out and touching the windowpane, I knew it was still bitter cold outside. The world beyond my windows had that bleak look of frozen desolation. Low-hanging clouds were bulging with snow, and if it fell as it was threatening to, I'd probably have my beautiful chandeliers for another twenty-four hours. Electricians were a sensible breed, and foul weather would keep them home rather than have their small vans play slip-and-slide. Besides, you waited for them, they didn't wait for you. But after everything that happened yesterday, I knew they would arrive.

I was wide-awake, having spent most of the night crying off and on like a complete fool. But in the morning light I was coming to the conclusion that what was there to cry about really? Because there was nowhere to sit except on a mattress and box spring? Because my clothes were in cardboard boxes all around the bedroom, dropped un-

ceremoniously in piles by the burly movers? Because all my family photographs were in a stack on the kitchen counter, their silver frames all
confiscated? Because there was no flat-screen television with which
to start my day with Matt Lauer and all my imaginary friends on the
Today Show? Please. It was easier to specify what remained than what
was gone. And there was nothing to be done about it anyway.

"Get out of bed and start your day," I said out loud to myself. I
rolled to one side and then pushed myself up into a sitting position. I
had not slept on a mattress and box spring on the floor since my college days, and as I struggled to rise I realized those days were a very
long time ago. My knees creaked, my balance was definitely off, and I
stumbled to the bathroom like an old, arthritic lady. I looked dreadful
but it was perfectly understandable. But I still had clean towels and I
hoped that a hot shower would get me moving.

I stood there under the hot water for much longer than usual, continuing to count my blessings. Isn't that what people were supposed
to do in trying times? Well, the list of my blessings was short but it
was not an insignificant list. I had my health, I wasn't ugly, and I had
a reasonable sense of humor and respectable brains. Good health was
a wonderful asset, not to be taken lightly, and good humor would see
me through this impressive morass of utter and complete bullshit I
was facing. On the material side of the ledger, I could add my diamond studs and diamond ring. And a nice watch. There was some
other jewelry but it probably wouldn't amount to much if I tried to sell
it. I imagined that our leased cars would surely be repossessed but that
was all right with me. I had never been a car person anyway. In fact,
I made a mental note to call Bergen Jaguar and Globe Motors to just
come pick them up. And after yesterday, mark that as the intergalactic
benchmark for a bad day, I was un-insultable, which I was pretty sure
wasn't a word and I didn't care one whit. It didn't matter if I did care.
The facts were what they were. At least I had the beginnings of some
sort of a plan.

I brushed my hair up into a big barrette, pulled on a pair of pants and a sweater, and wondered how long it would take for the swelling in my face to go down. I looked like a bloated trout. Every time I cried, since I was a little girl, my face would get blotchy and my eyes puffed up like I'd been on a bender. Come to think of it, Patti, Mark, and I did put the almighty hurt on three bottles of wine last night. Maybe that had something to do with the ruddiness of my complexion. But let's be honest, if ever there was an occasion that merited overindulgence, yesterday had been the ultimate one.

By the time I reached the kitchen to try and rustle up some sort of a breakfast, snow had begun falling in earnest, and Patti and Mark were coming in the door with a box of doughnuts; a bag of paper cups, napkins, and spoons, and a huge Box o' Joe from Dunkin Donuts; the *Bergen Record* and the *New York Times*. It was just before seven.

"Morning," I said. "You two are sure up with the birds! How are the roads?"

Patti gave me a peck on the cheek and then stood back and looked at me.

"The highways are probably fine but the neighborhood? Not so great. Next time you buy a house, make sure there's a politician on the street."

"Yeah, then you get plowed out first."

"By the way, shugah, you look like who did it and ran, girl," she said. "Lipstick." She reached in her purse and handed me a tube.

"We're supposed to get twelve to eighteen inches," Mark said and we all moaned.

"Somebody *did* do it and ran," I said, using her tube of Chanel Ballerina. "But! On the bright side of things, those nice men from the D&D Building left us some mugs and a few other things on the verge of recycling." I took three mugs from the cabinet. One had the faded image of Jane Austen's face plastered on it, another one had some bit of trite philosophy printed on its side, and the third one was from the gift shop at Radio City Music Hall. All of them had a significant chip or two. "Can you believe they didn't want these?"

"No taste," Patti said.

Mark gave me a brotherly hug and said, "We brought doughnuts."

"Yay. No carb left behind. Definitely my kind of breakfast," I said.

"Listen, Cate," Patti said, handing me a steamy cup of deliverance, "we don't want you to worry. You've been through enough. When the kids leave today, you're going to come and stay with us for a few days or for as long as you'd like to sleep on a sofa bed with a metal bar jamming your back."

I giggled at that. Mark and Patti lived three blocks away in a picturesque house for normal, sensible people (not a crazy, over-designed, waste of money, brand spanking new, with a five-car garage, home theater, tennis court, swimming pool, fountain out front spewing water day and night, wireless McMansion like mine), whose greatest selling point was an elaborate gourmet chef's kitchen with four ovens, two dishwashers, three sinks, and a huge marble slab for making Patti's infamous featherweight pastry and gorgeous cakes. Most women, myself included, would love a kitchen like that, because it would inspire you to tie on an apron. My witty, irrepressible sister Patti was a classically trained, well-known pastry chef who baked like an angel but only when she felt like it. She had declined countless offers from the Food Network for her own show, because she wasn't interested in becoming a celebrity. To put this in perspective, two years ago she made Martha Stewart's birthday cake at Martha's request and billed her. Martha's people were aghast that Patti sent a bill and Patti just laughed.

"Pay the bill," Patti said and they did. "Does Martha Stewart get up in the morning and go to work for free? I don't think so."

I greatly admired her sense of self-worth. Even Martha Stewart couldn't take her somewhere, especially if Patti wasn't interested in the trip. She charged so much money for wedding cakes it literally gave me hives to think about it. They had no children (their choice) and no pets (Mark is allergic to any and all creatures with dander), and as a result they had money to travel to all the exotic spots on the globe to sample and study their sweets, the one thing of which I was a little jealous.

"Well, I have to say. It's good to see a smile on your face," Mark said.

"Yeah, well, I think I'm pretty much out of tears, you know? They seem to have dried up."

"Yesterday was a little rough," he said.

"I'm married to the King of Understatement," Patti said. "It was like the worst day ever. Like something out of a Stephen King novel."

"Yeah, but you know what?" I said.

"What?" they said together.

"I'm gonna survive. Us Mahon women are built from pretty strong stuff, stronger than I would have thought. I mean, listen, who would *believe* what happened yesterday? It just doesn't seem possible."

"Cate?" Mark said. "These days, people are losing their houses and all their possessions right and left. What happened to you is not actually all that unusual, except for the baby pictures and the floosies in the office colliding in one spectacular graveside shit storm. Want a chocolate doughnut?"

"Like we already forgot the details?"

"Are you kidding?" I took the doughnut from him, ate it in two bites, and then I licked my fingers until all the sugar was gone. "Losing the house and everything we owned was bad enough but I agree, meeting Addison's whore was a nice touch and learning about the secretary and the other women he . . . what? What are y'all thinking?"

Patti and Mark had the strangest expressions on their faces, as though they were hiding something from me.

"Come on," I said, "what's up with the weird faces? What's going on?"

"You tell her," Patti said.

"This is why we came over so early," Mark said. "I couldn't sleep last night worrying about what you were going to do about paying your

bills. So I got to thinking and then I remembered something that happened when we were at dinner in the city a few months ago."

"And?" Patti said, opening her eyes wide and flailing her arms as if
to say *come on already!* "I swear to God, Mark. He is the slowest story-
teller in Bergen County. Quit prattling!"

"Excuse me, ma'am, but the details are very important here," Mark
said and continued. "So we're at Le Bernardin getting ready to lay waste
to some mighty fine black bass and I'm reading the wine list. I said to
Patti, gee, honey, remember that Pomerol we bought for like fifty bucks a
bottle back in '94? She says, yes, dear, although I'm not entirely confident
about her honesty on that one. You know? I mean, *yes, dear* is pretty much
thrown around the house without a lot of veracity attached to it."

"Puhleese!" Patti said. "He thinks he's the only one who remembers anything about our wine collection. Believe me! I *know* what the
man spends."

"And *I* know what *you* spend, too!" Mark wagged his finger at Patti.
"Well, anyway, don't you know it was four hundred dollars! The same
maker and the same year!"

"Basically, what he's telling you is that . . ."

"Ahem!" Mark said. "This is *my* story, not yours."

"Sorry," Patti said. "Just get to the point! Jeesch!"

"Cate? You're sitting on a gold mine downstairs. Addison's cellar is
probably worth a hundred thousand dollars! Maybe two."

"Maybe four!" Patti said.

"So what are you two thinking? That I should run out in the snow-
storm and sell it on the corner? Don't you know that the sheriff said
they were sending a special wine mover with a refrigerated truck to get
it?"

"A sommelier repo guy?" Patti said. "I didn't know they had those."

"I'm not saying that you should sell it!" Mark was getting excited.

"He's thinking you should swap it," Patti said. "It's kind of inge-
nious, really."

"What? Swap it?"

"Listen, the liquor stores open at nine. I've got the Expedition, right? That thing can go anywhere in any kind of weather."

"Yep, it sure can," Patti said.

"I'll go pick up twenty cases of something decent and we just switch it! How clever is that?" Mark was smiling from ear to ear. "We put your wine in our cellar temporarily, sell it either to a broker or at auction later on down the line, and that'll put a cool twenty-five thousand in your pocket. Maybe fifty! So what do you think? Smart, right?"

Silence hung between us for a moment while I tried to figure out if they were serious.

"Can you drive the Expedition to hell? 'Cause that's where y'all are going."

"What do you mean?" Patti said, completely mystified by my apparent lack of enthusiasm for their plan to send me to jail on top of everything else.

"Do you understand fraud? Great God, Patti! Mark, if we switch the Chateau Magnifique 1980 for the House of Mediocre Rat Piss 2010, it's fraud, it's a felony, and it probably breaks about another twenty laws. Good grief, y'all!"

All the air left the room in a great whoosh to be immediately replaced with yesterday's heavily laden gloom.

"She's right, Mark."

Mark, looking crestfallen as I pulled the plug on our adrenaline-pumping life of crime, shook his head in agreement.

"Damn it all! I thought it was such a great idea," Mark said. "I mean, wine? What regular judge in a New Jersey bankruptcy court knows jack shit about the value of rare wine? You know those guys don't drink anything but whiskey. Probably. Maybe single malts."

I was now doubly appalled that my heretofore saintly brother-in-law would assert that those learned gentlemen of the bench, in whom our society places a powerful sacred trust, were to be found after hours down at some seedy pub on the corner, knocking back shots of Jack Black and perhaps even doing something as commonplace as playing darts. Shocking.

"But maybe not. Come on, Mark. That's a very dangerous assumption to make. With all the business they're doing these days? You said it yourself. Bankruptcy courts are crazy busy. And those judges aren't exactly a bunch of dummies, you know. It would take those guys all of about a week to get up to speed and get their own reality show on the topic. *The Jersey Judges Do Vino!* Besides, all they'd have to do is subpoena the books or whatever it is that they do to the auction houses and the big distributors around here."

"She's right, Mark. It would be like, *Oh, Mrs. Cooper, we see here that on such and such a day you sold twelve cases of pinot to so and so . . .*"

"You know, you can stop all your robust agreeing with your sister any time now, Patti. I get the picture."

"Oh, come on," I said, seeing that Mark's pride was nicked. "Have another doughnut. They're good for you."

"Right," he said, defeated, and stuffed an entire jelly doughnut in his mouth.

"Look," I said, "I'm going to sell my diamonds. They've got to be worth a nice chunk of change. And I've got about twenty thousand dollars in my safe."

"Where's the safe?" Mark asked.

"Behind a fake wall in the wine cellar."

"You'd better empty that pronto," he said.

"I'm going to do that this morning. There's cash in the bank but I'm thinking anything with Addison's name on it is going to be frozen."

"Count on it. And everything else is held jointly, I imagine?" Mark said, turning his attention to the newspapers.

"Naturally," I said and they rolled their eyes to the ceiling. "Stupid, I know."

"A woman should always have her own FU money," Patti said.

"You're right. That's what the twenty thousand is but in this situation it's clearly not enough. I just need to get a job and find a nice little place to live and I'll be fine."

"Right. And what do you think you'll do for a living?"

"I don't know. I haven't worked that part out yet. I've been a little busy."

"True," Patti said and smiled at me. "Well, if I were you I'd bail on this whole town. Maybe I'd even bail on the state. There's no real reason for you to stay here anymore, is there?"

"Well, excuse me, but *you're* here. And where would I go anyway?"

"Well, there's Aunt Daisy, don't forget. I talked to her right before the funeral. Did I tell you that?"

"Um, no. Wait, maybe you did. I can't remember."

"Poor thing. She was just sick about not being able to be here with you and the kids. But, with her broken foot, you know she can't get around very easily or drive. Anyway, she needs somebody to help her with the Porgy House and all her other houses."

Our aunt Daisy, who raised us after our parents died and considered herself to be my children's grandmother, was something of a legend. She was known for her crazy hats and her even more colorful personality. Aunt Daisy purchased numerous rental houses over the years and had become the single largest property-holder on Folly Beach. I knew she had bought the Porgy House, which sounded like a good name for a butcher's shop to me, and for the life of me I didn't know why she would want such a funny little place. But it had historic value, as it was the place where Dorothy and DuBose Heyward composed the lyrics for *Porgy and Bess* with Gershwin. And it was true that she was getting older. Ella, her closest friend (read: life partner), had to be eighty-something, so she couldn't possibly be much of a help.

"Why in the world did she ever buy the Porgy House? It's so plain."

"Well, she's got her thing for *Porgy and Bess*, you know. She's always been crazy for anything about the Gershwins or the Heywards and I think she's got a little museum going or something like that. Anyway, you might want to pay her a visit for a while, you know, clear your head?"

All of this was certainly something to think about.

"And abandon this lovely climate?" I said sarcastically.

"Right?"

"No doubt some vitamin D would do me good."

"That's for sure. Mega doses. Hey, listen, you could help her with all those rentals, I think she has about twelve. That's a lot to handle at her age."

What *would* I do for a living? Like my daughter, I had that handy degree in musical theater, but I was a little long in the tooth to buckle up my tap shoes. But there were other things I had always wanted to do in my life and I imagined I would sit down, make a list, and weigh it all very carefully.

"Maybe. I'll have to think that one over. You know, after a death you're not supposed to make any changes for one year."

"And do what? Starve in the meanwhile? That's a load of nonsense."

"Good point," I said and knew she was right.

Meanwhile, while I considered my almost nonexistent options, I set up paper cups of oatmeal with raisins and honey for them to micro-wave. When Sara, Russ, and Alice got up, there would be something warm to put in their stomachs. I wondered if Aunt Daisy would even *want* me there. It suddenly occurred to me that this was a good time to clean the freezer, since I was going to be leaving.

"Hey, Patti?"

"Yeah?"

"You might want to look in my freezer and in the pantry to see if there's any food you want. I know there are about a dozen containers of chicken stock and there's pesto, too. And while you're in there see if there's any breakfast sausage. Russ loves sausage, you know."

"All men do," she said.

Over the next hour, I cooked sausage in the microwave on paper towels and buttered toast while Sara, Russ, and Alice drifted in, took a cup of coffee, and drifted back to their rooms to have a shower. No one was happy about the snow or particularly enthusiastic about the oatmeal. But we did manage to make three pounds of the sausage disappear, picked up from the griddle on the back of the stove with our fingers, stuck between slices of toast like a sandwich, and held in paper napkins. We were in post-traumatic tailgate mode. Plus the plates were gone.

"I'll bet you a buck that our flight's gonna be canceled," Russ said, watching the snow falling through the kitchen window.

"I'll call the airline," Alice said.

"Oh, man!" Sara said, looking out the window. "I am so screwed."

"Maybe not," I said. "You're probably flying a big plane that goes on to Tokyo or somewhere. They usually take off no matter what the weather is."

"Maybe we can get a flight on a bigger jet to Atlanta or Charlotte and then drive back to Charleston," Russ said to Alice.

"I'm on hold," Alice said.

There wasn't a lot of snow on the ground then, maybe an inch or so, and over the next hour of fierce packing and frantic checking with the pathological liars who worked for the airlines, who finally picked up and said everything was on time and running even slightly ahead of schedule, it was decided that Mark would drive them all to the airport in Newark before the tri-state area turned completely white. If they had a problem they would call us and we would rescue them. And if a rescue *was* necessary, we would all reconvene at Patti and Mark's so at least we could have a meal at a table and follow the news about the weather on a blooming television.

"I wish I didn't have to leave you now, Mom," Sara said. "It's too soon!"

"Darling, there isn't much you can do anyway. And we can talk on the phone all you want with my unlimited weekend minutes!"

"I'm glad you still have a sense of humor. I'm just thinking maybe I can get a job as a bartender. They're supposed to make bank."

"Give it a try," I said. We had talked, Sara and I. She knew the Gravy Train had not just pulled into the station, but it had jumped the tracks and rolled down the cliff, never to return. "Our new reality sucks."

"Yeah, it does but I just feel bad about leaving you now. I mean, there are probably other shoes to fall, you know?"

"Drop. Shoes to drop." My lovely daughter was known for mixing metaphors. "You don't worry about me, sweetheart. As things unfold, I'll keep you posted."

"Promise?"

"Cross my heart," I said and made an X with my finger over the spot where my terrified and very insecure heart was lodged. I loved my children so very much and it was so hard to send them back to their lives. A part of me felt like if I could just hang on to them that things might go back to normal. The rest of me knew better. Our family was irrevocably changed now and it was hard to see a future that was anything but unnerving. At least for me.

We hugged each other with all our might and I kissed their cheeks before they went out the kitchen door with Mark.

"If you want to talk about anything, *anything at all,* just call me, okay?" Alice said.

I saw Patti raise an eyebrow in my direction and I just smiled. I knew the child meant well but it would be a subzero day in the deepest valley of Hades before I'd reveal any fears or doubts I had to her. Too inappropriate.

"I'll call you when we land," Russ said, knowing I prayed like a cloistered nun on Good Friday while my children were in the air.

"That would be great, hon," I said.

"Me too," Sara said.

"Good," I said. "Travel safe! Love you!" in one breath and in the next they were gone.

"*If you want to talk about anything, anything at all, just call me,*" Patti said in her squeaky soprano voice. She was perched on our low breakfast counter, swinging her feet in the open space below it.

"Listen, you terrible old biddy, that child forgets that she's not my equal but I think her heart is in the right place."

"Oh? She has a heart?"

"Probably. And the last thing she needs is a neurotic mother-in-law destabilizing her life with whining and wailing."

"If you say so, but still, don't you want to just slap the crap out of her?"

"About every five minutes. But I know she can't help herself so I try to keep my gears in neutral."

"You're a better woman than me, Cathryn Mahon Cooper. Listen, have you done any packing?"

"My clothes are in boxes all over the floor of the bedroom."

"Let's fill your SUV up and start taking stuff to my house."

"Okay. No! Wait! I can't go yet. I didn't even see Albertina yet this morning!"

"Well, you'd better tell her to hustle herself home because the weather's not getting any nicer out there."

"You're right. I'll call her on the intercom."

There was no reply when I buzzed her room.

"I'm just gonna go and check on her."

"She's fine," Patti said.

Patti always thought everyone was fine but then she'd never had children to give her panic attacks or found her husband dead, hanging by his neck.

I moved quickly up the back stairs to the third floor and heard the shower running and her singing something in Portuguese. Albertina had a pretty voice, as clear and feminine as could be and I stood there for a moment listening. She had probably never smoked a cigarette or screamed her head off at a rock concert. Suddenly, I could envision her singing to her babies as I had when mine were little. Oh! What a sweet time in my life that had been. So sweet. In my mind's eye, it was twenty years ago. I was rocking my children at night to help them settle down for bed. I became sentimental and nostalgic. The time had gone so quickly and I would've given anything in the world right then to time-travel to those days even for just five minutes.

Russ was a man now and Sara was a young woman. Sara was going to find her way into the world like we all do. Until Addison's suicide, I had not really been worrying about her too much as I had when she was younger. But how would losing her father this way impact her in the long run? Russ seemed happy in his life but I worried about him for the same reason. I wondered if and when he and Alice planned to have children. I knew the answer for the immediate future was no time soon, because he stammered and turned red when I asked him, which I tried not to do every time the question popped to mind. The question came to mind every time I heard his voice or saw his face. It was all about Alice establishing her practice and she wanted to wait for a while, until they saved money, until the yard was fenced in, until what? Well actually, I had to give Alice her due. Her womb was her own private property and if she didn't feel ready for motherhood yet, then she was right to wait. The world did not need any more mothers who didn't want to be mothers. But I was filled with longing to hold a baby in my arms and I hoped that she would soon feel the same way. *Dear Lord, please don't let their children have Alice's unfortunate disposition. Thank you, Lord, Amen.* I frequently said little prayers like this to hedge my bets with the Almighty.

When I heard the water stop I waited a few minutes and then rapped my knuckles on the door.

"Good morning!" I said.

The door edged open and there she stood in a towel with clouds of steam all around her.

"Do you need me, Mrs. Cooper?"

"No, I'm sorry to disturb you. I just wanted to let you know that I'm going over to Patti's with a carload of stuff. If the wine movers show up early, just show them where the cellar is, okay? And call me on my cell if they do. And the electricians. FYI, there's some fabulous oatmeal, well maybe not so fabulous, in the kitchen. Just nuke it for a minute. And it's snowing like the devil outside. I'll be back. You take your time. No rush! No rush at all!"

By three that afternoon, the streets were plowed, all of my personal possessions, the contents of my safe, and the children's belongings that they wanted were all piled up in Mark and Patti's basement, and Albertina was safely home with her children. We hugged and promised to keep in touch. As she was leaving she put a business card in my hand.

"What's this?" I said.

"This is the number for the piano repair company."

"Oh! Tina! Thank you. Oh my God, what am I going to do without you?"

"You'll do just fine, Mrs. Cooper, but I'm going to miss you a lot."

"Me too."

When her car pulled slowly away from the driveway I burst into tears one more time. Patti threw her arm around my shoulder and gave me a squeeze.

"Doors close so others can open, you know," she said.

"I know that but hellfire, do they have to be so hard to close? She was my dear, dear friend."

"I know, I know. This is so hard."

"Yes. This is so hard. I hate Addison."

"Me too."

Patti and I had returned my SUV to my house and took another walk around. The electricians were there, doing their reprehensible best on removing the lighting and the home theater components. Another team of men were breaking down the gym equipment and I wondered how they'd ever get it put back together again. And what would the banks do with all the stuff left behind—old Christmas decorations,

old bicycles, curtains of no value, CDs, old linens that I didn't want . . .
I imagined they'd bring in a Dumpster. It was sort of amazing how
quickly you could pack up a life when you were only taking the things
you really wanted. We had simply left all our clothes on their hangers,
tying their necks with garbage-bag twist ties like the dry cleaners did,
and covered them up with lawn-size black garbage bags. I walked away
from all of Addison's clothes, because Albertina said she would give
them to her church. We tied a ribbon around all of them with a note.

Mark took Addison's golf clubs that had been overlooked yesterday.
He couldn't resist and I didn't blame him.

"Just take them," I said.

"Do you think I'm a crook? I mean, we were exactly the same
height and it would be a shame. But if you're not one hundred percent
comfortable, just tell me and I'll put them back."

"Good grief! Is your widdle bitty conscience having a renaissance?"
I said.

Mark's face blanched.

"Come on," I said. "They're used anyway. And Addison would want
you to have them. If we leave them here they'll wind up in the garbage.
Besides, you don't know what I have."

"What?" he said and the color in his face returned.

"My piano. It's out being repaired. Tell no one. The banks can't
have it. Screw 'em. I don't know how much they're going to charge me
to fix it but . . ."

"Don't worry about it. I'll take care of that one. You're sure you don't
want to switch some wine?"

"Oh, Mark." Mark was going to cover my piano repairs? Thank
heaven!

Earlier around noon and over some deli sandwiches they brought
in, Patti had asked for the tenth time, "How much stuff do you have
left to pack?" *How much more* became the mantra of the day.

There were about five inches of snow on the ground and going back and forth to their house was starting to become a real challenge, even with four-wheel drive.

"Not a whole lot. I mean, the kids left what they wanted on their beds, Albertina boxed it up. I told them I'd send it to them tomorrow. Weather permitting, of course." I said that and remembered I had just forty-eight hours to vacate and I wanted to go over the house a few times. The clock was ticking too fast. "Jesus, Patti, do you think they'd throw me out in the snow like the freaking little match girl?"

"No. Maybe. How the heck should I know? But I know this—the longer we let this drag out the worse it's gonna be on you. Emotionally, I mean. FYI, I took your saffron. That stuff is way too expensive to leave."

"Definitely. Gotta love your practical side. And you know what?"

"What?"

"I'm gonna call Aunt Daisy tonight. I think I'm going back to Folly."

CHAPTER SEVEN

Setting: The Porgy House kitchen, condensed-milk cans, a large sack of potatoes and onions, loaf of bread, carton of eggs, bananas.
Director's Note: Photos of the Porgy House kitchen on the back scrim. A photo of Jenifer as an infant and show Dawn Hill, their North Carolina home. Switch to the dancing.

Act I
Scene 4

Dorothy: It was always a struggle to figure out what to cook for supper, when we lived on Folly. Some days the kitchen seemed like another planet to me where I wandered around like an alien, unable to tell a good onion from a bad turnip. That's when I made soup. Onion, water, done! On other days, when the pantry was just about bare, I felt like Harry Houdini, producing a meal from thin air. Thank heavens for condensed milk and potatoes. Anyway, surprises and miracles happened in my kitchen on Folly Beach. And no one ever died from my catch-as-catch-can cooking skills, well, no one I knew of anyway. As a rule, small portions of blandness did not kill.

Oh, sure, breakfast was easy enough to put together—a few fresh eggs from Romeo, the island egg man, a slice of toast, a glass of juice. Or cereal! What an absolutely brilliant invention were cornflakes? With sliced banana? Even I could handle that. And our midday dinner wasn't completely beyond my capabilities either. I just always kept it simple because of our budget. Besides, DuBose and I kept a strict regime, being ever-vigilant of our health. On Sunday, if we weren't invited to dinner with friends or his mother, I might bake some chicken or pork chops with steamed rice and maybe I'd boil up a head of broccoli. No cream or sauces. Nothing spicy. Our digestive systems would have rebelled. We were not accustomed to much more than a little butter or the smallest sprinkle of salt.

When the day was at an end and I had to produce yet another meal I always wished we could just forget it. And sometimes I was just so tired. Another meal? Didn't I have a full-time job, a young daughter whose care was almost solely mine, and a house to run as well? Sometimes, when I was on the verge of exhaustion, I wondered why women found managing a household so attractive and that's when I would think about Jo Pinckney and just how smart she really was to never marry. Honestly, some days it was all just too much, especially when my head was deep in the process of creating a new story.

But on most days I took my domestic duties in stride. DuBose wasn't fussy about the state of the house or his meals. Often, I made sandwiches or plates of sliced leftovers from the previous day. If there were any to be had, that is. If I did not plan for leftovers, which I never seemed to calculate quite right, there would have just been more cornflakes! It seemed to me that I should've been able to come up with a more satisfy-ing plan, so sometimes I served a dinner meal for supper and just quick sandwiches for our midday meal, especially if my writing was going well. To stop writing around noon to cook a hot meal usually meant my workday would come to an end, because it was hard to change gears and cook and then change them again to return to my writing table. This is sounding confusing, even to me, but the point is that I felt that the more time I spent out of the kitchen the better it was for our health, our finances, and our careers.

Oh, those were the days! Such sweet days! DuBose and I were married for seven years before we were finally blessed with a child we brought home at first to our farm, Dawn Hill in Hendersonville, North Carolina, and then to our little cottage surrounded by pines and live oaks on Folly Island. The days we spent with Jenifer on Folly are still the happiest ones I can remember. She was such a sensitive child, prone to inexplicable forgetfulness and episodes of vagueness, well, we hoped the salt air would be good for her.

Maybe it was the latter part of March, 1934? Well, it was the time we were waiting, almost pacing the floors really, to hear if and when Mr. Gershwin would grace us all with his royal presence. At my urging, DuBose had been writing to him all the time, enticing him with stories about the exotic and primitive practices of the Gullahs. He told him that he had a Negro church he desperately wanted him to come and visit. The members of this congregation danced something called the "double clap" when they were moved by the spirit. I had seen it and it was indeed powerful, in fact, I had seen people faint from the frenzy of it. DuBose was certain the dance and the music had survived intact from their African roots, because there was nothing like it in the whole canon of American liturgical music.

And there was another, more sensual kind of dance he discovered as well. He felt very strongly that it would be the perfect number for the scene of passion between Crown and Bess. Surely old George wouldn't be able to resist it, especially when DuBose described the mood of the dance to him as "phallic." The term made me slightly uncomfortable but DuBose seemed convinced that everything about the Gullahs was

sexier and more exciting. The way they dressed, the way they walked . . .
he really believed when they played their gospel music, the Holy Ghost
came down to them for a visit. And when they played the blues, they
hoochie-coochied, and the next thing you know, they were . . . well, I
could never put it in writing, I mean I can't say it!

Ah well, between us, sometimes I wished it *was* contagious. DuBose
longed for a whopping dose of the virility he witnessed in the Negro men
he knew from his time working on the docks as a young man. He deeply
envied their masculinity. I guess you'll think me wicked for saying all
this but DuBose frequently said it himself. He blamed his ancestors for
not having had that quality to pass on to him. Too much reticence and
not enough electricity! They could sign the Declaration of Independence but did the whole lot of the Heywards ever have any fun? Did they
ever just let it all go?

Fade to Darkness

CHAPTER EIGHT

Road Trip

There had been many phone calls back and forth to Aunt Daisy on Folly Beach. My dear sweet aunt immediately warmed to the idea of a visit, possibly an extended visit, and if I would just move back for good, she would have been tickled pink. No one loved a project like Daisy McInerny and apparently, in her mind, I had become her next one. "You come home to me!" she said. "I'll make your bed myself! And I'll plump your pillows! Oh, how I've missed my girl. That dirty rotten son of a bitch!"

I didn't know whether to fall to my knees in gratitude for her generous affection or to laugh my head off at her naughtiness. Aunt Daisy would never let a trifling thing like demure behavior get in the way of speaking her mind.

"I thought maybe I might try to stay for a week or two just until I can get the bats out of my belfry and figure out what I'm going to do with myself," I said.

"What? Honey baby, you just get yourself down to Folly as fast as you can and you don't worry about another single thing, do you hear me?"

"Oh, Aunt Daisy! You are the greatest woman who ever lived on this earth."

"That's probably true, if you don't count people like Mother Teresa." I could hear her giggle and I thought, wow, this is what a generous heart is all about. I hoped it would rub off on me. "And, heavenly days, Cate. You've had nothing but one terrible shock after another. You need some peace! I'm going to tell Ella to bake you a pecan pie!"

A pecan pie was the cure for anything. For some families it was chicken soup but for mine it was a gooey rich filling of Karo syrup, butter, sugar, and pecans all nestled into a gel against a crust made with lard. If I was really on a bummer I could eat a whole one. Okay, not in one sitting but a homemade pecan pie would see me through just about any seventy-two-hour dilemma.

Sara thought it was a great idea for me to retreat to Folly Beach, too.

"Mom, seriously. You need to get the heck out of New Jersey. Your whole entire world besides me, Russ, Aunt Patti, and Uncle Mark just Apocalypsed! Take a break! You know? Maybe I can find some cheap tickets and come down for a few days. I'll make you one of my special cocktails and we can stay up all night . . ."

"Yeah, great! So how's that bartending thing working out?"

"Mom! I'm a mixologist!"

"Right, right. Sorry."

"I'm making some serious dough."

"Well, praise the Lord for that."

And I spoke to Russ, who was perfectly sanguine as most men are about a parent coming to town. In fact, he could see no reason why a basket of fried seafood wasn't the perfect solution to anything that ailed me.

"We'll go to Bowens Island! It'll be like old times."

Wasn't that the typical male response? The stomach speaks. I had to smile at my boy.

"Absolutely," I said and sure enough my traitorous mouth began to salivate.

Bowen's Island was the most diminutive of all the islands in the land, so small that in the old days the island itself was said to practically disappear when the tide came in. There, in a tiny, very undistinguished house passing for a restaurant, one that had escaped the attention of the health department for decades and any touches of gentrification from a decorator since its very inception, you could eat your fill of delicious shrimp so fresh, fish so exquisitely moist, and hush puppies as big as your fist, for a pittance. I mean, a plate of fabulous fish and grits for ten dollars? Even in my newly impoverished state, I could pick up that check.

So, with those conversations, observations, and conclusions, my immediate future had been more or less decided but the deal was clinched when I took an unfortunate but necessary short ride to Forty-seventh Street, the diamond district in New York City. Any woman would hate to part with her diamonds and my heart was heavy, but it was abundantly clear to me that I had to sell my ring and studs. After all, they were just *things* that could be replaced if my financial situation changed.

There in the kiosk of a well-respected diamond dealer, I. Friedman, leaning against a glass showcase crammed with estate pieces from another era, standing there with my sister Patti by my side, I learned from Corey Friedman that my diamonds were fake. Yes. Fake.

At first, I was stunned. Patti gasped and, to give you some idea of the gravity of the moment, she did not say one word. A terrible silence filled the air. There we were, two well-dressed middle-aged women, and I was obviously the victim of some kind of disgusting, horrible scam. I could feel my blood pounding in my ears. Here it was again. More treachery. More deception. One more betrayal from Addison, The F-ing Scoundrel, formerly known as The Deceased.

Then I remembered the night I gave them back to him. It was like watching the rerun of a movie in my head. Over dinner not too many years ago, he took my original diamond engagement ring and my smallish diamond studs into his hands and stood. With a glass of an '83 Haut Brion in one hand and my treasures in the other, he delivered an announcement that to honor our twentieth anniversary he wanted me to have something spectacular. Absolutely spectacular, he said, worthy of a queen, something worthy of The Queen of HIS World. This was done with so much theatrical flourish that you could almost hear the New York Philharmonic playing in the background. I had believed him and I even wept, hoping against the odds that this was my old Addison, trying to make amends for all the many other outrages with a grand gesture meant for me.

FAKE!

Unbelievable. Struggling to steady myself, I fought hard not to burst into tears for about one minute and then my heart abruptly changed. How very desperate had my husband been to do such a thing to me? It was absolutely just beyond pitiful.

Suddenly, I felt awful for the poor jeweler who had to deliver the news. His face was deep red and there were tiny beads of perspiration across his forehead. He had probably seen this kind of thing before. Maybe a lot. He took a handkerchief from his back pocket and wiped his face. Talk about an awkward moment?

"I could give you a few hundred for the mountings," he said. "I'm terribly sorry."

"No, it's okay. Not your fault. Let me think about it. Thank you," I said, "thanks for your time."

Patti, my Mortification, and I stepped out into the street. The cracked sidewalks were frozen to a dull gray, bumpy and uneven from the remnants of ice, salt, and sand. The wind whipping down the canyons of Manhattan nipped our cheeks, chapping our lips. I was so upset I could barely make eye contact with my sister.

Patti said, "Maybe we should check with someone else. I mean, he might be wrong. He was pretty nervous."

"He's not wrong. I mean, sure let's check, but he's not wrong. I just know it."

"Addison. That son of a bitch," she said.

"No. Well, yeah, he was a son of a bitch but the poor thing. How low! He must have felt so low when he did this."

"Humph. That depends on what he needed the money for. I mean, if he was buying cocaine or something, it wouldn't have bothered him one bit. Or if he was paying that woman's mortgage . . ."

"Oh, hell. You're right. Probably safe to say that by the time he pulled this trick his moral compass had dissolved into a puddle of very smelly crap."

"That's for sure. Want to go get a cup of coffee? Get out of the cold for a few minutes? Then we can go check with someone else?"

"No. I think I'd just like to go home, or back to your house, eat and drink neurotically and go to bed early. In the fetal position." I sighed so hard that my frosty breath looked like a mushroom cloud and then I sighed the same way again and again.

Patti looked at me then, worried that I might hyperventilate and aware I was headed to the abyss of despair. She gave me a stern look that said *we'll have none of that* and looped her arm inside the crook of my elbow and we leaned into the bitter wind together, pushing against its strength, heading back to the garage where her car waited and then back to New Jersey.

"Here's the good thing," I said to her in the car as we reached the other side of the George Washington Bridge.

"Let's hear," she said.

"There's nothing else to take or sell. This is the bottom."

"Life can be so unfair."

"You think I don't know that?"

It took about a week to make all the arrangements but I was finally ready to go. Mark had helped me buy a used Subaru for eight thousand dollars with only fifty thousand miles on it. In his estimation that was practically a new car. It was in good enough shape for a prudent widow or a starving artist, and if I could drive it to South Carolina without wrecking it, it would be all I needed to toot around Folly and Charleston for at least a year or two. I had taken almost all my designer clothes and handbags to a consignment shop called Second Acts, and if they were able to sell some or all of it that would give me another few thousand dollars, I hoped. Besides, what was I going to do with Valentino wool suits and Armani heavy sweaters in the humidity of the Lowcountry? I didn't need cashmere-lined gloves, cashmere wraps, and lined wool trousers, either. I'd perspire to death. I kept a sensible St. John black dress and jacket in case I had to go to another funeral or in case a prince materialized and invited me to a black-tie dinner. And I packed a few other accoutrements to remind myself I was a dignified woman. It was strange to let so many of my possessions just go in such a short period of time but it was also kind of liberating, like being born again, naked and free.

The morning I was to leave, I was up before the sun. My plan was to start early and drive straight through what we estimated would be about a thirteen-hour drive, depending on the traffic on I-95. My new old car was already packed. Mark had strategically loaded and reloaded my gear in such a way that I wouldn't have any blind spots. He had checked my window-washing fluid, the oil, the tires, and everything he could think of, including updating the emergency roadside kit with new flares. And he gave me a AAA card for national roadside assistance. *This* was why I loved Mark. He cared how you fared in the world and when I watched him repacking the car for the fourth time I thought again what a wonderful father he would have made. But then I reminded myself that if you didn't have children you might have thought they were a liability, because to be honest even I had friends whose children gave me nightmares. But that was rare. They could also be your greatest asset.

I dressed quickly, rolled up my pajamas, and dropped my cosmetics in an old canvas tote bag Patti gave me, a souvenir from a contribution she made to PBS. Even though I knew I was facing the endurance contest of the year to make that kind of drive alone, I was psyched. Sort of.

The truth was that part of me longed to get as far away from anything that had to do with Addison. I was sick in my heart over it all and I did not think I could bear another piece of bad news. The other part of me was looking forward to getting away from the terrible winter weather. My skin was so dry that it would drink whatever moisturizer I fed it only to feel taut again in just a few hours and then it flaked. Oh brother. My legs flaked like that character Pig-Pen in *Charlie Brown,* throwing off a cloud of dust in the air when I pulled off a pair of tights. Gross. My hair had static electricity no matter what I did to it. I was tired of numb fingers and toes, wheezing allergy attacks from wood smoke and wet leaf mold, but my number one, all-time feature of winter that I would not miss was the stinging shock to my hand when I walked across carpet and touched a metal doorknob. I hated it when the electricity ran from my fingers up to my elbow. It made me cuss every single time.

So the idea of leaving those aspects of Yankee living in the dust for a while and swapping stories with Aunt Daisy and Ella over a pile of roasted oysters or a bowl of stew was appealing, especially to a wounded soul like me.

I'd take long walks on the beach, warmed by the gentle winter sun and command my body and soul to soak up every salty benefit it had to offer. I'd think my future through and try to plan the next chapter with a lot more care. My life was my own now and what it would be would be what I would make it. But the other part of me knew that that very idea of finding happiness and contentment was wildly optimistic considering I had almost no resources to draw on except the wisdom of an aging old-maid aunt, her companion, and what I could muster on my own. Sure, I'd gladly help Aunt Daisy until her foot healed. I'd help her until she closed her eyes on her last day on earth if she wanted me to, but staying there and managing real estate for a living was about the last thing I wanted to do with myself. So, with mounting trepidation and enough nervous energy to light the city of Chicago, I was resolved to at least take this sabbatical and see what I would find on Folly Beach.

I smelled bacon frying—a powerful aphrodisiac if ever there was one—and hurried down to Patti and Mark's kitchen to have some breakfast.

"You think I was gonna let you leave without filling you up with pancakes and bacon?" Patti said.

"I'm really glad you didn't." I gave her a smooch on the cheek and poured myself a cup of coffee.

"I MapQuested your trip," Mark said, "and if you want, I'm happy to give you my portable GPS. It's no big deal."

"You are a dear, Mark, but I'm just heading straight down I-95 until I reach Aunt Daisy's and I know the way like the back of my hand."

"Right. I know. And you could always ask for directions if you need to," Mark said.

"No! Don't stop except for gas and don't talk to strangers and for God's sake don't stop at a truck stop! Bad things happen at truck stops, you know."

"Yeah, especially since I'm driving this hot car and all. They'll probably hijack it and me and this will be a short story. The end." I smirked at her and she shook her head.

"Just don't do anything stupid, okay? Like sit on a public toilet seat anywhere! And call us?"

"Don't worry! I know how to hold my purse and tinkle in midair!"

"Please!" Mark said in mock horror. "Tinkle?"

Patti and I made nasty, nasty *ew* faces at each other.

"I might stop and spend the night around Richmond if I'm getting tired. If I do I'll call you."

"That's a really good idea," Mark said. "Something like ten percent of all road accidents are caused by falling asleep at the wheel."

"Yeah, but three times as many men as women," Patti said and I stared at her as if to say, how in the hell did you know that? "I looked it up on the Internet."

"Oh," I said and was astonished to see that they had put more actual effort into my trip than I had. But they had done so to bring facts and statistics to light. And because they loved me. And in the end, this was a hallmark day.

We were all busy sighing and smiling, sighing and smiling. Mark was saying that he would be in touch with Dallas and Mel regarding Addison's estate but we all knew there wasn't anything to be gained there, that is, no inheritance for me or for the children. I gave Mark power of attorney so if there were documents for me to sign he could do that for me. More sighing, more smiling. Don't worry, don't worry. Bankruptcy is not the disgrace it used to be. Let's see what your real liabilities are, if any, probably nothing. Well, you can't get blood from a stone, Patti said and we smiled and sighed some more.

We were convinced this was the best possible decision for me for the short term. It wasn't exciting or uplifting, because it didn't fit the normal categories of why one usually took a road trip with all their belongings. I didn't feel like Katharine Hepburn playing Jane Hudson in the old fifties movie *Summertime,* the one where the schoolteacher goes to Venice, the trip of her dreams, to fall in love with some gorgeous Italian man.

Nope. I was going to my aunt's house on Folly Beach in an old Subaru. The truth was something had to be done with me and this was the most benign choice, couched in the excuse of taking care of Aunt Daisy.

I overate at breakfast, probably because of nerves and the fact that I had not indulged in blueberry pancakes since December, when Patti made them for all of us on Christmas morning. God, Patti was lethal in the kitchen. And there was the fact that when the meal ended, it would be time for me to go. Time to go and let go. Well, I had told myself that this was just going to be a trip and not necessarily a permanent move. I could tell myself anything I wanted to but it was plain to all of us that this trip had every possibility of becoming just that. And along with that new home address came an avalanche of other considerations, not the least of which was how would I adjust? Exactly how small would a new home have to be so that I could afford it? Two rooms and a hot plate? Well, all of that would be based on what I could earn. Doing what? This whole adventure and its background music produced a whopping case of acid reflux. Ugh. I noted that for the foreseeable future I should eat lightly. And before I got on the road, I'd stop at a CVS for some TUMS.

We hugged and hugged and Patti slipped something in my pocket.

"Wha . . . ?"

"Shhh! Later!" she whispered.

"Oh, Patti!" I was tearing up again and so was she.

"Stop!" she said. "Look, you can always come back here and live with us."

"Oh, right! That's not too screwed up or anything. Mark would shoot both of us after a week!"

"No, seriously! I'll teach you how to make cupcakes. They're all the rage now."

"Cupcakes," I said, thinking how ironic it would be to actually be able to support yourself making something like multitudes of cupcakes. But then, years ago, Pet Rocks, Zoo Doo, and Beanie Babies put some guys into the millionaire's club, as did Chia Pets and any number of weird fads.

"Yeah. Cupcakes."

"We'll see. I'd better get going. The sun's up."

After many oaths to be careful and to call and yes, to be careful some more, I finally cranked up the car and pulled away from Patti, Mark, and my former life in Alpine, New Jersey.

Why was it that I had so many ambivalent feelings about New Jersey until I was leaving it? Now, for the first time, I began to make a list of the many things I'd surely miss—riding my car through swirling leaves down the Palisades Parkway when the Canadian maples turned red and the towering oaks became gold, all the great Italian food, diner food, and sushi, and hiking Eagle Rock Reservation, the first snowfall of the season, crocuses poking their tiny but hopeful purple tight blooms through the last snow of the season promising spring's return, the bridges, the views, proximity to Manhattan with all the temptations and thrills to be found there—Lincoln Center, Broadway, the museums, Carnegie Hall, on and on. The best of this and the best of that—world-class everything. Yep, I'd miss it a lot but since I couldn't really afford the tolls much less the parking or the tickets or the meals, I was reconciled, almost, to a period of peaceful harmony and introspection.

Indeed, I spent the first night in Petersburg, Virginia, at the Ragland Mansion, a true piece of Americana, for the reasonable rate of eighty-five dollars for the night, including breakfast. Dinner was a small amount extra and would I like to have dinner? I would. My knees were so cramped I had to stop driving for a while or I'd never stand upright again. I took my overnight bag up to the Magnolia Room and wished I'd had my camera. It was buried somewhere in a box in the car. There was a king-size iron bed from New Orleans and several nineteenth-century gouaches of Naples and Capri on the walls. A charming fireplace, aglow from the small gas flame that danced around the cast-iron log. Best of all, there was a deep bathtub calling out to me to come back soon for a long, hot soak.

"I'll be back, honey," I said to the tub and was happy to see a container of sea salts on the corner shelf, to which I could help myself for a mere five dollars.

I emptied my pockets on the dresser and there was the envelope Patti had given me earlier that morning. I had forgotten all about it. I ripped it open and inside was two thousand dollars in crisp one-hundred-dollar bills, with a note that said, *Remember these two things: there's big money in cupcakes and sisters are forever. xxx*

For the millionth time, I choked up and cried, thanking God for giving me such a wonderful sister. I called Patti right away and promised to save the money to use for something important.

"Spend it however you want," she said. "I just wanted to be sure you had some emergency cash."

I didn't even know what to say. She made me feel suddenly empowered to go and do something, something big enough and grand enough to make her proud of me. The most I had hoped for since Addison's death until that moment was some measure of emotional stability, to quickly achieve financial self-reliance, and to regain my self-respect. But Patti's generosity gave me new strength.

I would be damned if I would let her hear me crying over her gift and I struggled to make laughing sounds to make her think I was just happily surprised and grateful. I knew how much flour she had to sift and how much sugar and butter she had to cream to stash away that much money to give away as a gift. I also knew then that she had not told Mark, because otherwise they would have given it to me together. I wondered how that was, to spend your life with someone from whom you kept all the facts. Maybe everyone had secrets. Addison certainly had had his share of them. Boring old me never had anything going on that was exciting enough to conceal. Hopefully that would change. In fact, I would make it a point to test my limits!

After Patti and I said good-bye, I called Aunt Daisy to say I'd see her the next day. She congratulated me on my level-headedness. I wasn't being so level-headed at all. I was totally exhausted.

"I don't believe in driving at night. Too many crazy truck drivers on the road, all hopped up on something!"

"You're probably right about that," I said. I knew the kitchen was closing, so I said good-bye to her, too, and ran a brush through my hair.

Downstairs there was a ballroom, a solarium, a library, and the walls and decorative ceilings—all of it with innumerable architectural details. It fascinated me, because it was so old and all done by hand. Hundreds of wood rosettes decorated the huge beams, probably hand-carved on the spot by an immigrant from Italy or Poland, some poor fellow perched up on a scaffolding, who spoke two words of English. You could almost feel the ghosts of all the craftsmen and artists who had made this home so beautiful. There I was, recently sprung from a culture that screamed NEW, and Lord, OLD was so much more warm and appealing. It was absolutely charming and I wished suddenly that I had more time to spend there, just to sightsee, since Petersburg, according to the brochures by the front door, had more eighteenth-century homes than anywhere else in the country. Somehow, and by God's grace, that devil Sherman missed it.

To my delight, I was not the only guest of the Ragland Mansion. There was a family from Pennsylvania there with their children, traveling to Washington, D.C., to see all the monuments and the Smithsonian. All of them had red hair, shining like new copper pennies, and the map of Ireland all over their faces. I had forgotten about spring breaks and winter breaks for schools. Those days were behind me as were so many things, which gave me a sentimental pause, remembering my trips to Boston and Washington with my children. Not now and not ever again. Now I was The Widow. Not to be confused with the merry one. Traveling alone. *Tell us your story* . . . Thankfully, they could not have been less interested in me. I could've been a Russian spy or an escapee from a mental institution for all they knew. But then, would my future be anything more than occasions where I was the silent bystander, of no interest to anyone? Would I shrivel up with each passing holiday until I was a wizened old crone? Screw that, I thought, I ain't gonna let that happen. Hell, I used to dance on Broadway! I had a story! I'd find my way. I would.

The good news was that the McDonough family was a highly conversational and energetic group of five, who kept the innkeeper busy all through dinner, peppering him with questions about the history of the house, local points of interest, and were there any nuts in the bread, because Junior, their five-year-old mouth-breather kid whose finger rarely left the inside of his nose, was deathly allergic. I kept my novel open under my left hand, and avoided them all. The meal was actually pretty good—roast beef, mashed potatoes, and some kind of mixed vegetable casserole. Dessert was a simple baked apple with a cinnamon stick propped inside against its missing core like a straw, and I washed it down with my third glass of a mediocre red table wine that was there for the taking. It's good for my cholesterol, I told myself. And my attitude. And after my date with the soaking tub, I slept like someone had shot me dead.

The next morning arrived, bright, clear, and beautiful. I was downstairs in the dining room again, reading the local newspaper, munching away on a warm cranberry-pecan muffin and drinking a mug of delicious coffee laced with almond, when Junior the Allergic appeared at the breakfast buffet without the benefit of adult or sibling supervision. I watched his germy little hand approach the muffin basket in slo-mo, all the while he was eyeing me, just daring me to say something. I knew his kind. But, still, I had a conscience.

"There are nuts in them," I said.

"So?"

"So, you're not my kid, but I just thought you might want to make an informed decision about how you die."

"Oh." The hand retreated.

"You could probably get pancakes, if you asked nicely. You know, use the magic word?"

"You mean *please*?"

"Yeah, that's the one. Works like a charm. Usually."

"Okay," he said and practically ran through the swinging door to the kitchen, oblivious to the possibility that someone on the other side may have been charging through to the dining room with a tray of something fragile or a tureen of boiling grits at the exact same moment.

God protects children and fools went the saying, or something like it, because just as I was finishing up my breakfast, having amused myself over the local Police Blotter Report in the paper, Junior reemerged with the chef and a platter piled high with steaming pancakes, dripping with butter and maple syrup and sausage patties glistening with grease. Junior carried a large glass of chocolate milk and I thought, oh boy, somebody's stomach is gonna be begging for mercy before they get to the Lincoln Memorial. In that moment, I was not nostalgic for the days of mothering young children. Not in the least.

"Have a great day!" I said and smiled at the little redheaded, freckled sack of hell.

The rest of the day should be easy, I thought. Straight down I-95, bang into I-26, whip over to Highway 17, and then get on Folly Road. I'd be at Aunt Daisy's by eight, still in time for supper and to begin the next leg of my odyssey.

Around one o'clock I stopped at a Cracker Barrel for lunch and to fill up the car with gas. I looked around the gift shop to see if there was something I could bring my sweet aunt, well, maybe *feisty* is the better descriptor, something she'd really want. Naturally, there were lots of things from which to choose: cast-iron cookware; a wall clock that looked like Felix the Cat with eyes that darted left on *tick* and right on *tock*; ceramic cookie jars; aprons, towels, and oven mitts that matched; coffee; packaged mixes for cakes and breads; relishes; music; and every kind of old-fashioned candy under the sun. She would probably not want any of it, because like most people over the age of whatever-the-age-is-when-you-get-peculiar, she was very, very particular. I'd buy her something when I got to Charleston, maybe an armload of flowers and a dozen Krispy Kreme doughnuts that I knew she loved. Ah, Krispy Kreme. Every girl should have a guilty pleasure, no matter her age.

It was around seven-thirty when I rolled into the parking lot of the Piggly Wiggly on Folly Road. My intention was to zoom in, scoop up several bunches of flowers and a box of glazed sin, and zoom out, but as you might imagine, that never happens. I hadn't been to the Piggly Wiggly in years, and Ruth's Pimento Cheese Spread, the Pig's own brand of breakfast sausage, a jar of pickled okra, and White Lilly Flour seemed to jump in my basket as soon as they caught my eye. I bought a can of boiled peanuts (sacrilege, but it was February and raw ones didn't come around until summer), a bag of barbecued pork rinds, a box of MoonPies, and a six-pack of Cheerwine. All I needed was a loaf of Little Miss Sunbeam white bread and I was set for the duration. And cereal, instant coffee, and skim milk. Addison loathed instant coffee. It occurred to me while I went through the checkout line that the flowers I had chosen were pretty pitiful and that I, The Widow who was no longer accountable to anyone, was no better at making healthy choices than the kid at breakfast in Virginia, but then I wasn't going to eat all this mess at the same time. I would allow myself to indulge in it all bit by bit. It was a good thing my pants had five percent spandex woven in the fabric.

It was very chilly outside, probably somewhere in the forties, but cold and damp enough for gloves. So I pushed the two bags and the flowers into the back of the car, hopped in, cranked it up, stepped on the gas, and bam! I hit something. Hard. I looked behind me again and there was a huge SUV awfully close, in fact, right on the right side of my back bumper. Shit. A wreck. Great. That's just great, I thought, just what the doctor ordered. I pulled back into my parking space and put the car in park. I really didn't need this and I don't know why but I burst into tears. Boy, I thought, for someone who never had a history of tears, I had developed some impressive waterworks. But I forgave myself, thinking I was probably overtired from all the driving and just overwrought from the most recent events of my miserable life. All that said, I put my head on my hands that were resting on the steering wheel and sobbed like a four-year-old.

Did I even have collision insurance? Was it my fault? Jesus. Couldn't life cut me some slack? Just a little slack for The Widow please?

There was a tapping on my window and I didn't want to look up. But the tapping continued and I picked my head up, sniffed like a stevedore, wiped my eyes, and lowered my window. There stood the most gorgeous man I have ever seen, with the most sympathetic eyes.

"Are you all right?" he said.

"Yes. No. Yes. No," I began to babble. "Look, my husband just died like ten days ago and I just drove here the whole way from New Jersey to stay with my aunt on Folly and I'm just so tired. I'm so tired." I took a deep breath and waited for him to tell me that I had caused at least a thousand dollars worth of damage to his car but he was just looking at me so I added, "And he left me with no money, too. Our house was foreclosed on and I lost everything, *everything* I ever owned except for what's in the back of this *stupid* car that I bought because it was all I could afford." I reached for the box of tissues I had on the passenger seat, pulled two out, blew my nose, and wiped my eyes.

"Holy smoke, ma'am, that's awful. Sounds like you need a break."

"Right? But no breaks for me! I still can't believe what's happened to me, but hey," I said and tried to smile, "some days you get the bear, right?" I opened my door and got out, my knees somewhat wobbly with shockwaves from the accident. "Let's see what happened to your car."

"It's no big deal. Really it isn't."

I closed my door and stood next to him. Good grief, I thought, this guy is electric or something. I mean, it had been years since I had been around raging testosterone. Well, I shouldn't say *raging* really, more like *any.* Yes, *any noticeable testosterone emanating from men* would actually be the more appropriate way to put it. I was long immune to the allure of any of Addison's friends or any other men who came and went in my life. Who was this guy?

"Wow," I mumbled stupidly, looking at him and alternately appraising the scrape across his left rear bumper, hoping he would think I meant the damage. "Look at your bumper," I said, thinking it might help clarify that The Widow wasn't on the prowl. Yet.

"Entirely my fault. I backed out without looking," he said. "By the way, I'm John Risley."

His fault? I sighed with relief. John Risley. Nice name. Was John Risley trying to spare me the expense of the repairs? He was about my age, I thought.

"Cate. I'm Cate Cooper." I smiled at him. I must've looked like a refugee from Fright Night. We shook hands and then stepped back to examine the cars again. My taillight was in pieces on the ground. And my bumper had a crack in it. "Have to fix that, I guess."

"I'll take care of it," he said. "Don't worry."

"Gosh, that's okay. It's nothing really."

"Look, my car belongs to the college . . ."

"What college?"

"The College of Charleston."

"Oh."

"I teach there. Anyway, our insurance will cover it. I don't know if your bumper needs to be replaced but it looks like a maybe. We can find that out. If you'll just give me your number, I'll call you tomorrow and get it all taken care of right away."

He took off his gloves to pull out his wallet to get a business card and there it was. A wedding ring on the left hand. I knew this was completely ridiculous but something inside of me sank.

"I just need a good night's sleep," I said, which probably sounded like a stupid thing to say. I took his card while I dug around in my purse for a piece of paper, deciding to use the receipt from the Pig.

"You too? I haven't slept through the night for about fifteen years," he said. "Do you need a pen?"

"No, thanks." I leaned on the hood of his car and wrote out my cell phone number. "Yeah, sleep's a precious commodity these days. My mind just whirls around all night. I should write a book."

"Shouldn't we all? I'll call you in the morning?"

"Sure."

"You sure you're okay?"

"Yeah, thanks. I'm fine. Just beyond exhausted in mind, body, and spirit, but other than that?"

"Cate? I'm really sorry about this."

"No sweat, really. I needed a jolt."

"Right. Okay, then . . ."

He smiled at me again, climbed into his SUV that was heavy-duty enough to pull a trailer of horses, started the engine, and then he drove away into the night.

"Wow," I said.

Inside of twenty minutes I was climbing the steps up to Aunt Daisy's front porch. I had called ahead to say I had been delayed by a fender bender but save me a plate of whatever they were having and I would see them very soon.

All the lights in the house were on and I rang the doorbell. I was excited then, smelling the salt rolling in from the ocean, feeling the dampness swelling my hair. I felt myself sliding back to my childhood and I remembered being really young and how complete I felt then. Maybe this would be good for me, to be here, to remember who I had started out to become, to find that girl and resuscitate her, see if she had any life left in her. Maybe if I could find her I wouldn't feel like an old, used up, and fractured middle-aged woman. Maybe I'd try to figure out a way to stay until I could put myself back together again. I heard uneven footsteps.

"It's open! It's open! Come on in! Come in out of that cold!"

It was Aunt Daisy, of course, hobbling toward the door. I tried the handle and the door opened with no problem. I stepped inside, adjusting my eyes to the bright lights.

"Hey!" I said. "Look who's back just like the flu! How are you?" I hugged her so hard I thought she might break but I was so filled with relief to be there at last.

"Close that pneumonia hole!"

I closed the door behind me as quickly as I could.

"Oh! My dear girl! How I've missed you! Let me look at you!" She stood back to give me the once-over and the tears in her eyes tumbled down her cheeks.

"You can't cry, Aunt Daisy! Don't! Believe me! I've shed enough tears for both of us, enough to last all our lives!" I hugged her again and we made our way toward the kitchen, from where the smell of something wonderful was beckoning us to follow. Good grief, we were surely turning into a bunch of weepers.

"Oh, shoot," she said and pulled a tissue from her sleeve to blot her eyes, "look at me!"

"You're fine! How's that foot?"

"Like hell. Hurts like hell." She blew her nose. "I'm just a sentimental old fool!"

"No. You're not. You're perfect. Now, what do I smell?"

"Okra soup. What else? In this weather? It's so damn cold you could lay down and die."

"Well, don't do that! I couldn't handle another funeral quite yet. Hey, Ella! You're here!"

Aunt Daisy's companion and partner of forty years stood there with her hands on her hips, grinning wide. There was a warm pecan pie on the sideboard that I could smell from across the room.

"And just where else would I be? We can't have Miss Daisy running around in that cast, falling down and breaking her other foot, too, can we?"

"Ella? Are you making us martinis or what?"

"Yes, Your Highness!" Ella mumbled.

"I heard that! I finally moved her in," Aunt Daisy said. "After all these years? Let 'em talk and see if I care!"

"That's right!" I said. "Wait till the neighbors hear what happened to me, you two old scandals will look like Republicans."

"Grey Goose good for you?" Ella said, shaking the martini shaker like mad.

"Anything. Believe me. For the first time in my life I can honestly say I have earned a cocktail."

As she poured the drinks out into three martini glasses, I realized the shaker was meant to look like a penguin. It seemed to me I had seen one before, ages ago.

"How cute is this?" I said. "Where'd you find it?"

"Catalog," Aunt Daisy said. "Restoration Hardware, I think. Maybe Target?"

"Ever since she became an invalid . . ."

"I am not an invalid!"

"All she does is sit around and order frivolous junk from catalogs, HGTV, QVC, and the Internet," Ella said and Aunt Daisy pouted. "Did you see the doormat with the smiling shrimp?"

"You said you liked the penguin," Aunt Daisy said.

"Well, *I* think it's adorable!" I said, wondering if the two old biddies went at it around the clock and how long I could bear it before it got on my nerves.

Ella carefully passed me a glass filled right up to the rim and one to Aunt Daisy, too. We held them up to toast.

"What are we drinking to?" I said.

"Welcome home, Cate," Aunt Daisy said. "We have missed you more than we can say!"

"Yep, it's fuh true, like we say down 'eah in the Lowcountry. More than we can say."

"Thanks," I said and took a deep sip, vowing to let them bicker all they wanted and I would never say a word.

Over dinner we talked about the recent days, finding Addison, the funeral, his whores, his maybe-love child, the foreclosure, my diamonds, moving—the whole horror show was briefly revisited right up to my car accident of that evening.

"His name is John Risley. He teaches at the College of Charleston," I said.

Aunt Daisy and Ella put down their spoons and looked at each other. For the first time since I had walked in the door, the chatterboxes were dead silent.

"Yeah, so, John Risley's one gorgeous devil," I said. I looked at them still staring at each other. Then they finally turned to me. "What? He's married! And hello, I've been a widow for less than two weeks. Although, I gotta say that if he got lost in the night and fell in between my sheets, I wouldn't have him arrested."

I thought that was a pretty witty line for the old girls to chew on but they were definitely chewing on something else.

"Okay," I said, "let's have it. He's an ax murderer?"

"Oh, no, darling," Aunt Daisy said with the most curious smile. "Yes, he's married but not exactly. Anyway, we know John really well. He brings students out to the Porgy House all the time. We'll move you over there tomorrow morning. I'm afraid you'll be seeing a lot of him."

"Oh, okay, so that's not the worst news. But what do you mean he's not *exactly* married? I saw the ring on his hand."

"He married a kook!" Aunt Daisy said.

"Hush your mouth! She's not a kook, she's sick. She's in an institution for the criminally insane, Cate. Been there for years. And she's probably not coming out."

"Why? What did she do?"

"He won't talk about it," Ella said.

"But maybe you can find out!" Aunt Daisy said.

"Good grief!"

"Would you like some more soup?" Ella said.

"Is there anything left in that shaker?" I said. "And maybe I'll have a piece of that pie."

CHAPTER NINE

Setting: The Porgy House, the Heyward bedroom.

Director's Note: Photos of the Porgy House fireplace, the poker, and wood floors. At the end of this scene, the kitchen table with peanut butter and milk. Dorothy in a nightgown and robe.

Act I
Scene 5

Dorothy: It was so quiet and remote that living on Folly Beach could be lonely and even frightening sometimes—one night I was convinced there was an intruder in our house.

I said, "DuBose? Are you asleep, DuBose?" I whispered as quietly as I could. Nothing. I poked his shoulder until he stirred.

"Yes. No, not now. I'm awake. What is it?"

"Shhh! There's someone in the house!"

I guess he decided to humor me because he rolled over, stood up, put on his slippers and his robe and went to see. I heard him padding across the upstairs living room, and Jenifer's room, and I could hear him on the steps, going downstairs making all the noise he pleased! Was he crazy? He was not even tiptoeing! And then I realized what he was doing. He didn't want to surprise the robber. If this criminal who sneaked in our house heard him coming, he'd have a chance to run out of the back door. Then no one would get hurt! Brilliant!

I could hear him opening closet doors and closing them shut again. He was going to wake up the whole island! I was holding my breath, listening for any other sounds beside the noisy commotion he was making. I thought I heard breathing but then I realized it was me doing the breathing and I thought well, thank God, because this whole business was enough to give me a darned fatal heart attack.

I heard something else from the kitchen, something muffled. Then there was a slam. The back door. Then it got quiet. I thought, oh no! Now DuBose is dead, bleeding from the head, lying in a pool of his own blood. There was blood everywhere! I knew it!

Now I *had* to hurry downstairs and save my husband. Oh, dear God! Jenifer was upstairs! What if the thug was still in the house? After weighing both sides, I decided to go it alone. There was no reason to wake her up and hide her in the closet, was there? Wouldn't this monster see her unmade bed and figure out there was someone else in the house? *Wait!* What if he had come to kill us and kidnap her like that Lindbergh baby? Oh, sweet Mother of God! Please pray for us!

I didn't even stop for my slippers, but I picked up the poker from the upstairs fireplace and sneaked across the floor. It creaked. I cringed, stopping and waiting for a second to see if I could hear anything downstairs. Silence. So I continued toward the steps and made my way down them, as quietly as a palmetto bug.

I could see the warm yellow glow of the overhead light in the kitchen as it cast itself in geometric shards across the floor and out into the room where I stood. My heart was in my throat. I tried to slide along the wall, not breathing, and peeked in the room from the corner of my eye. There was my darling DuBose, sitting at the table eating a sandwich.

"What on earth are you doing?" I said with my hand across my racing heart.

"Eating a peanut butter sandwich and drinking a glass of milk. Can I make something for you?"

"Since when do you eat peanut butter?"

"Since now, I guess. It just seemed appetizing."

"So, there's no robber, no killer here to murder us all?"

"Nope. Just a raccoon in the garbage bin outside. We can clean it up in the morning."

"I'm going back to bed."

"Are you sure? This is awfully good."

Men.

Fade to Darkness

CHAPTER TEN

The Porgy House

It was seven in the morning. I was in the kitchen getting fatter by the minute, bingeing on the sweet mysteries of leftover pecan pie, nearly euphoric from its healing properties. Pecan pies, especially the ones that Ella made, lifted my spirits to such spiraling heights I decided that if I could, I would have a slice every breakfast for the rest of my life. But, my confessor would be glad to know, I was sipping hot coffee with skim milk to compensate for my sins.

The house was dead quiet and I moved around like a little mouse in socks, gliding silently on the lemon wax of Aunt Daisy's highly polished heart pine floors. To the outside observer it might seem odd for a newly widowed middle-aged woman to sock-skate across her auntie's floor but it was what I had done as a child on these very same floors and I was home again. Besides, you should never pass up an opportunity to dance.

I put my plate in the dishwasher, careful not to rattle the racks, refilled my mug, and walked gingerly out toward the living-room doors that led to the enormous front deck suspended high over the dunes.

From that vantage point, the sweeping water view was so pretty it took my breath away as it always had every single time. Aunt Daisy's simple deck ranked high among my favorite places anywhere in the world. It filled me with such peace to watch the ocean, dimples glistening and currents moving, demanding my undivided attention, and my undivided attention it would have. This was where I would park myself until Aunt Daisy and Ella were awake.

I had the doorknob firmly in the clasp of my hand. Just then, right before I could turn that doorknob, I swear to you that in that very split *second,* I heard rushing, clomping footsteps overhead, a triple beep, and then Aunt Daisy's voice.

"Alarm's off!" she called out.

The woman had eyes in the back of her head. How else could she know that I was about to trip the alarm? Maybe she heard a floorboard make a familiar creak, but could her hearing be *that* good at her age? No. I was more inclined to go with the eyes-in-the-back-of-the-head that she had grown specifically for the difficult and challenging job of raising Patti and me. She was omniscient, like women can be, innately knowing all and seeing all.

"Thanks!" I called back to her. It occurred to me that our world today was pretty darned precarious if my aunt felt she needed an alarm on Folly Beach but that's how the world had changed. Everyone everywhere was at risk all the time. If it wasn't Al Qaeda scaring the liver out of you to take a plane to some benign place like Omaha, it was teenagers who'd rob you blind in your own house so they could get high on meth or whatever it was our young druggies of today ingested for sport.

I opened one of the French doors, let myself outside, and stood there, some twenty feet above the Atlantic. I looked around for a moment and then made a beeline to the railing, leaning on it, scanning the beach. It was empty except for a few dog-walkers and runners. The morning fog was disappearing by the minute, giving way to blue skies, and there was no doubt, it was going to be a beautiful day.

I counted three container ships out near the horizon. They were fully loaded with heavy cargo and riding low in the water, probably on their way to Germany to deliver BMWs or to parts unknown with whatever we were exporting these days. Gorgeous. South Carolina had certainly come a long way from the days of tall sailing ships carrying cotton, rice, and indigo back to the mother country. Yes, she had. Yet, though those days were centuries ago, the historic images of tall ships were very easy to visualize, highly polished wooden vessels, gleaming brass fittings, stark white sails unfurled, taut, their cheeks filled with easterly wind, keeling and moving briskly across the water . . . there was something romantic about living in a port city. Ports were not stagnant. They were always in motion, engaged in their own particular endless rhythms. Movement was the soul of their very nature and I loved it. I loved the waters of Charleston's song most especially because she had saved me from despair so many times.

When I was a little girl I spent hours wandering along the edges of this very shore, my sneakers sinking in the soft sand, my footprints filling quickly with the rising tide. It was hypnotic, watching tides roll in to wash the shore with their swirl and froth. The water chased the flocks of tiny sandpipers away, back into the salty air and they landed some twenty feet down the shoreline. Then the water pulled back only to slide in again, over and over, in its own measured time, covering the beach inch by inch, until it reached its high-water mark.

Low tides, most especially after storms, revealed treasures sprinkled along the shore—shells, bits of seaweed, driftwood, and so on. These were the things Patti and I gathered and saved. We held conch shells, whelks really, to the sides of our heads to hear their secrets. We decorated our elaborate sandcastles with moon shells and cockles. With the tips of our fingers, we carefully pried sand dollars from the mud they suckled for nourishment and safety, strung them across the deck railings, and before long the merciless sun bleached them to chalk-white. During the years of a good haul, we suspended our sand dollars from thin satin ribbons and hung them on our Christmas trees. Other times we broke them apart to find the five doves of peace that Aunt Daisy told us were in there. For us, for all of us, Folly Beach was filled with a kind of sacred majesty and in return for our homage she gave us endless rewards.

After our parents died, Patti and I would sit on this very same beach, usually on an old palmetto log that had washed up from another island. Those were terrible days. We'd damn our lives, and try to find a dream for our futures. Dreams eluded us. Blinded by salty tears and wiping runny noses on our sleeves, we would tell each other that there had to be more to life than grief. We would argue with each other, swearing that if there was a god somewhere who actually loved us, then surely he wanted us to be happy, at least some of the time. Where was this god anyway? Strangely absent. So we came to the beach to hide from the world and cry our hearts out or sometimes just to kick the sand or to run like maniacs until we were gasping for breath and our sides ached so badly we doubled over in pain. You might say it was our adolescent version of primal scream therapy. It worked, somewhat, but now I think whatever relief we found, we found only because we had each other to which our fractured hearts could cling. Sometimes we would sit there until it was dark. And Aunt Daisy and Ella would coax us with the sweetest words they knew to please come back inside the house for supper. On occasion, and especially in the early days when our wounds were still fresh, we'd be greeted by the parish priest, sitting at the kitchen table, drinking coffee and having a piece of Ella's pie. He'd try his best through diplomacy and guilt to talk us into becoming more active in the church, to join CYO—the Catholic Youth Organization—or the Regina Mundi Club. Aunt Daisy would stand behind him, rolling her eyes, and at some point she would say that, well, it all sounded fine but for now seeing us on Sunday was probably all he should expect, but he was welcome to stop by any time he was in the neighborhood. We were so grateful for her understanding that we couldn't stand one more thing.

I know that all sounds depressing but getting through those first birthdays and Christmases or holidays of any kind without our mom and dad was unbelievably painful. We couldn't show them our Halloween costumes or share our candy with them. Ever again. We couldn't make them cards on their birthdays or bring them school projects to admire or pick black-eyed Susans for them in the summer. Ever. We didn't know how to live without them. We belonged to them. And try as we may have tried to transfer all that longing and need to Aunt Daisy and even Ella, who was around more and more, we were inclined to hide our feelings from them and to make them think we were getting along all right. *We're just fine!* After all, Aunt Daisy took us in. And we loved her for it.

Besides, Folly Beach wasn't exactly crawling with therapists who specialized in the treatment of children in those days. Even if it had been, we weren't the kind of people who paid other people our hard-earned money to listen to our problems and help us understand tragedies that could not be reversed. We were far too pragmatic for that sort of self-indulgence, having been cut from suck-it-up cloth. We learned that you never got used to losing your parents. You just got used to the pain.

I was six and Patti was twelve when our mother died from breast cancer. She was robbed of her life when she was only forty years old. Lila. Beautiful Lila. She always put off going to the doctor for check-ups and so forth, saying she felt perfectly fine. She played tennis all the time and even belonged to a waltz society, which caused Patti and me endless giggling to see her twirling in the wacky dresses she wore. Skirt, skirt, and more skirt! But other than that one embarrassing deviation from our ironclad definition of what normal mothers were supposed to do for a hobby, she was tanned, toned, and fit from head to toe, defying her actual age from every angle. By the time her cancer was discovered it had metastasized to her lymph nodes, liver, and brain.

Patti said our mother's illness lasted only eight weeks. I don't remember the timeline. I just know that right after she died, I began to dance, saying I was dancing for her. Dance became the prism through which I looked at my world and the only way I could find it bearable.

It made Patti cry every time I said I was dancing for Momma, but Aunt Daisy and Ella said it was good for me and they wished Patti would dance, too. But Patti preferred to bake. It all started with the Easy-Bake Oven, moved to Toll House cookies, and led to zillion-dollar mega wedding cakes. No one who knew our family in those days would have laid a nickel on the table to bet that how we coped with the deaths of our parents would shape our careers.

When Momma was diagnosed, we began spending more and more time with Aunt Daisy, because Dad had to work.

Our father traveled for a living, so we spent more and more time at Aunt Daisy's house. He was a pilot for Pan American World Airways and flew all over the world. One night, just two years after we lost our mother, our father died in his sleep of a heart attack. He was in Singapore. I still remember the hullabaloo it was to have his body returned to us and how hysterical Aunt Daisy was with the American embassy and the airlines. They say it took weeks to bring him home. Red tape. So! That's the short version of what happened to our parents. I still have no memories of either funeral and it's probably just as well.

I don't like to think about those days. What's the point? But Patti and I get mammograms religiously every year and we try to do a lot of cardio and eat heart-healthy meals. Well, most of the time when we're not eating cake and pecan pie. Or sausage. Or waffles.

Anyway, all that said, from a very early age, we came to the beach to unburden our young souls, to find some kind of comfort in nature and from each other. We were too young to fully comprehend that life goes on and the world doesn't really care about your personal sorrow. It just kept turning. There was always someone to consider who had less, some poor soul in a worse situation to pray for, and we were constantly told that we should be grateful for what we had. And we *were* grateful, but that doesn't mean it wasn't a struggle to hold ourselves together, keep our grades up, and lopsided smiles on our faces.

I remembered then how the kids in school pitied us and how I hated their pity because it was false. Children are so cruel and when we were labeled as unfair game for the usual bullying, sarcasm, and backstabbing that went on among girls, they ostracized us as weird. They called us The Bummer Sisters behind our backs but we knew it. Who knows? Maybe they thought our situation was contagious or that we could use our loss to some advantage over them. All their mean-spirited childish quarantine really accomplished was to drive Patti and me closer together. Those were the days that Patti became elevated to the status of the ultimate big sister and that poor Aunt Daisy learned what it was like to raise long-eared mules.

Today it was nearly impossible to remember our parents beyond their faces frozen in time in the scrapbooks Aunt Daisy kept and the few pictures we had. It wasn't like Aunt Daisy didn't do everything she could to give us a stable and loving home. And when Ella was there, she was an angel to us, helping with homework, listening to us, or cooking something delicious to eat. But it wasn't the same thing as having our own two healthy parents in our life and we all knew it.

Funny, I didn't seem to need to dance like crazy to rid myself of the hangover of Addison's death. An unconscious sock-slide across the floor had seemed perfectly appropriate. The only thing I felt for Addison was seriously pissed off. Maybe I'd simply had enough of death for one lifetime and by the time he took the leap into the next world, I'd certainly had enough of him. The crazy selfish son of a bitch.

Even though it was just forty degrees, I shivered a few times and moved back from the railing to a chair at the table in the sun. Forty degrees in February in New Jersey would be considered a sign of early spring and here it made me have chills if I was in the shade. I took a few more sips of my coffee and thought about Patti up there in the frozen tundra of Alpine and all the misery that came with winter. Black ice. Furnaces that sputtered and failed. Slippery roads. And being so damn cold your teeth clattered if you had to walk across a parking lot. I should call her, I thought, and let her know I'm thinking about her, tell her I love her and rehash my drive down here once more. I wished then that she was here. Last night we had spoken briefly, briefly because I drank two of Ella's martinis and there was no point in trying to have a real conversation with anyone after that. She knew I was alive and here safely and she was relieved and satisfied. I would call her later. I wasn't getting up then. I was too comfortable sitting there, my head thrown back in the warmth of the sun, like a lizard. Later on I would retrieve my cell phone from its recharger, plugged in somewhere in the house, somewhere between the vermouth and the olives. Ahem. I would call her later.

"What in the *world* are you *doing?*"

It was Aunt Daisy's voice right behind me. She startled me so that my body lurched, throwing the remains of my coffee into the air and fortunately not on her. Or me.

"What? Hey! Good morning!"

"You'd better put a hat and sunglasses on your head or you're going to look like me before you know it!"

"You're probably right. Not that looking like you is a bad . . ."

"Oh, hush! I know what you mean! I'm a thousand years old. You think I don't know I have a few wrinkles? Prune face, that's what. And this wattle?" She flipped the hanging skin beneath her chin and laughed. "Never mind my upper arms. You want more coffee? Ella's making breakfast."

She stood before me like an obelisk fashioned of milky-pink marble pulled from the depths of the quarries decades upon decades ago. Her hands were firmly planted on her hips.

"Well, I think you look great. Maybe I'll get another shot of coffee but I don't really feel like break . . ."

"Yes, you will! We all need breakfast, otherwise our blood sugar plummets before noon and we get all cranky. Besides, you can't live on pecan pie, no matter how good it is."

"Well, I sure would like to give it a try," I said and stood up to give her a peck on the cheek.

"Me too." She sank into the chair next to mine and put her mug on the table. I sat again. "But I'd get as big as a house. So now tell me. Did you sleep well?"

"Like a stone."

"Good, good. After breakfast, I want to get you moved over to the Porgy House. I think it's best if you have your own space. Besides, all my rentals are full."

"Well, that's a lucky thing, isn't it? I mean, who rents a house at the beach in the winter?"

"Honey, this is Folly Beach. *Everyone* wants to come here. Remember? We're a bargain next to the downtown B&Bs. And the hotels? Forget it! Sky-high! You'd think only millionaires can afford a vacation!"

"Well, especially *these* days . . ." I was thinking about the god-awful unending recession.

"What? That's just ridiculous! No, no. I'm busy all the time, calling the housekeepers to come clean up after the last tenants and get ready for the next horde, coming with five more people than they stated on the contract and nasty old dogs that aren't allowed. I had one renter last month who brought their pet boa constrictor."

"What? What. Are. You. Saying? A boa?"

"Yes! They said, *Oh, don't worry. Walter's in his cage.* I said, *Oh really? I feel much better! Get Walter and his cage outta here on the double or y'all can leave right now!* During the summer it's ten times worse. So, I stop by unexpectedly, you know, on the excuse to see if they're happy, bring them brochures of things to do and then I count bodies and pets at the same time."

"Well, maybe I can help you with some of that. You know, the spy stuff."

"That would be a blessing, Cate. I mean, there's not much to it. Just some running around that . . . well, obviously, my running days are on hold until this silly cast comes off."

"Yeah, that's pretty clear. So how much longer is it supposed to be on?"

"I don't know. I go back to that damn fool doctor sometime next week. I wish they'd just give me the one you can take off so I can get a decent shower! I'm so tired of wrapping my leg in dry-cleaner bags and rubber bands, you can't imagine!"

"Actually, I can. I wouldn't like it, either."

She stopped and looked at me. I knew she wanted to ask me something that she didn't quite know how to ask.

"Come on, Aunt Daisy. I can smell your wood burning. What's on your mind?"

"It's none of my business."

"Let's make it your business. I don't mind."

"All right then. I want you to tell me how someone as smart as you are got completely bamboozled by that son of a bitch Addison Cooper. And Lord love a duck, I probably shouldn't say this, but Ella and I never liked him one damn bit. I mean, look, I understand a little bimbo on the side. It's not nice, but I get it. I even understand a love child—it happens. And I get the chasing skirts in the office. Men can be very stupid about their you-know-whats. They all think they're made out of gold!"

"Boy, that's for sure."

"Amen. And nobody understands how a business can fail any better than I do. I've been to the edge and back one hundred times. But here's what I don't get. Tell me how he leveraged your *whole* life, your house, your furniture, your *everything down to your lightbulbs* . . . tell me, number one, how he got that one by you and number two, why weren't you even suspicious?"

Wow, I thought, wow. Like I had not thought this through for almost every waking minute since I found his body? She must have thought I was the biggest idiot to ever draw a breath. Suddenly I didn't want to talk about it.

"Eggs might be good for me. You know, protein?"

"Well, as I said, Cate, it's none of my business. I know that."

I didn't know how to respond, so I just said, "You know what, Aunt Daisy? I don't know the answers to your questions. That's one of the reasons I came here, to try to figure that all out. I mean, you're right, it's bad enough to lose everything, including your husband, his reputation, which used to be something else entirely, stellar, in fact, and then to realize all of it was going on right under your own nose. And as far as borrowing money against the house, he must have forged my signature."

"My word! The skunk!"

"Exactly. That's all I can imagine, because Mark said the banks would've required two signatures. But who knows how elaborate his shenanigans were? How deep does that river of deception run? I learned about it all in a seventy-two-hour tidal wave until there wasn't a glass left in the house to fill up with liquor to chug or a bar stool to fall off of if I did. It doesn't really matter how he got away with everything, does it? It doesn't matter anymore, because it's a fait accompli. But I'm still a little shell-shocked, to tell you the truth. Yeah. I'm shell-shocked."

Aunt Daisy looked at me for what seemed like forever, planning her response. At first, she had been angry for me and even with me but now she saw me as I was. Damaged. Floundering.

"Truth," she finally said. "Do you *want* to know the truth?"

"Right now? No. I don't. Somewhere between Charlotte, North Carolina, and the outskirts of Charleston I decided that maybe the best thing for me would be to get into some heavy denial and tell myself this isn't my fault. Otherwise, I think I might crack into a million little pieces."

Aunt Daisy looked at me again with watery eyes, their once-blue color faded from age to a soft dove-gray. She leaned forward, taking my hand in hers. "It's not your fault."

I thought I would break down then. "You really don't think it was?"

"I do not think it was your fault. Any of it. And if you had your suspicions about things, and I'm sure you did from time to time, it would be only natural to sweep them under a rug."

"You know, I'm sure Patti told you, he was really changed."

"Stress. Stress does that to people. Why, he, he . . . he took his own life, Cate. He must have been completely, completely defeated."

"He didn't know how to lose, Aunt Daisy."

"Loss is a bitter pill. A bitter pill."

"Especially for someone like Addison. He was a very proud man. Don't you know he probably went through every possible scenario he could think of to save himself and our house?"

"Of course he did." She patted my hand and I looked down at hers. Aunt Daisy's knuckles were swollen and arthritic and probably ached all the time. After a moment or two she stood up and rubbed her hands together briskly to warm them. "Come on, now. Let's get some break-fast into you and get this day moving. Ella will tan our hides with a switch if we don't gobble up every crumb and tell her how wonderful it is."

"Aunt Daisy?"

"Yes?"

"In the end, I didn't like him, either."

"Well, now we're getting someplace."

"And what am I going to do if that woman with the little boy turns up?"

"We'll deal with that if and when the time comes. That's why God invented lawyers."

"I'm not so sure that was God."

So, while we talked about my children and Patti and Mark, we ate Swiss cheese omelets and rye toast and drank glass after glass of fresh-squeezed orange juice.

"I do love me some orange juice," Aunt Daisy said, sounding like a silly young girl from the 'hood.

She was so funny sometimes.

"You know, Cate," Ella said, "your aunt was voted the number-one supporter of the Marsh Tacky Association and they sent us a bushel of oranges."

"And I got a plaque! Don't forget I got a plaque! A nice one, too, with a little three-dimensional brass horse on it. I'll show you later."

"Humph," Ella grunted. "She needs another plaque like a hole in the head."

"You two," I said, remembering Aunt Daisy's wall of fame in her office. "Listen, why don't you let me clean up the kitchen and y'all can go get dressed?"

"She's pretty particular about her kitchen," Aunt Daisy said, hooking her thumb in Ella's direction.

Ella smiled, shook her head, and pushed back from the table.

"I'll inspect it later with my magnifying glass. Come on, Old Cabbage, let's get moving."

"Old Cabbage?" I said.

"It's what Prince Phillip calls Queen Elizabeth!" Aunt Daisy said, beaming. "I saw it in that movie *Queen*."

"Helen Mirren," I said. "Love her."

"We saw it ten times," Ella said. "That woman was so good, wasn't she? Made me want a Corgi."

"Oh, now!" Old Cabbage said. "That's what we need is a dog! Cate? Did you hear what she said?"

I giggled.

"Mirren's a genius. Like Meryl Streep," I said. "They really and truly can make you believe they're somebody else."

"That's why they make the big bucks!" Ella said and turned to Aunt Daisy. "You want me to help you with that cast or what?"

"Are you telling me what to do?" Aunt Daisy said. "Because when the day and time comes that I need someone to tell me what to do, I'll let you know."

"She's impossible," Ella said, pulling a dry-cleaner bag from the stash of them in the pantry closet. "Come on!"

I could hear them bickering all the way up the stairs and I couldn't stop laughing. They weren't really bickering though. It was how the old cabbages showed their affection for each other.

After I wiped down the last counter and turned on the dishwasher, I repacked my overnight bag and went outside to assess the damage to my car in the daylight. It was pretty banged up alright. Well, at least it gave me an excuse to see that nice guy again. What was his name? I pulled his card from the side of my handbag. Risley. John Risley. The gorgeous married one with the legally insane dangerous wife. I wondered if I would hear from him. I had to get my car fixed before the bumper fell off onto the street but the last thing I needed now was a fling with anybody. Even if he did have the most beautiful eyes I had ever seen on a man.

I heard a door close from under the house and looked up to see Aunt Daisy leaning on Ella's arm as they made their way from the elevator. All the new beach houses had elevators now, which would have been considered nothing short of ludicrous when I was little. But when Aunt Daisy renovated her house and had it jacked up to the required height to meet the code, she realized she wasn't getting any younger, so an elevator was added to the architect's plans. It was also very handy for them when they went to Sam's Club or Costco and came home with tons of paper towels, cases of water, and whatever else they stocked up on in case of an emergency.

"You follow us!" Ella called out.

"Okay!" I called back and started my car.

We drove the short distance down West Ashley Avenue to the Porgy House and pulled up in the yard. On the way over I sent a quick text message to Russ to let him know I had arrived. Maybe he and Alice would like to get together? It would be interesting to see how my relationship with Alice might develop. Dear God, please send the Holy Spirit to imbue my soul with charity. Thank you. Amen.

Ella went to the front door and began fumbling with keys, trying to find the right one. I hopped out to help Aunt Daisy and she turned around, eyes narrowed and focused on my bumper.

"You can't drive that car in that condition," she said. "And you'll get a ticket in about two seconds for not having a taillight!"

"Yeah, you're right. But your friend Mr. Risley promised to call today and get it fixed."

"My friend? Humph." She raised her eyebrows and said, "We'll see just whose friend he is soon enough!"

"Oh, please," I said but I was talking to her back.

Ella finally got the door open and came back to help Aunt Daisy navigate the stairs but of course Aunt Daisy was already halfway inside the house. Between her cane and holding on to the handrails there wasn't much that could stop her from moving when it suited her but any fool could see she really was incapacitated by her broken foot.

"I'm fine! I'm fine!" she said, calling out to Ella, who was turning on all the lights inside the little house.

A funny thing happened then. When the sun came from behind a cloud and through the trees, the ugly little weather-beaten cottage became adorable. It was absolutely charming and I was completely surprised by it. I felt an instant psychological lift as though this house was going to be my friend. But I knew the insides were very old, the plumbing and so forth, and I wondered how I would fare, trying to cook in a kitchen from the Dark Ages. This whole scene was going to be a cosmic test of my true mettle.

I stepped inside to a small living room that had been set up like a miniature museum exhibition, with Heyward and Gershwin paraphernalia all around on easels. There were playbills from the original production of *Porgy and Bess,* original copies of piano sheet music for "Summertime" and other hit songs from the musical. There was a glass case that held small glasses for cocktails and a decanter collection.

"I don't think they used this room too much except to pour booze," Aunt Daisy said. "Come see the kitchen."

"Quaint," I said. "My piano should go in this room." I reminded myself to talk to Mark about shipping it down here.

"Maybe."

"What piano?" Ella said.

"My mother gave it to me when I was little."

"This house don't need a piano!"

"Why?" I asked.

"Hush, Ella! That piano is an heirloom! Anyway, I've kept everything this way on purpose. Can't you just see Dorothy Heyward standing here making supper for DuBose and Jenifer? Although, I understand she wasn't much of a cook. But this is history! Isn't it exciting?"

"Oh, goodness yes!" I said to make her happy, but if I had known the words to the song from *The Rocky Horror Show* I would have entertained them with my version of "The Time Warp."

The kitchen was, well, really sort of pathetic compared to my Rolls-Royce kitchen in New Jersey. There was an ancient white ceramic sink on the far wall to the right of the back door. In the center of the left wall was a white stove with one oven, and a cabinet and a counter stood to the right. A white refrigerator stood to the left of the stove. Both appliances were from the fifties or sixties and could be replaced with period examples if this place was to be a museum. But I decided to keep my mouth shut for the moment. A round pine table stood in the center of the room with a few chairs. Any one of the home decorating programs on HGTV would have eaten this room alive, taking it on as the almighty challenge. But the apple-green trim was certainly authentic to the period and I wondered how I might help Aunt Daisy enhance the décor. Anthropologie sold those hand-embroidered dish towels that were reminiscent of the thirties. And mercury-glass plates would look good on the plate rack. I had seen them in some catalog in pink and green, if memory served me. And there were the flea markets. Maybe I'd make this kitchen a project. It could be charming.

Aunt Daisy and Ella were already outside on the side porch.

"What's that funny look on your face, Cate? Is my funny little house already working its magic on you?"

"Maybe," I said and thought maybe it really was.

Aunt Daisy and Ella exchanged knowing looks. Perhaps there was more to the house than I knew but it didn't matter. I was anxious to get settled. I had to unpack my car and I wanted to call Russ again and Patti. Then I realized that if I had all that to do I had better set up a time to meet with Mr. Risley before the day got away from me.

As if she was reading my mind, Aunt Daisy said, "If you have to leave your car in the shop overnight, you can use mine. I can't drive now anyway! Go look around upstairs. You can bunk anywhere you want but if and when groups come through . . ."

"I know, I know. Don't worry. I'll make my life disappear so much that they'll think DuBose and Dorothy are in the room next door."

"Well, actually, they are," Ella said and laughed so hard I thought she had lost her mind. But Aunt Daisy was laughing, too.

"Okay, you two! What are you saying? This little place is haunted?"

"You'll have to see for yourself!" Aunt Daisy said.

They smiled a little too serenely for my nervous system and left soon after that, handing me the key.

I went upstairs to see what my choices would be and I quickly decided to sleep in the bedroom in the back of the house. It faced west, so the sun wouldn't wake me up in the morning. And it was next to the bathroom, which had a claw-foot tub and no shower. Well, I thought, I'll just buy one of those rubber things from the hardware store that clamps over the faucet so I can wash my hair. Then I thought, Honey? You sure have come a long way from having your hair blown out at a salon three times a week, haven't you?

"Thanks, Addison. You stupid jerk," I said to an empty room.

The rest of the morning was spent trying to figure out what to do with my meager belongings. There was a tiny two-room guest cottage in the backyard of the house, which I had yet to examine, which I thought might be good for out-of-season clothes and some boxes of books. There was really no point in unpacking every last thing, because surely I wouldn't be here that long. I went out there to see what kind of shape the guesthouse was in and, to my surprise, there were hundreds of conch shells in there all over the floor and not a closet to be found. It occurred to me then that Aunt Daisy had mentioned at dinner last night that this was where Dorothy and DuBose did their writing. That must have been true, because between the tiny windows and the miniscule rooms that were no larger than jail cells, I could not envision anyone living in there comfortably. It must have been murderously hot in the summer, too, because there was very little ventilation.

I was musing over the details of the Heywards' life and my cell phone rang. My caller ID said College of Charleston. I am embarrassed to admit this but there was a distinct fluttering in my stomach. I wasn't too old to flutter.

"Hello?" I said, trying to sound normal and not giddy.

"Hi! Remember me? This is the guy who creamed your SUV at the Pig last night? John Risley?"

"Oh, yeah! I remember you! How are you?"

"Still feeling awful about it and wondering if I can come pick you up and take you to the body shop and maybe out for lunch or something? I don't have any more classes this afternoon."

"Sure! Yeah! Why not?"

We decided I'd meet him at Taco Boy, we could eat there and I'd follow him to the body shop. Then he'd bring me home to Aunt Daisy's. When I told him I was staying at the Porgy House, he was stunned.

"Well, my aunt Daisy McInerny owns it."

"Well, it's a small world, that's for sure. I know Miss Daisy really well! I teach the Charleston Literary Renaissance at the college, in addition to creative writing and some other things when they need me to. But I love the Porgy House! I bring students out there all the time."

"Yeah, she told me that last night. Well, okay then. I'll see you at one?"

"Yep. I'll be there."

We hung up and my first thought was what in the heck is the

Charleston Literary Renaissance? How could I have missed a whole *renaissance*? Oh. Wait. I was shuffle ball changing in a black leotard and pink tights, singing my heart out in auditions and trying to get into Juilliard. Oh, so what, I told myself. He's not going to ask you to write a paper, for heaven's sake! He just wants to fix your car!

I got there at about five minutes past one, not wanting to be the first to arrive, which was really stupid, because he had to be completely unaware that I had entertained any kind of lewd thoughts about him. It was dark inside. I looked all around at the faces in the crowd and couldn't recognize him. But then a man at a table in the back stood and waved. It was him and for some reason, I wasn't nervous anymore.

"Hey! How are you?" I said, fumbling around with my sunglasses and purse. I didn't shake his hand or give him a hug, because both seemed like a weird thing to do. But I smiled at him and he smiled back, seeming happy to see me, even though it was going to cost him time and money to do so when he didn't know me from Adam's house cat. Okay. Maybe I was still a little nervous.

"So, you're Miss Daisy's niece. How about that?"

"So far it's worked out okay," I said. Don't be a smart ass, I told myself. "Actually, Aunt Daisy raised me and my sister Patti after our parents died. She's pretty amazing."

"Yep, she sure is. You grew up on Folly?"

"Yeah, well, to the extent that I ever grew up . . ." You sound like an imbecile, my inner voice warned. "I mean, living on the beach keeps you young, you know?"

"Yeah, I think it does. Keeps you lighthearted anyway. So are you a surfer?"

"No. My sister surfed. I danced. Musical theater variety of dance."
"Ah!"

A waiter appeared to take orders but I hadn't even looked at the menu.

"Drinks?" said the deep-tanned, multi-tattooed, and dyed-blond ponytailed waiter, who obviously surfed whenever possible, all year-round, hence the tan. He was adorable and exactly the kind of young man that my Sara might fall dead in love with and take another ten years off her poor (literally) mother's life.

"Iced tea?" John suggested.

"Sure, why not?"

"Sweetened?"

"No, thanks," I said and thought, gosh, I'll have to get used to drinking iced tea in the winter again. There were a lot of things that were going to take getting used to, such as the freedom to go to places like Taco Boy, which was basically a beachside restaurant, which is also to say they served pretty cheap good food and the whole place smelled like salt and beer. Which I loved. If I had ever brought Addison Cooper to a place like this he would have informed the Health Department that there was a situation on Folly they might like to look into. Then he would have put on an Hermès ascot, which he never wore, just to be obnoxious, some attempt to look like the millionaire from that old television program *Gilligan's Island*.

"Did you hear me?" John said.

"God, I'm sorry, my mind just drifted. What did you say?"

"I said, I'm ordering some guacamole and the taquitos to begin and I think the sautéed shrimp taco is pretty great. We could share some quesadillas, too. And the chili con queso with chorizo. Love that. Or you just order whatever you feel like."

"I think that sounds perfect!" I heard myself say and had no idea what I had just agreed to. To be truthful, I was staring at his hands, which were large and masculine and beautiful and I wondered if they corresponded to other body parts, which people always said they did. I was being ridiculous.

"Okay!" he said and rattled off what sounded like enough dishes to feed six people.

"Awesome," the Heartbreak Kid said. "I'll be right back with your drinks."

When he had walked away, John looked at me and I thought holy hell, it might take every bit of strength I had in my body, but even if my clothes blew off in a hurricane, I was not having an affair with a married man. N. O. WAY.

"Tell me everything about you, Cate," he said. "I want to know who you are."

Oh great. That was all it took, that one simple request was all it took for me to understand that I had no idea anymore who I was. Moreover, how many decades had it been since someone wanted to know about me?

We had lunch, made pleasant conversation, not too heavy, drove to the repair shop, and he brought me back to Aunt Daisy's. I thanked him, died internally one thousand times to see him drive away, took Aunt Daisy's car, and bought groceries. Later I called Russ to let him know the mother ship was out on Folly if he and Alice wanted to have supper one night, that it would be great. And I called Sara and even though I didn't want it to, the story of John Risley slid out and she asked me if my heart was all aflutter for him. Of course I denied it, ha-ha, don't be silly, I said and I knew she was upset with me. Then I said that she *had* to come to Folly for Easter and how was the mixology business coming along? Hmmm? But my face was in flames. *Who is the Risley guy, Mom? No one, sweetheart, no one.* And I passed on dinner with Aunt Daisy, ate a peanut butter sandwich and a glass of milk for supper, soaked for hours in Dorothy Heyward's bathtub, and didn't fall asleep until after three in the morning, worrying about what would become of me. And what was I going to do about John Risley? The greater question was would I have the opportunity *to do* anything about him? I needed to talk to Patti. Where had the day gone?

CHAPTER ELEVEN

Setting: The Porgy House upstairs parlor, daybeds and afghans.

Director's Note: Photos of the book *Imitation of Life*, Fannie Hurst, Zora Neale Hurston, Claudette Colbert, Langston Hughes, Sterling Brown, *Porgy* playbill on the backstage scrim. Then photos of the music room, where the barware and brandy were kept. Now to photos of younger Dorothy in Puerto Rico, New York, and finally a photo of Josephine Pinckney. All DuBose Heyward lines spoken off-stage.

Act II
Scene I

Dorothy: It was that same winter, not long after the night I heard all the crying that DuBose thought was a cat but I knew better. I was thinking about the nature of Fate.

We were in the upstairs parlor, curled up on our own daybeds. During the winter we used them as sofas, but on many of the steamy summer nights when there was not a breath of air to be found indoors, we simply rolled the daybeds out to the porch and slept there, dreaming of wonderful things, lulled by the sounds of the ocean across the street and cooled by the gorgeous salt breezes. Not so *that* February. It was *cold*. The supper dishes were put away, a small fire burned in the fireplace, and we were warm and relaxed, each of us absorbed in our reading, with afghans covering our legs and feet.

"You must be enjoying your book, little one," DuBose said. "I haven't heard a peep from you in over an hour!"

I moved my bookmark to the page I was reading, closed the book, placed it by my side, and sighed a long sigh of exasperation or frustration. I knew DuBose was not entirely sure which it was.

"I'm not sure if I like it or not but I can't put it down!"

I was reading *Imitation of Life,* a novel published the year before that was the subject of wicked high praise from *some* quarters and suspicious derision from others. Some people said it was a sensitive story, one that portrayed the race issues carefully and truthfully. Others said it stereotyped the African Americans and the idea that black people wished to be white was racist and absurd. I was beginning to think it was wonderful and well done.

"Well, you've heard about the author? Fannie Hurst? She's all involved with the Harlem Renaissance."

"Good for her," I said.

"No, seriously! I think I heard she even had Zora Neale Hurston working for her doing secretarial work or something," DuBose said. "The world is changing every day and right before our eyes."

"Yes, but is that change for the better? They're saying that Claudette Colbert is going to play Bea in the film. Can you imagine?"

"She's very pretty."

"I guess so, if you like that slick kind of Hollywood look. Big eyelashes? Shiny lips?"

"She's not nearly as pretty as you are, dear."

"Humph. You know that movie is going to come off as a, well, a racist disaster, polarizing everyone one more time. I mean, your buddy Langston Hughes liked the concept fine until that mean old Sterling Brown clobbered it."

"The devil has a special place in hell for critics of all types," DuBose said.

"What's that again?"

"I said, the devil has a special place in hell for critics of all types."

What a marvelous and consoling thought that all the critics might actually be in hell. We'd certainly wished them there often enough!

"I'll say. We had some of the same kind of rubbish over *Porgy*. Remember? It takes *place* in Charleston but it can't be *performed* in Charleston? Bigots. It's so wrong."

"I wish I *could* forget! I'm going to pour myself a little bit of brandy to warm my bones. Can I get some for you?"

"Oh, why not? Now I'm all riled up again! I mean, DuBose! Listen! What's life without risk?" I threw back my afghan and stood, slipping my feet back into my flats. The floors of the house were cold and drafty.

"Pretty darn dull if you ask me. Nothing ventured, nothing gained."

"I'll come with you. Maybe I'll have a pretzel."

"This book really has your motor going, doesn't it?"

"Yes. Look, all this brouhaha is a little bit like saying that you can't write about Italians if you aren't Italian. Or that you can't write about women if you're a man! It's just ridiculous!"

DuBose opened the cabinet and took out two snifters. He reached for the decanter of brandy, removed its heavy top, and poured out a measure with his left hand. I stood there ready to help him. DuBose's left arm had been greatly compromised by polio when he was a young man. Fortunately or by necessity he was right-handed. We didn't talk about it and he was very modest, keeping it hidden as much as possible. But the task was completed without incident and he handed a glass to me.

"You're right, my dear! Here's to taking a leap, to taking chances with words and in life!"

"Cheers, darling! Cheers!" We touched the sides of our glasses and took a small sip. "Oh, DuBose! That's so perfect! I can feel the brandy warming me up all over!"

"Good, sweetheart! Shall we check on Jenifer?"

"I'll go. In a minute. DuBose? Do you remember *my* big leap? When I left the University of Minnesota and moved to Puerto Rico?"

"I didn't know you then, little Dorothy."

"Oh, phooey! You know the story well enough."

"But tell me again!"

He was humoring me and I didn't even care.

"Oh, you . . . all I'm saying is that there *is* such a thing as the hand of Fate or something because think about it. When I was in Puerto Rico at Uncle Charles's house I wrote that mess of a play? Then I had the pure temerity and stupidity to send it to Professor Baker. I remember that all I wanted to do was be in New York City. Oh! I wanted to be in New York so badly!"

"You are a born playwright, my dear."

"Thank you. But remember? Professor Baker told me to keep at it so I went to Columbia? And there I wrote *Jonica* and that landed me at MacDowell! If I had not taken that risk, I would never have met you! Don't you see? Sometimes Fate pushes you to take a chance on something in life and it can make all the difference!"

"Thank heavens you had the courage to roll the dice!"

"Yes! Or you would have married Jo Pinckney!"

"What? Ho! I don't *think* so! I was not meant to marry Jo."

"That doesn't mean you never *considered* it."

DuBose paused for a moment and I could see his wheels turning. He always wondered how was it that women were so sly and clever? How did I know things I had never been told? There was no real reason for me to be jealous of Jo Pinckney, her social standing, or her intelligence. But I kept my ear to the ground and the gossip mill said that Jo's mother had made it plain ages ago when DuBose was scratching around Jo's door that he didn't have enough to offer her daughter and that was the end of that business. They remained good friends to this very day. Besides, he knew Jo was happier to be single, to entertain *numerous* gentlemen, and to have her freedom to travel the world. I hope you all got what I meant to imply.

"The moment I met you, my dear, the whole world stopped spinning and I knew I was meant to be with you."

I smiled then, reasonably placated and satisfied. It might have sounded like baloney, but in my heart I knew it actually was true. DuBose and I *were* meant for each other.

"We even look alike," I said with obvious pride.

"Yes, yes, we do. Ah, Dorothy. Come now, tell me. What's bothering you?"

"There's going to be a drastic change, DuBose. Something or someone is coming. I can feel it in my bones."

"A storm?"

"I don't know . . . something . . . someone. I don't know."

"Hmmm. And your bones are never wrong."

Fade to Darkness

CHAPTER TWELVE

The Piano

I slept until past ten o'clock in the morning, which wasn't a particularly long stretch, considering I had not nodded off until long past the witching hour. There was so much to do today. No. Wait. No, there wasn't. Beyond seeing about what I could do to help Aunt Daisy and maybe checking on my car, my dance card was empty. This was going to be a problem. If anything was going to happen in my life, to me and for me, I was going to have to plan it and then make it happen. Day two on Folly and it dawned on me that this new existence, *if* I stayed around here for any length of time, this unexpected second act of my life could turn into a state of withering desolation if I wasn't careful. Great. Nice thought.

It was a good thing that Aunt Daisy needed my help, because truly, otherwise, what was I going to do with myself? Mourn Addison? Well, I sure wouldn't find Aunt Daisy or Ella in that camp, would I? I wasn't surprised at all when she said she never really liked him. Addison's brand of hauteur bordered on a kind of social terrorism and could be a turnoff to a lot of people who didn't know him. I always believed his posturing came from his fully loaded buffet of deep-seated insecurities and usually found him funny, because the way he preened and posed was just ridiculous. But no more. Every single thing about him was less funny now. By a lot. Everything.

Under normal circumstances I'm sure I would have mourned him like crazy. If he had died ten years ago I would have worn black for years, but given all the recent revelations, how was I supposed to behave? Maudlin and bereft? But I didn't exactly feel like throwing on a short red dress either. My Widow Thermometer hovered somewhere between extremely subdued and very sad but I had frequent spikes of fury about the deprivation and poverty in which he had left us, never mind all the mortifying betrayals and the morass of lies. But honey? We were poor now. Like Aunt Daisy used to say, and still would say even if the queen of England was standing in the room, I was so poor I didn't have a pot to piss in or a window to throw it out of. I don't care who you are and what kind of luxury you've been showered with, what Addison did to all of us was really pretty terrible. Make that *very* terrible. I gave him the best years of my life and this was how he treated me. No insurance. No nothing. Not even a roof. If I didn't have family to turn to I would have been homeless. I wondered if I would ever reconcile my feelings enough to forgive him and I thought then that no, no I would never forgive him. I felt like such a fool. And stupid. How could I have not known what was happening?

But when it came to discussing Addison's life and death with the children, I knew I still had to be a poker player, the standard-bearer of graciousness and forgiveness. They had never and would never hear me speak ill of their father. Wasn't what I preached the place from where the children would take their lead? No, they were not so young or impressionable anymore. Well, Sara cared what I thought but I was sure that Russ, under the laser focus and Svengali direction of his mental masseuse of a wife, had already drawn his own conclusions. He had yet to return my phone call, too. Maybe he had been out late last night. Maybe his team had a game. He would call eventually. I was sure of that. Boys didn't call their mothers every five minutes. Girls did.

I filled the old kettle, placed it on the back of the stove, and put a slice of bread in a creepy-looking toaster oven I had discovered in the cabinet. After I knocked it against the wall of the sink, checking for spiders. No spiders. I opened the new box of cereal, poured some in a bowl, and covered it with skim milk. While I stood on the back porch, shoveling bran flakes in my mouth, and waiting for the water to boil, I decided that as soon as I'd drunk a cup of coffee I was going out to buy a newspaper. And a coffeemaker. And a toaster. I wasn't destitute yet.

The yard was a mess. It appeared that a raccoon had made himself at home in the garbage can last night. But there wasn't much to clean up, just some paper that I had used to wrap things and the paper towels I had used to wipe down the counters. I'd have to get one of those elastic straps people used to keep the lid on cans. What did you call them? Well, I'd just go to a hardware store and ask.

The kettle began to go insane with its high-pitched whistle, so I spooned a heaping scoop of coffee crystals into a mug and stirred them around in the boiling water, lacing it with a generous pour of fat-free half-and-half, which definitely seemed like an oxymoron if I'd ever heard of one. It didn't smell that bad at all.

Somewhere in the distance I heard a rooster crowing like mad and wondered who had chickens in their yard? And how often did that crowing happen? Wasn't it supposed to be only at dawn? That could grow to an annoyance. Quickly. I wondered if the raccoon that got into my garbage had ever bothered the chickens down the road. I think I heard somewhere that the crazy bandits like pullet eggs better than anything in the world and they didn't mind snacking on the mother, either. How could such an adorable little animal be so nasty?

I rinsed my dishes—no dishwasher—and went upstairs to dress. My cell phone was ringing. It was Patti calling.

"Hey you!" I said, happy to hear her voice. "What's going on?"

"You're asking me? Nothing. High today of fourteen. It's colder than a whore's heart. That's what. How's it going at the Porgy House?"

"Well, to be honest, and I know beggars shouldn't be choosers, it's about ten steps above camping. But it's actually pretty sweet at the same time. I mean, it's old, you know? Nothing in here post-Eisenhower. But, well, I like it. You'd think an ex-princess like me would be miserable, digging around under the mattress for peas."

"Truly."

"I mean, we're talking no dishwasher. No shower."

"No shower?"

"Yup."

"Wow. Dishwasher, who cares? It's just your own mess, which can't be much."

"Right. And if I wanted to make a big dinner I could, I'd just have to be hyper-organized, because it's about the size of a Manhattan studio apartment kitchen."

"That would kill me."

"No, it wouldn't. You, of all people, would adapt."

"Humph. How's the oven?"

"June Cleaver used to make Thanksgiving for Wally and the Beav in it."

"That's when ovens were really ovens. Remember Aunt Daisy's was like thirty years old when we were kids? That thing baked a perfect cake."

"True story. Now they make appliances to wear out in five years. Ah, Patti. There's so much wrong with the world. So much."

I could hear her laugh a little and thought I was glad I could spread a little mirth in her direction. It would make her worry less about my mental health.

"Well, we can't change it, honey. But! There is some news on this end."

"Tell it."

"Your piano is ready. What should we do with it?"

"Hmmm." I thought about it for a minute and then said, "How much do they want to ship it?"

"Nada. Mark's got it covered."

"Really?"

"Yeah, he didn't tell you but he ripped off a case of LaTour that was in the garage. He says it was worth a load of money."

"That dog! Ship it to the Porgy House. The front parlor needs something jazzy and it's from the thirties, I think. So it would probably look amazing here."

"So? I gather then that you're thinking of staying there for a while?"

"Yeah, I guess. I mean, it's not like I have so many choices."

"Well, you have to stay there long enough for me to escape this wretched cold weather and come visit for a few. Right?"

"I'd love that. No lie."

"Okay! Done! I'll tell Mark to ship the piano to Folly and I'll go online and look for a deal on a ticket."

"Thanks, doll. So what else is happening?"

"Well, tell me about the *aunties*. Are they still as feisty as ever and are they still picking at each other like a couple of woodpeckers?"

"Did you say *peckers*?"

"You're disgusting!"

So we giggled at my locker-room humor, talked for another ten minutes about whether I had seen Russ yet and how's Sara and how much damage was there to the Subaru? And, of course, who was John Risley?

Patti laughed and said, "So, he's like Dr. Love, right? I can hear it in your voice."

"What the EFF is the matter with my voice? Sara heard some funny thing in my voice too. What did I do wrong?"

"Nothing. When you get excited, your voice goes up higher. It always has. So gimme the juice on him!"

My voice. Another traitor I needed to watch.

"Patti? I haven't been here long enough to know where all the light switches are. If I have any juice, even a drop of it, I'll call you pronto. Scout's honor."

"You were never a Girl Scout."

"Moot point."

I had decided that my thoughts late last night about John Risley were too premature to have any kind of a sensible or meaningful discussion about them. The potential situations that drove me insane in the middle of the night often disappeared in the morning. I'd wait and see. I might have been exaggerating his appeal in my mind. A couple of fish tacos and some guacamole did not a relationship make, sayeth the soothsayer. But if he so much as touched my arm, I knew I was calling Patti and screaming like a diva. We hung up and I punched in Aunt Daisy's number.

When I asked her what I could do to help her that day, she didn't hesitate.

"I've got new tenants moving into the Jolly Buddha this Saturday. There was a problem with one of the bathrooms. Some rotten kid stuffed LEGOS in the toilet and flushed it. Thank you! Water everywhere! If you could meet the plumber over there, it would be such a help. He's supposed to be there at noon sharp. He promised. Just stop over and I'll give you the keys."

"I'll be there in half an hour."

Just as I was pulling out of my driveway, my cell phone rang again. My caller ID read College of Charleston and I knew it was Risley.

"Hey!" I said. "How are you?" My voice was definitely higher.

"I hate caller ID. Takes the mystery out of everything. I'm fine. You?"

"Good, good! What's going on?"

"Well, I was thinking that if you're free, after classes this afternoon we might take a ride out to the body shop and visit your car."

"You mean, like going to see someone in the hospital? A corporal work of mercy?"

"Yeah, I guess. You know and then we could go get a glass of wine or something?"

This following flash of thought blasted through my brain: I had not expected anything like an invitation to imbibe or to spend any kind of time with him doing something that could be misconstrued to look like a date to rear its head so soon. BUT! If I blew him off I knew he might never ask again. AND! What was the harm in having one glass of wine? BUT! He did have that big boldface **M** tattooed on his forehead, didn't he? AND! Hadn't I taken a vow to myself? SO WHAT? I told myself, this is the twenty-first century and it's a glass of wine, not room service in a no-tell motel with mirrored ceilings.

"Should we bring my poor Subaru flowers and candy?"

"No, I think just our presence will help her heal, just knowing we cared enough to show up."

"You're a little nuts, you know."

"Uh-uh, I'm not the crazy one, but that's another story. I'll pick you up around six? The body shop stays open until nine."

My cell phone pinged in my ear to tell me that I had another call. This sure was a busy morning. Now, here's something about my techno-capabilities you may as well know. I don't know how to use the call-waiting feature on my cell phone. So I hung up on Risley.

"Got another call! Gotta go! See you at six!" I clicked off, knew he thought I was abrupt or a spaz, and just as suddenly I heard my boy's voice.

"Hi, Mom!"

"Hey, darling!"

"Welcome back to South Carolina!"

"Well, thanks honey! How's everything?"

"Great! We played Wando last Friday and kicked their miserable butts."

"That's great, sweetheart."

"Yeah. The mighty Trojans ha! We beat 'em by twenty. Smoked 'em."

"That's a win for sure." But that's a most unfortunate name for a team, I thought.

"So, what are you doing tonight, Mom? Alice made this huge casserole out of chicken and broccoli and I don't know what else is in there but it smelled good. Want to come over for dinner like around six?"

"Oh, Russ, I'd love to but I can't."

"Wait a minute. Is it this John Grisley getting in your life?"

"R. Risley. Where'd you hear about him?"

"Sara."

"Oh, please. I had a wreck with the man and . . ."

"You had a wreck?"

"Fender bender. No biggie. We're going out to a body shop in the sticks of Ladson to check on my car and then we were going to just get coffee or something and maybe a bite . . ."

"Hey, Mom? I don't care if you have a date. In fact, I think you should get yourself out there again. Why not? It's not like Dad was the ideal husband or something. If you go out to dinner it won't bring Dad back to life, right? Now Sara? She's of *another* opinion."

"It's not a date."

"Mom! I don't care if it's the most smoking hot affair in the history of the planet! It's your business. Come tomorrow night then! How's that?"

"What does Alice think?"

"About what? Your *it's not a date* deal?"

"Yes. I mean did Sara call y'all all upset?"

"You could say that but Sara is still majorly immature when it comes to anyone's happiness besides her own. She can't help herself. And my lovely Alice has an opinion about everything, as you know."

Was he getting a bellyful of Doctor Know-It-All?

"True enough. What did Sara say?"

"She just thinks it's too soon for you to be going out with a man. You know, she's still pretty messed up about Dad. I'm a lot less emotional about it."

"And Alice?"

"Believe it or not, she feels sorry for Sara."

"Oh my! That's a first."

"Sort of. I mean, she says Dad's death is complicated, which it is, and that everyone needs to be in touch with their true feelings to get the right kind of closure and move on in a healthy way."

"Oh, I see."

"Look, whatever. It's how Alice makes her living. She means well."

"I know."

"I mean, Dad was who he was. I always wondered how you dealt with his insanity. Too much BS for me."

"Russ? You're going to see that in a long marriage, if you're lucky enough to have one, you have some good years and some not-so-good years. If you really love your family, you try to endure the difficult times, because it's important to hold families together. Your father did the best he could. He was under tremendous stress . . ."

"Yeah, I guess so. But he brought it all on himself, didn't he? He sure was one crazy sumbitch."

"Is that the Southern term of endearment for son of a bitch?"

"Yeah. It might be."

"Well, son, try to remember the many good things your father did for us. It's not a black-and-white world. But don't focus on the dark stuff. It wasn't *all* his fault, you know. The housing market went south and banks made a lot of mortgages they shouldn't have and believe me, no one knew the economy would go to hell in such a blaze of glory."

"Blaze of shame is more like it. I'm so glad I teach high school and that I didn't get an MBA. You have to wonder how those guys on Wall Street live with themselves, right? No conscience."

"That slices it about as thin as you can."

"So, you'll come tomorrow night?"

"Absolutely! What can I bring?"

"Just bring yourself."

During the time these phone calls came and went, I had traveled the distance between the Porgy House and Aunt Daisy's and pulled up into her driveway. I hurried up her steps and right into the house through the unlocked door. Aunt Daisy was in her home office, going over a bank statement.

"Morning! Your door was unlocked!"

"Oh pish! Ella went out for the paper and must've forgotten to lock it. She's as senile as the day is long. I thought you'd never get here!" Aunt Daisy said, as though I had just been to Tibet and back. "Are you hungry?"

"No, I ate, thanks. Sorry I took so long. My phone didn't stop ringing."

"Who called?"

"The world."

"Uh-huh."

"Well, my world is small but chatty."

"Humph. I see. Well, here's a check for the plumber. And the keys. I really appreciate you doing this. Just get a bill from him so I can enter it in my books. I always worry about being audited. Besides, this is not one of my houses. I just manage it."

"No problem. Then what? You bill the owner?"

"Are you kidding me? I deduct it straight from their share of the rent! If I wait around to get paid from all these people with their second and third and fourth houses, spending their winters jetting down to Palm Beach and out to Aspen or Arizona and wherever the hell they go to give their happy place a little scratch, you'd be sending my deposit slips to the Pearly Gates!" Her arms were whirling around while she spoke.

"You're too funny!"

"Listen to me." She wagged her finger at me. "I'm gonna tell you something and don't forget it. Ever!"

"Okay?"

"The poor people don't pay their bills because they don't have the money. But the rich people don't pay their bills because they don't want to!"

"You might be right. But wouldn't you consider yourself to be rich, too?"

She harrumphed again. "I'm nice and comfortable and that's all. You mark my words! Awful! Rich people are awful!"

Evidently my sweet old Aunt Daisy, who was as rich as cream, had rolled out of her bed on the wrong side.

"Well, come on now, not all of them. I think you're pretty nice! Anyway, give me the address of the house and the plumber's number in case he doesn't show and I'll go take care of this."

Aunt Daisy looked at me and sighed, smiling at last.

"It's such a comfort to have you here, Cate. You just don't know."

I knew I was witnessing a master manipulator at work but I didn't mind it at all. Wasn't manipulation how a lot of things got done in this world? Besides, maybe I'd learn a thing or two. I blew her a kiss and left.

The Jolly Buddha was on East Arctic Avenue right where Aunt Daisy said it would be. I knew this place from my childhood. It was a small house up on stilts with red doors, not to be confused with Elizabeth Arden. Classic Folly Beach—two-million-dollar rustic, charming, inviting, sort of a house you'd never find in Palm Beach. But Palm Beach attracted a different kind of resident, who in all likelihood would not be found on Folly anyway unless they were shipwrecked.

The plumber was nowhere in sight. Big surprise. This was like déjà vu all over again, like Yogi Berra says. I guess there was no escaping this part of life when there was property to manage. But dealing with workmen was in the sweet spot of my limited skill set. I pulled out my cell and tapped in his number. He answered right away.

"Hull-*low*," came the deep voice.

"Hi! This is Cate Cooper calling. Daisy McInerny's niece? Is this Lou?"

"You got him." Brooklyn. I would've bet my life on it. "I'm on the way now. Had a backed-up sump pump that wouldn't cooperate this morning."

"No problem. About how long will you be?" I used my mother voice, the one that's stern but not rude.

"Fifteen? Twenty minutes? Depends on traffic. I'm downtown. Seems like I spend half my life fixing sump pumps downtown."

The water table in Charleston was so low that after a big rainfall you could almost make yourself believe you were in Venice.

"Yeah, I'll bet. Well, don't worry. I'll just wait."

We hung up and I thought, you know what Lou the Plumber? You've got a phone, use it. Tell me you're running late. That's all. Simple courtesy. But nooooo. Make me chase you, right?

Tradesmen were notorious for making you wait because they were out saving your world and their time was more important than yours. Unfortunately, at this particular moment, his time *was* worth more than mine by around a hundred dollars an hour. So I checked out the bathrooms and sure enough, the water in one of the toilets was right up to the edge. I wasn't touching it. Nasty. Then I decided that whatever plumbers charged, they earned it.

I definitely remembered this house from when I was a girl. It wasn't the Jolly Buddha then or maybe it was but in my memory it was just a cottage without a name. All summer long this house and dozens of others like it were filled with families and children, arriving on one Saturday and leaving the next. Their rambunctious voices, raised in laughter and games, traveled over the dunes to Patti and me as we walked by on our way to Center Street for ice cream or whatever nonsense we were after. I could remember hearing them then, teenagers in bathing suits, shouting from the balcony upstairs to someone on the deck below. I always wondered who these people were, where they had come from, wishing to Patti that we could go there and play. She would tell me I was crazy, that you couldn't just waltz into someone's house and expect them to be glad to see you. It was trespassing and stupid and undignified. But those were the days when we were pretty well convinced we were no longer entitled to accidental happiness. I shuddered remembering how sullen we were when we were alone with each other. Thank God that part of my life was in the past. Wasn't it?

I continued snooping around. The kitchen had been recently renovated, had new countertops and a brand-new stainless-steel refrigerator. Everyone seemed to think that stainless-steel appliances were the ticket to heaven. I had a higher appreciation for the table with various styles of retro wooden chairs, all lacquered red. Very slick, I thought. And clever. The bedrooms were all comfortably furnished with new striped bedspreads and vivid artwork decorated the walls. Everything was clean and although it was an old house, it wasn't musty like many beach houses are. When all the doors and windows were opened wide, and the ceiling fans were spinning, it must have been wonderful to listen to the ocean and feel the breezes moving through the rooms especially in the fall and spring.

You didn't have to live in a palace like Aunt Daisy's to enjoy the best aspects the island had to offer. The magical air on Folly Beach was everywhere, a powerful drug that could make you forget there was a world on the other side of the bridge. That was why people were so passionate about this place. It made them forget all their troubles by simply washing them away on the turn of the next silvery tide.

I walked out onto the deck, down the steps, and, lo and behold, there was a gray cement statue of the Jolly Buddha himself, rooted in the sandy yard facing the ocean. His robes were flung back revealing his well-fed protruding belly. His arms were stretched over his head and his face was filled with happiness. Maybe I could learn a thing or two from him as well. Garden statuary of gnomes and deer, geese and fairies, angels and squirrels were peculiar to me but the Jolly Buddha had my attention. Maybe it was okay to get a little bit fat on the pleasures of the world as long as you did no harm, as Buddhists preached.

I looked at him for a few minutes almost as though I expected him to tell me what to do with my life. Then a truck pulled up in front of the house and there was the recognizable loud metal clang of an unevenly hung car door slamming.

I rushed up the steps to see our plumber peering through the glass-covered screen door.

"Come on in!" I said and gave him the once-over. Smiling Lou was about my age, spiky salt-and-pepper hair, gelled to a sheen. In his day? I'd have bet my front teeth that he took in more skirts than Saks Fifth Avenue. Lou the Dude was in the house.

"Thanks," he said, stepping into the dim light of the foyer. "Where's the problem?"

"Right in there," I said, pointing to the bathroom.

He walked into the room, presumably took a look, and came right back out.

"Gotta get my snake," he said. "I'll be right back."

One hour and forty-five minutes and $130 later, Lou had his check, I had a bill marked *paid,* the Jolly Buddha was locked up tight, and I was walking up Aunt Daisy's steps, starving like an animal. She hobbled to the door and opened it.

"I'm going to give you a key," she said. "This is ridiculous."

"Probably not a bad idea anyway," I said, thinking if they needed me in the middle of the night, it would be good if I could get in. "Do you have any bananas?"

"Of course! I always have bananas. Gotta watch my potassium. Hell at my age I gotta watch everything. I probably need to hire a night watchman just to make sure I'm still breathing."

I giggled and she smiled at me. She was glad that I took her ongoing harangue about the pitfalls of aging in the right spirit.

"Can I make you a sandwich?" I said.

"Yes! I think a sandwich might be very nice! And there's some left-over thirteen-bean soup in there, somewhere."

I dug around in her refrigerator, found the soup and a wedge of cheddar.

"Grilled cheese?"

"Why not?" she said. "It's the perfect weather for hot soup and a grilled cheese sandwich."

"What about Ella?"

"She's gone to the city to see her eye doctor."

"Oh, I see." I thought that was marginally hilarious but Aunt Daisy just shook her head. "Get it?"

"Everybody's a comedian," she said. "All we do anymore is go to doctors. A big day is a doctor appointment and lunch downtown at Joseph's or SNOB's."

"Where's the bread?"

"In the breadbox. Where else would it be?"

"Right." I took out four slices of white bread and dropped a tablespoon of butter into the frying pan. "So, is everything okay? With your health and Ella's?"

"She's got cataracts and glaucoma, high blood pressure and high cholesterol. So do I. And we take an aspirin a day so we don't get a stroke and some other damn fool pill to improve our memory, I forget the name of it."

I giggled again.

"How's that one working?" I said. I sliced the cheese and put it on the bread in the pan.

"Not so hot, huh? Wait! It sounds like that Alaskan woman with the whiny voice, the politician . . . Sarah Palin . . . Cerefolin! That's the one! Whew! I still have it together!"

"Aunt Daisy? You've got it together better than I do."

"Yeah, well, you'll be all right. Let a little time pass." She said this and quickly changed the subject. Aunt Daisy's coddling days were behind her. "Anyway, we've got these plastic containers with little pillboxes for each day of the week like I used to have for my old dog, Manny. Remember him?"

Manny was her sweet black lab, who lived for almost eighteen years. And I say *who* not *that* because he was like a person in so many ways.

"He was a great dog," I said.

"He was the love of my life," she said. "Ah well, we're getting older, Cate, but the alternative stinks, too."

"Yes, it does. But you're not going anywhere for at least another fifty years." I flipped the sandwiches onto two plates and stirred the soup. I stuck the tip of my finger in the pot. "I think it's hot enough. You want to check?"

"You can't tell if the soup is hot enough? Where's your confidence, girl?" She was a little incredulous. She poured two glasses of tea over ice and put them on the table. It was barely fifty degrees outside and I could hear the fronds of the palmetto trees slapping the sides of the house.

"It left with the repo guys." I sat down opposite her, opened my paper napkin on my lap, and lifted my glass of iced tea. "Getting windy out there."

"Humph. It's the beach."

"Right. So, Aunt Daisy, let me ask you a question. What do you know about the Charleston Renaissance?"

"The what?"

"The Charleston Renaissance. I don't know a thing about it. In fact, I've never heard about it. I just thought it might be something interesting to learn about. That's all."

"Oh, sure. You think I was born yesterday? This is about John Risley isn't it?"

"I guess so."

"He's calling on you and taking you all around the town and you don't want to look uneducated if he asks this renaissance business? Is that it?"

"I guess so, yeah."

"Girl! Don't you play cat-and-mouse with me!"

"Sorry."

"Humph. Well, I was just a little girl at the time so I didn't know there was a renaissance going on, either. But! Ever since I bought the Porgy House, I'm learning something new all the time. This soup is too cold."

"I knew it. Give it back. I'll nuke it."

She passed me her bowl and I put mine and hers in the microwave, setting the timer for one minute.

"Well, you can sure learn a lot from our Mr. Risley. He lectures all over God's green earth about it. Basically it was a period of time, the twenties and the thirties, when there was a creative fire lit under a lot of aristocratic backsides and a bunch of new thoughts were thought."

"Like what?"

"Like the Civil War was actually over and maybe segregation was wrong. You know, these are sensitive subjects that took some getting used to."

"Yeah, but the Civil Rights Movement didn't really get going until Kennedy was in office."

"I told you it took a while. The seeds were planted much earlier. Anyway, there were lots of interesting people coming and going in Charleston and, of course, that's when Gershwin came to Folly while he and the Heywards were working on the music for *Porgy and Bess*. It was 1934. I was only about eight. Hell, I can't remember anything from yesterday, much less 1934."

"Oh, come on, Aunt Daisy. Throw me a bone."

"My mother, your grandmother, used to say she had no idea that the crazy bohemian man running around without his shirt on was George Gershwin himself! Every time she told that story she would hold her heart and pretend to swoon."

"It must have been a pretty exciting summer."

"I imagine so. Ask Mr. Risley. He'll tell you all about it."

"I'll do that." I looked out of the window at the rustling trees. It was after two and beginning to look like winter again in the fading afternoon sun. "I'm seeing him tonight."

"Big surprise. The Merry Widow rides again!"

"Oh, Aunt Daisy. Hush! It's not like that at all. I think he feels bad about the poor widow's car and who knows? Maybe he's just lonely."

"Somebody's been bit by the Love Bug."

"Oh, Aunt Daisy . . ."

"You can't help it, honey. I knew this would happen. So did Ella. It's like he's been down here just waiting for you to show up. We decided a long time ago that you two are perfect for each other."

"How do you figure that?"

"Because your personalities are absolutely compatible, you have so much in common that it's frightening, and because neither one of you has ever had a real love."

"I loved Addison. No one, even you Aunt Daisy, no one can ever say that I didn't. Especially in the early years. The last few years are debatable."

"All right then. But this is what Fate looks like, Cate. Think about it. He even ran into you, literally, before you could even get to this island."

"Okay, let's say it's Fate. I've been a widow for about fifteen minutes and he's got a wife in the nut house. I'm not touching a married man. No way."

"Great God! Of course not! You're too old to be jumping in the bed with a man anyway! It's nasty!"

"What? I'm not even fifty!"

"Well, maybe then . . ."

"Stop! I'm not talking about sex, for heaven's sake. I'm saying I shouldn't be running around with a married man. It's not nice."

"Nice? Nice? Listen to me. I'm an old lady who's done a lot of living and who's been a bit of a scandal, too, when I felt like it. Standing on your self-righteous indignation won't keep you warm at night. You and Mr. Risley were M. A. D. E. for each other."

"OMG."

"OMG is right. Go home and wash your hair."

"Right. I'll buy a toaster tomorrow."

It was six o'clock on the nose when John Risley pulled up into my yard, got out of his car, and knocked on the Porgy House door. Okay, I told myself, be calm. My hands were damp and my pulse pounded in my ears. There was no medicine yet invented that could calm me down, at least none that I had around the house. I pushed my hair back from my face and opened the door.

"Hey," I said, standing back. "Want to come in?"

Aunt Daisy was right. This was Fate.

CHAPTER THIRTEEN

Setting: New Hampshire.
Director's Note: Photos of MacDowell Colony, Josephine Pinckney, and Elinor Wylie fill the backstage scrim.

Act II
Scene 2

Dorothy: We should probably have a word about some of these other Poetry Society and MacDowell characters while DuBose isn't around to throw in his opinion. Not that I don't want you to have DuBose's opinion. It's that this is *my* moment to crow and sometimes . . . well, it just seems like I have a hard time being heard. Also, I have the advantage of distance of time now, so I can look back much more objectively and tell you how they all shaped each other's work.

Before I met DuBose, he was here in Charleston running an insurance company he founded with a family friend Harry O'Neill, who was actually the artist Elizabeth O'Neill Verner's brother. DuBose didn't need a formal education. He was so naturally curious he educated himself. Then as you know, in 1920, he founded the Poetry Society with John Bennett, Hervey Allen, Josephine Pinckney, and some others. It was the founding of the Poetry Society that was the primary reason he was invited to MacDowell at all.

Well, while he was there that first summer building up a network of talent to invite to Charleston to speak, he got his head turned by that bohemian poet Elinor Wylie, just like the rest of the men there. This was before we were a couple. I mean, Elinor was beautiful and brilliant but she was a calculating vixen, always setting her sights on other women's husbands and don't you know, she got three for herself! She did! That's quite a tally for the 1920s, when divorce was an absolute scandal. And according to the gossip, she also had more than a passing fondness for DuBose, explaining to him exactly what free love meant. Well, news of that little educational experience traveled back to Charleston and set the tongues on fire like a Pentecost Sunday and they're still wagging today!

Here's something most people don't know. After DuBose and I were married, Josephine Pinckney told me about Elinor trying to seduce DuBose and I just kept that little gumdrop to myself. Like I didn't know? I was there! I mean, it didn't matter if Jo was really trying to rattle our trees, because despite Jo's high opinion of herself, I knew DuBose. He wasn't going anywhere. I'm sure he was very flattered by Elinor's attention and if anything went on between them it was none of my business anyway. That's what I politely said to Jo and for once, she closed her sassy mouth, blinked her big blue eyes, and had nothing more to say on the subject ever again. At least, not to me.

By October of 1922, DuBose was writing poetry, *stunning* poetry all the time, and together with his great friend Hervey Allen he published a small book of their poems together called *Carolina Chansons*. It sold so well everyone was absolutely astonished, especially Macmillan who was their publisher. That was the same time I got a letter from him asking if there was a chance for us. I must not have replied quickly enough because the next letter informed me he was escorting Josephine to a party! But I didn't worry. I knew DuBose's heart was mine.

By then, DuBose's business was becoming rather successful, because my DuBose had wonderful natural instincts and he was keen on the details. But he was *miserable*. In all his letters and when we met the next time at MacDowell, all he could talk about was how he wanted to be a serious poet and that the business of insurance was suffocating him. All I could think about was when we went back to MacDowell, was Elinor Wylie going to pop out from behind the curtains, drag him into the hydrangeas, and have her way with him? After that summer, I encouraged him to quit, because I really and truly believed he was talented enough to make a living as a writer of poetry and maybe of prose as well.

But I can't take all the credit for DuBose walking away from business, because I think life at the MacDowell Colony also played a huge part in stoking the fires of his ambition. I mean, there we all were—artists, writers, painters, composers, dancers—creative types of all kinds, summering together in the beautiful countryside of New Hampshire, practicing what we loved during the day and then getting together in the evenings, entertaining each other with our work and stories of our experiences out in the greater world. He was surrounded by people who were supporting themselves with their art and he wanted to be one of them. He wanted to be worldly, too.

Anyway, it was pretty heady stuff, I'll tell you, and some pretty big egos and ideas floated in and out of the rooms every hour of the day and night. So why would someone who was obviously as talented and as sensitive as DuBose want to leave a creative paradise to go home and sell car insurance? It made perfect sense to me that he should at least *try* to give it a go. So, after we became engaged, I promised him I would take care of him. I think those were words he had been waiting to hear all his life. I might not have been as imposing a character as his mother, Janie, and I might have been an orphan, but I was not without certain resources.

Anyway, knowing the sexist and tawdry nature of a theatrical life as well as I did, and I was always dead-set on having a theatrical career, what were the odds that someone as genteel as DuBose would come into my life? I could go anywhere on his arm.

Fade to Darkness

CHAPTER FOURTEEN

About Dorothy

Look, here's the terrible and wonderful truth. When I opened the front door and he stepped inside the Porgy House, John Risley smelled like something so good I wanted to get that smell onto my skin and spend a serious amount of time inhaling it. Giving his neck a basset hound slurp also crossed my mind. Even in my state of sudden onset of a feral giddiness, I knew there was no way to do that without him noticing. But! The mental image of lunging with a flailing tongue twisted my facial muscles to hold back a burst of nervous laughter. I was in deep *merde* and nearly unable to handle the sudden and overwhelming urges to behave like a demonic whore.

I am also fully aware how completely juvenile, inappropriate, and ridiculous this all sounds but that's exactly how it was. Haven't you ever smelled something that gave you a jolt, made you stop to think of some childhood memory of wild honeysuckle or a kind of candy or the sweet rubber of a favorite toy? Weren't you immediately time-traveling back to the schoolyard or the playground or the Christmas morning and weren't you almost knocked off your feet from how fast and how total the distraction was? Your body is in the present but your nose and mind are decades away. They say smell is the most powerful of all our senses and I was just reminded again that it must be so by whatever it was that John Risley had slapped on his face after he shaved. The scent didn't remind me of anything from my childhood, yet it was just that striking and familiar. I could barely concentrate on anything else.

And all the while I struggled to get a grip on what remained of my composure he was nonchalantly going about doing the normal things a gentleman of the South does when squiring a lady around for the evening. He had opened my car door, adjusted the seat so I'd be at the safest distance from the dashboard, invited me to take my place, smiled at me like the old cat that swallowed the canary while I situated myself, and then he closed the door. It was impossible to tell if he was even moderately rattled by my cologne or shampoo or the combination but he *did* seem inexplicably amused. That gave me comfort and hope.

The whole way out to the body shop we made small talk and smiled and smiled and smiled. Man, pheromones are some powerful juju. Very powerful. It wasn't like I even had a choice in the matter. I was attracted to him like tiny vulnerable iron filings are drawn to a big old macho magnet.

Fate was on my side. My car still wasn't ready.

"Gosh! That's too bad," I said to the mechanic, trying to sound sincere, but Risley was not fooled.

Whatever part they were waiting for still had not arrived. That was okay, because it meant Mr. Fabulous and I could use the delay as an excuse to see each other again. At least that was what I hoped John was thinking, because I was thanking the good Lord for granting me some extra time. I surely did not want this grand and glorious maybe-not-exactly love affair to evaporate before it even made it for a spin around the dance floor. Right now the relationship felt like a buoy, wobbling over choppy white caps. It needed a chance to right itself, grow some legs, and grant me a plausible excuse to let nature take its course even though I knew the whole idea of a love affair with this gorgeous man was too ridiculous, too soon for me, and let us not forget, immoral to boot. You see, if time was on our side, too, then eventually I would hear some authentic and valid reason why John was still married to this woman who was institutionalized, one that would forgive the onslaught of thoughts that were transforming themselves by the minute into intentions. I was a nervous wreck.

And then I posed the question to myself in one fleeting thought of how would things have played out if I had met John Risley while Addison was alive? Would I have ignored any and all thoughts, twitches, and pangs and would I have walked away with my conscience intact? That was an impossible decision to make, because I had never felt anything like this before.

"Just give me a call," John said to the mechanic and we got back in the car.

John decided we should have dinner at the Red Drum in Mount Pleasant. I was fine with his choice. It was pretty amazing to learn that Charleston had a chef who had trained at the Culinary Institute of America living and cooking right under our nose, only to find out we had a few of them.

"Yeah, the chef at McCrady's too. There are probably a half dozen CIA chefs in town and another dozen or more from Johnson and Wales."

"Wow," I said, sounding really stupid and uninformed.

He laughed and said, "No! Charleston has become quite the foodie destination for chefs and patrons as well. There's the whole Food and Wine Festival that happens every year and then remember Johnson and Wales was here for maybe twenty years or longer."

"What happened to them?"

"Moved to Charlotte but I have no idea why. I heard that North Carolina offered them some sweet deal, like ten million, to make the move and then they reneged. Same story with Bank of America. I don't know all the details."

"Aunt Daisy says you should never trust anyone north of Columbia."

"Aunt Daisy is right! Anyway, I just know some of the faculty stayed behind and cut a deal with Trident so now there's still a cooking school here. It's kind of amazing, you know? This town really has come into its own. Everywhere you turn there's an interesting restaurant with a hot young chef cooking up something floating in a froth or finished with a coulis or some fancy, high-toned thing."

"Well, I say bravo to all of that!" I hoped I sounded enthusiastic but that wasn't what was running through my mind. Yeah, big hairy bravo, I thought, so tell me about your wife, Mr. Risley. Tell me about *her*.

We arrived at the restaurant, turned the car over to valet parking, and went inside. The lively and stylish southwestern-flavored bar area was teeming with people of all ages and I thought, well, at last there's a fun place where I could come for a night out, maybe with Patti when she came for a visit, and we wouldn't look like a couple of pathetic cougars on the prowl. The pretty and congenial youngish hostess led us to a nice table. As I followed her across the dining room, John's right hand was lightly touching the small of my lower back in an unmistakable proprietary way, a gesture that meant nothing more than we were together and he would be the guy to catch me if I should trip. I liked the whole idea of it, ceremonial or not, and thought, wow, Addison Cooper had not held my elbow or the small of my back in eons. In fact, I felt a twinge of sadness as I realized how long it had been since there had been any token of affection coming my way except from my sister, my children, my housekeeper, or my caterer.

My sex life was buried in a wasteland of mothballs and if I left it there it was by choice, not by necessity. I knew that but I was still grappling with the cold facts of the day—recent widow and married man. It just couldn't be a good idea.

John, thankfully, was oblivious to the churning wheels in my head.

"The bartender here makes a drink he calls a Magic Margarita. Want to try one?" Risley was scanning the menu in such a way that I knew he was familiar with it.

"Does it have tons of alcohol in it? Because I haven't had a drop of tequila in years. You'll have to carry me out of here."

"I don't think they're as dangerous as all that."

Too bad, I thought and said, "Then why not? I could use a little magic in my life."

"Couldn't we all?" He closed his menu, signaled our waiter, and said, "So what are you in the mood for? Seafood? Chicken?"

"What do you recommend? You've been here, right?"

"Yeah, about a hundred times. Most of the waitstaff used to be or still is a student of mine. Including this fine young lady."

"Hey, Professor Risley! Great to see you!"

"Good to see you, too, Ms. Geier. Cate Cooper, this is Christi Geier, she was in my playwriting class. How's law school?"

"Nice to meet you Ms. Cooper. Ah, it's the LSATs, sir. Going to give them another shot. So, what can I get for y'all?"

"The LSATs. They can be rough. Good luck. So how about a Magic Margarita for my friend and a Dos Equis for me?"

"Sounds good. I'll be right back with some chips and salsa."

"Thanks," Risley said and turned his attention back to me. "So, tell me about growing up on Folly Beach. That must've been incredible. The Edge of America and all that. Was it?"

I looked at John Risley and then around the dining room for a moment, pausing to frame my answer. I decided to just tell him how I felt at the moment, which I was somewhat unsure about, because I had not been leading the most reflective life until Addison died.

"You know what? I think my childhood was probably like everyone else's. There were some fabulous things about it and some really challenging moments, too. I mean, there were a few episodes in there where Folly felt more like the Edge of the World than the Edge of

America, you know, like we could fall off at any time and you know, spiral out into deep space."

"We?"

"My older sister Patti and me."

"I always wished I had a sister. Or a brother. I'm an only child."

"Being an only child has some real advantages, doesn't it? I mean, I would've been a disaster without my sister telling me what was wrong with me all the time but there were definitely times when she probably wished she had the bathroom to herself and . . ."

John laughed and said, "Well, it was great for me at Christmas but hard to navigate the Department of Great Expectations."

"Every kid in the world has to pass through the Department of Great Expectations."

The chips arrived, brought by a very young waiter, and he sort of plunked them in the middle of the table along with some pretty appetizing green sauce for dipping. Then a moment later the drinks appeared via Ms. Geier and she placed them in front of us.

"Thanks," I said.

"Sorry it took so long. The bartenders are slammed. Okay! Got a few specials for you tonight," she said and began describing the intergalactic heights to which the chef planned to elevate the unsuspecting humble tilapia and how the ceviche was going to change the way we viewed southwestern cuisine, especially now that it had collided into a spectacular fusion of chilies and seafood from the pristine waters around the Lowcountry. "And, not to be overlooked are some mighty fine spiced shrimp, wood grilled and finished off with a cilantro garlic butter and that comes with a side of sweet corn pudding. Of course there's always the South by Southwest Mixed Grill . . ."

"I'm full from just listening!" I said.

John shook his head, smiling at his former student. "I always said, Ms. Geier, you should go into theater. You're missing your calling. Do we really need more lawyers?"

Ms. Geier grinned and said, "I don't know, sir. I hope so. Y'all need a few minutes?"

"No, I think I'm all set. How about you, Cate? See anything interesting on that menu?"

"Sure, I'm thinking the ceviche to start and the Hawaiian sunfish? How's that sound?"

"Very good! And you, professor?"

"I'm thinking all that effort on the tilapia shouldn't go to waste and I'll have the day-boat scallops to begin."

"Perfect! I'll get your order right into the kitchen."

"Thanks," John said, watching her scuttle away. "She's a real talent. Would've made a great playwright."

"Hmmm," I said. "I always wanted to write a play, a big musical with great choreography like the old days or maybe something for the screen."

"And why didn't you? Cheers!"

"Cheers!" I said, touching the salty side of my glass to his frosted mug with a musical clink. "Well, I started down that road but then I hit a few twists and turns, you know, marriage, children . . ."

"So did Dorothy Heyward."

"You mean DuBose Heyward's wife?" I took a large sip of my cocktail. "Gosh! This is really delicious. But wait, she *was* a playwright." Even I knew that much.

"Yep. I know. Dorothy Heyward *always* intended to be a playwright, from the time she was a little girl but the facts of her actual career make for a very interesting saga on their own."

"Tell me the saga," I said, feeling infinitely more relaxed as the alcohol entered my bloodstream.

"I don't want to bore you . . ."

"I don't think you could, but I'll let you know if you do. I mean, I really am interested."

"Okay. So, in the very beginning of her career one of her professors urged her to get to know the theater from the inside out."

"Good advice. You should always know the business inside and out."

"Definitely. So somewhere in between the time she went to New York to study playwriting at Columbia and when she went to Harvard to join George Baker's famous Workshop 47, she got herself cast as a chorus girl in a traveling show."

"Seriously? I danced in plenty of chorus lines, including the play *A Chorus Line,* for the exact same reason! So, how did she like it?"

"Hated it. Thought it was demeaning to be a chorus girl, especially back then, in the vaudeville days, when theater people were suspect anyway. I think the whole theater world probably *was* a pretty sexist environment then."

"This would have been what year?"

"Early twenties. The story goes that in this particular play, all the girls had to enter the stage in their underwear, carrying a little suitcase and wearing high heels. Then all the girls would file down into the audience, pull out a dress from their suitcase and, get this, sit on a man's lap so he could button her up the back of her dress."

"You're kidding, right?"

"No."

"I am beyond stunned. How many laws would that break today?"

"About a hundred, I'll bet. Talk about creating a hostile work environment?"

"No lie. That was a pretty gutsy thing to do for her time, wasn't it?"

"Yes, it definitely was. Especially given her background. She grew up on the right side of the tracks with her aunts. She lost her parents when she was a young girl . . ."

"What?"

"But her aunts seemed to have done an amazing job of giving her a cultured life."

"Aunts?"

"Yep. I mean, she began going to the opera as a child and later she was sent to universities and so forth. And this was in the day when women rarely went to college except to become a teacher or a nurse. Dorothy was encouraged to be creative. Her whole family was very musical."

"Was *she*? Dorothy, I mean. Was she musical?"

"Not so much. In her papers she talks about the fact that she had a tin ear and couldn't play any instrument very well, except for the piano, a little."

"This is sounding creepy—like you've been reading *my* diaries, professor, not Dorothy Heyward's."

"I thought you might find her history interesting."

"I do. Where are these papers?"

"Right here in Charleston. They're all in the archives at the South Carolina Historical Society downtown. For a slight fee, like five dollars, you can go read them and *you* really should. After all, you're living in *her* house."

"You're right, you're absolutely right."

"Yeah, they were quite the couple, old Dorothy and DuBose. She was definitely the pepper in his pot."

"And him? What was he like?"

"Well, I think he can be described most politely as a man of his time."

"That's pretty cryptic."

"Yes. Because I think people should draw their own conclusions about others, especially when it comes to relabeling Charlestonians with aristocratic backgrounds."

"So, what you're really saying is that anything less than veneration of Mr. Heyward could be considered desecration of something sacred?"

"Exactly. Look, among other things, here's the guy who allegedly put Charleston on the map again with *Porgy and Bess*."

"What do you mean *allegedly*?"

"DuBose published the book *Porgy* in 1925, not the play."

"Then who did? The Gershwins?"

"Nope, the play *Porgy* appeared on Broadway in 1927. Gershwin's play didn't run until 1934. And you should know, DuBose dropped out of school at fourteen and went to work in a hardware store. Then on the docks. Then in insurance."

"But Dorothy went to Harvard . . ."

"My goodness! Miss Cate Cooper! You are one quick study!"

"Do you understand this kind of talk is practically treason?"

"What? What did I say? I didn't say a thing! You did!"

"Holy moly. John, this is serious."

"Yeah, it is. Would you like another drink? I'm gonna have another beer."

I looked at the bottom of the inside of my glass to see that I had all but chugged this, my Magic Margarita. I wasn't feeling magical but I surely knew that John Risley was capable of pulling away the curtains and exposing the Wizard of Oz. I was fascinated.

"Yes. Yes, I would. Thanks. Maybe a glass of white wine? Like a pinot grigio?"

John turned away and scanned the restaurant and after a minute he made eye contact with young Ms. Geier. My wine and his beer were ordered, our appetizers and entrées came and went, and I listened with both ears. I had found a new purpose for the days and weeks ahead. As we talked some more about Dorothy and DuBose Heyward, many other characters of their day came exploding to light, exploding because that was the way John presented them.

The members of the Charleston Renaissance and especially the Poetry Society of South Carolina were like a little army of determined carpenter ants, chewing their way out of the final mounds of Civil War ashes, through the poverty of the Great Depression and into the light of modern day—a new day. Their collective mission was to look to the future, to find everything about it worth living for and to take their artistic colleagues from every discipline of the arts from all over the country, bring them to Charleston, educate her citizens on what was happening in the larger world, and move forward. Whew! Now, there's a mission statement, if I ever heard one.

When John spoke of these people—John Bennett, Josephine Pinckney, Hervey Allen, Beatrice Witte Ravenel, and others—he became contagiously animated. His eyes danced and he leaned in across the table in conspiratorial whispers when he talked about the alleged private life of Laura Bragg or when he revealed the secrets of Julia Peterkin.

"You make it sound more exciting than Woodstock," I said and we laughed.

"It was."

"I want to know everything about it."

"I'll make an historian out of you before I'm done. If you stick around long enough, that is."

"I think I'll be around for a while."

Driving home across the Cooper River Bridge, high above the port of the City of Charleston, for perhaps the hundredth time in my life, I was struck by the great beauty of the shipping industry. Even with some of the container ships in their weathered state, I thought they were all beautiful. So many rested below us, docked overnight for an evening of shore leave, waiting for cargo that would come in the morning, waiting for the harbor captain to give them the signal to ship out, just arriving from Belgium or Port Elizabeth, or perhaps bound for someplace exotic like Singapore.

"It's always something to watch, isn't it? The port, I mean," I said.

"Yeah, it's irresistible to me, too. All those people, all that cargo, coming here, going somewhere else. Nothing stagnant about harbor life, that's for sure."

"That's the attraction, I think."

"Definitely. That whole industry has changed so dramatically since technology moved into our lives. But, like a lot of things, the more it changes the more it stays the same."

"I like being able to rely on things staying the same, well, I used to anyway," I said and then realized how pitiful that must have sounded.

John was quiet then and I thought, oh Lord, he's probably worried that I'm getting emotional. Men hated it when women let their feelings get the better of them. I had probably just ruined the night by reminding him about the loss of Addison, that I was broke, and that I was mortified by my changed circumstances. He was deciding then and there that I was too much trouble to get involved with. I probably was. He was probably wondering what I did to make my husband want to kill himself. Good grief, I thought, I'm not only a broke widow, I'm also damaged goods. Maybe dangerous, too.

My paranoid indulgence was for nothing. Just as I turned to him and was about to launch into an I'll-survive explanation for what I'd said, he reached his hand out to cover mine and gave it a squeeze.

"Look," he said, "I know it hasn't been easy lately. It's okay. Anyway, sometimes change is good."

"Maybe."

"No, not maybe. Definitely. I mean, look, how do you know what's going to happen to you now? The universe, or whatever you believe in, might have something unbelievably wonderful in store for you."

"I have merely retreated to the familiar and I believe in God, just so you know. I grew up Catholic, but in Aunt Daisy's Leftist cafeteria sect."

He laughed then, a hearty laugh that had been unused for a while. I began to laugh, too. The pall was officially lifted.

He said, "I want to hear all about *that*."

"In between history lessons?"

"Anytime."

We finally pulled up to the Porgy House and I was safely home, back on Folly Beach. There was nothing darker than a beach on a moonless night, and at the door, I fumbled around in my purse to find the keys.

"You need a porch light," he said.

"Boy, no kidding!"

"I can take care of that. I mean, it's no big deal. I go to Lowe's all the time."

"Thanks. But I don't know if it would be historically correct. Aunt Daisy doesn't want anything changed."

"Oh, well, maybe the Heywards used tiki torches. Let's find out."

I giggled again. God, I was glad he had a sense of humor. What's worse than a humorless man?

I finally found the house key and unlocked the front door. Rather than invite him in (dangerous territory), I decided it was wiser to just say good night so that the evening would end on a high note. I turned to face him only to see him retreating down the steps.

"I had a great time," he said.

"Me too," I said but there was no mistaking the disappointment in my traitorous voice.

He stopped and turned around. "What's wrong?"

"Wrong? Nothing! Nothing's wrong. I just thought, you know, well . . . I thought, well, okay then. I had a great time, too!"

"Did I do something wrong?"

"Wrong? Oh! God, no! No! I don't know what I was thinking!"

He looked down at the ground and then up to me and shook his head, incredulous that a woman could get the whole way to my age and still not have one shred of cool in her arsenal of social skills.

"Do you want to invite me in?" he said.

S. H. I. T.

"Well, of course I do but I'm not sure what to do about that because you know you're . . . well, you know . . ."

"Married?"

"Well, it crossed my mind. And I'm, well, you know . . ."

"Unsure of what would happen?"

"Oh, no . . . I mean, yeah, that, too."

"Look, we're not kids, Cate. It's gonna happen . . . you and me, that is unless I am reading the signs wrong."

"Oh, no. You read well! Yes, you do . . . but I . . ."

"You're nervous and you don't want to get involved with a married man?"

"Yeah, that's about . . . yeah."

"There's an explanation."

He began walking toward me and up the few steps until he was right in front of me in my personal space that was, believe me, completely unviolated by his close proximity. He took my face in his hand and with his other hand he reached for the small of my back but this time it wasn't a ceremonial touch. He pulled me into him and honey that man laid his lips on mine and I never even had a second to shut my eyes. I thought I was going to die, but I didn't and then I got so excited to realize what was happening and thinking this might be the only time I ever got to do this with him so I kissed him back and surprised myself that I was instinctively kissing him like I was a starving animal. Maybe I was. It appeared that he was starving, too.

"Wow," I said when he finally stood back.

"Wow yourself," he said. "Who taught you how to kiss like that?"

"All Catholic girls are sluts. Didn't your momma ever tell you that?"

He laughed so hard then and I did, too. We laughed, teasing each other, until tears ran down our faces.

Do you know how long it's been? Are we teenagers or just manic? Or maniacs? The last time I even kissed anyone was . . . who remembers? Is it the Magic Margarita? Oh my God! That was crazy!

"So! Listen!" he said with some seriousness. "Here I was thinking I'm not going to reveal the story of my life to you if the kissing ain't no good but I think we're *okay* there. Whaddya think?"

"I'm thinking I might need a cardiologist. No lie! Feel my heart!"

He was about to place his hand over my heart, which was conveniently located under my left breast, and I thought, shit, he's gonna know my puppies are store-bought.

It did not appear to matter.

My heart was banging against my rib cage something fierce and I was still out of breath.

"Wow. I don't think you need a doctor but you might want to join a gym," he said with a straight face.

"Up yours," I said and began to calm down. Sort of.

"Actually, normally it's the other way around. Want to have dinner tomorrow?"

"Can't. Seeing my son and his wife."

"Then, the next night?"

"Without a doubt."

This time he was leaving. I wasn't stopping him. We'd had our fun, well, we'd learned what our real fun might be like and it was enough to know for the time being. Besides, I wanted to make the Heywards' bedroom look something more than it did, you know, flowers or candles or some atmospheric enticements from this century. Not that we would need much encouragement. Holy hell. I would have to give the personal grooming issue some immediate and thorough attention. Holy hell. Holy hell. Holy hell.

And speaking of the Heywards, I fully intended to find the South Carolina Historical Society building and spend the day there digging around. I wanted to understand why John was so passionate about this period of Charleston's history but what I *really* wanted to know was why would a woman who had a classical education let her high school dropout husband take the bulk of the credit for her work? Or did she? Was it just a perfect collaboration? Because of the times in which they lived? Was that what had really happened? I suspected there was more.

CHAPTER FIFTEEN

Setting: The bathtub at the Porgy House.
Director's Note: Photos of Hanovia's Alpine sun lamps, the *News and Courier*, and the streets of Folly paved in oyster shells on the backstage scrim.

Act II
Scene 3

Dorothy: Like I did on so many weekends, I got up early to take a hot bath, deciding to let DuBose and Jenifer sleep for a while. It was a Saturday and there was no reason to rush headlong into the day like the house was on fire. The fog and damp continued to hang over the island as though it had taken up permanent residence and I probably could have convinced Jenifer that we were actually in London.

The wind last night was fierce, thundering around the house like the Four Horsemen of the Apocalypse! I was surprised and believe me, very glad that Jenifer slept through it. In fact, DuBose slept soundly, too. I was the one up and walking the floors.

Island winters were very different from island summers when the beaches were stuffed with cars and sunbathers and everything was light and full of optimism and liveliness. Winter was its opposite, undeniably strange in the early morning and at night the fog rolled in and out on the tides. It was hard to believe there was a world out there over the bridges and down Folly Road. We were so very isolated. But we loved the isolation. It was wonderful for our imaginations.

And it was wildly changeable. By midday the sky could be a blazing blue with a sun that warmed you all over, so much so that you didn't even need a sweater. But not that morning. It was simply miserable outside, a real Ohio winter day of the sort I remembered from my childhood.

I knew that DuBose's arthritis had to be troubling him, because my rheumatism was bothering me, not that the medical establishment seemed to be able to define the differences between them to me. It didn't matter. It was pretty obvious that cold dampness aggravated our conditions. But I loved being on Folly Island in every season and I didn't like to complain, because it didn't change anything if I did. And it wasn't as if we had not taken advantage of every alternative treatment there was. I had tried everything from ordering Hanovia's Alpine cockeyed sun lamps out of a catalog to every diet in the world designed to reduce the inflammation in my joints. So had DuBose. Nothing really helped. We finally came to the conclusion that staying as thin as possible, being physically active, and taking aspirin was the best course. I normally weighed about eighty-eight pounds and DuBose could not have weighed more than one hundred and twenty-five. (Of course his tailor cleverly padded his jackets to make him appear to have a more manly physique!) And hot baths helped us, too.

So that morning I soaked in a steamy bubble bath until the water was cool and I drained the tub a bit by removing the stopper with my big toe and added more hot water, turning the faucet with my big toe as well. I did this over and over until my skin looked like prunes. I finally got out, feeling ever so much better. I covered myself with great puffs of bath powder and thought about what I would make for dinner.

This whole living on a shoestring business was beginning to be a trial but it was useless to complain about that as well, because it would only depress DuBose. What could he do? The whole country was still in a slump since the Crash in '29. If only the Gershwins would finish the score for *Porgy and Bess* so we could get it up on the stage. Nine years! But did George Gershwin need money? No! He was flying high on *Rhapsody in Blue*! Our situation was not his problem. Ah well, when *Porgy and Bess* was finally up, people would come to see it in droves and *then* we'd be in the chips again. Golly! Have patience! I told myself this all the time. Patience, patience.

Then I remembered I had split peas soaking from last night and I thought about how good the soup would taste with ham. The recipe I had yielded six servings for about eight cents a bowl. That was almost as thrifty as my vegetable soup, which also tasted better cooked with a ham bone for flavor. Didn't a ham bone make everything taste better? (And don't fret, the recipes for all of my budget meals are in the back of your program, too.) Anyway, I thought I just might take a walk down to Mazo's Grocery to see if he had a smoked hock that fit my budget. And some cornmeal. I'd make a pan of cornbread in my cast-iron skillet. The walk would do me good. Moving around to work the kinks out of my bones always made me feel better.

So I bundled up and made my way down the road leaving my husband and daughter in the Land of Nod under piles of blankets and quilts, still fast asleep. As I walked along, I wondered if the streets would always be paved with oyster shells. I loved the crunch of them beneath my feet. I would just hate it if anything here changed. This was one of the many things I loved about Folly. Streets with oyster shells, wooden sidewalks on Center Street, cars on the beach, and the goats people kept to landscape their yards. Yes, goats! You never saw that in Ohio. I even loved the two-tiered buses, with their tasseled shades, that brought us deliveries from Charleston. And I adored the fried chicken from the Magic Lantern. We stopped there for dinner every time we went to Charleston for drinking water. Now, hauling water in jugs was a definite inconvenience but if we lived in the tiny downtown area where the water was potable I wouldn't have the thrill of watching the sun glisten all over the oyster shells. Walking down Atlantic Avenue was like walking on miles of pearls and that made me feel like a queen.

I stopped by Mr. Spradling's house to see if he had an extra copy of the *News and Courier* he could spare and he did indeed, for the price of a nickel. We were not regular customers but since the Donahue family was out of town he was happy enough for me to take it off his hands.

"How's that playwrighting going?" he asked.

"Well. It's going well."

"That's good. Give my regards to Mr. Heyward."

"I'll surely do that."

Most people on the island and, to be honest, most people in South Carolina couldn't understand why anybody in their right mind would pay money to go see a play about African Americans. But all those same people would not be able to answer that question unless they went to New York City to see a performance. In South Carolina it was against the law for African Americans to perform in a white theater. Not only did the general public rail against the idea of seeing actual blacks on the stage, but they also could not fathom what was so interesting about the Gullah culture that a gentleman like DuBose Heyward with all of his pedigree would waste his creative energy to write about such an insignificant topic. Insignificant! Can you fathom such a thing? They probably thought it was my Yankee influence bringing his talent to ruination. Not so. Not so at all.

DuBose was an intellectual who found the world of the Gullah people to be not only an endlessly fascinating subject but also that their culture was actually enviable. He longed, I mean *longed* to live that same spirited life he was forbidden to have. I think I mentioned that but you know, these days . . . I can't remember everything quite as well as I used to.

Although, at times, DuBose could be very narrow-minded about social boundaries. But who doesn't do a little talking out of both sides of their mouth? Back in early 1923, which wasn't so long ago, I had written him saying I had a delightful lunch with a Negro woman. At the time, I was still studying at Columbia. He wrote me back in that *tone* he sometimes used, saying he knew I could not have seen this as an *absolute impossibility* because I am a *benighted Yankee from the Midwest*, whatever that meant! Was he *forgiving* me? Then he warned me she would be in my room next. I got the gist of what he was saying and didn't like it. His words contradicted his wide-eyed soul. But there were scads of people who thought that way even in Ohio.

Unfortunately, it was the prevailing wind of the time in which we lived and although the wind had begun to shift, it wasn't a change sufficient enough to make a noticeable difference in our society. So, I did what I normally did when something didn't suit me. I ignored it, filed it in the back of my head, and wrote about it later on. After all, like my grandfather used to say, "The pen always has the last word."

Fade to Darkness

CHAPTER SIXTEEN

Grandma

Old people can be sage-like and wonderful but they can also be as persnickety as the day is long. Obviously, I was still using Aunt Daisy's car and she claimed she didn't mind at all. But I thought I owed her the courtesy of letting her know I was going to take it downtown so I stopped by her house to tell her. I mean, I wasn't driving her car to Miami or Albuquerque but I knew her meticulous (read: persnickety) nature and thought she'd appreciate knowing its whereabouts. And in her mind, going downtown, which was in reality a mere fifteen-minute ride, had become quite the trek. I also just wanted to see how she and Ella had fared during the night. They didn't need caretakers. Yet. But while I was sloshing around in Dorothy Heyward's bathtub that morning, singing "Summertime" over and over to the ethers, it occurred to me that considering all Aunt Daisy had done for Patti and me, a little unobtrusive oversight of their days and nights was a tiny but potentially important compensation.

The front door was locked so I rang the bell and Ella let me in.

"G'mornin'!" she said.

"Hey! How're you?" I gave her a peck on the cheek.

"Good, honey. Just roasting a pork shoulder and cooking some greens for supper. Your aunt is in the living room with her foot propped up. Finally! I keep telling her she's got to rest it, but you know *her*!"

"Yep! I sure do!"

Aunt Daisy was wearing a sweatshirt from the College of Charleston with a Cougars baseball cap, sitting in a big upholstered armchair, working the *New York Times* crossword puzzle in ink. I loved that she worked the puzzle in ink. She always claimed it was so she could read what she had written but I thought it reflected her decisiveness. Once Daisy McInerny put it in writing, it was so. I mean in all my life I was always reluctant to argue with her. It just didn't pay.

"Well!" she said and put the newspaper on her hassock. "Look who the cat dragged in! How was your dinner with our Mr. Risley? Did you get the poop on his wacky wife?"

"I'm working on it," I said. "I just stopped by to see if y'all need anything from downtown."

"Sit a minute! Where're you headed with your pants on fire? *Ella! Make my niece one of those cappuccinos! She had a hot date last night and I want her to give us all the juicy details!* Here, I got you a key." She pulled a key on a chain from her pocket and tossed it to me.

"Ooh! One cappuccino, coming right up!" Ella called out from the next room.

"Thanks. There's not too much to tell, really. We went out to the repairman to see how my car's coming along and some part they need isn't in yet."

"That's fine. The part my foot needs isn't in yet either."

"Getting restless, huh?" I said.

"Humph," Aunt Daisy said. "This gee-dee foot of mine."

"You have no idea," Ella said and put some kind of a microwave coffee concoction in front of me. "Driving me crazy," she whispered behind her hand.

"I heard that! You think just because I'm old and decrepit that I'm deaf, too?"

"Apparently not," I said and giggled.

Aunt Daisy's face softened and she smiled then, her shoulders relaxing. All these two old girls needed was an agreeable buffer. And it had to be annoying to be hobbling around in a cast for weeks on end. I would've been impossible to live with.

"So where'd you go for dinner? Someplace romantic I hope?"

"Oh please! No, actually, we went over to Mount Pleasant to this very cute place called the Red Drum. It was good. Sort of Tex-Mex meets up with the Lowcountry. I liked it a lot. When y'all feel like a night on the town, I'll take you over there." I took a sip of Ella's version of cappuccino and decided one sip was more than plenty. It was truly wretched.

"I don't like to drive at night anymore," Aunt Daisy said.

"Me either," Ella said. "I see things in the street that aren't there."

"Humph! I wouldn't get in a car with you after dark for all the tea in China," Aunt Daisy said to Ella.

"And I don't blame you but who invited you anyway?" Ella said to her and then turned to me. "Is she turning into a mean old biddy or is it my imagination?"

"She might be a mean biddy but she's not old," I said.

"Hush your sassy mouth! You're not too old for me to turn over my knee, you know."

Aunt Daisy was smiling but you could sense the Grim Reaper blinking and lurking behind every doorway and in each and every shadow in Aunt Daisy's house, taking away her freedoms one by one. And Ella's. That's how old age was, chipping away at you, bit by bit. If you're lucky. No one in my family had ever liked to talk about it, to admit they saw changes in their abilities to go and do as they pleased. But I guessed Aunt Daisy and Ella were fed up a little.

"Well, the dark doesn't bother me," I said, "so I'd be happy to drive."

"Speaking of night, can we get back to your evening with the professor? Did you have a wonderful time?"

"Yes, I sure did."

"And are you going to see him again?" Ella asked.

"Yes, I definitely am."

"Okay, give us the dirt. Did he try to put the moves on you?" Aunt Daisy said with the most serious face, the kind you reserve for depositions with the FBI.

"Aunt Daisy! Good grief!"

"I'm just telling you, my dear, don't squander your flowers!"

"What?"

"Oh, stop it Daisy! Let Cate have her fun! See what I mean? O. L. D."

"What's *squander your flowers* supposed to mean?"

"It's a line from 'Dusk,' a poem DuBose Heyward wrote. Read it and see for yourself. Only decent poem he wrote if you ask me. Anyway, you should memorize it if you want to impress Mr. Risley."

"I'm not worried about impressing Mr. Risley, Aunt Daisy." I already took care of that, I hoped but did not say. Nonetheless, I wrote the name of the poem on the back of a receipt I found in the black hole of my purse and hoped I'd be able to find it again.

"Well, good. I'm just saying . . ."

"I think I know what you're saying. But anyway, by coincidence, we had an amazing discussion about Dorothy and DuBose Heyward at dinner last night, so amazing that I'm taking myself downtown to read the Heyward papers at the Historical Society."

"And then what?" Aunt Daisy said. "You gonna write a book about them?"

"That's highly doubtful. But I have this nagging question that keeps running around in my head and if I don't find out the answer it might drive me crazy."

I told them what John had told me about the huge disparities in

Dorothy and DuBose's educational backgrounds and that I didn't quite believe that Dorothy didn't do more than just help with DuBose's writing. They looked at each other slack-jawed and stunned.

"My stars!" Ella said. "I've worked in a library all my life. I've read everything there is in print about them. I never *thought* to wonder about that. If you're right, Cate . . ."

"It just would be amazing to know, wouldn't it?" I said. "I'm not sure if it's true, but maybe I can find out. Anyway, I'm going digging. It will give me something to talk about with John."

"Women have to do everything," Aunt Daisy said. "It wouldn't surprise me one little bit!"

"Me either, but then the larger question is *why? Why would she do the lion's share of the work and let him take all the credit?*"

"Who knows?" Aunt Daisy said.

During the drive downtown I kept thinking about the Heywards. From what I understood so far from John, DuBose, his sister, and his mother's inherited social standing had been almost completely truncated by their financial deprivation. Basically, like they say down here in the Lowcountry, they were po'. It would have been very important for his family's pride to try to reclaim their position within Charleston's circle of old families. So then, if that was true, how would Dorothy, a Yankee from Ohio, fit into that plan? And was there a plan? And if there was one, was it openly discussed and was Dorothy aware? Probably not, I decided, because if I had learned anything in all my years growing up in Charleston, even though I was out on Folly Beach, it was that it was poor manners to speak of your losses and certainly money was rarely if ever discussed. I could see the Heywards stiff-upper-lipping it until such time the society hounds caught the scent of improved circumstances to a degree that would welcome them back into the downy bosom of the circuit. That was the scenario that made the most sense to me. Well, I would see what I would find.

I located the South Carolina Historical Society's imposing but compact building with ease. It was right across the street from the Mills House Hotel on the corner of Meeting and Chalmers Street. I parked in the hotel's parking garage and made my way there, enchanted in the moment by the ancient cobblestones that paved Chalmers Street. How lovely! Cobblestoned streets made me sentimental. Once all the streets of Charleston were probably paved with the ballast of old ships, or oyster shells or just packed dirt. But cobblestones, pretty as they were, were the devil to deal with. They had to have wreaked havoc on the ankles of humans and beasts. I was pretty certain they still sent more than one high-heeled tourist, out for an innocent night on the town, right to her knees. But they were lovely to look at, even the ones that held cement mortar in between their uneven edges. I had never really thought about them before, where they came from and so on. It was sort of like when you lived around New York you never went to the top of the Empire State Building or rode the Staten Island Ferry. You took so much for granted. But it seemed to me then that they looked like river rocks. Maybe they were. I'd have to ask Risley. He'd know.

I rang the bell on the ancient door and waited for a few moments for someone to answer. I was met by the smiling face of a pretty young woman whose name tag read MARY JO FAIRCHILD.

"Come in," she said, "welcome!"

"Hi!" I said and stepped into the foyer. "I'm Cate Cooper."

"And I am Mary Jo Fairchild. What can I do to help you today?"

"Well, I was hoping that I might be able to read the papers of Dorothy and DuBose Heyward."

"Absolutely! That's why we're here. Just sign in there . . ."

I signed the guest book, followed her inside, and she explained the library's rules to me. Purse goes in a locker after I give her five dollars, notes are only taken in pencil, no cell phones please, use only one file at a time . . . I thought that it was probably pretty standard protocol, not that I would have known the difference. Believe me. The process I thought would be so intimidating could not have been easier. In no time at all, I was seated at a large table reading a letter from Robert Frost himself to DuBose Heyward. I held the *actual* letter in my hands. It just seemed too wonderful to be true and I have to say, the moment made me feel a little light-headed. That was only the first file from the first box of documents and I had already bumped into Robert Frost. Amazing! What else was in these boxes? Plenty, I'd bet.

After Robert Frost, I tackled the file of correspondence between DuBose and George Gershwin, and there were many letters to read. There was one most important one though, the one that would change the Heywards' life and seal their fate forever. In its text, Gershwin tells DuBose that he is thinking of setting *Porgy* to music, saying that the story is the most outstanding one he knows of about colored people. I read on. Every now and then I would flinch from the language Heyward used referring to people of color or the condescending tone in his letters to Dorothy but I had to keep reminding myself that he was using the accepted terminology and customs of his day. The 1920s were nearly a hundred years ago and many things were decidedly different then. Life in Charleston was multilayered and each of those strata followed a strictly prescribed code of conduct. I mean, the only time you'd see a black woman in a white woman's house was if she was doing the laundry. On the other hand, DuBose had no compunction about visiting and participating in an African-American church service and bringing Gershwin there, too. There were social lines drawn all over town, neighborhood by neighborhood, races divided, ancestors compared, judgments made. But more than that, it was as though everyone worried that they were being watched by some invisible Etiquette Queen and King who would pulverize them to charred smoky bits if they stepped out of line.

Lord knows, DuBose stood on social ceremony in all his letters to Dorothy, being painfully correct, not too personal, and no one would have accused him of being romantic. To be honest, I gagged a little every time I read that DuBose sent his mother's love along with his.

I mean, for the life of me, I don't know how Dorothy figured out he was serious about her unless they sneaked off behind the barn when they met at the MacDowell Colony and carried on like lovers do. And for some reason I doubted that there was very much hanky-panky happening between them. From their photographs they both looked pretty prim. And there were a lot of photographs of DuBose—studio portraits, to be specific. Apparently, he liked his own looks. Hmmm, I thought, what gentleman of that day had their portrait made so frequently?

I couldn't wait to read Dorothy's letters to DuBose. All I could find of hers thus far were cocktail recipes, budget recipes, diet information, and some correspondence with a friend from the MacDowell Colony named Dorothy DeJaggers, who seemed to be a bit mad. Was she? And then there were some letters to and from the headmistress of Jenifer's school and a plea to Dr. Karen Horney, a noted psychiatrist in New York, to please take Jenifer on as a patient. Apparently, although Jenifer made wonderful marks in her classes, she had some behavioral issues and severe absentmindedness. All that was very interesting but it wasn't what I was looking for and I wondered if I would ever find the answer to my question.

There were still boxes of papers to read. Hopefully there was some romance in them. Something!

I read on. The next stack of letters concerned Al Jolson, who wanted to play Porgy—and he would do it in blackface—so eagerly that he formed his own production company with Rodgers and Hammerstein, intending to cut Gershwin out. That took some brash nerve. But blackface? At first it seemed so offensive to me but then I was reminded by Mary Jo that there were laws in those days that forbade black actors from performing on a stage in a theater attended by white patrons. I knew that but had forgotten it. In my mind's eye I suddenly remembered a movie with Jolson singing "Swanee" and I shivered.

"That's why *Porgy and Bess* was never performed here in Charleston where it was written until there was an anniversary revival of it in 1970."

"It seems so crazy now, doesn't it?"

"Yes. It surely does. Anyway, it didn't matter because DuBose was adamant that the actors would all be black or else no play."

"Well, you have to give him credit for that kind of foresight."

"His mother hammered authenticity into his skull from birth."

"I'll bet!"

And as the day went by, I began to understand all the reasons why DuBose was so heavily influenced by his mother, who I decided early on was a meddler and a Bossy Boots nonpareil. They had been very wealthy once but the Civil War left the family nearly destitute. Their financial gloom was further exacerbated when DuBose's father was killed in a factory accident when DuBose was just a toddler. When there's no money you do what you have to do and you hang on to what you've got. In their case all they had left was the glory of the historic deeds of their ancestors. So his mother held her head high and took in boarders at their beach house, ironically named Tranquility, on Sullivans Island but she also wondered aloud *who was going to cut her fingernails?* Gross, I thought. But the answer to that would be DuBose, who became the consummate momma's boy.

Janie Screven Heyward was as resourceful as Scarlett O'Hara, seemingly helpless but really the proverbial iron fist in the old velvet glove, doing everything she could to put food on the table for DuBose and his sister. She even stood in the lobby of the Francis Marion Hotel and recited poetry in Gullah for tourists who were passing by, for what pocket change they would spare. That had to be completely demoralizing for someone who considered herself to have the bluest blood in town. But her lobby recitals led to parlor performances in private homes and whatever other honest work she could find until DuBose became a young man. She had surrendered her pride for her son and daughter and they owed her a great debt.

At fourteen, DuBose dropped out of school, because he had to help support the family. He sold newspapers, eventually finding work in a hardware store and later on the docks as a cotton checker. I was so deeply engrossed in spying on the Heywards that I thought I could have spent the rest of my life reading about all of them. No wonder Risley was so consumed. They were real characters who took dangerous risks and somehow life had worked out for them. But, they had no way of knowing at the time that ridicule and more poverty wasn't waiting for them at every turn.

Mary Jo was passing by with an armload of books to return to their proper shelves. I stopped her to ask her about DuBose's education and the story on his mother, two of the curiosities in my mind.

"Got a minute?" I said.

"Sure. How's it going?"

"Well, I have to say, it's a little overwhelming! I mean, just how poor were the Heywards?"

"Good question. I know it's been said that many nights DuBose went to bed hungry. But in those days, around the Depression, Charleston was still dealing with the poverty from the Civil War. People said the Great Depression went almost unnoticed in Charleston."

"*That's* poor."

"Yep. But most people were in the same boat."

"Mary Jo?"

"Hmmm?"

"Do you think DuBose's mother encouraged him to drop out of school?"

"Well, there's nothing in these papers that directly says that but I've always thought so. I mean, he wasn't a very good student and he was sick all the time, so what was the point of going to school? And she needed help."

"I guess. I'm just trying to get a sense of who they really were, Dorothy and DuBose, I mean."

Mary Jo put her books on the table and sat down in an old oak chair opposite me.

"Well, their reputation was that they were both terribly shy and self-deprecating. Very sweet."

"Oh, please. I've read enough here to know that isn't entirely so. I mean, they were diminutive in stature . . ."

"Between us? I think he might have had a food issue."

"Yeah, there wasn't enough to go around."

"That, too. Although in those days, thinness was definitely equated with chic."

"It still is. For women anyway."

"Yes, well, I've thought about them a lot. Seems like he sure wanted to look dapper. But then there was the health thing, with both of them really."

"How bad was it?"

"Well, he had typhoid fever, dengue fever, terrible polio, and a whopping case of arthritis. Plus his left arm was a fright. Check out the boxes of pictures with Gershwin. And she had some very high blood pressure and impressive rheumatoid arthritis. She was frequently on bed rest because of exhaustion. I think they thought in those days that less weight on your joints would ease pain."

"You also go to bed if you're weak from hunger."

"True. You know, it's like they're still here, in these walls."

"No. They're out on Folly Beach. And I have this peculiar feeling that Dorothy is trying to tell me something. I'm living in the Porgy House on Folly. Did I tell you that?"

"No! Oh my! Is that what brought you here?"

"Yes. That and I've made friends with a fellow from the College of Charleston who thinks I'd find them fascinating and I do," I said and Mary Jo stood then. "Do you think I could have a box of letters from Dorothy to DuBose?"

The afternoon was fading and soon I would have to leave but I wanted to take a fast look at Dorothy's letters first.

"There are none."

"What?"

"Yep. DuBose didn't save her letters. She saved his."

"Oh no." The son of a bitch, I thought, isn't that just like a man?

"Well, it is actually interesting, because it might suggest that he never thought her letters would be the subject of any research or debate."

"Or maybe because he didn't want the world to see how brilliant *she* was?"

"Now, there's a thought. Who knows? Maybe *she* destroyed them after he died? Remember she outlived him by twenty years."

"Why would she do that?" I said, a little saddened by the suggestion.

"Who knows? Maybe because she wanted the world to remember him as the genius, not her?"

I sat there for a moment, considering the weight of what she suggested. Then I began gathering up my notes and pencils but was suddenly overcome with surprise and confusion. Had Dorothy Heyward destroyed her own letters because she loved DuBose Heyward that much? What was she trying to do? Control the spin? Why, when she seemed to me, at least thus far, to be such a bold and liberated woman for her time . . . why would she hide her light under her husband's bushel?

Had I just stumbled on the greatest love story in Charleston's literary history? If so, just how could I prove it?

Later, as I drove to my son's house, I tried to shift my attention to the evening but the truth was that I was almost completely preoccupied with my search for the truth about Dorothy. It just didn't make sense to me but then there were boxes left to read. So I shoved it to the back burner in my brain, pulled into my son's driveway, and thought, *oh, my, what a simple house they have.* If I'd had my old wallet, I'd have made them a gift of some serious landscaping.

I rang the doorbell. Russ answered.

"Hi, Mom! How are you? Come on in!"

"Good, baby. How're you?"

I stepped across the threshold and into their living room, hugged my son, and heard Alice's footsteps coming toward us.

"Hi, Cate! Welcome home!"

I really wished she'd call me something else.

"Thanks, Alice," I said and gave her a maternal hug, patting her shoulder. "Well, now! Don't you both look wonderful?" I stepped back, looking at their genuinely happy, youthful, smiling faces, thinking how important parental approval was at every age.

"Thanks, Cate! And so do you, all things considered," Alice said and Russ shot her a death-ray look. "I mean, the long drive and all the terrible things, you know, Addison's suicide and . . ."

I was thinking, why is she bringing this up? I mean, let's just relive it all one more time and have a nice evening, okay? When Russ was uncomfortable with a situation he rubbed his hands on the sides of his pants. I guess I was staring at her with a very furrowed brow, because Russ was rubbing his legs and his palms.

"You're gonna start a fire," I said.

"Right! Why don't I get you ladies a drink? Glass of wine, Mom? Alice? You want a glass of tomato juice?" Russ said, smiling, seeing precisely why Alice compromised my sense of humor.

"Why, I'd love that, Russ! Thanks! What smells so good? Gosh, your house looks so pretty!"

No, it didn't. It was as sterile as an operating room. Didn't they have any tchotchkes? I forced a smile, walked by Alice, and followed my son into the kitchen. My poor son.

"I made fish sticks," I heard her say in a tiny voice. "And a pot of grits."

And it isn't even Friday, the Catholic in me said to no one. Wow. Fish sticks.

We made it to the dinner table, which, for the record, was set by

someone who did not share the domestic goddess's propensity for anything that smacked of style or beauty. That would be Alice. The mis-
matched forks were jumbled with the knives on the right, and a bottle
of ketchup was in the middle of the table along with a paper napkin
holder and a bottle of Texas Pete's Hot Sauce. There was at least one
stain on every place mat. But I held my tongue. The ketchup was for
the fish sticks and Texas Pete was there to enhance the collard greens
from the plastic quart container that came from the Bi-Lo, reheated in
the microwave and served in the same container it traveled in. Again,
I held my tongue and thought, well, maybe I would teach Alice to
cook. And to set an inviting table. At the same time I taught myself,
that is. I mean, I was a reasonable presence in the kitchen, especially
with holiday meals, and I could do some pretty interesting things to a
chicken . . .

"Mom? Did you hear what I said?"

I was winding a wad of collards around my fork, thinking about the
slow-cooker recipe I had for coq au vin.

"Oh! I'm sorry, sweetheart! I was just thinking that it's been years
since I had collards and grits and I love them! They're really delicious,
Alice. Just the right amount of salt and just the right consistency . . ."
They were staring at me with the strangest expression. "What? What
did I miss?"

"We're having a baby, Mom. We're pregnant!"

"*You are?*" WHAT? I was stunned. "Oh my God! Russ! Alice! Oh!
This is *wonderful* news!" I shot up from my seat, I don't know what
possessed me, but I hugged Alice and kissed the top of her head. Then
I ran around the table and pulled Russ up into my arms and hugged
him, too, for all I was worth, I hugged my boy. All at once I was filled
with a flood of joy and I didn't quite know what to do with myself. I was
going to be a *grandmother*!

"Oh, my God! I'll learn to knit! I'll learn to crochet! Have you told
Sara?"

"No, you're the first person we've told. Well, Alice called her mom but that's different, right?"

Actually, I was glad she had told her mother first. It was the right thing to do. If Sara had called her mother-in-law before me I would've cut her throat. Of course, her throat had not been jeopardized thus far.

"Oh, Alice! Dear child! Is your momma thrilled? Oh! What a stupid question! Of course she is!"

Alice smiled and turned her head to the side. "She's very happy."

Her mother, Maureen, lived in St. Paul and I knew she'd be coming to visit as much as she could. I'd have to help them fix up a guest room. And a nursery! A *nursery*.

"Old Maureen almost burst she was so excited," Russ said. "Yeah, I'm gonna have me a boy to shoot hoops!"

"What if he turns out to be a she?" I said, still smiling like . . . I can't even tell you how I was smiling. From my toes up to my face? Inside and out?

"Can't happen! I'm having a boy first. Then Alice can have all the girls she wants."

"Guess we'll have to fence the yard this summer," Alice said.

"Oh, honey, don't worry yourself about a fence. There's time for that yet. And how do you feel? Are you feeling all right?" I reached out and put my hand on her arm. She did not recoil. This was a good sign.

"I feel great, actually." She smiled and I realized her complexion had a new opalescent glow. Too bad I couldn't bottle it. "I really feel fine. A little more tired than normal, but that's all."

"Well, isn't this just wonderful? This is just wonderful."

"I was worried you wouldn't be so happy," Alice said, perfectly straight-faced.

"Oh, Alice." I looked at her and thought, okay, this is it, you confrontational little so-and-so. Assuming she carries this child to term and delivers? She's in my life forever. Sometimes a baby seals a marriage. It happens with royalty all the time. I cleared my throat. "Alice?

I am *very* happy. I could not *be* happier! Wouldn't you say this family *needs* a piece of *good* news? And this is the *best* news! It really is, darlin'!" I almost choked on *darlin'*, but I decided immediately on hearing their news that from that moment forward, I was going to be the model in-law, which I thought basically required saying only positive things and saying very little at that.

"Let's call Sara," Russ said.

Russ dialed Sara's number and put her on speakerphone.

"Hey, sis! I'm here with Mom and Alice and we've got some news!"

"Yeah, what?" Sara said, without an ounce of enthusiasm.

"We're having a baby!"

Silence from California.

And then, after an uncomfortable pause, "That's so not funny, Russ."

Russ picked up his cell phone and clicked a button, making it a private conversation in case Sara said something ugly about Alice. "Come on, Sara, you're going to be an aunt!" He listened to her, nodding his head and saying, *I know, I know, unbelievable, right? September. Yep.* Then he covered the phone with his hand and gave it to Alice. "She's psyched. She wants to congratulate you."

I watched Alice's expressions as she spoke to Sara. She seemed deeply satisfied with herself. That was reassuring to me. It was good for a woman to have confidence when she is preparing to bring a child into the world.

The rest of the evening, which included a room-temperature peach pie from the store and vanilla ice cream, passed as though I was in a dream. What other dramatic changes were in store for me? My children? I was still fighting to regain my bearings from losing Addison and everything else and it didn't matter at all to the world. Not one bit. The world continued to turn and life continued to go on. My son was going to be a father. Addison would've been so happy to know it. Look what he was missing. The idiot.

I had hoped so hard against their denial of readiness that they would have children and soon. I wanted Russ and Alice to know the kind of deep joy and happiness that only comes with a family. And while I looked at the world very differently than my daughter-in-law, she made Russ happy. That was what mattered.

"You'd better call Aunt Daisy," I said. "Wait till she hears this!"

CHAPTER SEVENTEEN

Setting: The Porgy House in the music room.

Director's Note: Photos of cardboard theater, cardboard actors, a soup tureen, and Jenifer on the backstage scrim. Voices of Jenifer and DuBose from off-stage.

Act II
Scene 4

Dorothy: I remember like it was yesterday. No change in the weather. No change in our moods, either. Our ship had yet to come in. We had consumed vast quantities of split-pea soup, more from boredom than from hunger, and we didn't know what to do with ourselves.

DuBose was as sulky as I had ever seen him and Jenifer was whiny. I thought I might go a little crazy. Cabin fever, I thought, that's what we've got. A colossal case of cabin fever. But it was cold and drizzling outside and no weather in which to send her out to play. She would catch her death and then give it to us!

Then I remembered the theater I had when I was a little girl. It was made of cardboard as were all the characters. Every day I wrote a new play and made new characters, forcing my family to attend the performances. I would make one with Jenifer and we would while away the hours reenacting fairy tales until the sun came out. Brilliant!

I remembered that I had some corrugated cardboard boxes whose present use was to hold old clothes I intended to take to the church for the poor. I dumped the contents of one of those boxes on the bed in the room downstairs opposite the kitchen and rattled through the kitchen drawers until I found my serrated knife. I cut off the flaps, turned it upside down, and cut out almost all of one side leaving some edges to be like stage wings. Then I cut a hole in the top of the box, through which I could lower my cardboard characters like puppets, their backs secured to pencils with tape.

I searched the pantry for some paint and all I had was some poster paints, old pots of red, blue, and yellow, almost dried up from neglect. I boiled some water, added a little bit to each pot, and shook them like mad. Then I covered the kitchen table with newspaper and called Jenifer.

"What is it, Mommy?" she said.

"We're opening a theater!" I announced and put her to work, painting the building in red and blue stripes with yellow stars scattered all around.

Her eyes lit up and she clapped her hands. Jenifer was delighted. Here was my child, whose attention span was about as short as it could be one minute and in the next she was lost in space, completely absorbed in our project. That short attention span and spaciness would cause her trouble later on and all through her life. But then? We passed that afternoon and so many others, stretched across the living-room floor on our stomachs, lost in the world of princesses and every fantasy a childhood could hold. When all our stories were exhausted, we began to make up new ones. DuBose watched and listened, applauding at the end of each performance, praising Jenifer's ingenuity and natural gifts he claimed she inherited from me.

"No doubt you'll have a spectacular theatrical life, little one!" he said.

"Oh, no, Daddy. That's your life and Mommy's. I'm going to be a ballerina," Jenifer said with solemn determination and then she rose on her toes, pirouetting across the room.

Fade to Darkness

CHAPTER EIGHTEEN

The Moon

"What? I can hardly believe it!" Aunt Daisy said, practically breathless, having thrown herself back in her chair from the news, slapping her hand across her heart.

I had suggested to Alice and Russ that it would be thoughtful and yes, respectful to take a ride out to Folly to tell Aunt Daisy and Ella the news in person. I had called Patti and told her myself and she almost fainted.

"So, they have a sex life," she said deadpan.

"Apparently," I said and we broke into a fit of laughter.

"My God. Now what? Are you going to get a blue tint for your hair?"

"You know, I've got a body part you can kiss, too!"

So the next evening, before I met up with John, we were all gathered in Aunt Daisy and Ella's kitchen, sitting around the table eating, what else, but a freshly baked pecan pie, still warm from the oven. We were all going to be diabetic soon but nonetheless, I had called ahead to Ella and begged her to make one and told her there was wonderful news, news truly worth celebrating.

"It'll be on the table by six o'clock," she said. "Don't y'all want to have dinner?"

"Well, I'm seeing John and . . ."

"Shoot. I ain't getting in between you and that man. Not me!"

"There's nothing to get in between," I said hoping that my words were a lie.

Anyway, I was all dressed (not to kill but hopefully to seriously maim) and ready to go out with John so I just drove over and met them at Aunt Daisy and Ella's beforehand. I don't have to tell you that I did not put on lipstick or cologne. I didn't want to hear about it and Lord knows, in my family someone always has something to say.

"It's true!" Russ said. "We're having a baby, Aunt Daisy. Isn't it great?"

"Mother McCree! I never thought I'd live to see the day when you were old enough to get married, much less have a child!" She sighed heavily and then, the sentimental nature of the moment getting the better of her, she smiled wistfully. "God, oh how I wish my sister was still alive for this. I miss her something awful right now. I really do."

"I miss her too, Aunt Daisy," I said, smiling. "But you did the heavy lifting with Patti and me so you deserve the spoils. Anyway, you have to believe she's up there somewhere watching over us all the time, don't you?"

"Humph," she said with a grunt.

So much for Aunt Daisy's spiritual side.

"She's watching alright," Ella said. "You *have* to believe that or else what are you going to do?"

"Oh, I prefer to howl at the full moon," Aunt Daisy said, straight-faced. Then she cut her eye at me and said, "So, *somebody's* gonna be a grandmother!"

I laughed and looked at Alice. "And somebody else is gonna be a mother!"

"I sure am," she said. "This pie is so awesome. Do you think I could have another little piece?"

"You sure can, honey," Aunt Daisy said. "You can have the whole thing!"

"Just a forkful," she said.

Ella got up, took Alice's plate, and cut her another big slice. As she handed Alice the pie, she leaned in and said, "You carrying a girl chile. Uh-huh, got you a girl!"

"Oh, come on," Alice said. "You couldn't know that."

"Aw, come on, Aunt Ella," Russ said. "I'm hoping for a b-ball buddy!"

"Ain't no reason why that chile can't play ball, but she's a girl all the same."

"How do you know, Ella?" I said.

"'Cause she's cravin' *shugah*! Boys want pickles. Girls like sweets. Mark my word! Y'all all see *what* come September!"

"No point in debating with Ella on that," Aunt Daisy said. "She calls 'em all the time and guess what? It's the only thing we never argue about."

"'Cause I'm *right* all the time and you know it," Ella said.

"Did you hear me disagree with you? You going deaf now, too?"

We all laughed and I stood up to leave, taking my plate to the sink to rinse.

"Where you headed, Mom?"

"Humph," said Aunt Daisy, with her eyes widened to capacity and rolling around for emphasis. She certainly was opinionated tonight.

"I'm having dinner with John Risley."

"Oh," Russ said. "Well, that's great. Have fun!"

"Thanks. Listen, if your sister calls, you might want to keep that detail to yourself."

"Oh, *heeeere* we go again," Alice said, and put her fork down.

"What does that mean, Alice?" I said.

Now, wouldn't you think that a twenty-eight-year-old young woman would have more manners than to voice an opinion about her mother-in-law's social life in front of everyone? Pregnant or not, shouldn't there be some kind of a filter between her hormonal brain and her flapping jaw? Apparently not.

"I'm just saying that to ask Russ to lie for you? It's not a good thing. That's all."

Would it be so terrible if I put just one strip of duct tape over her mouth?

"*You're just saying?* Well, that's nice. *Listen,* Alice, I'm not asking Russ to lie for me or anyone else. I just don't think it's necessary to go advertising every piece of information you have. Sara is very sensitive and I don't want her upset."

"Don't worry, Mom. I won't tell Sara."

"What if she asks?" Alice said.

"Then you just say you don't know."

"That would be a lie," Alice said, finishing off that unnecessary but irresistible second piece of pie.

"No, sweetie, that would be *discretion.* Big difference. Now, if any of you ever see me having dinner with a known criminal then please, be my guest and alert the authorities. Anyway, he's a friend and that's all. It's nice for me to have a friend, don't you think?"

I forced myself to giggle so that she wouldn't feel like it was a direct insult or reprimand and would then take it in stride. I winked at Russ, who was grinning, thankful that I had not really taken Alice to task, evidence of my vow to walk softly but think whatever I wanted. Let's be honest, everyone knew what I thought of Alice, because it was a widely shared opinion.

"Ah, well, okay kids. I'm going to be on my way. Thanks for the pie, Ella. Y'all have a great evening! Oh, by the way? The piano is coming soon. Aunt Daisy? You don't mind if I park it at the Porgy House for a while do you?"

"Absolutely not," she said. "That's your little red wagon."

182 / DOROTHEA BENTON FRANK

"Oh, my! Well? Whatever that meant!" I gave her a little kiss on the cheek and left.

I returned to the Porgy House, freshened up my face, spritzed all the important targets with cologne, and then went downstairs to look around the downstairs den. The piano would have to go in there. The stairs that took you to the larger room upstairs were definitely too narrow and frankly, I wouldn't ask the deliverymen to even chance it. They would be singing soprano in a choir. Even so, I'd have to make room in the cramped downstairs. I was thinking of different ways to rearrange things when John knocked on the door. I ran my hands through my hair and answered it.

"Hey! Come on in," I said.

He breezed past me, smelling predictably addictive, and then turned to face me. "Wow, you look so pretty! What did you do?"

I just stared at him.

"That didn't come out right," he said. "What I meant was, you're always pretty but I thought maybe you'd done something to yourself? You know, different hairdo or something?"

"Pink lipstick, but it's not new," I said. "Bobbi Brown says you should always wear pink lipstick because it brightens up your face."

"Well, I'll have to try that," he said.

"Oh, please." I shook my head and said, "Let's get out of here."

"Yes, ma'am!"

There was very little traffic on Folly Road and we were just sailing along. I fell in love with the landscape every time I came this way, crossing the little bridges, spotting the snowy white egrets standing majestically in the quiet marsh and the occasional great blue heron swooping by.

"Beautiful, isn't it?" he said.

"Beyond," I said. "I can't tell you how many times I tried to remember all of this and describe it to someone but there are no words."

"Yeah, you really have to see it to believe it."

"And every time of year is different . . . so pretty."

The marsh grass was a beautiful tawny color, like the fur of a chinchilla. Whether it was green in the summer or brown in winter, it always seemed like you could just run your hand across it and it would feel so good, like streams of silk. The reality was it would cut your hands to ribbons while you sunk into the pluff mud, waving goodbye cruel world, and banks of coon oysters wouldn't even blink as you went down, never to be heard from again. Take my word for it: don't wear your good shoes clamming. In fact, if you ever *do* go out in the marsh, make sure it's dead low tide and don't bring those shoes into your house. Ever. Unless you like the smell of sewage.

"How was your day?" he asked.

"Fabulous. I'm going to be a grandmother!"

"Oh Cate, how wonderful!"

"Yep, in September!" I was thrilled. "And I spent the better part of the day today and yesterday at the Historical Society, reading until I was bleary-eyed."

"Fantastic! I want to hear all about it."

"Dorothy and DuBose were a couple of real characters, but you already know that."

"Yeah, but I am anxious to hear your take on them."

He began whistling a tune.

"Well, somebody's chipper over there, Mr. Bluebird!" I said.

"And why shouldn't I be?" he said as he stopped at a traffic light. "I'm with you and we're going to have a fabulous dinner together and talk about my favorite subject in the world!"

"I'm beginning to understand the obsession. Reading those papers is like eating potato chips or buttered popcorn. Once you get started . . ."

"Yep! That's what happens. Most people don't take the time or have the time to do what you're doing right now, but wouldn't it be a great way to spend vacations? I mean, visit different cities and read what they've got in their libraries and special collections of other people's papers?"

"I don't know. I mean, I'd like to visit a lot of places like Angkor Wat and Patagonia and the Galápagos Islands but on the other hand, you're probably right. There are so many thoughts I have about Dorothy and DuBose, Dorothy especially. But I wouldn't be able to verify my suspicions unless I went to Ohio and dug up all of her childhood and got the scoop on her aunts. I feel like Nancy Drew on one hand and like a cheesy reporter for a creepy tabloid on the other."

"Cheesy reporter?"

"Yeah, you know, out in Hollywood there are these crazed paparazzi who go through people's garbage cans, looking for receipts to see how much money they spend on clothes and count their liquor bottles to see how much they drink?"

"And their mango skins to see what's in their smoothies?"

"Exactly! How do you decide who someone was, based on the papers they leave behind? It's impossible. Especially in this case, because I don't think Dorothy wants me to know all about her."

"Why do you say that?"

"There are too many holes. Stuff that's missing. And things that don't add up."

The traffic on Folly Road grew heavier and then it seemed like we caught every single traffic light.

"Hmmm. By the way, we're going to a very cool restaurant. The Wild Olive. It's out on Maybank Highway. It's actually real Italian, if you can believe it."

"Oh, come on. The only Italian food in Charleston is Pizza Hut."

"Not true! There are a few now. Anyway, they have this chef, a guy named Jacques Larson, and he's great."

"A French guy cooking Italian? Come on."

"Nope, he's from Iowa but he trained with Mario Batali . . ."

"No kidding?"

Well, of course, all you have to do is mention Italian food and the next thing I know, I'm salivating, my stomach is growling from massive hunger pangs, screaming to be fed, and I'm already trying to decide what I want to eat before I even see the restaurant much less a menu.

"Was that *you*?" he said.

"Yes," I said, embarrassed to death.

"Holy hell! Do you want to stop for bread? I mean, can you make it there?"

"You're hilarious, Risley. Anybody ever tell you that?"

"Yeah, all the time." He was so pleased with himself. So pleased.

"Listen to you! All that rumbling from such a little person."

He reached over and gave my leg a friendly slap. It was funny but about every two minutes my stomach would start wailing again. And John would snicker and I would tell him to knock it off.

"This is truly disgusting," I said.

"There are some crackers in the glove compartment," he said.

I looked and there were a few packaged saltines in pairs, left over from a chili order at Wendy's.

"Fine," I said. "Great."

"But I can pull into the 7-Eleven if you think you'd like me to. I mean, you know, feed the beast?"

"Just shut up and drive, okay?"

We were both laughing at that point, because what could you do? I turned up the radio. This had happened to me before and it was usually the result of too much acid and not enough carbs. Maybe. Honestly, who knew why it happened but I hated it and wished my digestive system hadn't started going into overdrive when I was planning to become The Seductress that night. Some siren I was.

We finally pulled into the parking lot of the restaurant and got out. The building was white and new, beautifully lit and landscaped. I had no idea it even existed.

"When did they build *this* place?" I said.

"I don't know. A year ago or maybe a couple of years ago?"

"So many things have changed since I grew up here," I said.

"You've been spending too much time in enemy territory," he said with a chuckle. "I can show you wondrous things in the Lowcountry! You'll think you're in . . . well, it's the Lowcountry and that's it."

"But it's the updated version?"

"Exactly."

Inside, we were shown to a table for two that was very nicely tucked away near the bar. Once again, as we crossed the dining room, John's hand was resting on the small of my back. How and why had I ever lived for so long without any of these small demonstrations of affection? It just goes to show you that you can get along on very little.

We scanned the menus and I was drawn to the pastas.

"Wow," I said. "I'm thinking about a big ole bowl of spaghetti and the house-cured salumi with the . . . well, with the stuff that comes with it."

"And I'm torn . . ." John finally settled on the braised meatballs and polenta. "I'm having mussels to begin," he said.

I'm having muscles later, I thought and did not say. Anyway, I loathed mussels and hoped I could watch him eat them without getting ill.

"Sounds good," I said.

He ordered a bottle of Chianti Classico and we got down to the contents of the bread basket. As soon as the wine was poured, John said he wanted to propose a toast.

"Sure! To what?"

"I say let's drink to the memory of the Heywards, John Bennett, Josephine Pinckney, and . . ."

"Hold it right there, Dr. Renaissance. It's all I can do to hold the Heywards in my head!"

He laughed and said, "Okay. To Dorothy and DuBose!"

"How about just *to Dorothy*? DuBose is not exactly my favorite guy right now."

"All right, then, to Dorothy." We touched the sides of our glasses and took a sip. "So, do you want to tell me what poor old DuBose did to offend you so? We certainly have become a bit judgmental haven't we? A few hours in a library and one of Charleston's greatest icons is a scoundrel? 'Fess up, woman! What did you find?"

"Oh, please. Make fun. I mean, you're right, of course. I'm no expert but the facts are a little strange. Where to start?"

"Start anywhere."

"Well, all right. I'm assuming you've read everything they've got down there. Is that right?"

"Yeah, and everything from Harlan Greene and James Hutchisson and Barbara Bellows . . . but I'll admit, it's been a while. I can give you their books, too, you know, to round out your education."

"That would be great." I took another sip of wine. "I'm really loving this whole era, the beautiful gowns and the way women wore hats and gloves and what went on. Okay, so look, here's the first thing I'm sure of. I am absolutely convinced that Dorothy Heyward was in love with DuBose like Cathy was with Heathcliff. Like Scarlett, like Anna Karenina, like Juliet . . . I mean, her love for him was epic, the stuff of the greatest classics in the whole of time. Obsession! Totally consuming obsession."

"And what's the matter with that? Isn't that how a woman should love a man?" John had this tiny little smile creeping across his face.

"God forbid. That kind of love is a lethal prescription for misery. It's what got me a room at the Porgy House. I mean, if you find yourself falling for someone, really falling? You'd better keep both eyes open."

"I'll keep that in mind. Anyway, tell me more."

Our appetizers arrived and I tried not to look at his so I dove right into mine, taking a bite of the chicken livers on crostini.

"Wow, this looks perfect. Okay, so, as you know, Dorothy got shuttled around from one aunt to another during her childhood and then shipped off to a boarding school, right?"

Then it happened.

"Yes. Say? Would you like a mussel?" John offered me one, with the dark slimy bulbous thing hanging from the tines of his fork like a horrible goober on a miniature gigging pole.

I gagged a little but held on.

"Uh, no, thanks. Listen, you may as well know, the only way that thing is getting in my mouth is if it can fly. Have you ever cleaned one of those bad boys?"

"Can't say I have."

"Yeah, well, it's a totally nasty trip. They've got this beard you have to remove and then this blue cone-shaped phallic thing you have to pull out . . ." I shuddered. "Sorry."

"Gross," he said. "That was truly gross. Maybe I'll have carpaccio instead. Does raw meat bother you?"

"Not at all."

He signaled for the waiter and explained that he had changed his mind, they could charge him for the mussels but I was offended by their presence and this was a very important night. The waiter, thoroughly confused, took them away and promised to take it off the bill anyway.

"Jesus, Risley, I'm sorry. You must think I'm really crazy . . ."

"No. I know what crazy looks like and you're not it."

I paused then and looked at him, pushing my platter of antipasto toward him to share.

"Have some. Please. You want to talk about her?"

He helped himself to a slice of mozzarella and a piece of red pepper.

"I'll tell you about her. I promised you I would if you'd like me to, but finish telling me about Dorothy and why DuBose is such a bum."

"Okay," I said and helped myself to more wine. He took the bottle right out of my hand and poured it himself.

"Forgive my oversight, ma'am."

"Thanks. Well, first of all, I think that having some sense of permanence, you know, a place where she truly belonged, was the most important thing in the world to her. And I think being respected and famous in the world of serious literature was *way* too important to him. And when they met, she had this great education, she was a promising playwright, and she probably had wads of money that was left to her. He was adorable, soft-spoken, and most likely very attentive and probably had a pretty sophisticated demeanor."

"So, he's a bad guy *because . . .*"

"He saw her as a ticket for him and his momma out of poverty. That's not to say he didn't care for her. I think he must have, because in all the old photographs and press he sure *seems* devoted to her. But she had been treated like an orphan . . ."

"Well, she *was* one."

"No, I know that, so was I, so maybe I'm sensitive to that. But here was someone who also appealed to her intellectually, socially, and yes, despite all of his grotesque infirmities, he appealed to her physically, too. *She,* who had *never* enjoyed anything close to great health, was in *far* better shape than he was. She could save *him.* Women adore saving men. And he needed saving."

"From what?"

John was smiling and relishing his carpaccio, picking up the parmesan shavings with his fingers. He was clearly enjoying himself.

"Poverty. His mother. The ravages of polio and all the other diseases he had in his life. And professionally, too."

"And what did she get out of it?"

"A home. And the great satisfaction of restoring his family's name in Charleston and helping to build his name in the literary world and in the theatrical world. And she got the love of her life."

"So, you think he married her for her money?"

"Yep. Definitely. I mean, he was living with his momma! And the fact that she understood writing for the theater and had a real gift for it. Dorothy was happy for him to give up his business and try to live on only what they earned. And she was meek enough to stay in his shadow and let him be the star."

"You think DuBose wanted Dorothy's thunder?"

"No, I just think it was there for the taking and he took it but he always kept her at his side. Look, you don't have to read very far to discover how ambitious he was. What man has his portrait made that often? What straight man, anyway?"

"There were rumors."

"No kidding?"

"Yeah. I mean, the guy was a shrimp with deformities and so soft-spoken people had trouble understanding him. Oh! You'll love this! When they started up the Poetry Society, he went around with this petition for incorporation asking people to sign it and they thought they were signing up for a Poultry Society."

"That's pretty funny."

John sat back in his chair and stared at me for what seemed like an incredibly long period of time. I just continued eating, finishing up the last of the olives and caponata, waiting for him to say something.

"You know," he said, "I'm not sure that I agree with what you're surmising about them but here's something. I don't think contemporary historians have ever looked at their marriage and career from *her* point of view."

"Well, that's not hard to believe, because her letters to him were destroyed. He probably dumped them so his Nosy Nellie mother wouldn't read them."

"Maybe." John laughed at that.

"Or, she threw them out after he died, trying to cover her footprints so he could be all shiny and bright when he took his place in history next to Gershwin."

"Maybe. I mean, what if that's all true, everything you're proposing?"

"Who cares?"

"Well, I do. And you know what else, Nancy Drew?"

"What?"

"So would others. Who cares if it's speculation? This story would make a wonderful play for Piccolo Spoleto Festival. I mean, you said *you* wanted to write a play, didn't you? Give it a shot!"

"Oh, no, I couldn't. I mean, I don't know enough. And isn't it sort of treasonous to screw around with DuBose's reputation?"

"Absolutely not. Have you been to the theater lately? *Nothing's* sacred. I say, go have a ball!" He reached across the table and took my hand in his. "I'm not kidding, Cate. Do it."

Holy hell, wait until I told Patti about this. I was holding hands with this gorgeous man who was telling me to become a playwright. Maybe I would! I looked at his hand and thought, wow, it's beautiful. I loved the shape of his fingernails, the light brown color of his skin . . . the waffle of my virtue was gaining speed.

"Well, I'll think about it. Anyway . . ." Our entrées arrived and the aromatics of pancetta and pecorino riding on the steam rising from my spaghetti were divine. "This looks amazing. Italian food in Charleston. Wow."

Our waiter grated some additional cheese on our food; then he stepped back.

"Buon appetito!" he said and walked away.

"So, John?"

"Ah! Yes, you want to know about Lisa, I guess?"

Her name was Lisa.

"Yeah, well. Yeah." I wound several strands of spaghetti around my fork and blew on it. "Hot."

"Lisa is in a small hospital slash jail where she will spend the rest of her life."

"What's the story?"

"The story. Well, we got married right out of college. We were young and foolish. We were living in Maryland then. She was working for an insecticide company and I was teaching ninth-grade English. For a while we were getting along just fine and then she started acting paranoid and accusing me of running around on her."

"Were you?"

"God, no. I was working every minute I could, trying to save money to buy a house for us. Anyway, one night I came in sort of late and she flew at me with a knife, saying she was going to kill me. I got the knife away from her but then she kept on screaming and it became obvious to me she didn't know who I was."

"She snapped or something?"

"Yeah. So I got out of there and went to a buddy's house to spend the night on the sofa. The next day, I went back to get a change of clothes and she acted like nothing at all had happened. When I asked her about what the hell she was trying to do, she didn't know what I was talking about."

"But, she must have."

"Well, who knows but anyway, I stayed with her. Then the same thing happened a few more times so I moved out. She refused to see a doctor or anyone. I felt terrible for her but I couldn't live like that."

"Who could? Where was her family?"

"Father took off when she was a kid and her mother was basically a street person in Salem, Oregon, making jewelry with beads made out of recycled paper, selling the stuff for whatever she could get."

"You mean useless?"

"Exactly. Anyway, Lisa wanted us to get back together and all that but I said no, I really didn't think it was a good idea. And, there were lots of hysterical phone calls and crying and I just held my ground. I mean, I was as nice as I could be. I kept telling her she needed help but she refused, saying she was fine. Somehow she continued to function. Then one day all the phone calls stopped."

"And you had not filed for divorce yet?"

"No. I didn't have money for a lawyer and I wasn't seeing anyone so it didn't matter. Anyhow, she found out where I was living and one day when I was out . . ."

"So she was watching your house?"

"Had to be. Anyway, she climbed in through my kitchen window and poured thallium into my grapefruit juice. Then she left."

"Nice. Very nice. That's an insecticide, I assume?"

"Yes. It's rarely used these days."

"The world's probably better off for it. Then what?"

"I came home, drank part of a glass, thought it tasted funky, then my stomach started killing me. I thought I was having an appendicitis attack so I went to the emergency room. They did blood work, found traces of the poison in my bloodstream, and called the cops."

"Holy hell! So, did you say you thought it was her?"

"No. Stupidly, I did not. Look, I felt bad for her, you know? And I thought well, it won't happen again. But it did. Then I realized she really *was* trying to kill me so I let the police search my house. They found all kinds of forensic evidence that nailed her. She was convicted but sent to a high-security hospital instead of a jail. Anyway, she's not coming out."

"How do you know? I mean, don't people go to a hospital to get well and go home?"

"Yeah, but apparently she tried to stab a few of the orderlies with a fork and she's had some other issues with other patients."

"So she's violent."

"Very. And delusional."

"Gosh, that's so sad. So, how come you never got a divorce?"

"For a lot of reasons. First, I struggled with the whole *in sickness and in health* part of the vows. I thought if I don't forgive, I will become angry and bitter. Then, as I began to teach at a college level, I realized it was probably better if my rambunctious coeds thought I was married. And now, I can't get the ring off. Seems like my knuckle grew. I mean, I could have it cut off, I guess, but there's never been a reason to."

"Oh." I understood now and didn't feel so guilty.

"Oh? Oh, I see what you're thinking. I got close a couple of times but life always got in the way of serious commitment for me. You know, either I moved or they moved or something."

"Wow." That was very disappointing news. After all he'd been through, the chances of him ever making a commitment were probably greatly diminished. What good-looking straight man with a job makes it to his age without a family? One who doesn't want one. I was fore-warned but not completely discouraged.

"Okay, I can hear what you're thinking. Listen, I'll make you a deal."

"I'm all ears, Risley, and this had better be good."

"When you get rid of yours, I'll get rid of mine."

I looked down at my left hand and there it was. My wedding band of disappointment. My phony diamond, that unforgettable deception, was in a box somewhere, packed with other costume jewelry. THE TALE OF THE WIDOW AND HER INFAMOUS CZ was another story to tell him on another night.

There would have to be some kind of a ceremony to mark my lib-eration from the confines of my inglorious farce of a marriage. Maybe I would wait for Patti to come to town. We could stand on the last tiny bridge to the island with a couple of lit sparklers and a thermos of something wicked and toss the lying thing over into the water. Or maybe I would toss it from the Ravenel Bridge. It was higher and would be more dramatic. This required thought.

"It's kind of like a battle memento, isn't it?" I said and smiled.

He looked at me and smiled so sweetly that I believed then that his relationship with me was going to be different from all the others. I knew it. I did. Okay, I didn't know it but it didn't really matter because I was already in the soup. The way we were looking at each other? All I could think about was how we would be together. We may as well have already been in bed. And soon we were. But here's how the evening progressed.

First, I put my fork down and John immediately said, "You don't want dessert, do you?"

And I said, "I was thinking of something else but if you want dessert? I don't mind if you do."

"Let's polish off this bottle. I'll just get the bill, and let's get out of here. I have some ideas of how we might spend the rest of the night, too." He signaled the waiter with the universal check mark written in air and the waiter nodded. "Before we go, I mean, since I laid it on the table about Lisa, is there anything you want to tell me about your husband?"

"Well, his name was Addison, he killed himself, which I think you know . . ."

"God, no. Actually, I only knew that he was deceased."

"Yes, well, lemme tell you, committing suicide was the only noble thing he had done in years. Very few people mourned. My children did, of course. But not many others. I don't miss him one little bit, which surprises me sometimes. That's not to say finding him wasn't a terrible shock, but I am sort of over that now. I think. But the reality is that he was such a terrible husband for so long that I am more relieved than anything else. The Tale of Addison Cooper is a really strange story about arrogance and self-deception, but yours is actually more bizarre."

"Well, it's not every day that your spouse tries to murder you. What did he do for a living?"

The waiter placed the bill on the table; John glanced at it and put his credit card down.

"He ran a private equity firm and managed a portfolio that was once worth about twenty billion dollars in assets. His friends and former partners think he found out that he was going to be indicted for every crime in the books he cooked but he preferred to die rather than go to jail. How stupid is that?"

"Seems like a drastic way to deal with things, doesn't it?"

"To say the least. Maybe someday I'll tell you just how unbelievable he was. And I was so busy trying to keep him calm and keeping things going I had no idea how much trouble he was in."

John poured out the last of the wine and I took a sip.

"I've always thought that life's a gift, you know?" he said. "I think it's better to try and work things out, even with the IRS if, God forbid, they came knocking. But then I've always been a pretty modest guy in terms of my own ambitions. I just don't have some burning desire to own a lot of worldly possessions. I mean, don't get me wrong, I like nice things but you should own your stuff, it shouldn't own you."

"And you see, that's where he was, dead center in that trap of defining himself through what he could own, *and* what he could get away with. I remember the day we were moving into our house in Alpine, which was quite the fantastical over-the-top testimony to Addison's success. My brother-in-law looked at the house and back to him and said, *So Addison? How much is enough?* You know what he said?"

"I couldn't begin to guess."

"Right? I remember this like it was yesterday. He said, *Mark? Enough? Double what I have at any given moment in my life.*" I shook my head. "My brother-in-law is a perfectly wonderful podiatrist and he does very nicely, but he just blinked his eyes and let out a low whistle. He looked up at the house and then back at Addison again and slapped him on his shoulder and said something like *better you than me, pal.* Anyway, my family thought Addison was pretty funny and generally a great guy at first but then something happened to him. He became someone else."

"And that new Addison wasn't so great."

"Not so great? No, he was intolerable but at least he didn't put poison in my juice. Jeesch! I have to remember to count my blessings."

"Truly. So not only did you lose your husband, your whole life is now completely different. You weren't exaggerating that night at the Pig, were you?"

"Not one bit." I took a drink of water. "Yeah, it's just me and the Heywards down at Porgy's. But some of my family is here and that's awfully nice."

"I'll bet so." He reached across the table and put his hand over mine. "So you're really feeling okay?"

"Well, yeah. I mean, I haven't been with another man in decades so I'm a little nervous."

"Don't be. I think you're amazing."

"Well, I think you are, too. You know, I keep thinking about all the possibilities."

"You should be really. Who knows? You could be the next Lillian Hellman!"

Well, that wasn't exactly the response I sort of hoped for. But I took it in stride.

"Or Dorothy Heyward."

"That's right. Look, I can help you get started. I mean, I teach creative writing, you know."

"Would you? Gosh. That is so nice! I mean, if I can find the courage to try . . ."

John added the tip, took his receipt, and stood, coming around to pull my chair away from the table.

I stood and he put his finger under my chin and said, "Ms. Cooper? I have not met someone like you in so long I cannot say. But I have this funny feeling that you're going places with your ideas on the Heywards and I want to go with you."

"Oh, John," I said. Someone had not just an interest in me but also a little faith.

This man was going to be mine, somehow, some way, I was going to make him mine. Actually, so far it didn't appear that he would put up much of a fight.

"It's dark," I said, when we went outside to the car.

"Dark enough to steal away into the night and throw caution to the wind?"

"How fast can you drive those clichés?"

We laughed then, completely comfortable with each other, knowing full well what we were about to do. To sleep with a man after knowing him for such a short period of time was not like me at all, because I never had, but I hadn't been single for decades. Besides, if television represented real life, this was what people did in 2010. They had spontaneous sex. To be honest, at that moment? I was going for it. I'd debate the sense of it later.

Along the road we'd steal a glance at each other and smile. We were excited. It was cold and most of the way home we could see our breath. But this time I had the key to the front door in my hand before we got there and we walked right in like we owned the place. There was only a small light coming from the kitchen, but it was enough to cast a faint glow across most of the first floor. He disappeared upstairs. After all, John knew the house better than I did. He had been coming here for years. Wait! What was he doing? Getting undressed?

"Hey, John? Would you like a glass of something?" I called out. "White wine? I've got a bottle here in the refrigerator."

Suddenly, I was getting very nervous. Maybe it wasn't the right thing to appear to be so cavalier about something so important. No matter what they did on HBO or in the movies, I didn't want to make a mistake and then be embarrassed if he never called me again. He'd show up with students and I'd have to hide in a closet. What if he had a sexually transmitted disease? Like herpes or something or that awful HPV virus or what if he had a weird one? I'd heard about that, you know, men with weird ones were all over the place.

"Not yet," he said. "Why don't you come up here? I want to show you something."

Oh, God, come *on*! What was he going to show me? *IT*? My mind was racing. Okay, I said, get a grip for God's sake. What's he going to do? Jump you? That's ridiculous! So I took a few breaths, got the bottle, two glasses, and the corkscrew. Then I inched my way toward the dark stairs, turning on the light switch.

"Turn off the light," he said.

"Why?" I said, hoping I didn't sound as frightened as I was becoming. What was he doing? I made my way up to the second floor, slowly. "Where are you?"

"I'm in the living room."

Good, praise God, I thought. He's not in a bedroom.

"Come see!"

There it was. The fullest and largest moon I had ever seen, hanging over the ocean, rising in orange and then turning gold. It was absolutely gorgeous.

"Oh!" It was simply amazing.

"Here, give me that," he said, taking the bottle and glasses from me. "I remembered the paper said it was a full moon tonight and boy, it sure is something, isn't it?"

While I stood there, dazed by the spectacular display seemingly just across the street, John popped the cork, poured two glasses, and handed me one.

"Yes," I said and took a sip. "It looks like it's coming to get us."

He pushed away my hair and kissed the back of my neck.

"It's okay, Cate. You're safe with me. I promise."

I turned around to face him and met his beautiful hazel eyes. His face was illuminated in the moonlight. I believed him and let him kiss me, which I already knew was going to be a pretty pyrotechnical experience. It was. I was still holding my glass, groping around for the edge of the bookcase so I could put it down. I thought I had it and I didn't. The glass shattered into a million little pieces and wine went everywhere.

"It's okay," I said, in between some unbelievable groping and struggling for breath. "They're really cheap."

"I'll buy you a dozen tomorrow," he said and ran his mouth down the side of my neck.

"You don't have to," I said and let him pull my sweater over my head.

"But I want to," he said while I unbuckled his belt and unzipped his trousers, with every intention of checking out the goods. Bad girl, I thought. Things appeared to be in working order.

"I know you do," I said and thought, screw it if he never calls me again.

And that was it. We hurried to the bedroom where I slept, kicking off shoes, pants, his shirt . . . we were shedding as we went, hands everywhere . . . I pulled back the covers as fast as I could and rushed around to the far side.

"Where are you going?" he said.

"I just thought . . . you know, that's your side and this is my side? What?"

"You come right back over here," he said, looking very serious and breathing pretty hard. "You can pick your side later."

"Right!" God, I was so awkward. But it didn't seem to matter except in that split moment.

I wondered if the neighbors could hear the bedsprings squealing and making a racket or us moaning, screaming the occasional *Oh! Yes! God!* I had a fleeting thought that the bed was going to collapse as it rose and fell in rhythm like the bass on a Barry White CD, the head-board banging the wall like twenty hammers. Would I have to repaint? I got my leg tangled in the sheets and he ripped them away and threw them all on the floor along with all the pillows. It was insane. All I can tell you is that about an hour later, when I was lying there in the crook of his arm, covered in sweat, glad to be alive, dying for a glass of water and smelling like something only Satan would recognize, I had an im-portant realization. When doing this dance, it was a far better decision to let John Risley take the lead. Whew.

CHAPTER NINETEEN

Setting: The Porgy House in the music room at the piano.

Director's Note: Photos of book jacket of *The Country Bunny and the Little Gold Shoes*, the "Summertime" lyrics, the MacDowell parlor, Marjorie Flack, Janie Scriven Heyward, Eugene O'Neill, and Pearl Buck on the backstage scrim. Voice of DuBose comes from off-stage.

Act II
Scene 5

Dorothy: I thought it might be important to tell you one last detail about my mother-in-law, Janie, because DuBose was an honest man and I know he would want the facts set straight. When our Jenifer was a little girl, Janie would make up stories for her, like grandmothers do all the time. But there was one in particular that Jenifer loved her to tell over and over again. It was called "The Country Bunny and the Little Gold Shoes." The last time we were at the MacDowell Colony, we were all gathered in the parlor, quite happy, listening to each other telling stories and applauding loudly after each impromptu performance. Then DuBose got it in his mind to tell a children's story. He had everyone in the palm of his hand as they heard about the struggle of the poor little rabbit to become an Easter Bunny and how wonderful it was when she did. Afterward a good friend of ours, the illustrator Marjorie Flack, came up to us and insisted that DuBose write it down. Well, he did and it only took him two hours to do it! Of course, Marjorie illustrated it and Houghton Mifflin published it and it's the only book by DuBose that never went out of print. It's also the most money he ever earned in two hours. Anyway, I just thought the old girl should get her due. *The Country Bunny and the Little Gold Shoes* was completely Janie's creation but DuBose was given the credit. She never complained one bit. She knew that anything she could do to further DuBose's reputation and his earning power was good for all of us. It was the one and only issue on which we always saw eye-to-eye.

And while we're on the subject of credit being given to the right people, we need to talk about some of the lyrics to the songs in *Porgy and Bess,* because it will help show just how crazy and unpredictable the whole creative process is.

It was another terrible night of fog and rain and the temperature never climbed above forty degrees. We were out on Folly in that same little house that we paid for with the proceeds from *Porgy* the play and some royalties from the book as well. It's still my favorite place I have ever lived. Anyway, we were having cocktails, martinis I think, and I sat down to the piano and began to play a little tune, just a few notes really.

And DuBose said, "Don't be blue, little Dorothy, soon it will be summertime and we'll be living calm and easy!"

"Humph," I said and sang along with my few little notes. "Summertime and the living is easy!"

"Play that again," DuBose said.

So, I did. I could just hear it in my head like someone was singing it to me. He got very excited.

"What is the matter with you, DuBose?"

"I *like* that, Dorothy! Summertime and the living is easy! I'm going to send it to George! Can you write down the tune?"

"Of course I can!"

"I think this could be the beginning lyrics for a great song for *Porgy and Bess!*" He refilled his drink and mine and took a pad and pencil from the desk. He was suddenly very animated. "Let's see! What happens in the summer? Corn grows way up high!"

"So does cotton," I said. "Well not so high as corn, I'll admit, but it gets as high as it's going to, doesn't it?"

"Yes! Yes, it does! And what else? We go fishing!"

"Yes, when you walk down by the gullies and docks you can see all the little fish jumping in the sun!"

"Well, I suspect the poor little fellows are jumping because they're trying to avoid being eaten by a bigger fish. But I'm writing this all down . . ."

And he wrote it all down and sent if off to George, who, along with his brother Ira turned it into one of my favorite songs in the whole play. And, lo! Guess what? They gave DuBose credit for cowriting the lyrics! Isn't that swell? Isn't that just the grandest thing? DuBose said oh, no no, he didn't want the credit but they insisted. They absolutely *insisted*. George may have been a bit of a scene-stealer but his brother Ira was one of the finest men I have ever met and both of them had a terrific sense of fairness.

I'll tell you this. DuBose could have been anything he wanted to— he was already a poet and a novelist of adult and children's books and now he was going to be known as a lyricist! I was so proud of him. Oh! And he was a screenwriter, too! He wrote a script for Eugene O'Neill's adaptation of *The Emperor Jones* for film, but he didn't really enjoy the work so much. Eugene was an old classmate of mine. I introduced them to each other and I always wondered if DuBose was jealous of him.

Even though that didn't end so well, DuBose tried screenwriting again for Pearl Buck's *The Good Earth* and that was kind of a disaster, too, because they had twenty other writers working on it. In the end his name didn't even appear in the credits, which he was glad of, because he didn't like the movie at all. Anyway, the point is that Hollywood never really valued its writers much, which if you think about it makes no sense whatsoever. You could have all the Clark Gables and Vivien Leighs in the world but if the words they spoke didn't enthrall you, what good was the movie? No, I don't care what any of those Hollywood fools say, you have to start with a good story and that story is nothing without good writers.

Fade to Darkness

CHAPTER TWENTY

The Piano

The movers pulled into the yard at around three in the afternoon and began to slowly unload the truck. They were supposed to have been there at noon, but I imagined they stopped for a nice long lunch somewhere and then had a nice long nap by the side of the road and then stopped for ice cream, so three was about right. I just loved waiting around for people to show up. But actually, on that afternoon, I was preparing dinner for John and I wasn't going to let anything ruin my good mood. What was I cooking? Roasted chicken, mashed potatoes with gravy, salad, biscuits, and Ella was making us a pie. It was a foolproof menu and there wasn't a man alive who didn't love biscuits and gravy.

And, at last, the blessed movers had arrived. I stepped outside into the brisk afternoon air to watch them.

I couldn't help but to stop and reflect on my piano's long and checkered history. It was the only thing of any consequence I still had that my mother gave to me. It probably wasn't worth much but, you know how it is, it had great sentimental value. When I was just a little girl, I had pounded away on the keys in the house where I grew up, eventually learning to play simple pieces under the earnest tutelage of some poor bespectacled old man whose jacket smelled like mothballs and breath like peppermint. It's funny what you remember and what you forget. Then it moved with me to Aunt Daisy's where I continued my lessons but I took up dance with a vengeance. In its next incarnation, my piano became Addison's jumping-off point in Alpine, New Jersey. Now my piano was back where it started on Folly. Full circle. I was dragging that thing around with me like Marley's chains, except that Marley wasn't so fond of his chains as I was of my piano. I loved it.

My childhood home, just an old clapboard house up on stilts, was washed away by a hurricane years ago. But I remember clearly how the piano came into our family. My mother bought it used from Siegling's Music House for my birthday the last year she was alive. I'm told that she always thought I had some musical aptitude and that she thought every house should have a piano, because it added dignity to the home.

Aunt Daisy has pictures of it positioned in the living room of that house but when I look at them I can hardly remember being there, sitting on that bench, practicing scales. I was so little when my momma died and then Daddy, it's hard to remember much of anything about how life was and there were so few artifacts remaining to jiggle my memories.

Even the land where the house once stood was completely eroded away, which had happened to lots of property on Folly Beach in its history. Beach erosion, which travels from north to south, was great for Seabrook and Kiawah Islands, because they picked up acres upon acres of accreted land traveling with the tides from Folly Beach. But it was devastating for our residents, because the jetties around Folly Beach blocked incoming sand from Sullivans Island. So, as a result, from time to time, second-row houses became prime real estate when the neighboring cottages across the street literally fell apart and into the sea. In any case, the hurricanes and erosion surely served as a Buddhist reminder about the impermanence of all material things.

But the sea-salted population of Folly Beach was nothing if not stoic. They simply shrugged their shoulders, told their stories, laughing and happy at their great fortune to be alive, and then they rebuilt on other land bought with the settlements from their insurance companies. "It's why we pay our premiums," became an often-used explanation for why no one worried too much about the weather. Hurricanes were usually simply an irksome fact of life and, to be honest, some of the construction on Folly Beach was, well, long past its prime anyway. In almost every single case, the new homes were sturdier and certainly much prettier than the old homes.

One of the deliverymen came up to me to scope out the destination.

"Where do you want us to put this, ma'am?"

"In the first room, under the window on the far left wall," I said. "You're welcome to have a look."

"Thanks," he said and stepped inside the door. He came back out, nodded to me, and called out, "Okay guys, let's get this baby inside."

Speaking of island construction, the Porgy House was as ancient a beach cottage as there was left on the whole island and I would bet you a dollar that you couldn't find a right angle in the whole place. The way the house had settled in the sandy yard, probably sinking by a hair each year over many decades, had left the floors sloped and everything just a bit off-kilter. These varying depreciations of symmetry gave the house a distinguished character all its own. In the short time I'd been there I had come to feel some real affection for all the crooked windows and the musical creaks in the floorboards. After all, I was walking the floors where Dorothy and DuBose drank cocktails with George Gershwin and wrote the quintessential theatrical work that burst forth from the Lowcountry of South Carolina like a rocket to Mars. If that couldn't inspire me to at least try and pen my own play, what would?

I watched as the men groaned under the weight of the piano, pulling it up the steps on a heavy plywood ramp they carried for just these kinds of occasions and then as they lowered it onto a heavy quilted mat they used to slide it across the floor and put it in position. You could keep that job. My back hurt just watching them.

They unbuckled and pulled the canvas belts from around the piano and lifted the quilted blankets away, folding them as they went. She sure was *yar*. (I've always wanted to use that word ever since I heard Katharine Hepburn say it referring to a boat in *The Philadelphia Story*. It's probably a nautical term.) Anyway, I was thrilled with the glossy patina of the cabinet and the fact that they had not retouched the CUNNINGHAM PIANO CO. gold-leaf signature that was slightly faded from the years. Cunningham Piano Company, coincidentally also from Philadelphia, has been building pianos for symphonies, academies, and concert pianists since the 1890s and they were treasured by those who played them. Considering my rudimentary skill level, I was humbled to own one.

Every ivory and ebony key was immaculate and, miraculously, the bench still held all my old sheet music under the seat, which in the haste and tumult of that horrible day Tina had forgotten to remove. I couldn't wait to sit down and play, even though the sound of my playing would surely send all the neighborhood cats screaming up the trees.

"Can you sign here?"

"Sure! Wait just a minute." I ran upstairs and got my wallet to give them a tip. Fortunately, I had just made a withdrawal from the ATM, so I could give them a twenty. Now, I know, twenty dollars sounds like a lot of money for a widow of greatly reduced circumstances to be throwing around but it was to be divided among three men and when was the last time I tried to pick up a piano?

"Here we go." I signed the receipt and handed the man with the clipboard the money.

"Thanks a lot, miss," he said and went to join the others, already waiting in the truck.

I closed the door behind him and looked at my beautiful Cunningham, standing there all shiny and new-looking and wondered if I should give the room a fresh coat of paint. This is what happens when you start redecorating—you bring in new throw pillows and then you want to throw the old sofa out the back door. Ah well, I told myself, maybe it was because the piano was new to the room, still a stranger, and I should give my eyes a few days to get used to it and then decide. But one thing was certain, I wasn't going to let the memory of Addison Cooper's death spiral of insanity sully the regard I felt for my most important heirloom. The piano was washed clean of any sign of him and maybe in time I, too, would remember only the good things from the good years. One could hope.

I decided to call Patti and let her know that it had arrived in mint shape.

She picked up on the first ring.

"So, missy?" Patti said in a sassy, merry voice. "Just how long am I supposed to wait to hear from you? Do I need to go find a new best friend now that you're gone?"

"Don't you dare," I said. "I'd die."

"*I don't knooooow . . .*" she said in a singsong warning.

"Oh, please," I said. "We can't replace each other anyway. Who're we kidding?"

"I guess you're right. So what's going on?"

"Well, first of all . . ." I told her about the piano's arrival in such perfect condition and thanked her profusely.

"Don't thank me. Thank old Ebenezer! I still can't believe he prepaid the shipping. But, he did take that wine."

"And maybe because he took Addison's golf clubs and maybe he found out they're worth like half a zillion? He must have thought he owed me something."

"Yeah, probably. I married the last man on the planet with a conscience. But you know, not a day goes by that he doesn't ask me about you and if I've heard from you and how you're doing."

"He's really a precious guy, Patti. You're very lucky."

"Yeah, I know. So he's a little tight with his money? You never get it all with one man."

"Well, he has it all with you! Ha! So, when are you coming to see me?"

"How's next weekend?"

"For real?"

I got very excited then. For the month since I had arrived here my new existence had everything in it except Patti.

"Yeah, I want to see how our sweet little Alice is doing . . ."

"You're terrible," I said.

"And the professor . . ."

"Listen, he's unbelievable." I told her all about John and his plans for my future as a playwright but I didn't tell her about, you know, about us *moving the earth.*

Then she asked.

"So? Did you throw him down yet?"

"WHAT? What kind of a crazy question is that? I'm . . . speechless!"

"So, you did, huh? Wow. Tell me, what's it like to make love to somebody new? I've been with Mark for so long I can make out a grocery list in my head and still not miss a thing. So how is it?"

There was no point in withholding anything from Patti. She knew anyway.

"Fucking fabulous, and the word order doesn't matter."

"OMG! Listen to you, you old perimenopausal slut! I'm telling!"

"Yeah? Go ahead. Tell the world! Listen, at my age? I'm going to do exactly what I want to do. Yeah, I finally am. But I wouldn't bring it up to the kids quite yet."

"Of course not!" There was silence for a second or two and then she said, "Well, it's about time you took your life back."

Is that what she thought? The more I thought about it I realized she wasn't wrong.

"Well, if you meet him you'll see why I'm so, so . . ."

I could hear her gasp.

"Jesus, Cate! Are you in *love* with this man?"

"I don't know. Maybe. I mean, I could be at some point. Not now, of course . . ."

"Too soon . . ."

"Of course! It's too soon. But you'll see. He's . . . well, he's not like anyone else I ever dated. That's for sure. But Patti, I have to tell you, he's not divorced. I mean he's not really married, but he's not divorced." I then proceeded to tell Patti about Lisa.

"I'm changing my ticket. I'm coming Thursday. Maybe Wednesday. This is worse than I thought."

"Actually, you're going to find out it's better than you thought possible. You can bring Mark, too!"

"Are you losing your little cat-eyed marbles? You think I want to spend the whole time I'm with *you* worrying about if *he's* entertained? No way."

We laughed again and I said, "Look, get yourself down here as soon as you can. We'll talk about all of this over some good but moderately priced vino."

"We should've switched the cellar. Mark was right."

She promised to call me with her final reservation information. I would pick her up at the airport. She could stay in the bedroom across the hall and it would be like old times. We'd be girls again. For a few days, we'd be girls.

It was time to put the chicken in the oven. It was already four thirty and he was supposed to arrive at six. I wanted the place to smell like roasting garlic and onions when he walked in the door. I wished there was a separate dining room, but alas, there was none. So for that evening we would eat in the kitchen. The table was set and I had to say, while it wasn't something that would have thrilled Addison Cooper, I knew John Risley would appreciate every effort made on his behalf.

Earlier in the day, while I was shopping at the Piggly Wiggly for dinner, I bought a two-slice toaster, a drip coffee machine, a couple of inexpensive pots, and a cast-iron skillet. I also picked up some red and white dish towels, two red pot holders, and four red place mats. In a final nod to extravagance and in the name of beauty, I parted with ten additional dollars for a bunch of red tulips, hoping there was a vase in the house. I had checked out the flatware, dishes, and glasses and thought, well, they were good enough for a college student and they would have to be good enough for tonight. Spending money made me nervous and even though I was giving Aunt Daisy dozens of hours of help with her business we had yet to discuss a salary or any kind of compensation. After all, I was living in the Porgy House rent-free. But at some point I'd have to do it or get another job. I had to consider things like health insurance for Sara and me. It was foolhardy to be without it and I knew Addison's policies had a time limit. I'd have to ask Mark to look at all of that for us, because reading insurance policies and trying to make sense of them made my teeth hurt. I think that's a pretty normal reaction for most people.

I was just putting the plump, herb-stuffed bird in the oven and closing the door when I heard a voice.

"Anybody home?"

It was Ella.

"Hey! Come on in! I'm in the kitchen!"

"I've got your pie."

"Pecan?"

"Lord, no! I can't even *look* at a pecan for right now. Too many pecan pies, even for me." She delivered it in a sweetgrass basket lined with a red-and-blue plaid kitchen towel. It looked like something out of *Southern Living* magazine. "No, I made an apple pie this time. Is that okay?"

The minute she folded back the towel, the smell of apples and cinnamon filled the air and my mouth started to water. The way my salivary glands reacted to Ella's baking? You'd think I'd spent the last twenty years in the woods, wandering aimlessly, starving and foraging, living on a few berries and roots. Actually, that wasn't too far off—the aimless wandering part, anyway.

I clasped my hands together and gave the glossy golden crust a good once-over.

"Oh, Ella, it's gorgeous. How can I thank you?"

"Humph. You can get your Aunt Daisy to a doctor instead of those Marsh Tacky Races down in Hilton Head. I don't like the way she's looking for the last week and I can't get her to go see her doctor."

I began to panic inside at the mere thought of anything being seriously wrong with Aunt Daisy.

"What are you saying? What kind of symptoms does she have?"

"Well, it started the night you, Russ, and Alice came over, after y'all left. First, she seemed sweaty, you know like flu. But it ain't flu. Then she starts getting all kind of cranky."

"More than usual?"

"A lot more. And I think she's running a fever. I see her taking aspirin and ask her why and she tells me to mind my own business, which isn't unusual for *her*. But something's wrong. I think her pressure is up. And her breathing ain't quite right."

"She's congested? Maybe she has bronchitis?"

"I don't know. Anyhow, she's determined she's going to get me to drive her to Hilton Head to watch these fool horses run on the beach and I just don't think she needs to go this year."

Aunt Daisy loved the Marsh Tacky horses and I knew why. They were like us—a little bit abandoned but adaptable in tough situations. Once, when we were sitting around talking, she told me that if a Marsh Tacky got caught in the pluff mud and started to sink, he didn't panic like a regular horse. He just lay down on his side and pulled his hooves out. Then he got up and went on his way. They were tough little fighters like Aunt Daisy and me, too, if I could remember how to fight.

"I'll talk to her. She probably *does* have the flu. In fact, I'll make her go with me in the morning. Who's her primary doctor? She's not still seeing Harper?"

"Yeah, God. She's the only woman her age I know that uses a pediatric allergy doctor but all these years after y'all all grown? You can't get her to change and he doesn't seem to care. Maybe 'cause she give him and his family a house last summer for two weeks. I don't know. Maybe he's her long-lost son. Here's his number."

Ella reached in the pocket of her cardigan and handed me the folded paper that revealed his office address and phone number in addition to his cell phone number.

"You're really worried, aren't you?" I said.

"I don't know, but I don't like what I see and I ain't no doctor to decide what's best."

"I'll call him tonight."

"Thanks, honey. That makes me feel much better. What time is Mr. Risley supposed to show up? Your table looks very nice, by the way."

"Well, thanks. Amazing what you can buy at the grocery store these days. He'll be here in an hour."

"Well, I'd better skedaddle and let you young people have your night."

She turned to go but I could see that she was filled with anxiety.

"Ella?"

"Uh-huh?"

"I don't want you to worry tonight, about Aunt Daisy, I mean. Let me worry for you."

"You're a sweet girl, Cate. That's a nice thing to say."

She went out the door and I followed her to the front stoop.

"Call me if you need anything, okay?"

"I will."

"And thanks again for the pie!"

She waved at me as she pulled away, leaving me to stew over the frailty of her position in the world. She had come here with Dr. Harper's number, prepared to ask me to step in and get involved with Aunt Daisy's health care. Life partners. That's what they were but saying they had a life partner didn't mean they didn't need anybody else. Had Aunt Daisy provided for her? I mean, was there an insurance policy naming her as the beneficiary? A will? Would she be able to stay in the house? Would it belong to her? How many houses did Aunt Daisy own at this point? If something happened to Aunt Daisy, which I could not fathom, would others step forward to put a claim on Aunt Daisy's assets? Like the IRS? Would her estate be obliged to pay exorbitant estate taxes because she had not put her affairs in order? Who was her executor? And, most important, how in the world did you approach a subject like that with someone who might be very ill but was as belligerent as Ella described? You did it tomorrow, honey. You approached these kinds of things delicately and with all the sensitivity you could muster. Tomorrow.

Meanwhile, I had a chicken in the oven and I was in need of a fast bath. My first thought was that if I ever had any money again, I was getting a place with a shower. Baths made a mess no matter how careful you were.

I dressed myself, after a careful but generous application of whatever body moisturizer they were selling in the bomb shelter–size for the least amount of money and targeted spritzes of the last of my Chanel No. 5. It wasn't going to waste. I wondered if there was a generic version of it out there in the world I could find for less. Not that I was *so* worried about my resources yet, but it couldn't hurt to be vigilant about these things.

Risley wasn't due for another twenty minutes so I decided to use the time to call Dr. Harper. I pressed his number into my keypad and, to my surprise, he picked up.

"This is Tom Harper," he said.

"Dr. Harper? You probably won't remember me but I'm . . ."

"Cathy Mahon? Caller ID, you know. The nice girl who ran off and married that old geezer? Addison, right?"

"Yeah, well, that old geezer bit the proverbial dust and I'm back in town."

"Oh! I'm terribly sorry! I didn't know . . . please accept my apol . . ."

"No, no, it's okay. Really." I stopped for a second and remembered I was a widow, not someone on a travel spree, dropping in on relatives for the fun of it. "Anyway, I'm calling you about my aunt Daisy."

I told him what Ella said and he was quiet.

"Could be anything. Why don't you bring her around in the morning and let me look at her. I'll do some blood work and we'll see what we've got going on."

I heard John's car door close. He had arrived. I opened the front door for him and before he reached the house, I thanked Dr. Harper and hung up, promising to be there by nine. I felt so much better.

"Hey!" he said, and handed me a bottle of wine. "What's happening? Boy! Something smells good. Is it chicken?"

"Yeah, but what about *this* chicken?"

"I've been thinking about *this* chicken all day," he said leaning down to give me a kiss. "Where's the corkscrew?"

"Did you say *screw*?" I opened the drawer, took it out, and handed it to him.

"Bad girl!" He shook his head, grinning. "You're driving me a little mad, you know. I mean, there I am sitting at my desk, grading papers on the importance of the Agrarian Poets, and suddenly a memory of us, you know, us . . ."

"No, I know what you mean." I pointed to the corkscrew and he slapped my hand. "You don't have to say the word."

"You are so bad tonight! What got into you?"

I just stared at him as if to say, whaddya think?

"Yeah, it's way too cavalier to just call it . . . anyway, you know, here comes this memory and I lose total concentration, I start reliving *the moment* and I'm worthless for the rest of the afternoon. It's like I'm possessed or something."

"Well, Risley? I hope you never call the exorcist. And, by the way, I am experiencing the same phenomenon. All I did today was think about the curve in your lower back. Aren't we a little old to be carrying on like this? I mean, what if we die in the middle of, you know . . ." I gave the corkscrew the hook of my thumb.

"I'm hiding this thing from you," he said, smiling. "Cate, if we die in the middle of carrying on I will be one happy dead man. But I don't think we're at risk quite yet."

"You know, I had all this fear and trepidation about us sleeping together so soon into our relationship and now I wonder what the heck was I so worried about? We're old enough to do what we want, aren't we?"

"Yep." He handed me a goblet. "And, we're also old enough to *know* what we want, too."

"So, we're not really a couple of impetuous idiots?"

"So what if we are? Who's going to judge us?"

I gave him a kiss on his cheek, we touched the rims of our glasses, and we took a sip.

"What are we drinking to?" he said.

In the few short weeks we had been seeing each other we had drunk to everything under the sun, including my car, which was finally fixed and parked outside. But more important, our attraction and affection for each other had grown into a full-blown romance.

"Let's drink to us," I said and raised my glass.

"To us! And to the night!"

"To the night!" I said and remembered my piano. "Oh! Let's drink to Cunningham."

"Okay. Here's to Cunningham! Who's Cunningham?"

I giggled and said, "Come! I'll show you!"

I took him by the hand back out to the front room where the *Porgy and Bess* display was.

He looked at the piano, dropped his jaw, and looked at me.

"Where did you get this piano?" he said in a somber voice.

"My mother gave it to me when I was a little girl. Why? What's the matter?"

"Do you realize this is the exact same piano that the Heywards and Gershwin used to write the music to *Porgy and Bess*?"

"No way!"

"Yes! The real one's on display at the Charleston Museum. I'll take you there myself and show it to you."

"Oh, come on, John. You're pulling my leg." He could not have been more serious. "You're not pulling my leg. This is a true story?"

"Yes, ma'am. True story. Same make. Same model. Probably the same year."

"Holy moly. My mother bought it for me from Siegling's Music House. It was used. I just had it cleaned and refinished. It was delivered this afternoon."

"Siegling's? You've got to be joking, right?"

"Why would I joke about something like that? I joke about a lot of things, you know, like my weight, my age . . . not pianos. No, can't say I ever made a piano joke."

"Right." John walked over to the piano and ran his hand across the top. "She's a beauty."

"It wasn't so pretty when I found Addison swinging over it."

"I can't even imagine how awful that must have been for you. I don't care if he was Genghis Khan."

"He practically was."

"What a moron. Cate?"

"Yeah?"

"This is a pretty eerie coincidence, don't you think?"

"Well, I didn't think anything until you said it was the same piano . . ." The hair on the back of my neck stood on end and I had a sudden chill. "Eerie, I don't know, but it's strange. That's for sure. When was Gershwin here?"

"The summer of 1934. He was here for seven weeks."

"Wow. In which house?"

"Well, the house he rented was blown away by Hurricane Hugo but he was in this very house on many nights."

"You know, I found all these cocktail recipes in Dorothy Heyward's papers at the Historical Society."

"Really? Gosh, if this room is where they had their piano and they probably *did* have it in here . . ."

"Yeah, because it would take daggum Harry Houdini to get it up *those* stairs."

"That's for sure. But I'll bet you they sat around this same room and drank whatever they drank. What *did* they drink?" John was getting very keyed up.

"Martinis. And a lot of weird punches they made with champagne and liquor."

"Well, maybe we should make martinis and drink them in their honor."

"Why not? Maybe a little one. Tomorrow I'll get us a bottle of gin or vodka and some vermouth and some olives, I guess?"

"I'll bring my shaker. Cate, this is really unbelievable. If I was a religious man, I'd take this as a sign from God."

"What? What sign?"

"Cate? I want you to listen to me, very carefully, okay?"

"Maybe I'd better get a little more wine for this?"

"Why not? I'll get it."

"I'm coming, too."

We went back to the kitchen where the potatoes were boiling away. I checked the chicken and it was golden brown. I was no Julia Child but if a woman couldn't roast a decent chicken she may as well turn her kitchen into a walk-in closet.

John poured me a little more wine and handed it to me.

"So, what are you telling me, Professor Risley?"

"I'm saying that all of this . . . this business of you and me and the Charleston Renaissance and this house and now the piano . . . doesn't it seem like we're pawns on somebody else's chessboard?"

"I like what's happening. I don't care if we're getting manipulated by some unseen force, do you?"

"Listen, there was this guy, one of the Fugitive poets, named Allen Tate, who also had an affair with a *nun* by the way . . ."

"A nun?"

"Yeah, a nun. He was a pretty wild guy for his day. He divorced his first wife, who he married twice . . ."

"He married the same woman twice?"

"Yep. And divorced her twice. Then he converted to Catholicism, married the nun, fathered a child when he was seventy years old, and oh, he was also married to the poet Isabella Gardner."

"Holy hell, Risley! Every time you tell me about these characters, they sure sound much more interesting than anybody *we* know, don't they?"

"Well, if you're into this stuff like I am, the answer is yes. Anyway, Tate was of the opinion that detachment, alienation, and living through tumultuous change are what distinguished a Southern writer from writers from say, the northwest. If that's not *your* situation, I don't know what is. If you don't get busy and write that play the unseen hand might decide we're not worth the effort of throwing all these signs our way."

"Well, I have been giving it some serious thought. And I've read all the books you gave me. There are about a thousand Post-it stickies on the pages."

"And?"

"And I devoured them. Speaking of devouring, do you want to eat? The chicken is ready."

"Which one?"

"Your choice," I said and laughed. "You sure are full of beans to-night."

I drained the potatoes and mashed in a whole stick of butter and some half-and-half with the back of a wooden spoon. The chicken was resting quietly on the cutting board, waiting patiently to be dismembered.

"So, tell me about your serious playwriting thoughts," he said, yanking a chicken leg away from the carcass with his fingers and taking a bite. "Wooo! This is delicious! But it's hot!"

"Thanks!" I handed him his glass of wine to put out his fire. "Oh, shoot. I forgot to make a vegetable!"

"Who cares? I'll just eat more chicken. Dang. This is so good! My momma used to make chicken like this."

"I'll bet she was a great lady," I said.

"She was that," he said.

Soon we were at the table, eating and talking like we'd known each other for a thousand years. We started to talk about my thoughts on the play. I told him I was thinking of an almost one-woman show, where we may or may not bring in someone to play DuBose in a few scenes and their daughter Jenifer in a few others. But mostly it would be Dorothy's story. In Act I, she starts out as an older woman, talking to the audience and remembering her life, telling stories about her great love for DuBose. Then she would also tell stories about his family and friends, his insufferable but completely forgivable mother, but the big fish would be Gershwin and how they worked together writing *Porgy and Bess*. In the end, the audience will understand that the real reason she gave her life and the credit for all her work to DuBose was that she loved him that much. It had nothing to do with the times or her gender or the fact that she was from Ohio. It was love. Period.

"I really think this is a beautiful piece of genius, Cate. You need to write this down, just as you told it to me. So, you know, if you take this idea, write it in the right format, polish it to death, and we manage to get it up on a stage during Piccolo Spoleto, I'm just thinking here, would this be something your daughter Sara might like to do? Play Dorothy, I mean."

"Wouldn't that be brazen nepotism?"

"Well, yeah it is. So what? If you're the director and I'm the producer, we can cast Adam's house cat if we want."

"Do you want pie? I'd have to ask Sara, but she'd probably go crazy to do it."

"Pie? Absolutely. But the next dinner is at my house. I have a dishwasher."

"And a shower. It's a deal. Hey, did I mention to you that my sister is coming for a visit next week?"

"No, but that's great! Can I take you ladies out on the town?"

"I don't see why not. Thanks! And did I tell you that Aunt Daisy isn't up to snuff?"

"What's wrong?"

"Ella doesn't know. She just told me this afternoon and she's pretty concerned about her. I'm taking her to the doctor first thing in the morning."

"Think we should check on her tonight? I mean, they're not exactly in their twenties anymore."

I weighed the choice of hopping in the sack with John before or maybe right after the dishes were done, or going over to Aunt Daisy's to see if she was really all right, for about two seconds and knew what we had to do. It wasn't even eight o'clock yet. Decent people didn't screw this early at night. It was gauche. And it was barely dark.

"You know what? We can take the rest of this pie over there, saying it was so good we just wanted to make sure they got a slice and then we can see what's up. What do you think?"

"Great idea. Let's go now."

I quickly wrapped the pie plate in aluminum foil, put it back in Ella's basket, and grabbed my cell phone and my purse. We were out of the door and over at Aunt Daisy's in a matter of minutes. I let us in the front door using my key.

"Anybody home?" I called out, expecting to find them somewhere watching one of their many televisions.

There was no answer so I called out again, but louder.

"*Ella? Aunt Daisy? Y'all here? It's Cate and John! We brought the pie over to share!*"

"This can't be good," John said.

I put the pie down on the kitchen counter and said, "I'm going upstairs."

"I'm coming with you," he said.

We hurried up the steps, calling out for Ella and Aunt Daisy to no response. Finally, I tiptoed into Aunt Daisy's bedroom and I could see from the doorway to her bathroom door, which was slightly ajar. There were her hat racks, filled with every style and color hat you could imagine.

"Come on now," I heard Ella saying. "Let's just sit still."

I went to the door and without looking inside I said, "Ella? It's me, Cate. Y'all okay?"

"I'm just trying to give Daisy a sponge bath to cool her down."

"Who? Who's there?" Aunt Daisy said.

Let me tell you, her voice did not sound right. Not one bit. I felt my chest tighten with panic. She wasn't gasping for breath but she sounded congested and out of it.

"Can I help you in any way?" I said.

"Maybe you can help me get her out of the tub. I got her in here but I can't . . ."

"No!" Aunt Daisy said. "I'm naked!"

I was going in and I didn't care if the whole world was naked.

"Please!" I said and swooped right into the bathroom. "Where's her robe?"

"In the wash," Ella said. "There's a big towel on that rack."

"Get out of here!" Aunt Daisy said.

She yelled so loudly that John came to the door immediately.

"What's going on in there?" he said.

"We're trying to get Aunt Daisy out of the tub and she's fighting us," I said.

The next thing I knew John was in the bathroom, pushing us aside and lifting Aunt Daisy out of the tub in one swift move. I put the towel over her for the sake of her modesty and she started to cry.

"I don't feel good," she said.

The sound of my sweet Aunt Daisy crying like a baby broke my heart. It made me want to cry with her.

"Something's terribly wrong," Ella said.

John laid Aunt Daisy on her bed, pulled her comforter over her, and felt her pulse. Then he felt her head.

"I'm calling 911," he said.

"*NO!*" Aunt Daisy said.

I had never seen her so agitated. Maybe she was afraid of the hospital?

"Ella? Let's you and I pack her a little overnight bag. Do you know where her medicines are? And her health insurance cards?"

"Yes, yes!" Ella said and began rushing around, getting what she needed.

"It's going to be all right, Aunt Daisy. I promise it's going to be all right."

"*NO! NO! NO!*"

She screamed *NO!* over and over again for the next five minutes or so until finally her yelling became a whispered but still desperate protest and then at last, she rested, falling asleep. Even in her resting state, I saw that she was drooling and her hands were shaking and I was afraid for her. Ella was nearly panic-stricken. I put my arm around her shoulder and tried to console her.

"She's going to be fine," I said.

"Dear Jesus, please save her! Please Lord! Don't take my Daisy away from me now!" she said, and began to weep. "Oh, Lord, Cate. What's happening here?"

I felt absolutely terrible for both of them and I was just as frightened as anyone else in the room.

"Come on, Ella. Don't worry yourself so. We're going to get her to the hospital and they will give her what she needs."

"I'll be right back," John said.

John ran downstairs to turn on the porch lights and to unlock the doors. We could hear the sirens approaching and, in minutes, Aunt Daisy was on a gurney and on her way to the capable hands of the Medical University of South Carolina in Charleston.

"You ride with us," John said to Ella and she nodded her head, grabbed Aunt Daisy's little overnight bag, and hurried out to the car with us.

It seemed like an eternity passed in the blink of an eye. We raced down Folly Road behind the screaming sirens and flashing lights, and yet another eternity passed until we reached the emergency room entrance, but we got there at last and stayed with her in a curtained-off area until a doctor came to examine her, minutes later. She was still asleep. John went to the desk with her health cards to fill out the forms and tell them what they needed to know.

At last a doctor pulled back the curtain and looked at Aunt Daisy and then to us. I was busy thanking God he wasn't just some medical student. He was a real adult. He asked us who we were.

Ella said, "I'm her best friend, Ella Johnson."

"She's way more than that," I said, completely unsolicited, and added, "and I'm her niece, Cate Cooper. My aunt is Daisy McInerny."

"I'm Doctor Ragone," he said and nodded to us.

I didn't know if the doctor understood what I meant but I wasn't going to let them shuttle Ella out of there just because they weren't related by blood or marriage. The doctor did not care one iota about any of that or that the woman in that bed was one of the most important people in my life. I started getting upset and bit my lip to hold back the tears I could feel getting ready to rise up and fall. John stepped back inside the curtain and put his arm around my shoulder, giving me a solidarity squeeze.

"Shhh!" he said to me. "It's all right. We got her here and she's going to be fine."

"She *has* to be fine. I can't stand it if she's not."

"Shhh," he said again.

I sighed so hard then. It had been a rough month for me, but this wasn't about me. It was my momma in that bed, not my birth mother, but the momma that had loved me all my life. I wanted her well and out of that bed as fast as possible.

Dr. Ragone began to examine her by taking her pulse.

"Ms. McInerny, can you hear me?"

"She's been really out of it," Ella said.

Inside of fifteen seconds, he slapped a pressure cuff around her arm and began pumping it up. Then he made a note on her chart, put his stethoscope in his ears, and listened to her heart. He made another note and looked up at us.

"Do either of you know what kind of medicines she takes?"

"Everything's in this bag," Ella said and handed the doctor a Ziploc filled with vials.

"What other kind of symptoms is she showing?"

Ella described all of Aunt Daisy's behaviors and her fever and spasms and everything she could think of to the doctor and he listened carefully, taking more notes.

"Do you know where she got that nasty gash on her arm? It's infected."

"I do and I told her that thing looked bad but she don't listen to nobody!"

"How did it happen?" Dr. Ragone asked again.

"Oh! She caught her arm on a splintered board under the house where she had no business being in the first place. It was raining and she wanted some paper towels from the storage room. I said *I'd* go for 'em 'cause her foot's in a cast . . . *oh, Jesus! We forgot to bring her cast!*"

"Don't worry," the doctor said, "we've got a few of those around here. But she won't need it tonight. I'm going to admit her to intensive care and run some tests."

"Intensive care! Oh Lord!" Ella said.

"Don't worry. I'm putting her there because she'll get the best care there. Her blood pressure is dangerously high and her breathing is very labored. She's definitely got some kind of an infection. I'm going to give her a breathing tube to help her get the oxygen she needs until we can get her fever down. You folks can go on home if you want or you can wait until we get her in a room."

"I'm staying," I said.

"I ain't moving from her side," Ella said.

"I'll go get us some coffee," John said. "If you leave here just send me a text where to find you, okay?"

"Sure," I said and took a deep breath, starting to relax somewhat.

It was going to be a very long night.

CHAPTER TWENTY-ONE

Setting: The top of a sand dune near the front door of the Porgy House.
Director's Note: Photos of the sunset on Folly, sand dunes, Romeo's Streetcar, George Gershwin, an alligator, Gertrude Stein, Edna St. Vincent Millay, and Amy Lowell on the backstage scrim. Voice of DuBose comes from off-stage.

Act III
Scene I

Dorothy: I remember one night, when the waiting for Gershwin was coming to a head, and after a quick dinner of leftover baked chicken and potatoes that was boring enough to peel the paint from the walls, DuBose and I were enjoying another spectacular winter sunset from the top of a sand dune no more than twenty yards from our front door. I surely did love the late of day after supper when it seemed like the world quieted down. I considered it my great reward for being industrious in the kitchen and tenacious in my dealings with Gershwin.

We were reluctant to venture too far from the house, because I had just tucked in Jenifer for the night and she wasn't always perfectly compliant with her bedtime. If she thought she had been left home alone she would be hysterical for weeks. That said, I calculated the odds and decided that the advent of the purple and red streaks that slashed the horizon . . . ? Well, were they worth risking the wrath of our high-spirited child with her tall tales? Neither DuBose nor I ever imagined the energy it would take to be parents. I was beginning to think she was too vague and forgetful for her own good and had no idea how to deal with that. I usually did a lot of sighing when the day was done.

"Look at this sky! I've never seen such colors!" I said.

DuBose laughed a little, charmed I hoped, that I was always so taken by the majesty of the sunsets. He took them all for granted I suppose, but now that he was seeing the Lowcountry anew through my eyes I thought well, maybe this part of the world seemed like a slightly different place.

"Mr. Heyward! Are you laughing at me?"

"Absolutely not! I am thinking that being here and in this moment, I am a very rich man." He smiled and dropped his chin in a manner that suggested knowing all the intimate details about me and stared at me lovingly with his enormous brown eyes.

"Oh, DuBose, you could coax the birds from the trees. You really could. Say, have you heard from George lately?"

"Yes, my little Dorothy. In fact, I got a letter from him today. How did you know?"

"I could feel the literal heaviness of its arrival in the air," I said and rolled my eyes toward the sky. "The importance of it, the vibration of his words on paper . . ."

"Oh, come on now . . ."

"Oh, all right. I saw the envelope under the egg carton from Romeo's. But before we get to King George, how is old Romeo? What did he have to say for himself? What's he up to?"

"Still living in his streetcar and still selling eggs. I was on my way to see Mrs. Rabon to collect the mail when I heard him calling out his song. *Romeo's got fresh eggs!* I thought, now, who could resist that?" He took my hand in his and kissed the back of it.

"Oh, DuBose. Hmmm. You're right. You know, Folly has such wonderful characters, doesn't it? So much color! Maybe we should write a play about it."

"Let's."

He took my other hand and kissed the back of that one, too. I thought well, someone has ooh la la on his mind!

"What's gotten into you tonight?"

"Moonlight." He raised his eyebrows and wiggled them like the evil landlord. "I am bewitched by you again!"

"It's not even dark yet, DuBose. And so, darling, there is no moonlight."

"A minor and very unimportant detail."

"Hmmm. Yes." Sometimes my husband was a romantic rascal. "Maybe I'll make egg salad for tomorrow's lunch. Jenifer loves egg salad."

"So do I. Even though it's probably good for my health."

"Oh, not after I'm finished with it." Somehow I could rarely get the right amount of mayonnaise in it.

Soon, the sun slipped away and the sky was still streaked with scarlet, mango, and another shade of red that was the color of a glass of old port wine. I leaned into DuBose and put my arm around his waist. "Glory, I could stay here all night but let's start back. This is so beautiful but I want to be able to hear Jen."

"All right," he said. We turned and began to climb down the dune. "You know, I love the beach here but we're going to have to be very careful about Jenifer playing in the ocean this summer."

"Well, of course we will but why in the world are you bringing this up now? It's the dead of February."

"Well, when I was over in Mazo's buying bread, I heard these two fellows talking about sharks."

"Sharks!" I stopped dead in my tracks.

"Yes. Sharks. Those dastardly things with the big teeth and insatiable appetites? I never knew about them, either, but it seems we've got a smattering of about ten different varieties swimming around here. Tiger sharks, bonnetheads, hammerheads, lemon sharks, blacknose sharks, and I don't remember what else but it's pretty frightening to consider, isn't it?"

"Mercy, DuBose! I doubt you'll ever see Jenifer or me in water above our *ankles!*"

"Me, either. But when old George gets down here this summer, he's definitely coming in June, I'll bet he dives right into the waves and swims to Sullivans Island."

So. He was definitely coming. I was very, very relieved and I had learned what I wanted to know.

"Mr. Rhapsody in Blue. Humph. Wait until he sees his first alligator! That will give him a little religion. So what did his letter say? You didn't tell me."

"Not much. He's working on spirituals for Act I. He went to see *Four Saints in Three Acts,* Gertrude Stein's new opera. Hated the libretto, loved the music. He sends you and Jenifer his best."

"That's nice."

"He's not much of a fan of Stein's writing anyway. Never has been."

"Well, I am," I said. "I think we should get her down here to speak at the Poetry Society, don't you?" DuBose held the front door open for me to enter. "Thanks sweetheart." I loved his impeccable Southern manners and thought many times that he could have served as the United States ambassador to anywhere in the world.

"You're welcome. Why not? I don't know how well she'll be received but no doubt she'll be more popular than, who was it?"

"Millay."

"Ah, yes. Edna St. Vincent Millay. *What* was it that she did that so offended our blue-blooded natives?"

"You don't remember? You must be *kidding* me."

He shook his head.

"Well, pardon me DuBose but a lady does not discuss her relationship to the cycles of the tides and the phases of the moon in mixed company or at *all* for that matter."

"Ah yes, *that's* what I was trying to forget. But I think our guest poet considered herself to be quite above anyone's disdain. She was a very free spirit, wasn't she? As was Amy Lowell . . ."

"Who smoked cigars and said that our gardens in Charleston weren't exactly dazzling? That's just poor manners if you ask me."

"I suppose . . ."

"I'll never forget how she asked everyone why she was never invited to dinner. How awkward!"

"Well, darling she's from Boston," DuBose said with his eyebrow in an arch, "and a scandal herself, to the Old Guard here anyway. She didn't know that we ate our dinners in the middle of the day. How could she? But she was invited to loads of cocktail parties."

"Yes. Yes, as I remember, she was everywhere. You know around ten years ago there was some fellow who claimed that cocktail parties were *invented* in Charleston. Do you remember that? Who was that man?"

"Don't know, but I daresay the poor man simply didn't understand the mechanics of how things are done around here. Which would be easy to believe."

"Well, it should have been plain to see, really. I mean, it's just a practical matter. Why shouldn't our help be able to go back home for the evening? Just leave us a haunch of something we can carve up and a good strong bowl of planter's punch and what else do you need for a party?"

I said that as though I had a liveried staff of ten at our cottage, waiting to carve and pour. Besides, we went to many more parties than we gave.

"You only need interesting guests."

"And maybe a basket of biscuits. Well, my darling DuBose, there's been no shortage of interesting visitors to this fair city. Anyway, I think Miss Stein is better heeled than Miss Lowell was and would make a wonderful guest. We'll have the whole town begging to come hear her."

"You might be right. I'll ask Bennett about it when I go into town. You know, we're awfully close to finishing up the libretto for *Porgy and Bess*. Awfully close."

"Praise the Lord!" I rubbed my hands up and down my upper arms. "Is there a chill in here or is it me?"

"No, it's chilly. Tell you what. I'll check the furnace and pour us a little cognac. How does that sound?"

"Oh, DuBose! You always know the perfect thing to do."

That's how it went with DuBose and me. Sweet and easy. I remember that night so well because we were that much closer to finishing *Porgy and Bess*, that much closer to Gershwin's arrival, and that much closer to some financial relief.

Fade to Darkness

CHAPTER TWENTY-TWO

The Hospital

We stayed at the hospital the whole night. Aunt Daisy was moved to intensive care and was receiving antibiotics and fluids through her IV. She had a heart monitor, a catheter, a blood pressure monitor cuff, and a pulse oximeter attached to her fingertip. The mere sight of the breathing tube scared me to death. The machines were blinking and making sounds in step with her pulse. Ella and I stood around the room waiting, waiting for what I'm not sure, but we waited all the same. Risley had fallen asleep in a geri-chair in the hall that reclined, and was snoring a little now and then. His snoring was the only thing that brought the occasional smile to our faces.

"He's a sweet man, huh?" Ella said.

"The sweetest," I said. "I should send him home. He's got classes in the morning."

"Let him rest for a little while," Ella said. "He looks so comfortable."

Completely sedated, Aunt Daisy was breathing a little easier but there was no other improvement that I could detect. And for as fright-ening as it was to see her in a hospital bed hooked up to all the ma-chines and apparatus that she needed, I was so deeply relieved she was here.

We took turns going in and out of the room, sitting with her, and Aunt Daisy didn't budge an inch or bat an eye. She was a very sick lady. Before long, the sun was coming up and Dr. Ragone came into the room.

"You're still here?" I said, following him inside.

"Yes. I never sleep."

Ella jumped up from her chair at the sight of him.

"How's our patient?" he asked her.

"Quiet as a mouse." She smiled at him.

"So, ladies, I wanted to stay until we got the blood work results because I was so curious. And here's the news. It's not meningitis, rabies, strychnine poisoning, or any of the other things that have these symptoms."

"Then what in the world? What does she have?"

"Well, in my thirty years of medicine I've only seen one other case of this and that's really why I stayed. I'm pretty sure it's tetanus. Do you know when was the last time she had a tetanus shot?"

"No, but we can call her primary-care physician as soon as the office opens," I said.

"Well, I put her on metronidazole, which is a broad-spectrum an-tibiotic that will take care of it if it *is* tetanus. I suspect that when she cut her arm she *probably* took a spill."

"She never said she fell down," Ella said.

"That doesn't mean she didn't," I said and Ella winked at me in agreement.

"So," Dr. Ragone continued, "I'm thinking she fell in a sandy area, some spores got into her wound and released bacteria into her blood-stream. That bacteria makes a poison called tetanospasmin, not that you'll ever come across that word again, but anyway it blocks nerve signals, causing spasms. The spasms are what got my attention. And the drooling. You don't usually get those symptoms with something like pneumonia. It had to be a poison."

"Gosh," I said.

"Gotta go to school for a long time to learn all this mess," Ella said.

"You're telling me?" the doctor said.

How many times had I watched the television doctors on *House* call a diagnosis of some obscure disease and they were right? It was *all* about the diagnosis.

"Who gets tetanus anymore?" I said.

"Not too many people, but what people *don't* know could kill them. First of all, tetanus shots are only good for about ten years. And second, tetanus bacteria can lie dormant in your yard for forty years. That's why I tell all my patients to get a shot on their thirtieth birthday, their fortieth birthday, and so on."

"That ain't no way to celebrate a birthday," Ella said.

"Then get it ten days later," Dr. Ragone said with a big smile. "I don't want you ladies to worry about Ms. McInerny. I'm pretty sure she's going to be fine. She'll sleep most of the day today. The sedative I gave her really knocks you out. It's better for her to keep quiet with that tube, you know? If everything goes well, I'll probably send her home in a few days but remember, she'll need to be in a quiet room with dim light. I'll give you a prescription for an ointment that should take care of that arm, too."

Ella had tears in her eyes. "I'm so glad you were here, Dr. Ragone. So grateful," she said.

"Well, thanks. And it's a good thing y'all brought her in because her symptoms could've become much worse in a hurry."

"Good Lord," I said. "Oh! What about her broken foot?"

"I'll have the geriatric orthopedic guy come around and pay her a visit," he said. He gave us a little wave and the door whooshed to a close behind him.

Ella narrowed her eyes and looked at me. "Who's that fool calling *geriatric*?"

"Really! He's got some nerve." I looked at my watch. It was just after five thirty in the morning. "I wonder if the cafeteria is open."

John was completely fast asleep in the chair so I left him a note. *Gone downstairs for breakfast. If you wake up come join us. xx*

We made our way down endless halls and elevators and found the restaurant. They were just opening up. There was a large lady there, an employee whose apparent job it was to load the buffet's steam table with large stainless-steel containers of scrambled eggs, grits, oatmeal, and so on. She carried out tray after tray from the kitchen and dropped them in their designated positions. She looked up through weary eyes, spotted us, and smiled sympathetically. We weren't the only ones she'd seen on the first light of morning, people straggling in through the doorways after being up all night, waiting for a doctor or a diagnosis or for their loved one to just open their eyes. How many people did she see, exhausted from worry, numb with fear. I realized then we were a familiar sight to her, Ella and me. Just two more soldiers from the countless ranks who scoured the fields for their maimed and dead, scooping them up, rushing them to safety. As good as the food was in their cafeteria, and it was reputed to be amazingly good for hospital fare, it would never attract an outside clientele. No one was there who didn't have to be. We were as sorry as we could be to have to say we belonged there.

"There's coffee," she said, and pointed to the hot-beverage area. "Y'all help yourself. We'll be opening up in just a few minutes."

"Thanks," we said, poured two cups, and went back out to the atrium to take a seat at a table.

We mixed the fake cream in our cups with wooden stirrers and sighed hard.

"What do you think?" Ella said.

"I think, I think . . . I'm thinking so many things. How about you?"

"I'm thinking what a damn fool I was to decide I could take care of her at home."

"Ella, I think it's really hard to know when it's time to call for help."

"I should have known."

"Not necessarily. I mean, look, if someone has a heart attack and they're lying on the floor then it's obvious. You call 911. But this was strange and mysterious. Me? I thought it was a bad case of the flu or bronchitis. I *never* would have guessed tetanus. Not in a million years."

"I feel so bad, I mean, I should have forced her to go to the doctor sooner."

"Ella! Quit blaming yourself. Didn't you give me Harper's number and wouldn't she have been in a doctor's office in a couple of hours anyway? You were on it."

"Okay," she said.

Ella looked so sad. I took her hand and said, "Look, what if she didn't have you? What if she was all alone? If you think about it that way, she's pretty lucky. Isn't she?"

A few minutes later I looked up into John's face. He had a little stubble but other than that he looked perfect. Because he was.

"Morning, ladies. How're we doing?"

"Okay, I guess. Did Aunt Daisy wake up at all?"

"Oh, Lord! She's gonna throw a conniption fit if she wakes up and finds out she's got a tube down her throat. Y'all? Mark my word! She'll rip that thing right out."

"Ella! Stop fretting so! The doctor said she'd sleep."

"Yes, don't worry. She's sleeping like an angel. A nurse came in to check her vitals and I told her what you just said, because that was the first thing I thought about, too. Anyway, she said they would probably remove it before Miss Daisy even wakes up."

"That would be a blessing," I said. "John, I can't thank you enough for all you did to help us. You were the guy on the white horse, saving the day."

"No big deal. I just did what I thought should be done, because I couldn't think of what else to do."

The logic of his words sounded so funny that we actually started to laugh a little.

"Maybe I need coffee," he said.

"You sit," I said. "Let me get it for you. What time's your first class?"

"Not until ten," he said.

I was going to bring him pancakes. And bacon. And sausage. And juice. And maybe just one biscuit for me.

"Ella? You want a scrambled egg sandwich or I can get you something else?"

"I couldn't eat a thing, honey, but thanks."

While John was eating his gargantuan breakfast, and I was picking on my biscuit, Ella went to search for a copy of the *New York Times*, saying that Daisy would be furious if she missed her crossword puzzle.

"This is delicious," he said. "Are you sure y'all don't want to share this?"

"No, thanks," I said, "I'm not that hungry, for some weird reason."

"Okay. Oh, since we all came here in one car I thought I would run y'all back out to Folly so you can get your car. How's that?"

"That would be great," I said, yawning. "Gosh, I need more coffee. All of a sudden I'm so tired I can hardly hold my eyes open."

"Big surprise! When's the last time you stayed up all night?"

"Prom?"

"Well, when I take you home you should try to close your eyes for a few hours."

"What? I can't do that, John. What if something happens?"

"Just leave your number with the nurses' station and they'll call you but the doctor seemed to think Miss Daisy was pretty stable, didn't he?"

"I think so. As long as she stays sedated, I guess. I'll ask them to put my number on Aunt Daisy's chart. I'm actually next of kin."

Ella returned and we decided to leave. It was seven then and time to go home, take a bath, and try to nap. But before I did all of that I knew I had to call Patti and my children and tell them what was going on. So they cleared our table while I ran back up to the ICU to leave my number and then we went outside trying to remember where we had parked the car the night before. The drive was quiet on the ride back to the beach.

First, John dropped off Ella and walked her inside just to be sure everything was safe. Then he came back outside to me.

"Do you know how beautiful you are; even when you've been up all night?"

"You know, Professor Risley, this is more than a crush."

"Yes, Miss Cate. I'm aware."

I let myself out of the car at the Porgy House and thought two things at once. One, every bone in my body was as stiff as a board and two, here I was, at my age and with probable arthritis in every joint I had and I was falling in love like a young woman. It made me so nervous to admit that to myself but I wouldn't have to tell anyone else until I was ready. This was the beauty of middle age. You knew instinctively when to keep your mouth shut.

I went inside and called Patti.

"Hey!" she said. "What are you doing up so early?"

"You're not going to believe this," I said and told her the whole story.

Patti was very upset. She made me stop and repeat what I had said several times to be sure she understood the facts. Her voice kept cracking and I thought she would start crying but she held herself together.

"Is she going to be all right?" Patti felt the same way that I did about Aunt Daisy.

"I sure hope so. I mean, the doctor seems to think she'll be fine but she's got a breathing tube, a heart monitor, an IV, and she's heavily sedated. So to look at her, well, it's a pretty frightening sight to see, lemme tell you."

"You know what? I'm coming down tonight. I'll call you back with my flights."

"Okay."

"Jeez, Cate, you gotta ask yourself what would you have done if John wasn't there?"

"I don't know. You're right. I mean, she could've fallen on the bathroom floor and broken her hip."

"I'll bet she was pissed that y'all saw her naked."

"Listen, she didn't even look that bad, thank God, and she probably won't remember anyway. She's a pretty sick woman right now."

"You're in love with this John fellow, aren't you?"

"Head over heels."

So much for playing my cards close to my chest.

Next, I called Russ's cell phone and left a message. Then, realizing he was already in school, I texted him, too. *Aunt Daisy's in the ICU @ MUSC. Call me.* He called me back right away.

"Mom! What happened?"

"Remember the night y'all came over to tell Aunt Daisy the big news? Well, later on she started feeling bad and Ella said . . ."

I brought him up to date and he was just as surprised as I was to hear that she had tetanus.

"Man! Of all the crazy things to catch. I'm getting a shot this week. Can we go see her?"

"Of course! I'm going back later on this afternoon to take Ella. Ella wants to hold a vigil and I'm not going to let her try to do that all by herself or she'll be in the hospital next for exhaustion."

"No! Of course not. Oh, man, wait till Alice hears this. Did you call Sara?"

"Well, it's five thirty in the morning in Los Angeles. I should probably wait awhile. But look, I don't think there's a reason to panic. I really do believe that Aunt Daisy is going to recover and be fine. It just might take a while, that's all. Oh, and Aunt Patti is coming in tonight."

"What? Mom? Is Aunt Daisy in worse shape than you're telling me? Is that why Aunt Patti is coming?"

"What? Oh, no! She was coming down anyway. She simply moved her trip up. Honest."

"Well, good then, good! It will be great to see her. She's the best."

"And she can split the vigil duty with us, too."

"Well, I gotta get back to my class . . ."

We hung up and I went upstairs to lie down on the bed. I fell into a deep sleep with no dreams until almost noon. When I began to awaken, it was a slow return to reality. I drifted back and forth between waking and sleeping for a while and suddenly I was dreaming about George Gershwin. He was downstairs playing my piano. It was some time in between night and day. (Oh, wait! That's Cole Porter. A little music joke. Sorry.) Okay, so in this dream it was a summer night. The doors and windows were all open and there was a gorgeous breeze. Dorothy and DuBose were there and so was Josephine Pinckney with her dog, a black spaniel named Peter, which is a stupid name for a dog, I remember thinking. The three of them were singing along with Gershwin, first "Summertime" and then "A Woman Is a Sometime Thing." They were so happy and in the next scene Gershwin was holding his head, as though he was in blinding pain. Then I remembered he died from a brain tumor and I woke up.

I finally got up to wash my face and still couldn't get Gershwin out of my mind. He wasn't even forty years old when he died. Thirty-eight, in fact. What a loss to the world. If he had lived until his eighties, how many more wonderful songs of his would we have had the thrill to enjoy? That saying, *only the good die young,* was too terrible. Certainly there had been so many musicians who died young and it made me wonder for a moment if the gift of musical composition came with a price. I mean, just like certain people walked into a room and saw things geometrically, because they had a mathematical bent, and others walked in the room and saw color combinations, because they were artistically creative in another way, did the gift of being able to compose extraordinary music cause an extraordinary strain on the body? Chopin, Bizet, Mozart, Schubert, Schumann—all of them gone at young ages. And in our time there was Kurt Weill, not to mention all the others whose personal excesses and dark forces got the better of them. Well, I thought then, what if the spirit of George Gershwin wants to take up residence in this house and play my piano? It was all right with me. I was happy to have him.

I changed my clothes and had a bowl of cereal and decided that although Sara worked until late into the night, she would surely be up by eleven, her time. I was wrong. It was a groggy voice that answered her phone.

"Mom? Everythin's 'kay? Oh man, what time is it?"

"Oh, sweetheart! I'm sorry to wake you. Do you want to call me back later?"

"No, it's fine. What's going on?"

"Well, it's Aunt Daisy . . ."

I told her the whole story and she became very upset as I knew she would, because Sara is probably, no *definitely* the most sensitive one in the family.

"Do you want me to come home? Or should I come? I mean, it's no big deal. So they'll fire me. I'm just a bartender, for heaven's sake. I can get another job tomorrow."

She had gone from the lofty designation of *mixologist* to the normal term of *bartender,* which told me she was becoming disenchanted with her work. I would talk to her about that another time.

"No, I don't want you to give up your job. And you know, it's not so great out there. You might *not* get another job so fast. Besides, Aunt Daisy is not in a life-threatening situation. If she was, I would tell you."

"I just hate being so far away. Something like this happens and I can't see for myself what's really going on. I just hate it."

"Well, precious, you'll just have to trust your mother. Or if you want, call Russ and ask him his opinion. He and Alice are heading over to MUSC after work this evening."

"How's she doing? Alice, I mean."

"She seems fine. A little fatigued but that's normal."

"I still can't believe Alice is pregnant. It's so weird."

"In some ways, yes. But you know, life goes on, doesn't it?"

There was a silence then and I knew what she was thinking.

"I miss Dad," she said. "I still can't believe he's gone."

"I know. It seems like it all happened in a bad dream, doesn't it?"

"I guess you don't miss him too much, huh?"

"Sara? I think the facts and details surrounding his death might be a little larger and more profound for me than for you or Russ. But you should never doubt the fact that he loved you and your brother very much."

"And you don't think he loved you, do you?"

"Oh, I think there was a time when he absolutely did. But I think he had too much terrible anxiety over the last years of his life and that anxiety trumped whatever feelings of affection he might have *ever* had for me. I don't think he did the things he did to deliberately hurt me. But any outside observer would say that *he* was absolutely his first priority. He had ceased to be a partner in our relationship years ago. And I can tell you this about his love for me—it doesn't matter anymore. I'm okay with it."

"Humph. You're in love with that John guy, aren't you? I can't believe you about *anything*. You're rationalizing having an affair with this guy for *some* reason . . ."

"Wait just a minute, young lady. You don't dare speak to me this way."

"Oh! I get it now! The reason you don't want me to come is because you're having this affair and you don't want me to see, isn't that it? Dad's been dead for maybe ten minutes and you're already involved with somebody else? Nice work, Mom."

"Look, Sara, I know you were never a morning person but this conversation is *out of control*. When you want to apologize for being so disrespectful and when you think you can have a reasonable discussion about your aunt Daisy's condition, call me back. In the meantime, I'm hanging up."

And with that, I pressed the end button.

And I felt terrible. I hated it when Sara and I had words. And I didn't know exactly why she thought it was all right to let whatever was rolling across her brain roll across her tongue and out into the air. She was her father's daughter if ever there was one. Like Addison, she had always had a problem with her mouth. Since she was a little girl, I would tell her that you just can't go around saying whatever you want to people without consequences. It had cost her many friendships and boyfriends and she never seemed to care too much. Their perceived transgressions only made her furious. In Sara's mind, she *always* thought she was right and she *had* to have the last word. It was more important to her to vent and to walk away, think things through and come back another day, making a different case for her point of view. She did not like to be on the receiving end of any kind of guidance from anyone. Ever. They say you can raise one hundred boys for the energy it takes to raise one girl and I think truer words were never spoken. I loved my ballistic girl more than anyone in this world, except for my son, and I knew her attitude got in between her and happiness but she was a grown woman and it would be up to the world now to teach her the lessons she needed to learn. All that said, I wasn't going to let her take a bite out of me whenever the mood struck.

Now, Russ? Russ was born easygoing and nonjudgmental. Oh, we'd had some issues like him not being forthcoming with a bad grade or him breaking curfew and when he was in high school, beer went missing now and then. But overall? He seemed happy to stay with the program and, mostly, he did what he was supposed to do. Maybe playing sports had a lot to do with it, because they put demands on his time

246 / Dorothea Benton Frank

that he had to meet if he wanted to play. But I will never understand why he fell in love with Alice and married her. He dated so many cute girls who were so sweet. Ah well, I'm not the only mother in the world who ever pondered *that* question.

My phone rang. It was the Confrontational One. I sighed and took the call.

"I'm sorry," she said.

"Okay," I said.

"I love you," she said.

"I love you, too," I said.

"You're sure I really don't need to quit my stinking stupid job and come to South Carolina?"

"Yes, I'm sure. Do you want to talk about work? How's it going?"

"It's going nowhere, that's how. I mean, you want to talk about doing thankless work with a bunch of drunks?"

She went on for at least fifteen minutes about her horrible lot in life and I listened like the dutiful mother should. Which is to say, I offered no unwelcome solutions.

"So what are you thinking about? I mean, is there something else you'd like to be doing?"

"I don't know! I don't know! I mean, the money's good but I'm so *tired* when I get home! I don't feel like getting up and going to auditions, if I even had them to *go* to that is. My agent hasn't done shit for me."

"Language!"

"Whatever. Anyway, maybe I should get another agent."

Okay, it's not like I never used the word myself but never in front of my children and I still believed that children were supposed to curse among themselves, not in front of adults. And here was another stellar example of Sara taking license. We are not and will never be peers.

"Well, honey, you're the only one who can answer that question." I could see then that since Addison's death, Sara may have been brooding all along. It wasn't easy to be so far away from home, especially when she lost a parent. Maybe a visit to the Lowcountry would do her some good. "Listen, how's this? When Aunt Daisy gets out of the hospital and comes home, why don't we find you a cheap ticket to come here for a few days? I think it would do her a world of good to see you. And Ella, too."

"Awesome! Yeah, I'd love that. Let me see when I can get some time off."

"Yeah. Just remember, there's no urgency, Sara. Honestly, there isn't. If, heaven forbid, her condition changes I'll get you here right away."

"Okay. Mom?"

"Yep?"

"This John is a nice man?"

"Let me tell you how nice . . ."

By the time I finished telling her about how he picked up Aunt Daisy from the bathtub, called 911, and then sat up all night at the hospital with Ella and me, her tune was in a different pitch altogether.

"Wow," she said. "Mom, he sounds like amazing."

"Look, there's no reason for anyone to get excited about John Risley. He is my friend and if that status changes, I'll let you know that, too." No, I won't.

"Yeah, I guess when you're your age, you have to take what you can get."

Now, what kind of an assessment was that?

"Um, I'm not so sure what that meant . . ."

"Wait! I meant, you know, you don't have, you know, sex and stuff."

"Sara Cooper! Go wash your mouth out with soap!" She should only know, I thought.

She laughed and said, "Yeah, I'll get right on that! See ya, Mom! Love ya!"

And the Contentious One was gone. For the moment. I had not

told her about my budding career as a playwright or Piccolo Spoleto or that John had suggested Sara to possibly play Dorothy Heyward. So far all I had were notebooks filled with notes and a lot of Xerox copies of Dorothy's and DuBose's letters. And I had not droned on about the Charleston Renaissance as I was now inclined to do whenever I got my hands on the mike. But I had raised her spirits and introduced the idea of me having a friend of the opposite sex in a way that I thought seemed reasonable and acceptable to her. No sex, huh? Is that what twenty-five-year-olds thought? That their parents didn't get it on like jungle animals? That *they* had cornered the market on that pastime? My children would drop dead if they knew. Drop dead on the floor.

I was still laughing to myself about that when I picked up Ella to go back to the hospital. She put a big tote bag on the floor in the backseat and got in the front with me.

"Did you manage to get a nap?" I asked her as she was buckling her seat belt.

"Well, I closed my eyes but I didn't sleep. I made a pie and brought it with me."

"What kind?"

"Pecan. It's so good. I think I'm gonna be taking the nurses a pie whenever I can so they'll keep an extra eye on you-know-who."

"Not a bad idea," I said. "Did you eat?"

"I had a banana and a glass of milk. Whenever I'm worrying about something I lose my appetite."

"Not me. I can always eat. Oh, I spoke to Russ and they'll be meeting us there at some point. And Patti is flying in tonight. She lands at six thirty so I'll be going out to pick her up and then I'll bring her downtown to see Aunt Daisy."

"That's good. Be so good to see her. And you talked to Miss Sara?"

"Oh, yeah. And she's marinating in a mood over me seeing John. I think she thinks I should be lonely and miserable, that it would be more suitable behavior for a widow."

"Humph. All them kids is crazy as a bunch of bedbugs, too, 'eah? They don't know how short life can be."

"They don't know a lot of things, Ella, but they have to learn their lessons in their own time."

"Isn't that fuh true? If you ask me, you became a widow a long time ago."

"You don't know the half of it," I said and nodded in agreement. "Sometime when Aunt Daisy is on the mend I'll tell you some stories that will curl your hair."

"God, I pray she's gonna be on the mend today."

"Me too. Sara wanted to come but I told her it wasn't necessary. Besides, she has to work."

"Well, she's got bills to pay."

"She'll come as soon as she can take some time off."

"I haven't laid my eyes on that child since I don't know when."

"Well, she's sure something else, I'll tell you."

"Humph. What's it like to be twenty-five?"

"In today's world? Must be hard."

We rode the rest of the short trip in relative quiet, just moving with the traffic. We were tired and anxious but both of us were so glad, so relieved that Aunt Daisy was in the hospital, where she belonged.

I pulled in the parking lot and found a space.

"You hungry?" she said.

"No, I grabbed a bowl of cereal. My stomach wanted breakfast."

This time it was easier to find Aunt Daisy's room and there she was, right through the window, still sleeping. We decided to deliver the pie and went back to the nurses' station.

The head nurse on duty was a beautiful young woman whose name tag read Tolli Rosol, RN. That had to be a shortened version of a family surname. I was guessing but it reminded me that down here in this part of the world we had more last names used as first names than any other part of the country. Unlike certain people in the entertainment world we didn't name our children after fruit and inanimate objects. We were insanely proud of our ancestors and went to great lengths to honor them.

"I'm Ella Johnson, Daisy McInerny's friend? And I made y'all this so you might keep checking on her. You know, make sure she's doing all right?"

"You really made this pie for us? That is so sweet! Thank you!"

"You're welcome. I'll bring you another one tomorrow."

"You do that and Ms. McInerny will get spoiled rotten," Nurse Rosol said.

"Humph," Ella said and smiled. "Too late. She's already rotten."

Ella and I went back to Aunt Daisy's room and resumed our positions. Ella went in for half an hour and then she came out and I went in. We did this Chinese fire drill of sorts until I was sick to death of my magazines and it was nearly five o'clock. There was no change in Aunt Daisy's condition whatsoever. The only sound was the steady bleep from her heart monitor.

"Do you want to go get a bite to eat? I've got about forty-five minutes before I have to go get Patti. And there's rush-hour traffic."

"I guess so."

Back in the cafeteria, we had a bowl of vegetable soup and a small mixed green salad that I devoured and Ella pushed around, barely eating at all.

"No good?" I said.

"Tastes like dishwater," she said.

"Yeah, it actually does but that's when I compare it to yours. Next to the one I make it tastes like heaven!" I looked at my watch. "I'll be back in an hour, if she's on time. Can I bring you anything?"

"No, honey. I still have my book to finish. But thanks and you drive carefully, okay?"

"Sure."

Ella was deep into Harlan Greene's *Mr. Skylark,* the story of John

Bennett and the Charleston Renaissance. It was in the Porgy House among Aunt Daisy's collection of books related in any way whatsoever to DuBose and Dorothy Heyward. She picked it up, saying if I was going to get myself all involved in this period of history, she wanted to know more, too. If I put all their laments of aging aside, Aunt Daisy and Ella fought hard to remain relevant and to keep their brains sharp. I had to believe it made a difference in their lives. They were good role models for everyone.

While I was cruising along I-26 in my car, I wondered then if there was anything in Aunt Daisy's rental properties that required immediate attention. I would ask Ella tomorrow when I went to pick her up if I could help her sort things out. That way, we could go through the mail, the voice mail, check her books, and try to keep things moving along. Patti would help, too. She ran her own business. She would know what to do as well. I couldn't wait to see my sister. There was no greater gift on this earth than a good sister.

I wasn't comfortable with Ella's plan to spend all of her time at Aunt Daisy's bedside. At her age it couldn't be good for her. We all knew how much she loved our aunt. She surely didn't need to prove it. I would talk to that nice nurse and see what she said. Tolli Rosol. Sounds a little like the name of a Swiss village! Musical!

I gave John a ring and he picked up.

"Hey," he said. "How's it going? Any news?"

"Not a peep," I said. "I'm on my way to the airport to get my sister."

"Oh! I thought she wasn't coming until next week. But I guess when she got the news . . ."

"Exactly. She changed her ticket the minute she heard. So, how was your day?"

"I'm going to bed early. I'm pooped!"

"That sounds like heaven but I'm afraid I'm in for another long night."

"You poor girl. You and Patti want to have dinner tomorrow night?"

"Absolutely. I'm dying for you to meet her."

"And tell her I can't wait to meet her, too."

"I will. So, I'll call you tomorrow when we get free?"

"You know, I'm so used to spending the nights with you I don't know what to do with myself this evening."

"Well, if you want to meet my precious son, his pregnant disagreeable wife, and my wonderful sister all in one fell swoop you know where to find us!"

"I'll see y'all tomorrow!"

We hung up; I pulled into the airport parking deck and found a spot. I told Patti I could meet her in baggage claim and when I got inside she had already arrived, and was there shooting the breeze with an ancient skycap.

"Patti! You're early!"

"Hey, you! Yep! We landed twenty minutes earlier than we were supposed to."

We hugged like we hadn't seen each other in a year.

"Who lands early? Musta caught a tailwind! Is this all your stuff?"

She had a roll-on bag and a tote bag, her overcoat, and her purse. Her roll-on and tote bags were lime green canvas with bright red yarn pigtails hanging from the name tags.

"What's this?" I said and gave the pigtails a flip with my finger.

"I want to be able to distinguish my bags from other people's bags. Why?"

"You're kidding, right?"

We hurried out to the car, threw her bags in the back, and got in.

"Wow, the temperature's so nice. This is like spring. I don't even need my coat. It's been under twenty in New Jersey all week."

"I don't miss that," I said and started the car.

"I'll bet. So, tell me the truth," she said, closing her door. "How's Aunt Daisy?"

"She's going to get better but right now, she's still pretty sick."

"Tetanus? Talk about scaring the crap out of me. Even Mark said I should get on the plane today. He sends you a smooch, by the way."

"And send him one for me. Look, if you wanted to get scared, you should've been here last night. Patti, holy hell. I hear those ambulances coming and all I can think about is Addison swinging from the rafters. It's been a very dramatic twenty-four hours."

"You poor thing. I'll bet it was awful."

"Yeah, it really was. But you know, as much as I hate seeing her in that bed and knowing what I know now, I am so relieved. She could've died, you know."

"That's what Mark said."

All the way downtown we talked and talked. I told her about my little tiff with Sara and that Russ and Alice would probably be at the hospital when we got there and that John was taking us out to dinner the next night. She was as worried as I was about Aunt Daisy but looking forward to seeing everyone just the same.

"So, you think it's okay if I rub Alice's stomach for good luck?"

"Oh yeah, Patti. You know Alice. She'd love that. I dare you."

"What's in it for me?"

"I'll make you breakfast in bed the whole time you're here. How's that?"

"Just remember I like my coffee with one sugar and my toast light."

"Sure. Big talk. Wait until you see the Porgy House."

"Dump?"

"No, not at all. It's adorable. Like a dollhouse."

"How's the piano?"

"Old Cunningham looks like she's as happy as a clam."

"A smiling piano. Only you would have a smiling piano!"

We arrived at the Medical University and saw Russ crossing the parking lot. I rolled down my window and called out to him.

"Hey! Russ! Wait for us!"

We parked and got out of the car and he hurried over to hug Patti and then me.

"Where's Alice?" I said.

"In the car over there," he said, pointing to his Jeep.

"What's she doing in the car?" Patti said. "Hey, congratulations again, by the way."

"Thanks!" he said. "I had the easy part, you know."

"Gross," I said. "What's she doing? Is she coming in?"

"No, she's afraid to come in."

"What?" Patti said and we exchanged looks about his wife's questionable behavior, which was almost never the thing either one of us would do.

"What's she afraid of, son?" I said.

"Germs," he said.

"Ooooh boy," I said under my breath and thought great, it was going to be one long hot summer until that baby arrived.

CHAPTER TWENTY-THREE

Setting: The Porgy House at the piano.
Director's Note: Show photos of the beaches of Folly Beach, the church, and then George Gershwin with DuBose and Dorothy sharing a cocktail on the backstage scrim. Voice of DuBose comes from off-stage.

Act III
Scene 2

Dorothy: I'll remember that summer forever, the one when George Gershwin arrived on Folly Beach, with his cousin Henry Botkin, supposedly to get down to work. We were away when George showed up but I had rented a little cottage for him. When we asked him what kind of accommodations he wanted, he was adamant that he wanted to live like the natives. I thought, okay, I can manage that. The place I found was within walking distance of ours but it had no electricity or running water. He wanted native? I found him native. Wasn't that terrible of me?

Surprisingly, there was no objection from him, probably because he fell in love with Folly Beach the same way everyone else does. But it had to have taken some getting used to for a city-slicker like him.

In fact, there was a story in the *News and Courier* that Ashley Cooper, the pseudonym used by one of our favorite columnists, came out to visit him, and George, ever the well-dressed man, appeared in a getup that he probably wore in Palm Beach—a sport coat and an orange tie! But soon he put his sport coat and orange tie in the closet and spent most of his time walking on the beach and diving into the waves. I think I forgot to tell him about the sharks.

Anyway, it wasn't long until George found himself a lady friend but as I hear it, she was not particularly impressed with him. She thought all his swimming and athletics were some silly attempt to make himself into a he-man. In fact, the rumor mill said that George spent more time swimming in the ocean and counting turtle eggs, painting watercolors, and playing golf than he did composing music.

By the time DuBose and I returned to Folly, George had a scraggly beard and he was as brown as a pecan. Well, DuBose was having no more delays and shenanigans from Mr. Gershwin, so the first thing he did was get him over to James Island where there was a huge Gullah population. He took him to schools and church services so George could see the "Double Clap" for himself. Don't you know George got so excited, he joined in? And, to his credit, George always left a nice donation so that word would spread and he'd be welcome to visit the next place.

I think the biggest disagreement between DuBose and George was about how much of *Porgy and Bess* should be sung and how much should be spoken like regular lines in a play. George wanted the spoken lines to rhyme, because that was the American operatic tradition. But I think DuBose wanted the actors to speak in straight Gullah, because that was authentic to the Gullahs of the Lowcountry. I said, gentlemen, this is your musical and you can do whatever you want. I don't think they were listening to me.

Then there was the argument of how much to keep and what to cut. The most unusual aspect of the writing of *Porgy and Bess* was that the majority of the time we were writing the libretto and some lyrics, we were in South Carolina and Gershwin was in New York. But George and DuBose devised their own notation system so that George and Ira could set our lyrics to music in the tempo we envisioned. Sounds wacky, but it worked!

So when George came down, I rented a piano for him from Siegling Music House, which was a real beauty, by the way, and we were to hear our lyrics set to his music for the first time. It was terribly exciting.

We went over to his cottage with some champagne and a shaker of something good and George played and played and played. It was so astoundingly beautiful and I was so moved that I cried like a baby. For the first time I saw George as he truly was in his heart. He wasn't just an egomaniac. He was a brilliant young man who loved his music and he loved to play it for you. Now I ask you. What's the matter with that?

Fade to Darkness

CHAPTER TWENTY-FOUR

The Sisters

We went up in the elevator together—Patti, Russ, and I—and I led
them to Aunt Daisy's room where Ella sat right inside the doorway,
staring at Aunt Daisy in her bed, no doubt continuing to chastise herself and praying Aunt Daisy well at the same time. It was plain to see
that nothing had changed. I tapped on the window to get Ella's attention. She came out, hugged Patti and then Russ. She had been crying
and I decided right then that she was not going to spend the night
there, working herself into a state of morbid anxiety and winding up
sick herself. It just wasn't a good idea.

First, Russ went in for a few minutes and then Patti took her turn.
When Patti came out she rolled her eyes at me and whispered, *holy shit.*

I nodded in agreement. Seeing someone you love in Aunt Daisy's
condition was a *holy shit* moment if ever there was one.

"I'll be right back," I said.

I slipped down to the nurses' station and asked if Nurse Tolli Rosol
was still around and she was.

"Oh, hi!" she said. "Just FYI? That was the best pecan pie I ever had in my life."

"Good, good! Ella will be thrilled to hear it. Listen, I actually wanted to ask you for a little help with Ella . . ."

She understood perfectly, because sentinel relatives and friends who held their posts like the Swiss Guards at the Vatican were a common occurrence and she knew exactly how to handle it.

"I'll give her about thirty more minutes, okay?"

"That would be terrific," I said, adding, "thanks."

And sure enough, about thirty minutes later she came strolling down the hall with Aunt Daisy's chart and stopped to say hello to everyone.

"This is my sister Patti from Alpine, New Jersey," I said.

"Oh! Nice to meet you," Nurse Tolli said. "I have a cousin in Summit."

"No kidding," Patti said, "small world."

"And this is my son, Russ, who coaches basketball at James Island and teaches, too."

"Really? What grade?"

"Tenth," he said and smiled.

"That's a challenge, I'm sure. And, Ms. Johnson? Did Cate tell you what I said about your pie?"

"She did," Ella said. She smiled and was all ears for the compliment to come. "Thank you."

"Well, it's true. Delicious! Now, y'all aren't planning to spend the night again, are you?"

"*I* most certainly am," Ella said and raised her chin a little. She didn't think for a minute that this little nurse was a match for her determination.

"No, you won't be doing that tonight," Nurse Tolli said.

"And why not?" Ella said, surprised.

"Because I'm here. Ms. McInerny is under total surveillance from my station. If her blood pressure changes one little bit or her tempera-ture goes up or down even one tenth of a degree, all my alarms go off. We're so high-tech up here in ICU it's better than having her own mother watching over her, believe me. And *you* need to get your rest because when she comes home you won't have *me*!"

"But . . ." Ella started to object.

"Besides, even though you all think she's asleep, she's sedated. She knows there are people around her and she won't rest as well with an audience. So, y'all are welcome to stay a few more minutes but let's let Ms. McInerny get her rest. I *know* you wouldn't want to impede her healing process."

"No, of course not," Ella said.

She spoke to all of us just as politely as I had hoped she would but Ella knew the nurse's comments were directed to her. Ella also knew this was an experienced nurse who knew what she was talking about. And it was obvious that our sweet Ella was bone-tired.

"I know what," I said. "Let's all stop somewhere on Folly Road and get something to eat. And, Ella, I'll bring you back here in the morning whenever you're ready."

"Besides, if you don't go home, how're you going to make us another pie?" my favorite nurse said.

"That one's all gone?" Ella said, perking up again.

"Not a crumb left," Tolli said so sweetly that it pulled my heart-strings. "Now, if y'all will excuse me I want to check on my patient," she said and slipped into Aunt Daisy's room. "Nice meeting y'all."

"Nice to meet you, too," Russ and Patti said.

Nursing was truly God's work. And this young woman was practi-cally glowing with a saintly presence, putting all our worries, but Ella's most especially, to rest.

"How about the Crab House?" Russ said. "It's not crazy expensive and it won't take all night."

"Alice isn't afraid of shellfish?" Patti asked. "You know raw shellfish can be dangerous in the first trimester. Smoked seafood, too. Not to mention sushi . . ."

"Oh great. Please don't bring it up," Russ said. "I'll encourage her to eat flounder."

"Yeah, and don't let her eat tuna salad, either," Patti said.

"Since when are you the OB/GYN nutrition expert?" I said.

"Oz was on *Oprah* last week while I was on the treadmill," she said.

"I hate treadmills," I said.

"Yeah, well, my walking buddy abandoned me and flew south," she said.

"I drove."

"Let's get a move on," Ella said. "It will do us good to have supper together. I know we ate a little something earlier but now I'm starving!"

I took it as a promising sign that Ella was so hungry. She felt relieved enough to get back in touch with her appetite. And the Crab House was fun. It would lift everyone's spirits.

Locals in Charleston usually go out to dinner on the early side, so it should have been pretty easy for us to get a table at eight thirty. But the Crab House was still filled with patrons eating and drinking and having a good time. After seeing Aunt Daisy, we needed to be surrounded by happiness.

We waited for a few minutes, got a table, and ordered drinks.

"I'll have a glass of the Raymond Sauvignon Blanc," I said, choosing from the list.

"Me too," Patti said.

"Iced tea for me," Alice said. "I can't drink alcohol."

"Oh, no problem," said the waitress. I could tell she was wondering if Alice was on the wagon, out of rehab, allergic, or what.

"She's having a baby," Russ said. "Actually, my baby."

The waitress cocked her head to one side and looked at Russ like he was warped to be telling her his private business that would be patently obvious as soon as Alice started to show.

"We're married."

"Well, good for you hon," the waitress said, without missing a beat.

Russ turned red. "And I'll just have an Amstel Light," he said.

"And for you, ma'am?" the waitress said.

"I'll have a Crab House Slammer," Ella said, looking up from the menu.

We all looked at her at once.

"What?" she said. "Y'all want to see my ID?"

"No! I think you should get whatever the heck you want," I said. "It's been a rough day."

"Absolutely," Patti chimed in.

"I'll get those drinks right out for you," the waitress said and left.

We all studied the menu, trying to make our decisions.

"So, Alice?" Patti said. "Tell me how you're feeling."

"I feel great, except that I want to eat everything in sight," she said. "I'm just really going to have to discipline myself so I don't get as big as a house, you know? Well, actually, you wouldn't know since *you've* never been pregnant . . ."

"How do *you* know?" Patti said, not wanting to miss the opportunity to stick it to Alice. "So, let me ask you this. Anybody rub your belly for good luck yet?"

"What?" Alice said.

"Ahem!" I cleared my throat and kicked Patti under the table.

"Ow! Sorry, so tell us how you plan to stay fit? Are there some new guidelines?"

"No, no. I'm just going to eat lots of protein and fresh vegetables and try to get some exercise every day. And sleep, which won't be a problem, because all I want to do is sleep."

"That sounds good, honey," Ella said, being nicer than my sister.

The waitress reappeared with a tray of our beverages and began putting them in front of us.

When she got to Alice she said, "I didn't know if you wanted lemon in your tea so I put it on the side."

"There aren't too many calories in a squirt of lemon, are there?" Alice asked.

The waitress looked up at the ceiling.

"You may squirt with impunity," Patti said, but she was smiling when she said it so Alice didn't think she'd been jabbed again.

"Actually, lemon juice is a natural diuretic," I said. "So, if your ankles get swollen this summer, make lemonade. Or eat asparagus. They help, too."

"I did not know that," Alice said. "Thanks for telling me."

"On the house," I said and smiled at her. After all, she was pregnant with my grandchild.

The waitress waited to take our orders.

"So, girls? What are we having?" Russ said. "I'm thinking seriously about the tuna."

"Who you calling a girl?" Ella said, winking. She raised her glass. "To Daisy, who would be right here having a martini if she could. Get well quick!"

"Amen," I said. "Here's to Aunt Daisy!"

And everyone touched the rim of their glass to another's.

"I'm having the shrimp platter with collards and grits," I said.

"That sounds good but I'll have the crab cakes," Ella said. "With red rice and collards. I've been thinking about the crab cakes ever since Russ said we should come here."

"So good. Coconut shrimp for me with fries and cole slaw," said Patti.

All eyes were on Alice.

"And you, hon?" said the waitress.

"Well, I can't eat tuna because of the mercury thing and all this other stuff is too fattening so I'll have the cheeseburger and fries with a side of mac 'n' cheese? That mac 'n' cheese isn't a big portion, is it?"

"No, no. You could barely feed a mouse with it," the waitress said.

"Eat what you want," I said. "You'll never be able to eat like this unless you get pregnant again."

"Yeah, but then you have to starve yourself to lose it all," Alice said.

"The weight will fall off of you like water," I said, wondering if the whole dinner was going to be monopolized by Alice's new favorite subject—herself.

It was.

We crawled through dinner, listening to Alice regale us on the topics of prenatal care, breast-feeding, Lamaze techniques, and her mother's advice. Almost every sentence she spoke began with *well, my mother says* . . . I thought, yeah honey, when you go into labor and your momma ain't here, you'd better learn how to spell *Cate*.

Hugs and good-nights for Russ and Alice took place in the parking lot and then we drove out to Aunt Daisy's and Ella's house. Except for a few choice remarks about Alice, the ride was pretty quiet. We went up in the elevator with Ella just to be sure there were no robbers hiding behind the curtains or monsters under the beds. It was just really lousy manners to let a woman of her advanced years, or a woman of any age, for that matter, enter an empty house alone. Plus, Patti said in the car that she wanted a Diet Coke in the worst possible way and of course I didn't have any at home and all the stores were closed. But Ella offered her a twelve-pack, because they had just made a Costco run and her pantry was fully stocked. So, we had our solution for Patti and our excuse to follow Ella in without making her feel like she needed special senior-citizen coddling.

"They're right in the pantry in the kitchen," she said, going from room to room, turning on lights and televisions.

"Thanks. Wow! The house looks great, Ella," Patti said. "Did y'all redecorate the living room?"

"No, not everything. Just changed the drapes and repainted."

Patti had her cans of Diet Coke balanced on her hip and she was standing by the sliding glass doors, debating opening them to take in the beach at night.

"Here," I said, "let me do that."

I took the drinks from her and put them on the coffee table and opened the doors. The salty air rushed in and the ocean was loud. It was high tide and the waves rolled in relentlessly, banging the shore and grabbing all it could on its way back out. We stepped outside.

"Holy mother!" Patti said. "Why is it so easy to forget how powerful this place is?"

"I don't know," I said. "The first morning I was here I stood on this deck and just looked out over the water, wondering why I ever left."

"Why *did* we leave?" she said.

"Because we were stupid knuckleheads, that's why. And we thought Nirvana was out there over the causeway, just waiting for us."

"You can say that again," she said. "Meanwhile, Nirvana was right here."

"It's the truth."

The door opened again and Ella came out to join us.

"You girls want hot chocolate or are y'all too old for that?"

"Not too old," I said. "Too fat."

"Oh pish!" Ella said. "Remember when I used to make it for you when you were little?"

"Yep," I said, throwing my arm around her shoulder. "I sure do. Your hot chocolate mended plenty of disappointments and broken hearts."

"Remember you used to put candy canes in it at Christmas?" Patti said.

"Only if you were *good*," Ella said, smiling.

"We were *always* good around Christmas," I said.

"That's why you only got candy canes in *December*!" Ella said with a chuckle.

"I *knew* there was a reason," Patti said.

"Come on, let's go back inside," I said, yawning. "It's late and I'm *completely* exhausted from last night."

"Me too," Ella said. "Sleep sounds like a good idea."

"Well, Ella, it's so good to see you," Patti said, giving her a hug. "I missed you."

"I missed you, too, girl. You are a sight for sore eyes."

I gave Ella a parting hug, picked up the Diet Cokes, and held the elevator for Patti.

Back at the Porgy House it was as dark as pitch and maneuvering the uneven ground with Patti's luggage was a bit of a minefield.

"Don't you have a porch light?" Patti said.

"Right? You're not the first person to make that remark. John said he was going to get me one and then we never got around to it. Well, so far."

I opened the door and flipped on the light switch, illuminating the exhibition room and my piano. Patti stepped inside, put her bags down, and looked around. I went back to the kitchen and turned on the light there, too, and in the back bedroom.

"Holy cow," Patti said. "This is a little weird. All this stuff?"

"It grows on you. You want a Diet Coke?" I said. "Come see the kitchen."

"Coming!" Patti walked right in and the first thing she did was open the oven door to inspect the insides. "Cate?"

"Wild, isn't it?"

"Totally. Ain't no way I'm leaving here without baking something in *this* baby."

"Be my guest," I said. I held a Diet Coke can in one hand and a cold bottle of white wine in the other. "Your call."

"Just gimme all the grapes and nobody gets hurt," she said.

I giggled and began the process of twisting out the cork.

"I'm good for about twenty minutes and then I am going to pass out facedown like a starfish." The cork came out with a loud *pop!* "Love that sound!"

"Me too," she said. "You have to be dead on your feet."

"Pretty much," I said, handing her a glass. "Here. Cheers!"

"Yeah, here's to Aunt Daisy getting the hell out of that place in one piece pronto."

"I'll drink to that," I said and we hoisted our glasses again. "Pretty scary, right?"

"Scary as hell," she said.

"And here's what's worrying me . . ."

I told Patti that besides the small concerns I had about Aunt Daisy's business, which she agreed to help me look into the next day, I was becoming more and more worried about her estate. Did she have a will, an executor, a plan? What would become of Ella if she went first and how did Aunt Daisy want her own eventual demise to be handled?

"I mean, those two operate like they're thirty-five," I said.

"True but I can't imagine this world without Aunt Daisy in it," Patti said.

"Me too," I said. "But either we're going to bury her or she's going to bury us."

"Look, she's a very smart woman. I'll bet she's got a will and an executor and she probably has even picked out the outfit, including a hat and gloves."

"Maybe. I hope you're right."

"I want everyone to have cake and champagne at my funeral," she said. "Lots of lovely cake!"

"Does Mark know this? I mean, I'll try to remember it but I don't plan on going anywhere until I'm two hundred years old and I don't know how good my memory will be then."

"Probably best if I write it down somewhere, huh?"

"Yeah."

"Okay, we're hilarious. So give me the short version of what's happening with lover boy."

"He's wonderful."

"Not that short. Elaborate, please?"

"He's trying to turn me into a playwright."

"Now *there's* a practical career. Is he nuts?"

"Right? Well, look, I'm also getting more involved with Aunt Daisy's business so I can pay the rent when I rent something. When she decides to pay me, that is. Anyway, writing a play is just an old dream of mine. And I came up with this idea."

"Let's hear," Patti said and sat down at the kitchen table.

"So, I'm living here in Dorothy Heyward's house . . ."

"Why don't you refer to it as Dorothy and DuBose's house?"

"I'll get to that. Anyway, John says *you know, you really should go down to the historical society and read all her papers.* So I did."

"And you found what? Are you falling asleep?"

"No, actually, I'm getting a second wind here. Probably the sugar in the wine. Who knows? Anyway, what I found in all those boxes and files were lots and lots of contradictions."

She refilled my glass and hers. I pulled a box of white cheddar Cheez-Its from the pantry closet, opening it and dumping a pile of them on a paper towel.

"God, I love these things," she said, eating a handful.

"Me too. In my old life we would've been picking these out of a Steuben bowl."

"And they wouldn't taste as good, either. Okay, gimme some contradictions."

"Well, there are all these recipes for soups and stews for a nickel a serving and two cents a serving."

"So they were broke? Writers starve. Everybody knows that."

"Yeah, but wait. When they got married, DuBose was living with his *mother*. And she was *quite* the force to deal with, too."

"That couldn't have been any fun for Dorothy. I mean, a married woman needs her own house."

"Exactly. One too many hens in the henhouse. So, listen to this. The first thing they do is build the mother a house on St. Michael's Alley and then they build themselves this gorgeous Federal-style house in North Carolina on ten acres or more—I can't remember exactly— but they had a writer's cabin in the yard and a little bridge over a stream and these huge fieldstone fireplaces. It was really something."

"So where'd they get the money for all that? We go from two-cent soup to St. Michael's Alley and the glam life?"

"Exactly! My theory is that Dorothy was loaded. Look, her parents were dead so she inherited whatever they had. *And* she went to boarding school in Washington, not cheap, and later she studied at Columbia University and Radcliffe College, which were also no bargains."

"Well, somebody had to pay for all of that."

"Right? So she came from money. He dropped out of school and worked some pretty low-rent jobs to try and help his mother put food on the table. I mean, DuBose and his mother and sister were so poor that his mother took in sewing and rented rooms but she also did some other pretty demeaning things, too."

"Oh, please tell me that she shook her tail feathers in one of those seedy bars up by the navy base?"

"You're terrible. No, she stood in the lobby of the Francis Marion Hotel and recited little rhymes in Gullah, hoping the tourists would give her a dime or a quarter."

"Wow. That's like being a beggar."

"No. That *is* being a beggar. Anyway, DuBose had all these lofty ideas about living his life as a poet . . ."

"While his mother is killing herself to pay for the gruel."

"Yep! So, he's going to make a living as a poet . . ."

"Now we're really talking two-cent soups."

"Exactly. I mean, DuBose knew how to be a little snob but he *really* didn't want to be poor. So, he struggled with the idea of a literary career, which he considered appropriate for a gentleman of his highfalutin background, versus what he considered selling out and writing something more commercial. Dorothy was the perfect solution."

"Because she arrived on the scene with deep pockets?"

"Yes. And she was already a commercial success as a playwright when they met. DuBose Heyward didn't have the first clue about how to adapt *Porgy* the book to the stage. Dorothy did it."

"You know, it's so funny, you never even hear her name. I always thought DuBose was the creative genius."

"Well, to give the devil his due, he *was* the one who had the very original point of view about the whole Gullah world that shaped the story of *Porgy and Bess.* I mean, DuBose took the accepted view at the time, which was that the African Americans were shiftless and lazy and sat around all day just waiting to please Massah, you know, Al Jolson in blackface, the whole minstrel thing?"

"I'm with you. Heck, Cate, it was almost that bad when *we* were growing up."

"Not with everyone. I mean, look at Ella and Aunt Daisy."

"What? You don't remember because you were really little but I remember that Daddy was more upset about Ella's complexion than he was with what went on between them."

"Come on."

"True."

"Oh, for heaven's sake. How stupid."

"That's right."

"That old skunk! All right, well anyway, DuBose turned the stuffy old Charlestonians on their ears when he described the black world as highly desirable, even enviable. He was completely enthralled by their passion for living, for religion, for love . . ."

"I'll bet that caused some talk around the old Yacht Club."

"Don't you know it? Well, from what I can gather, people from other places like Boston and New York thought he was avant-garde, but people here didn't understand what he saw in Gullah life that was worth writing about. So, it's safe to say that he was controversial."

"You got a picture of him?"

"Yeah, a bunch. In fact, there's one in the front room. Come on, I'll show you and then let's call it a night. I'll help you take your stuff upstairs."

We put our glasses in the sink and rinsed them.

"What's this room?" Patti said.

"That bedroom? Oh, that's where their help slept and supposedly that's the desk he used to write *Mamba's Daughters*."

"Humph."

"Yeah, that's what I say, too. Come in here and look at this."

I turned on the extra lights in the front room and turned out the lights behind us and pointed to a picture of DuBose with George and Ira Gershwin.

"That's him," I said.

"He looks like a total wimp," Patti said.

"Well, there *was* talk . . ."

"That what? He was gay?"

"There was that rumor but I don't think so. I think he was just a gold-digging, self-promoting, opportunistic, arrogant ass and also a total wimp."

"Oh! That's it? But not gay."

"I don't think so. But who knows?"

"Who cares?" Patti said.

"Not me."

"But you have to wonder what she *saw* in him?"

"That's easy. He had a name. And he *belonged* somewhere. She was as smart as a whip, an orphaned vagabond, and she wanted a life in the theater on the other side of the footlights."

"Like you?"

"No, she was totally amazing. I'm just a sniveling novice. But you see, DuBose could give her all of that. But here's the part I'll never understand."

"What?"

"She adored him. She absolutely adored him."

"She must have. Aunt Daisy always said there was a lid for every pot. Gershwin died young, didn't he?"

"Yeah, very. Thirty-eight. So did DuBose."

"Really? How old?"

"Fifty-five. Massive heart attack."

"And she never remarried?"

"Nope. She canonized DuBose instead. She spent the entire rest of her life protecting his name and making sure he got all the credit he was due."

"Now *that's* love."

"That's what I think, too. Come on, I'll even let you use the bathroom first."

All night long I kept waking up thinking I was hearing someone playing my piano. Of course that was ridiculous. And it wasn't like they were playing a whole song. It was a few faint notes here and a few hushed chords there. I thought, boy, Cate, you've got some crazy imagination and I made a mental note to buy earplugs at the drugstore in the morning.

I couldn't tell you when I finally fell asleep but I could definitely tell you when I woke up—it was when my cell phone rang at eight o'clock. It was Ella calling.

"Y'all want some breakfast? I've got my waffle iron heating up and there's a pound of bacon sizzling away in my big cast-iron skillet."

Waffles? Bacon?

"I haven't even seen Patti yet but I'll say *heck yeah* for both of us. Give us thirty minutes?"

"See you then!"

I threw back the covers and called out to Patti.

"Patti? Ella's making waffles. And bacon."

"I'm up!" she said. "Should we get dressed for downtown or are sweats okay?"

"Sweatpants are fine. Let's walk on the beach after we eat and then we can do all the other things we've got to do."

"Perfect. You've got sheet marks on your face."

"Big shock."

We pulled ourselves together in record time, hopped in the Subaru, and we were off. When we got there I emptied their mailbox and Patti picked up the newspapers. We went inside, using my key.

"Aunt Daisy gave you a key?"

"I thought it was a good idea for a whole lot of reasons."

"It really is."

Ella was in the kitchen watching the *Today Show* and turning bacon with a fork.

"Morning!" I said and gave her a hug.

"Sure smells good in here," Patti said and hugged her, too.

"Nothing on this earth like bacon. And I have an apple pie in the oven for that nice nurse. Why don't you girls make yourselves useful and set the table?"

"I've got the mail and Patti got the newspapers. No word from the hospital, huh?"

"Not a peep."

"That's good," I said.

Happy birthday from our friends at Smuckers! Here's Bessie Johnson as pretty as a picture. She's one hundred and four, still likes to go bowling and she sings in the choir! Never misses a Sunday! Willard Scott chirped.

"Humph," Ella said. "She looks like she's past dead, if you ask me! Listen to that fool man up there flapping his jaw. She sings in the choir? I'll bet they wish she wouldn't!"

"Yeah, and she bowls, too," I said. "That's gotta be fun to watch! These place mats okay?"

Ella nodded and I put them on the table.

"Someday they'll have you and Aunt Daisy on that show," Patti said. "Do you want me to melt the butter and syrup together?"

"Hush your fool mouth and hand me a plate, and yeah, melt it quick in the microwave," Ella said and shook her head, hooking her thumb in its direction. "Oh, Lord! It's so nice to have my two girls here."

In minutes we were seated around the table, drizzling hot buttery maple syrup over steaming waffles and snitching a slice of bacon with our fingers before the first waffle was cut. Patti poured coffee and I turned down the television.

"Let's bless this food with a little prayer for our Daisy," Ella said and we did.

Fully fortified by another hearty meal, Patti and I thought about taking a short walk on the beach. Ella adamantly insisted on cleaning her own kitchen. It didn't matter that Patti was an accomplished chef who cleaned and disinfected a kitchen like a surgical theater preparing to operate on the pope. Ella nearly always cleaned her own kitchen and when anyone else tried to help she twitched.

"We'll be back in thirty minutes then we'll run home and change and go downtown to Aunt Daisy? How's that?" I said to Ella.

"You girls go get a little exercise but don't be gone too long though. I want to get to the hospital before the morning slips away."

"Wait," I said. "We can skip the beach? Right, Patti?"

"Ella? We can take you downtown right now, and then come back," Patti said. "Would that be better?"

"No, I'm just, you know, a little uneasy. That's all. Besides, I can drive *myself* in my own car!" she said and I could see her anxiety all over her face. She would drive herself to the hospital, stay all day, it would get dark, she'd be scared to drive herself home. "I just want to wipe down my counters and start the dishwasher. You girls go on now."

"No way," I said, feeling stupid and guilty about not rushing her to Aunt Daisy's side. "You're right. Let's get you downtown. It would actually be better to walk later on when it's warmer anyway."

"Yeah," Patti said. "It's awfully foggy and damp and this morning my throat was a little scratchy. Probably better to wait."

"You girls haven't changed a bit," Ella said, pouring liquid dishwasher soap into its little compartment. "Always in cahoots with each other." She closed the door and turned it on.

"What kinda cahoots?" Patti said.

"I don't know," I said. "I don't know what she means."

"I'll get my coat," Ella said.

"Anyway, it's a waste of gas to take two cars," I said. "Russ will bring you home whenever you want him to."

"Why? Where are you going?" Ella said.

"John is taking Patti and me out to dinner tonight."

"Oh! Patti, wait 'til you lay eyes on this man. He's a *hunk*."

"A hunk, huh?" Patti said and laughed.

When we were in the car, moving down the highway that was indeed like a bowl of pea soup, I remembered to ask if Ella needed help with the bills and so on.

"Ella? Would you like me to spend some time going through the bills and see if anything's due? Check on tenants?"

"Oh, no, honey! I've got that all under control. Don't worry. But you're sweet to ask. I'll let you know if I need something."

"Okay," I said.

Well, that's good. Maybe they were more organized than I thought.

When we arrived at the Medical University, Patti got out of the car, too.

"Know what?" she said. "I'm just gonna run up there really fast to see how she did last night and I'll be right back."

"I can park and come up with you if you want," I said.

"Nah, you look like who did it and ran. I'll be two seconds!"

"Oh thanks!"

"Truth hurts!" she said and stuck her tongue out at me.

I lowered my window and called out, "How old are you?"

She turned to me laughing and slapped her backside, which was sister-code language inviting me to kiss it. I gave her the one-finger salute and hoped that Ella had not seen us. We were still not too old to catch the devil from her.

I looked in the rearview mirror and then the one on the visor. She was right. I looked like I hadn't slept in days. Gosh, what a whirlwind it had been since I arrived here. First, a car wreck that throws a new man into my life, next I find out I'm going to be a grandmother, then

John wants me to write a play, and I turn around to put Aunt Daisy in the hospital! Surely things would settle down now. What else could happen?

I listened to *Walter Edgar's Journal* on National Public Radio while I waited. I swear, if that man could bottle his voice he could make zillions but I suspected that was why he had his own radio program for so many years. He was so nice to listen to.

Soon Patti was back in the car.

"How's she doing?"

"She's awake. They took out the breathing tube and now she's got this thing on her finger, like a clamp. It measures her oxygen in her blood. She's very hoarse and oh, did I mention that she's pissed?"

"I'll bet she is."

"She wants ice cream and popsicles, and two vodka martinis, vodka because they can't smell it on her breath and we're to sneak it in to her in a thermos. And oh, if she doesn't get what she wants, she's getting out of that bed and walking home if she has to."

"God, she must be feeling better. And what else?"

"The doctor wasn't around but the nurse, that nice one from yesterday? She said Aunt Daisy is in for at least one more night. Her fever's down so she's responding to the antibiotic. They just want to be sure she's entirely out of the woods."

"Good. Was she happy to see you?"

"She wanted to know if I was here to claim my inheritance."

"Only Aunt Daisy would ask such an outrageous thing."

"And she wanted to know where the hell you were. Her words. I told her I just ran up to make sure she had a pulse."

"Nice one."

"She said to tell you that if you expect to inherit a dime she'd like to see you at her bedside. I told her you'd be back by lunch."

"Then we'll be back by lunch."

CHAPTER TWENTY-FIVE

Setting: Show slides of the theater in Boston, then of the theater district in New York.

Director's Note: Show picture of the Gershwins with DuBose at a piano and then a head shot of George.

Act III
Scene 3

Dorothy: When *Porgy and Bess* opened in Boston, we knew from the enthusiasm of the audience on opening night that we had a hit on our hands. Gershwin of course went out to take a bow and got a standing ovation. DuBose was there, too, standing behind him and you can hardly see him in the pictures. In any case, Boston loved it! But when the critics got hold of it they started to chew. Was it an opera? Not exactly. An operetta? Not technically. Was it a musical? Not really.

The critics worked themselves into a snit trying to decide whether it was a white show or a black show and all sorts of really stupid remarks were made. Rouben Mamoulian, who was our director, summed up the bickering pretty nicely. He said, "You give someone something delicious to eat and they complain because they have no name for it." Isn't that the truth?

Anyway, the Boston run gave us confidence for opening in New York and there was one thing everyone agreed on—it was too long. So George began hacking away at it and in my opinion I think he destroyed a lot of its integrity. The New York run was only 124 performances. Now that's great for an opera but not great for a musical. Needless to say, George and DuBose lost their shirts. Another problem was the segregation laws. Oh, what a mess that was, especially here in Charleston! It couldn't be staged here until what? 1970?

Anyway, poor old George was never to know what a controversial piece of theater he created with us. He was performing in Los Angeles, working on *The Goldwyn Follies,* and began getting these terrible blinding headaches. He said he could smell burning rubber all the time. He thought the headaches were a result of getting hit in the head with a golf ball. He complained of being extremely sensitive to light. People thought he was just being dramatic. But then he began to have seizures. Finally, during a performance, he collapsed.

Not to get too involved in medical terminology, which I can barely pronounce, the kind of seizures he had were called automatisms, which made him do very bizarre things. During one of these seizures, he opened the door of a moving car and tried to pull the chauffeur out. He said he had no idea why he would do such a thing. Another time someone gave him a box of chocolates and he smashed them up into a pile of goop and smeared them all over his body.

Doctors finally decided he had a brain tumor and they operated on him at Cedars of Lebanon Hospital. After the operation his temperature went up to almost 107 degrees and his pulse beats were almost 180 a minute. Poor George never regained consciousness and he died. He was only thirty-eight years old.

The world was robbed of his incredible genius and DuBose and I were shocked and inconsolable.

Fade to Darkness

CHAPTER TWENTY-SIX

Aunt Daisy

"I forgot my purse," Patti said.

"Where? At the hospital?"

"No, at Aunt Daisy's house."

"So, we'll stop and get it. I know the alarm code."

"Okay, thanks. I hate when I forget things. Don't you hate getting old?"

"No, I love getting old. In fact, I don't know which part of it I love the most. Maybe the sagging jowly thing. How about you?"

"I was thinking memory loss but on second thought I'm gonna go with memory loss."

"Nice."

We got back to Folly Beach and were approaching Aunt Daisy's house just as the mail truck was pulling away.

"I'll go get it," Patti said.

I pulled into the driveway and parked. I got out and stretched while Patti unloaded the mailbox.

"Boy, they sure do get a load of junk! There must be fifty catalogs here."

"Here, give me a pile of that. Ella said that ever since Aunt Daisy broke her foot she's been ordering stuff like a crazy woman. I think they breed."

"Oh, I see. Catalogs have a sex life now?"

"Yeah, they get it on like rabbits."

"You're truly demented."

We went up the stairs, I unlocked the door, turned off the alarm, and we dumped all the catalogs on the kitchen counter. An envelope fell out with my brother-in-law Mark's office address on it.

"Hey, Patti? Do you know why Mark would be writing to Aunt Daisy?"

"Nope." I handed her the envelope and she looked at it for a minute. "Let's open it."

"Are you crazy?" I said. "Aunt Daisy would have us arrested, after she kicked our butts the whole way to Iowa, that is."

"Yeah, she'd keep the cast on for that one. But what is Mark doing that he's not telling me about?"

"I don't know." I thought about it for a minute. What *was* Mark up to? "We could steam it open with the teakettle. I've done that before. You know, open it very carefully, read it fast, stick it back in the envelope, and iron it to reseal it?"

"Iron it? Nah. I never iron," Patti said. "I'll get the kettle going."

So, there we were in Aunt Daisy's kitchen like a couple of middle-school truants, waiting for the water to boil so we could see what that letter from the school principal was all about.

"So you *really* don't know why Mark's writing to Aunt Daisy?" I said.

"Nope. I don't have the first clue."

The kettle started pouring steam and I picked up the envelope.

"Well, we're just gonna find out," I said, and held it near the spout.

"Don't get it wet!" Patti said. "The ink will run!"

"Quit stressing and get a knife."

When it seemed loose enough we laid the envelope on the counter and carefully ran the knife between the flap and the envelope, pulling it ever so slowly and gently until it was open. Patti pulled out the contents. As she unfolded the letter, a check fell out, falling to the floor. I picked it up. It was a certified check for $100,000 from Aunt Daisy to someone named Heather Parke.

"Who the heck is Heather Parke?"

Patti was reading and practically gasping for air at the same time. *What? What does it say?*

"Oh my God! It was for that woman, that woman with the baby! Look at this!"

I stood next to Patti and read.

> *Dear Aunt Daisy,*
>
> *I am returning your check because after a lot of thought, some mighty serious soul-searching, and lengthy conversations with Addison's attorney Mel and his accountant Dallas we all agree that Heather Parke is entitled to nothing. Your generous offer to give her this money would only be the beginning of a life of torture for you and for Cate, because we are certain that she would return time and again to try to extort more money.*
>
> *History is replete with Heather Parkes, young women who make poor choices and wind up with unexpected dependants and eventual disappointment. Addison died bankrupt. If he had nothing to leave his wife and legitimate heirs, why would this woman and her bastard child be entitled to anything?*
>
> *Let her file all the lawsuits in the world. In Mel's opinion and in the opinion of his partners, her suit is without any merit whatsoever and would be thrown out of court. And Dallas, his accountant, says he will sign any papers necessary*

to show that Addison was indeed not only bankrupt but in
such financial ruin that it is unlikely he would ever have been
able to earn enough to satisfy his debts and be solvent again.
Finally, you most certainly have no obligation to this woman.
But your generosity is a testimony to your special nature and
it is what makes us all love and cherish you so . . .

"That little bitch! Did she contact Aunt Daisy directly?" Patti said.

"She must have!" I could feel my head starting to pound. "I'll kill her with my bare hands!" I meant it.

"We'd better put this back, Cate."

We quickly refolded the letter with the check and slipped it back in the envelope. Of course the glue had dried and wouldn't stick. Patti grabbed it and licked it, leaning on it with the heel of her hand to secure it. Finally, it worked in some places and the envelope didn't look as though someone had tampered with it too badly. I hoped Aunt Daisy or Ella would just rip it open and not give the seal much attention.

"You know what's in glue, don't you?" I said.

"Who cares? Here's my question for you. How are you going to keep your big fat mouth shut?"

"I don't know because I am seething."

"You're not going to be able to do that. I know you."

"Well, this was a pretty incredible secret for them to keep from me, wasn't it?"

"Keep from *us*, not just from you. I'm going to have a little chat with my husband and see just how this whole thing happened. He has to know everything."

"Want to go walk for half an hour? I think I need to, so when I face Ella and Aunt Daisy I can have on my game face."

"Yeah, let's do it."

We locked up the house and walked out to the beach. It was getting closer to noon and the tide was out. Low tide and a warm sun were a beautiful combination and I reckoned the temperature to be somewhere near sixty. I began walking quickly and I could see Patti was struggling a little bit to keep the pace and talk at the same time.

"I can't believe Mark knew about this and didn't tell me," Patti said.

"I can't believe that woman had the unmitigated gall to try and get money from Aunt Daisy."

"She probably hired some ambulance-chasing lawyer who took her case on contingency and he just figured he'd keep suing the next of kin down the line until he found some money," Patti said. "Can we slow down just a little?"

"Sorry. I'm so angry that someone would harass Aunt Daisy, I could just explode!"

"It's pretty horrible alright. Listen, she's just some tramp . . ."

"Patti? I don't care if she's a tramp who works as a stripper or a nice person who's a . . . who's a *pediatric hospice nurse!*"

"I'm not sure there is such a thing as a pedia . . ."

"*You* know what I mean. What's the *matter* with people? I still can't believe she had the guts to come to Addison's funeral!"

"Yeah, in that awful weather, too," Patti said and I knew she was trying to assuage my anger with a little humor.

"With *pictures!* I mean, of all the *crust!* And then, to get some lawyer to go after *Aunt Daisy?* Is she *kidding?* I'm so mad I could spit! Heather Parke. What a stupid name. Sounds like a garden in Scotland."

"Yeah, her middle name is probably Lavender," Patti said.

"Oh, shut up, you stupid ass." We started laughing then, like we always did when one of us talked the other out of anger or disappointment or any of the less welcome conditions that were visited on all of humanity. "Oh, Patti! What does this all mean?"

"It means my husband has a brain, Aunt Daisy has a heart, and Heather Parke has some pair of calzones."

"Great. All I need is a pair of red shoes and a dog named Toto."

Someday, when I was more secure, I was going to do something wonderful for my sister.

She looped her arm inside of mine and said, "Look, don't worry. I'll wrestle the whole story out of Mark and then we'll think of how to get her to leave Aunt Daisy and all other family members alone. There has to be a legal way to do it."

"I'd rather slap her in the face about a million times."

"You're right. That would be infinitely more satisfying. Now let's get downtown before Aunt Daisy slaps *us*."

"Hey! Are we really going to bring her a thermos of martinis?"

"Absolutely not. We'll get her popsicles," Patti said. "I'm in no mood for bullies. Or olives."

"Me either. Let's move it."

What happened next was *truly* like a scene from a play. The sisters, the two fiercely loyal felines from the sand dunes of Folly Beach, the middle-aged ones with dreams still in front of them to chase until their last breath, they power-walked, fast and furious, until they nearly collapsed at the bottom of the wooden steps that went over the white sand and scrub and buttercups that would be back to bloom in summer, climbing the flight of steps to their aunt Daisy's deck and returned, albeit begrudgingly, back to reality.

"I hate reality," I said to Patti.

"Yeah, Folly Beach is way better."

I knew we couldn't stop Heather Parke, the tramp with the supercilious name, from suing us until eternity. But she'd *never* see a dime from us and *I* was going to handle this from now on. Not Mark. Not Aunt Daisy. Not Mel and Dallas. Me. I'd find a free lawyer somehow, I'd ask John whom to call, and I'd file something in the courts to make her stop. Or at least to upset her enough to make her go away for a while. That decision meant I'd have to confront Aunt Daisy and tell her I knew what had happened. So what? I was old enough to know that the truth was nothing anyone should ever be afraid to face. Like Ella used to say when we were just little girls, *every back was fitted to the burden*. Well, I thought then, heaven knows I've carried plenty of burdens and I was still standing.

On the way to the hospital, Patti and I rehashed the letter and I told her my plan.

"You're right, of course. But remember, you've got the stash money I gave you for just such an emergency. If you need it to retain a lawyer, use it."

"I'm buying a laptop and a printer," I said, apropos of nothing.

"What?" she said, confused.

"How am I supposed to write the Great American Play without a laptop and a printer?"

"Holy Dorothy and DuBose, Batman! Go for it."

"You're such a jerk, did anyone ever tell you that?"

"Why no, but thank you very much!" she said in the worst Elvis imitation ever. "Thank you."

We picked up a box of popsicles at the 7-Eleven near the hospital and dropped them off at the nurses' station once we got upstairs.

"How's she doing?" we asked the nurse.

"She wants to know when we have happy hour," the nurse said with a straight face.

"She's feeling better," I said.

"And you'll be glad to know she doesn't need a cast any longer. The X-rays showed her foot has healed just fine. We fitted her with a rocking boot this morning, for a little extra support."

"She probably wanted to know how many colors it came in," Patti said.

"Boy, you really know your aunt!" the nurse said and took the popsicles.

We sat with Aunt Daisy while Ella went out to stretch her legs and get a cold drink. It was such a relief to see her with her eyes open and to hear her voice, even as raspy as it was.

"Where have you been?" she said, in a whisper. "Ella's boring me to death."

"You are incorrigible," I said, smiling.

"We got a late start," Patti said, as though she felt the need to confess. "And we took a walk on the beach to shake out the cob-webs."

Aunt Daisy nodded and then she smiled.

"Tetanus! Who knew?" she said.

"Yeah, talk about a long shot," I said. "The doctor said it was only the second time in his whole career that he'd seen a case of it."

"He's single," Aunt Daisy said.

I just shook my head.

"Listen, Miss Matchmaker, I've got enough going on with John Risley. He's practically sending me back to college with this whole Charleston Renaissance business. I don't *want* to go to medical school."

"I'm meeting him tonight," Patti said. "But here's the big question: Is he worthy?"

Aunt Daisy sat up a little and looked down her nose at Patti. Then she fell back into her pillows and began fanning herself.

"Got the message," Patti said and giggled.

"Oh, Aunt Daisy," I said.

There was no lack of drama in this family.

We stayed for most of the afternoon. Ella had returned and Aunt Daisy began drifting off to sleep.

"We're going to go back out to the beach," I said. "John's coming at six."

"Just call us if you need a single thing, okay? You've got our cell numbers, I hope?"

"I put them into Ella's speed dial," Patti said.

"I marvel at your tech talents," I said.

We got in the car and rather than rush right back to Folly, I had this nagging urge to swing by the Charleston Museum to see the piano.

"Do you mind if we make a stop?" I said.

"No, of course not."

"I just want to check something out before we see John tonight."

It was a short ride and in minutes I swung into the museum's parking lot and parked the car.

"This will take five minutes," I said.

We paid our admission and hurried upstairs.

"Remember the old museum on Rutledge?" she said.

"Are you kidding? Remember that mummy?" I said.

"That thing used to give me nightmares."

"Me too. You know, during the twenties and thirties the museum was run by a woman, which was a big deal at the time."

"I'll bet it was."

"Yep, Laura Bragg was the first woman in the country to run a publicly supported institution of science and natural history. And she was a *lesbian*."

"Oooh! Le Scandal!"

"Right? Lemme tell you, sister, back in the day? Charleston was wild! I could write a play just about her!"

"Who knows? Maybe you will."

"I just might. Where are we? I'm lost. I thought it would be in this room . . ."

Patti asked the guard to direct us to the piano and he pointed the way—after this gallery, turn right, two more galleries, turn right again . . .

Inside of a minute or two we were standing in front of the glass case that held the piano George Gershwin used to write some of the music for *Porgy and Bess*. It was identical to mine.

"How weird!" Patti said.

"It sure is."

On its top was a bottle of Rheingold champagne with two lovely cut-glass champagne saucers that looked like ones Aunt Daisy might have used decades ago for a special occasion. On the floor stood an old banjo and a cigarette in an ashtray rested next to the sheet music for "Summertime."

"I wonder who played the banjo," I said.

"Didn't lots of people play it then?"

"Yeah, but I never read anything about DuBose or Gershwin playing one."

"Maybe it's just a random decoration."

I walked around the side of the glass case and got a glimpse of the back. It was uncovered. Mine was covered with a panel of wood, finished just like the piano itself.

"Maybe. Hey, Patti. Look at this."

Patti came around and stood in the exact same spot where I was and looked.

"Cate? I think most upright pianos have an open back anyway."

"Yeah, I know. Usually they're up against a wall. And it's probably for sound, too. So why is mine covered up?"

"Mom or Dad probably had it in an open space or something. Aunt Daisy might know. Let's get out of here before we get stuck in rush-hour traffic."

I looked at my watch. It was almost four thirty.

"Too late. We're screwed," I said.

And, as predicted, we sat in bumper-to-bumper traffic, not arriving at the Porgy House until ten minutes past five.

"You take the bathroom first!" she said.

"Thanks! Maybe he'll be late!" I said, rushing up the stairs.

Patti and I made ourselves as presentable as we could in a short period of time and at six o'clock he wasn't there. Ten after six, no John. Six fifteen, no John.

"Should you call him?" Patti said. "You know, maybe he's got a flat or something."

"Nice girls don't call boys," I said. "You want a glass of wine?"

"You're not a nice girl. Call him."

"If he's not here in ten minutes, I'll do it."

I went down to the kitchen and poured two glasses of wine from the open bottle in the refrigerator. I tasted one and then poured them both down the drain. There was nothing quite like cheap wine that had been sitting in a refrigerator for a couple of days to make you want a Diet Coke.

Finally, there was a knock at the door, which he opened himself and called out, "Cate? Sorry I'm late!"

"I'm right here!"

He gave me a kiss and said, "Wow, you smell good."

The man was a veritable poet sometimes. Freaking Keats. But it should be noted that he smelled good enough to, well, you know what I mean. Pretty delicious is what, okay?

"Thanks! So, what happened? I was getting worried. You know, dead in a ditch?"

"Wild horses couldn't keep me away from you. Don't you know that by now? There was a terrible wreck on Folly Road and my cell is dead. How's Miss Daisy?"

"Doing great, thanks! She's probably coming home tomorrow."

"Where's your sister?"

"Patti? John's here!"

"Coming!" she called back and I could hear her feet scurrying about overhead.

"Oh! Guess what? We went to the Charleston Museum today and saw *the* piano."

"And?"

"You were right, of course. It is absolutely identical to mine."

"Isn't that something?" John said.

"Yeah, it's another one of those crazy coincidences."

"There are no coincidences, Cate. This is another confirmation that you are the one to write Dorothy Heyward's story. Plain and simple."

"I'm buying a laptop tomorrow," I said. "It's time."

"Hi!" Patti called out too loudly from the top of the steps. "Are y'all coming up or am I coming down?"

"Let's get going," I called up to her. "For the first time in my whole life, I skipped lunch."

"Starving?" John said.

"Like an animal," I said.

"Yeah, you are," he whispered, with a naughty expression.

"Hush!" I mumbled.

Patti hurried downstairs, took one look at John, and I wouldn't say she gasped or went all gooey, but there was a marked change in her normal demeanor. Maybe giddy was the way to describe her.

"It's nice to meet you," she said, in her usual way, but I knew better, because she was talking too loud.

He took her extended hand and put his other hand on top, holding on to it as though she was a rare and tender orchid he was protecting from a bruising tropical rain.

"So, you're Patti, Cate's *beautiful* sister I've heard so much about. You're much younger than I thought you'd be. You're a pastry chef, aren't you? How do you stay so . . . I mean, Cate said you were a knockout but she didn't prepare me for *this*! No, ma'am, she did *not* prepare me for this!"

Patti's eyes opened wide; she leaned her head to one side and said in a new voice, one just above a whisper, "Please marry my sister. We'd love to have you in the family. I'm not kidding."

Among the many qualities John Risley possessed, he was also able to lower the volume on my sister.

Massive giggles overtook us and countless disingenuous admonishments flew around the room like a swarm of crazy bees.

My sister's such a great kidder, making jokes all the time! Who's joking? For God's sake, marry her! Do you think your sister would have me? Are you serious?

On and on they went until finally I said, "All right, you two? We can plan the wedding over dinner, okay?"

"I'll make the cake. John, what kind of cake do you like?"

"I like every kind of cake," he said. "Whatever you make is delicious, I'm sure!"

"And you're so sweet to take us out to dinner. Can we make dinner for you tomorrow night?"

"I think that would be wonderful," he said.

"Have you seen the things my sister can do with a chicken?"

"Well actually, only once but I can't wait for an encore," he said.

"I'll make dessert. Do you like chocolate?"

"Hoo, boy," I said, and sighed.

I followed them, turning out lights, but leaving one on so I could find my way to the door in the dark. Patti was completely, totally, and thoroughly taken by John. I know this to be a fact because she kicked the back of my car seat about every two seconds the whole way downtown and she kicked my shins under the table all during dinner at Rue de Jean. And whenever she thought John couldn't see, she leaned over and pinched me. I was going to be black-and-blue if dinner didn't end soon. But truly? I was so happy, blissful really, to see that Patti approved so enthusiastically of him. For the very first time in my life I was with the right man. I had found someone who was genuinely right for me, my sister was talking like a normal person, and I was thrilled.

He was giving her the story on some aspect of the Poetry Society of South Carolina and Dorothy Heyward's involvement with the Dock Street Theater, even after DuBose was long gone. Patti was entranced.

"And I am insisting that your sister write her story," he said. "She's always wanted to write a play . . ."

"That's true," Patti said. "She made up tons of plays when we were kids but you should know she always gave herself the best parts. Just once, I wanted to be the princess, just once! But noooooo! Cate always got to wear the crown."

"Would you like some more wine, Cate?"

"No, thanks, two glasses are plenty. The crown was cut from cardboard and covered with aluminum foil," I said. "And just for the record, she never let me use her Easy-Bake Oven."

"So, you were a baker even as a child?" he said.

"Yes."

"Patti's always been brilliant in the kitchen," I said, thinking, oh Lord, how much manure can these two shovel in one night?

Apparently, their skills in this department knew no ceiling and they continued piling it on until we were interrupted by the jittery vibration of my cell phone, which I had left on in case someone needed me. It was Russ.

"Hey! Is everything okay?" I said.

"Oh, yeah, everything's fine. I just dropped Ella off and I wanted to tell you that Aunt Daisy was asking for y'all. That's all."

"How's she doing?"

"I'd say she's a little cranky but she's sure better than she was."

"So, we'll stop by. How's Alice?"

"Alice? Let's say we talk about babies a lot. Maybe nonstop. I mean, do I really need to know all this stuff?"

"Oh, honey, it's her first baby. She'll settle down."

"No, I don't think so. I mean, tonight at supper I said, *Can't we talk about something else?* She started crying and went in the bedroom and slammed the door. I finally just left to go see Aunt Daisy."

"Nice. Listen to your momma on this one. Before you get home? Buy her some flowers. And when you get there, tell her she's beautiful and that you're sorry. That's all."

"Yeah, you're probably right. I'll stop at the grocery store."

"And we'll stop by and see Aunt Daisy to tell her good night."

We hung up and I said to John and Patti, "It's only eight. We have one short command performance and then we can go do whatever y'all want to do. Go listen to some music or something?"

"Not a bad idea," John said. "There's a new jazz club on Market Street."

"Hey! Is paradise rumbling?" Patti said.

"No. My son is being insensitive and Alice is weepy. Classic first pregnancy baloney."

"Let's get going," John said. "We can't keep Miss Daisy waiting!"

"Boy, that's for sure," I said. "And there's a storm coming."

"Typical Charleston weather for this time of year," John said. "One day you're playing tennis or you're out on your boat and the next day it's freezing rain."

On the ride there, it had begun to drizzle and the temperature was dropping. We told John about how Aunt Daisy wanted us to bring her martinis and he laughed his head off.

"She is such an original character," he said. "So adorable. I just love her. Everyone does. You should see how she entertains my students when I bring them over."

"I'll bet so," Patti and I said.

Our chatter continued until we rode up the elevator together, which was always a somber experience at a hospital. We were feeling pretty good after a delicious dinner and some wine and I was looking forward to the rest of the evening. As we stepped off we saw Tolli Rosol, several other nurses, and orderlies rushing toward Aunt Daisy's room. We started running. I was thinking the worst and when I got there I nearly fainted from what I saw. Aunt Daisy was flailing her arms and legs, sitting up in her bed, choking. It was obvious that she couldn't breathe. She was choking!

"*What's wrong?*" I said to anyone who might listen and give me an answer.

"*Get them out of the room,*" Nurse Rosol said.

"*But what's happened?*" Patti said, just as panicked as I was.

"*Please! Leave so we can do our job!*"

John placed a firm grip on Patti's arm and mine and pulled us outside. We watched in horror through the window. The orderlies were restraining Aunt Daisy, whose eyes were bulging in terror and another person, a man who I assumed to be a doctor, was holding what looked like a big oxygen mask over her face, trying to attach it. At the same time Nurse Rosol was giving her a shot of something. It was all so horrible and I thought they would never get her calmed down, fix what was wrong, and come out of that room. I started to cry and then Patti did, too. John stood in between us with his arms around our shoulders, squeezing us in between our sobs. I felt so completely helpless. What if she died right in front of us? Should we call Ella? No, I knew we should wait, because we didn't even know what was happening to Aunt Daisy so what would we tell Ella? All we would do is frighten her and she was already at home for the night. *Oh God,* I thought, *please don't let this be it. Please save Aunt Daisy from whatever is happening!*

"Come on now, she's going to be all right," he said and I wanted to believe him.

I wanted to believe him with all my heart, but I couldn't, because his words didn't match what my eyes were seeing. Not even close. But a minute or maybe two passed and it appeared that Aunt Daisy was beginning to relax. They elevated the top of her bed and gently laid her back into her pillows with such tenderness I started to cry all over again.

Nurse Rosol turned to us and gave us a thumbs-up. Before I could even process the fact that we had gone from near-death to thumbs-up, she came out to speak to us, followed by the others.

"She's fine," she said. "She's absolutely fine."

"What *happened*?" I said.

I was still reeling. Nurse Rosol dug in her pocket and pulled out a couple of tissues, handing one to me and one to Patti.

"This happens all the time. Respiratory arrest. It's basically a blockage in the airway, usually mucus. The BIPAP machine forces air in, moves the blockage, and then she can breathe. She'll probably not need the BIPAP for more than an hour. I gave her a good dose of Ativan to make her relax and help her tolerate the machine. She's breathing normally now so that's a very good sign. I just want to have the doctor take a look at her."

"Does this mean she won't be coming home tomorrow?" I asked.

"Not necessarily but the doctor will make that call, not me. My guess is he'll want to keep her for another day just to be sure she isn't going to have another episode. Remember, the antibiotics are going to take care of the mucus. And believe me, this is a pretty common occurrence. I'll be right back." She went back to her station and picked up the phone, presumably to call the doctor.

"What do you ladies want to do?"

"I don't know," Patti said.

"I think we should stay until they take that thing off of her face, don't you?" I said.

"Patti? How does my future sister-in-law take her decaf coffee?"

"Any way my future brother-in-law thinks I would like it," she said and actually smiled.

So did I.

"I'll be right back," he said and disappeared down the hall.

"What a graceful, elegant man, Cate. I think you've found the real love of your life."

"Me too."

"And you know what's funny?"

"What?"

"Well, if I understood everything you were telling me about Dorothy and DuBose, you know, how she gave him all the credit for her work and was always promoting him and never herself? And she was the woman behind the man?"

"Yeah?"

"He's going to do that for you, Cate. He's going to help you become a playwright. You're going to have a whole new career. And even though he pointed you to where all the clues are about the Heywards' private life and even though he will probably help you through the whole, entire process, I'll bet you anything that he won't take one ounce of credit. He loves you, Cate. It makes me so happy to see you with someone like him."

"Thanks, Patti. I am *really* in love. It's a little scary."

"Honey, it *can't* be any scarier than Addison, okay?"

"Yeah, he was pretty much the benchmark for scary husband."

"But I have to ask you something."

"What's that?"

"What race is John?"

"His grandmother was an Inuit. Canadian. So he's part Inuit, I guess. But he sure is beautiful, isn't he?"

"Yes, he's gorgeous. Whatever he is, his DNA is the perfect genetic cocktail."

"You have no idea, sister, you have no idea." Patti shot me a look of *oh ho! And what secrets have you not told your only sister?* and I added, "That's all I have to say!"

The night flew by. We drank coffee and the medical staff came and went. Aunt Daisy slept, they removed the mask, and when we were comfortable that she was out of danger, we left the hospital to drive home.

It was pouring rain in torrents and the wind was gusting, swinging the traffic lights and bending the palmettos. I was glad that John was driving. I couldn't see the road five feet ahead of us. But it was late and there wasn't much traffic so we just drove a little slower. When we got home I told him not to get out, that we'd be fine and he didn't need to get soaked to the skin. I was exhausted, and despite the fact that I was not looking forward to telling Ella what we had witnessed, I felt so lucky and so very blessed. I could say that my life was coming back together with at least some shred of confidence. Patti reminded him about dinner the next night, thanked him, and we said good night. We'd talk in the morning.

Patti and I held our jackets over our heads and hurried to the door.

"Hey, Cate?" she said, shaking out her jacket over the kitchen sink.

"Yeah?"

"I gotta tell you, this guy John is a prince."

"I'm going to spend the rest of my life with him, Patti. I mean, it's almost like the hand of God is in on this one, you know?"

Patti shook her head at me and laughed.

"I think we'd better start going to church."

CHAPTER TWENTY-SEVEN

Setting: St. Philips Cemetery.
Director's Note: Photos of New York's theater district, cover of *Mamba's Daughters*, Folly Beach, Christmas in Florida, Janie, and St. Philips Cemetery in the backstage scrim.

Act III
Scene 4

Dorothy: DuBose and I knocked around the New York theater scene for a while after *Mamba's Daughters* had its run, and we suffered with the ridiculous relationship we had with our director Guthrie McClintic and his wife. We were in rehearsals and I really thought we should cut a scene. It was just too melodramatic. But Guthrie's wife was there, weeping at its perfection, and I just stood my ground. Don't you know he accused me of calling his silly wife a nitwit, which of course I thought she was one but I would never have said it. Anyway, he *threw a chair* at me, careful to miss me but I thought, *that's* it. I can go home to Charleston now and all you crazy people can have New York City. The only thing that saved *Mamba's Daughters* was Ethel Waters who sang the lead. Lord, that woman could sing!

And DuBose was feeling the same way that I was, so we decided it was time to go home. It was 1937 and he was offered and accepted a seat on the Carolina Art Association, which managed this very theater. A little later on, with money from a Rockefeller grant, the Dock Street was able to hire DuBose as the resident dramatist. Well, we worked together really. Our mission was to develop local talent, so twice a week, we'd gather up ten local aspiring playwrights and read what they had, critique it, and they'd go home and rewrite it. I loved the work and for DuBose it felt like the old days. We were supremely happy.

Of course there was nothing to prepare us for his mother's death. On June 10, 1939, Janie died from a heart attack. DuBose was devastated and the depth of his shock was a little frightening to me. He didn't want to work, he said he was too tired and didn't feel creative anymore. He started writing to his old friend Hervey Allen, who had moved to Florida, and during the Christmas holidays of 1939, DuBose, Jenifer, and I decided to visit them. Well, we had a wonderful time! Robert Frost was in town and we had the chance to catch up with him and everyone was so happy then. I thought, well maybe DuBose is going to come around. But when we returned to Charleston, DuBose became depressed again. He was worried about money. Janie had not left him very much, but she didn't have very much to leave anyway. We decided to sell Dawn Hill and we did. To be free of that burden should have cheered him but it seemed there was nothing that could. He was sluggish and blue and I was at my wits' end.

We were up in North Carolina, staying with our friends, the Matthews. I thought he should see a doctor before we went to MacDowell for the season but he refused. Finally, he agreed to see a doctor who was a cousin of his, Allen Jervey. Allen suspected a heart ailment but didn't think there was an imminent danger. But on the way home from the doctor's, DuBose had terrible chest pain. Margaret Matthew, my dear friend, drove him back to Allen at the hospital in Tryon and DuBose died there. Just like that. It was Sunday, June 16, one year and one week after his mother died. I was a widow and my daughter was fatherless, the same way I was when I was her age. Jenifer never spoke her father's name again.

We laid him to rest beneath the venerable oaks in St. Philips cemetery. You know, DuBose was not a regular churchgoer. So it didn't seem appropriate to have a big funeral in the church with music and hymns. But there was a poem he had written that I thought perhaps he might have written with himself in mind. It's called "Epitaph for a Poet."

> *Here lies a spendthrift who believed*
> *That only those who spend may keep;*
> *Who scattered seeds, yet never grieved*
> *Because a stranger came to reap;*
> *A failure who might well have risen;*
> *Yet, ragged sang exultantly,*
> *That all success is but a prison,*
> *And only those who fail are free.*

Fade to Darkness

CHAPTER TWENTY-EIGHT

In Control

The weather was not as violent in the morning as it had been the night before but the skies were still pouring plenty of rain. There was no sign of it clearing anywhere on the horizon no matter in which direction I looked. I got up with the birds, because since before the first ray of morning light crossed my floor at dawn, I had been worried sick that Aunt Daisy was down at MUSC all alone having another attack. Of course she had not, or the hospital would have called me. But as I lay there having all manner of paranoid fantasies, I couldn't get my mind to slow down long enough to go back to sleep. So I got up, dressed, put on a pot of coffee, and started rereading some of the notes I had on Dorothy Heyward.

Patti must've smelled the coffee in her sleep, because when the pot finished dripping here she came, barefooted, crossing the floor in her flannel pajama bottoms and a T-shirt, scratching her stomach and yawning like a teenager.

"Hey!" she said and gave me a hug. "You're up early."

"Yeah, I was thinking about Aunt Daisy. Respiratory arrest. Screw that! It scared me to death. Coffee's ready."

"Still raining. Wow." She ambled over to the windows and looked out. "The yard's a mess. I'm definitely not washing my hair for this weather. You want a refill?"

"No, I'm good, thanks. Listen. As long as we're up we may as well try to get Ella to Aunt Daisy's bedside as early as we can. When we tell her what happened last night, she's going to want to teleport herself there."

"You are right about that," she said and pointed her finger at me for emphasis. "Let me just guzzle a couple of mugs and wash my face."

"Take your time. It's just seven."

"Cool," she said and disappeared to the kitchen downstairs.

Dorothy, Dorothy, Dorothy, I thought, how would you like your story to be told?

And as if she was whispering in my ear I heard her say, *I was never as happy anywhere as I was with DuBose. And in this house. And on this island. Life without a great love is no life at all.*

I thought, well, sugar? If we can just keep the dialogue going, I'll have your story on paper in no time. I'd just be channeling Dorothy as soon as I got my laptop plugged in and when Patti went home, which would only be another day or two.

I went downstairs to get another blast of caffeine and continued thinking about Dorothy. We did seem to have an uncanny amount of things in common. Beyond the obvious similarities such as being orphaned and raised by our aunts, and having theatrical backgrounds and being widowed at a pretty young age, I'd been happy here, too. And, with Addison's horrible legacy, I'd learned I could be happy with a lot less, which was kind of marvelous to know, although I'd still say that having pots of money was better than not. But Dorothy knew that, too, didn't she?

So many nice things had happened in such a short time. I'd reconnected with the island and Aunt Daisy and Ella at a very important moment and I'd even made some headway with my wacky daughter-in-law, Alice. But perhaps most important, I might have found my great love right here, too. Yeah, for the foreseeable future, Dorothy Heyward and I had a lot to talk about. And I had hundreds of questions for her.

I called Ella at seven thirty, which, knowing her habits, seemed like a reasonable hour. She said she was just taking an apple-cinnamon coffee cake out of the oven for the nurses but that she had made one for us, too. We'd be there on the double, I told her.

In the car I said to Patti, "You know, lately, I feel like The Thing That Must Be Fed."

"Well, sorry for you, tootsie wootsie, but who could say no to anything coming out of Ella's kitchen? Count your blessings. You could be eating your own cooking all the time."

"You're right." I pulled in the driveway and said, "I think we'd better go in and tell her here, don't you? Better than in the car, don't you think?"

"Yeah, so we can stuff our faces while we do," Patti said and laughed.

So, we hurried through the rain, went up the stairs, and I let us in. Ella was predictably in the kitchen and as we all know, there is nothing on this earth to eclipse the smell of butter and sugar baking with apples and cinnamon.

"Morning!" she said and gave us a hug.

"This is what paradise smells like," I said. "I'm sure of it."

"I'm starving," Patti said. "Well, I'm not exactly starving but if I don't get a piece of that cake in my mouth *tout suite* I'm gonna start crying."

"Well, sit yourself down, chile, and let me cut you some. You want eggs?"

Soon the whole story had tumbled out across the table. Ella was unnerved by how quickly Aunt Daisy had been overcome by the respiratory arrest, and what the medical team had to do to get her breathing normally was just as upsetting.

"What if it happens again? I mean, what if we bring her home and it happens right here?"

"It won't happen here, Ella," I said. "She's on massive antibiotics that are flushing all the possibilities of that out of her system."

"Cate's right. Even the nurse said they wouldn't release her unless they were certain she was completely okay to come home."

Ella got up, wrapped the second cake for the nurses in foil, and said, "Let's move. I can clean this up later."

We got up immediately, put our dishes in the sink, and turned on the spigot. We knew that for Ella to leave a crumb on her countertops, she was gravely concerned about Aunt Daisy, and probably furious with herself for not having been there with her. I checked to see that the oven was off and Patti flipped the switch on the coffeepot.

The ride from the beach to Charleston was something of a challenge. The marshes were so swollen with rainwater and the tide was so high that the waters threatened to wash over the causeway and carry us away to Kiawah Island or Hilton Head. Driving took all of my concentration and focus, and Ella and Patti didn't say much as they knew I was working hard to keep us safe. But after a while my reflexes seemed to revert to auto-pilot and my mind started to wander. My new life, which was in so many ways the mature version of my childhood, seemed so natural to me. My re-immersion into Folly Beach and all its irresistible charms had been almost seamless. Watching the lone egret standing in low water and then lifting into flight like an angel, the twitter of a thousand birds in the early morning, the mango sunsets, the glisten of phosphorus on the ocean at night under a full moon that changed colors on its rise—these events, so specific to the Lowcountry—made me feel rich. But more, they reclaimed my weakened spirit that had so desperately needed assurance and gave me enough hope and strength to go on to try again. The stress of Addison, of pleasing him, impressing his colleagues, trying to live up to some impossible standard that in the end was completely frivolous and shallow—all of that was gone forever. There was nothing I'd left behind that I missed or felt I needed. I was perfectly happy, no, honored in many ways, to give some oversight to Aunt Daisy and Alice's health, more than thrilled to have John in my life and wherever it all led—the play, managing real estate, whatever curveball came my way—I was ready to take it all on. Relaxed and ready. And there was something else, too. I couldn't wait to hold my son and daughter-in-law's baby in my arms. I could not wait for that.

When we arrived at Aunt Daisy's room, we all filed in even though we were supposed to go in two at a time. She was sitting up in bed wearing a beret covered in flowers and working the *New York Times* crossword puzzle in ink. Her eyes twinkled with restored health and the kind of joy that comes when you realize just how very happy you are to be alive.

"Good morning!" she said, still slightly hoarse. "Do y'all know a four-letter word for a two-toed sloth?"

"Unau," Ella said. "She asks me this about once a month. I can't remember the Rhine tributaries or the Asian mountain ranges, but that sloth devil? I got him! So, Old Cabbage, I heard y'all had a party without me last night."

"Humph!" Daisy said. "Some party."

"But how are you feeling this morning?" I asked.

"Right as rain!" she said.

"Well, that's appropriate," Patti said, "because it hasn't stopped pouring for the last twelve hours."

"Yeah, there are palmetto fronds all over the roads and some live oak branches, too. All the gutters are flooded and, of course, Lockwood Boulevard is a swimming pool."

"I'm so glad you're all right," Ella said and took Aunt Daisy's hand. "I was worried sick."

We stayed for about an hour and then Patti and I left on the pretext of finding the right laptop and printer for me.

"So, our Mr. Risley is going to help you find a new career?" Aunt Daisy said.

"I doubt that much will come of this but I want to try. I mean, why not?"

"Why not indeed? You girls run along but bring me a surprise when you come back to pick up Ella, all right?"

"Time she start asking for sursies? Time she went home," Ella said. "Let's take this coffee cake to the nurses."

So we did and Nurse Rosol was glad to have it.

"Y'all are too sweet!" she said.

"Not them," Ella said, feeling full of beans after seeing that Aunt Daisy was going to walk out of there. "That's *my* coffee cake."

"Oh fine!" Patti said.

"When's Aunt Daisy going to be released? Any clue?" I said.

"I'd say, if she continues to do as well as she's been doing, probably in the morning after the doctor sees her."

"Well, listen, I just want to say thanks, I mean thank you sincerely for all you've done for Aunt Daisy. She's, well, she's the most important person in our whole family."

"It was my pleasure," Nurse Tolli Rosol said and I wondered if she could yodel.

I told Ella before we left that she should call us and we'd swing by to get her. She said she would.

The rain had slowed to an intermittent drizzle. The storm seemed to be moving north, toward McClellanville and Georgetown. There was some sunlight breaking through the clouds, sending radiant streams of light across the sky.

"Looks Biblical, doesn't it?" I said.

"Maybe it is," Patti said.

"What's the matter with you? Did you have some religious rebirth you haven't told me about?"

"Hell, no. But every time I come back here I'm reminded how

this place is closer to God than the congested, freezing-cold, super-competitive rat race I run," she said loudly enough to alarm anyone nearby.

"Inside voice," I said.

"We're in a parking lot," she said.

"Whatever. Had enough of New Jersey?"

"Yes. As soon as I get home and kill Mark for not telling me about Heather Whore, I'm putting the house on the market. I can make wedding cakes here and don't people down here get bunions and ingrown toenails? We're moving because there's just no point in being there without my family. I don't want to go back. Isn't that awful?"

"No. I know exactly what you mean. I feel alive here. I feel young here. And my reasons are a lot different from yours, but I don't ever want to feel like I did when Addison was alive. Not for another minute."

"It's a lot to think about," she said.

"Yeah, well, in my case, the thinking got done for me. Still hard to believe, isn't it?"

"Where's the closest Best Buy or Staples? You've got a new life to start living."

By late that afternoon I had my new computer set up in the bedroom downstairs, the one with the tiny desk. If that was the desk DuBose and Dorothy used to write *Mamba's Daughters* it was surely good enough for me. In fact, maybe it would bring me luck.

Patti was in the kitchen making dinner. My job was to make the salad, set the table, and be alluring. Clearly, she didn't trust my culinary gifts beyond poultry and I didn't care if she had to be the alpha chef. I called Russ, who said he'd be glad to collect Ella and bring her home and he reported that Alice's doctor was upset because she'd already gained eleven pounds.

"How far along is she?" I said.

"Seven weeks," he said. "That's a lot, huh?"

"Russ? You want to know the secret of how to get through this pregnancy?"

"The flower aisle at the Piggly Wiggly?"

"My genius son. Yes. We're going to get you on *Jeopardy!*"

"You know, you were right about bringing her flowers and telling her she was beautiful."

"Well, son? Think about it. She needs to hear it. Her entire body is working so hard to produce and support another life. Every hormone she's got is like a whirling dervish. So until she gets to about her seventh month, she's going to be a little extra touchy."

"You mean, I've got *five more months* of this?"

"No, my precious heart, if you're lucky you've got another fifty years."

"Oh, man."

"Listen to me, sweetheart, your life is about to change for the better in so many ways you can't even imagine. You're going to have a *child*! Your very own child to love and cherish and believe me, there is *nothing* in this world that can happen to you that will bring you greater happiness. *Nothing.*"

"Really?"

"Yes. Really."

"Yeah, I know. I guess. It's what everyone tells me. But it's a little scary, you know?"

"I'm right here for you, son, anytime you need me. I'm not going anywhere. You'd be a moron if you weren't a little nervous but don't let the changes in Alice throw you. This is the time for you to be the man, Russ. You know, the protector? If you think about it, she's going through this for *you* and for all of *us*. What more important contribution can a woman make to a family than a life? Try to be extra understanding and realize however quirky she might seem right now, it isn't you and it isn't her, it's her *body* sending her all kinds of messages she's never heard before."

"Like to start eating like a wolf?"

"Yes."

"Like to fall asleep all the time?"

"Yes, like the only time she's not talking about being tired is when she's asleep?"

"Exactly. What causes that?"

"I have no earthly idea. Ask the doctor. I'm sure there's a new study that says it's a vitamin deficiency or something. Anyway . . ."

I thanked him for seeing about Ella and I promised him I would take Alice out to lunch or for a manicure or for a walk on the beach and that I'd talk to her and more important, I'd listen to her.

"I love you, Mom."

"And, my darling boy? You're going to realize for the first time how much I love you when you hold your own child."

I could almost feel him blush, just thinking about his own little baby.

We hung up and John called just a few minutes later.

"Hey," he said. "How was your day?"

"Good!"

"How's Miss Daisy?"

"She's doing just great, thanks. Probably coming home tomorrow. How about you? How was your day?"

"Well, I got a really disturbing phone call from Camp Lisa. I don't want to . . . but well, the truth is I need to tell someone."

Camp Lisa was how he referred to the institution where his estranged insane wife resided.

"You tell me, John. It's fine to tell me anything. You know that." I thought, given Lisa's history, she probably tried to stab someone again.

"Turns out she's got Stage Four pancreatic cancer."

"Oh John. That's awful." It was about the last thing in the world I expected him to say.

"Yeah, she's going. I mean, you know, it's not as if I've had a thought, not a *single* thought of ever getting back together with her, because I knew there were absolutely no drugs or therapies out there that could cure her. And besides, I was all done with her the last time she laced my juice. How can you love someone who wants to kill you?"

"No, I know. I know all that. But still. What a shock."

"They wanted to know if I wanted to see her one last time and if not, what did I want them to do with her remains? Her remains. Gee, God. What a question. Anyway, she's only expected to live for a few weeks. At most."

"Jesus, John. That's a helluva phone call to get."

"Yeah, it was. I was sitting at my desk grading papers. Hopefully we don't get many of those calls in our lifetime."

"Hopefully you *never* get another one! What are you going to do? I mean, what do you think? Is she asking for you?"

"No. The doctor I spoke to said she's pretty out of it, conscious one day and then she sleeps for three. But I'm still in the records as next of kin so I got the call. So strange. I never thought it would end this way."

"I'm sure. Oh, I'm so sorry, darling. I mean, I'm sorry for her, too, you know?"

"Yeah, her life is a very sad story. Tragic, really."

"It is. Listen, speaking of shockers . . ." I told him the story of Heather Parke and he was aghast.

"See? People and their sense of entitlement! It's just incredible. The brazen thing."

"Yeah, so I think I need a lawyer to tell her to back off or else we're going to call the police or something."

"You know what? I know someone. Got a pencil? Here it is. Jennet Alterman. She runs the Center for Women downtown. No doubt she knows a lawyer who'll write a letter for you gratis. Here's her number . . ."

I copied it down and wrote her name next to it.

"But don't you love Aunt Daisy trying to get involved, not telling me and trying to fix it?"

"Your aunt Daisy is a G-flawless diamond, Cate. So, are you ladies still on for tonight?"

Diamonds. Humph. I hadn't told him the diamond story yet. I was saving that one.

"Yes! Absolutely."

He said he'd come by at six thirty. It was cocktail night. Did I have ice? He was bringing his shaker and we were making martinis and playing all the music from *Porgy and Bess* we could find in the house. And he was bringing me a stage play format to follow to write my first draft. Maybe he'd have two martinis, he said and was it all right to sleep on the couch?

"Of course! But I forgot to buy liquor!" I said.

"An insignificant oversight. You've had plenty to worry about and I have enough vodka in this house to share with everyone. My students actually give it to me for the holidays and when they graduate and so forth. Isn't that crazy? I probably shouldn't take it but I do. Anyway, don't worry. And I've got olives and vermouth. By the way, what are y'all cooking?"

"Lasagna. Garlic bread. Salad. Pound cake."

There was a pause.

"God, I'm a lucky man. I might get there on the early side if that's okay?"

"Of course it is!"

Patti stuck her head in the bedroom.

"Did I overhear favorable news?"

"Oh, Patti, come on. The poor woman is on her deathbed."

"Yeah, I know, it's disrespectful. Sorry. Is he upset?"

"I think he's more surprised than upset. There's no love lost between him and her."

"Well, let's be honest here. If she goes, you two could make it legal any time you want."

"I am not ready to even think about something like that. If I marry John it will be when everyone thinks we should have done it a long time ago. Besides, I don't *need* to get married again, do I?"

"No, you really don't. You've got a family and children and I suspect you're not going to starve. But I wouldn't string him along forever."

"Don't worry. I won't. But you know what? I don't think he's going anywhere. I think we are so groovy together that maybe this summer we'll take up surfing."

"I think you need to get your head examined."

"You're probably right. By the way, the lasagna smells really good, doesn't it?"

"Thanks. You know, sometimes I wonder if women ever do any-thing else besides grocery-shop, cook, eat, and clean up the kitchen. I swear it seems to take up way too much time."

John arrived at six with a cooler of ice and all the makings of a little bit of wickedness, including a manila envelope for me.

"Your homework's in there," he said.

"Ah! When's it due?"

"ASAP. There's a deadline for submissions. Thirty days."

"Yikes."

"Just write and don't worry about deadlines. It's content that mat-ters."

"Right. Okay."

In his cooler, resting on plenty of ice, were several brands of vodka, two kinds of olives, olive juice for those who liked it dirty, and a shaker that looked like a penguin.

"Aunt Daisy has the same shaker!" I said. "What is it with this penguin?"

"I brought this for you," he said. "It belongs in the Porgy House."

"Thanks, it's adorable!"

The evening began with necessary and serious discussions about Heather Parke and Lisa. He assured me that he didn't think Heather

had a leg to stand on in any court in the land. And that if I called
Jennet Alterman, all my fears would be put to rest. And of course, Patti
echoed his sentiments.

Patti and I reassured him that it was normal and perfectly all right
to be saddened to hear about his long-estranged wife's impending
death, because she was someone he once loved enough to marry and
because her story was so very heart-rending. There were few illnesses
more misunderstood and debilitating than mental disease. I promised
him that I would go with him or help him plan some kind of ceremony
for her, even if we were the only two people in attendance. Then we
talked about Aunt Daisy, her endless stamina and how grateful we
were that she would be home by tomorrow night.

"I just want to be like her when I'm her age," Patti said.

"I'd like to be her now," I said. "To the irrepressible Daisy McInerny,
Iron Woman 2010!"

"To her good health!" John said and we all took a sip of a martini
from the tiny glasses I lifted from the display case, ones actually used
by Dorothy, DuBose, and George.

With so many serious issues scratching at our doors, and ignoring
the fact that it was a weeknight, we threw caution and prudence to
the wind and let the evening have its way with us. Maybe because we
drained a full penguin, dinner was especially delicious. And of course
all of it was enhanced by my salad in a bag and the frozen garlic bread I
baked, fresh from the Pig's freezer to mine. We told one another the red
wine we drank was a health food and refilled our glasses as we saw fit.

We had so much fun, singing "Summertime" at the top of our lungs
and "Bess, You Is My Woman Now," and "I Got Plenty o' Nuttin'," and
all the songs I could limp through. But no one seemed to care that I
had not played the piano in ages or that we sang off-key more than half
the time. We giggled, ate cake with our fingers, and told each other we
still had it going on, wondering why Broadway had yet to call. I can't
remember who it was that first noticed we were standing in a puddle,

but I stopped playing and turned on all the lights. It was still too dim to see very well. Patti went to get paper towels to soak up the water.

"It's that window," John said, pointing to the window behind the piano. He put his hand back there and then ran it around. Then he got up close to the piano and pulled it away from the wall a little. "You're not going to like this."

"What?" I said, handing him eight or so paper towels to wipe up the windowsill.

"The whole back of your piano is warped," he said.

"Oh no! I just had it refinished!"

"I know. Tomorrow morning when the light's better, I'll pull this out and have a good look at it."

"Cate? You know what?" Patti called out from the kitchen where she went to throw the sopping paper towels away. "Maybe you can just pull the back off. You don't need it and it's not original to the instrument anyway."

"Maybe," I said. "Bummer."

"It's nothing that can't be fixed," John said. "Don't worry. This is no big deal."

"Cunningham? You're ruining my night," I said, and John gave me a hug.

As we all made our way upstairs to sleep, it struck me that we seemed to belong together, a small tribe of merrymakers. John was staying the night, because we agreed that his blood alcohol level might land him in the Big House if he got pulled over. I took some bedding and made up one of the daybeds in the living room for him while he looked on.

"DuBose slept here, you know," I said.

"Like George Washington?"

"Yep. We should put a plaque on the door. You know, if you're miserable out here all alone you can climb in the sack with me," I said, feeling silly and light-headed from the wine.

"Temptress that you are, I don't want Patti to be uncomfortable," he said. "When's she going home?"

"Day after tomorrow," I said. "You're right. I'm sorry. I'm a slut."

"Don't you go calling my woman names," he said, grinning at me. He sat on the side of the bed and pulled off his shoes.

"God, you are so gorgeous," I said, "move over."

"Go to bed, you bad girl. I'll have my way with you all weekend."

He stood up, pulled me to my feet, pushed my hair away from my face, and laid one on me.

I opened my eyes. "Okay, 'night!" I said, surrendering, and went to brush my teeth. If he had said *go sleep in the yard,* I might have thought about it. Good grief.

Patti was in the bathroom, drying her face.

"God, Cate," Patti said, "it's like I've known John forever. It's so funny."

"Yeah, we all just fit. It's just *right.* It's as right as old Addison was *wrong.*"

"God rest his evil soul; I didn't say it. You did."

"That son of a bitch," I said, "but I mean that in the nicest possible way."

"Amen."

Maybe because of the wine or because I knew that John was under the same roof, in fact just in the next room, I slept more soundly than normal. I got up as soon as I stirred instead of indulging my usual slugabed rolling around and trying to recapture the fragments of that last dream. It looked cold outside but at least it wasn't raining. We could use a nice day.

I slipped into the bathroom, not wanting to wake him or Patti and went about the usual business of my morning toilette. I left a new toothbrush and a razor on the counter for John. Then I tiptoed downstairs to get the coffee going. The kitchen was clean. I could not remember doing the dishes and I wondered if Patti and John had done them with-

out me. Hmmm, I thought, maybe all this conversation about Dorothy and DuBose is bringing them back from the dead? With sponges?
Nah, too far-fetched, even for me. But how wonderful would it be to
have a housekeeper who you never had to talk to, deal with, or pay? It
was a nice idea that could only happen in the movies, like that old film
with Cary Grant, *Topper*. Maybe it was something I could use in a play.
Like my daughter, I always woke up with one foot left in fantasyland.

Ah well, they'd be downstairs soon and all I had to offer them was
coffee and the remains of Ella's coffee cake. And then I thought of
Aunt Daisy and hoped she was coming home that very day.

Before John left, he pulled the piano out and had a good look at the
back. The towel on the sill was soaked through.

"That's a pretty impressive leak in that window," he said. "Better get
that fixed right away."

"Aw, shoot!" I said. "Look at the back! It's shot!"

"Yeah, but wait, look at this. The way it's attached is from *under*
the top piece. I can probably lift this whole panel off with a flat-top
screwdriver, fill in the holes with wood fill, let it dry, give it some shoe
polish, and you'd never know it was there to begin with."

"Oh, John! I'd be so happy!"

"Making you happy is what I want to do," he said and I sighed and
thought, when was the last time somebody said things like that to me?
High school, Tommy Brolling, backseat of a car, mission impossible . . .
sorry Tommy, wherever you are.

Patti cut him a big slice of her pound cake and another for Ella.

"I loved meeting you, Patti," he said.

"I think we'll probably see each other again," she said and hugged
him.

"I sure hope so," he said, "and thanks for a wonderful night."

We watched him drive away then Patti turned to me.

"You sly dog," she said.

"Woof," I said.

We got dressed, went to pick up Ella, and let ourselves into the house.

"Ella? Good morning! We're here!"

"I'm in here!" she called out.

Ella was in the kitchen, as always it seemed, watching *Good Morning America,* emptying the dishwasher and putting dishes away, giving them a swipe with a dish towel first.

"Does Willard Scott know you're cheating on him?" I said.

"No, and don't tell him but isn't that George Stephanopoulos the cutest thing?" Ella said.

"Yeah," I said.

"Yeah, he's a honey," Patti said. "I brought you some of my cake . . ."

"Thanks, Patti!" Ella said.

"Which is like bringing coals to Manchester," I said.

"Newcastle," Patti said.

"Whatever," I said.

"Y'all eat?"

"Yeah, we're good. You ready to go see the queen?"

"Yep, time to go check on the old cabbage," Ella said.

"Yep, and Mr. Stephanopoulos will have to find a new love," Patti said. "He'll live."

When we got to the hospital we found Aunt Daisy sitting in a chair in her room, dressed and ready to go. She was wearing a pair of maroon-colored sweats Ella brought her the day before, running shoes, a black wool beret, and black round reading glasses, doing the puzzle from the *News and Courier.* No cast on the foot.

"Looks like they're cutting you loose," Ella said, handing her the *New York Times* arts section, already folded into quarters.

"Get me out of here," Aunt Daisy said, "hospitals are for sick people."

"How about your bootie for your foot?" I said.

"I threw it out of the window," she said.

We looked at each other and knew she'd done no such thing but what she meant was, forget the cast. She wasn't wearing it and she didn't care. I got her a wheelchair for the ride to the car. She sat down like the queen of Mardi Gras and if she'd had strings of beads or hard candy, she would've tossed them to everyone. I had no doubt of that at all.

On the way out, we all hugged Nurse Rosol, who had been so wonderful to Aunt Daisy and nice to all of us, too.

"Thank you for everything," I said to her.

"I had to make sure Ms. McInerny got better quick or I'd weigh a million pounds! That was still the best pecan pie I ever tasted," she said.

"I'll send you the recipe," Ella said. She was so pleased.

"It's on the back of the Karo syrup bottle," Patti whispered.

"Hush!" Ella said. "She's giving away all my secrets."

When we got Aunt Daisy home, she was exhausted. We walked her slowly to her room upstairs. I knew she was tired because she was unusually quiet. I closed the curtains and Patti turned down her bed. Ella was with her in the bathroom, helping her put on a nightgown. The plan was that she would nap for a while and we would wake her up for lunch.

"I'm so happy to be home and in my own bed," she said, as I covered her up.

"I'll bet so," I said.

She put her hand over mine and held it. "Tell me," she said. "How's John?"

"John's great, Aunt Daisy, he really is."

"I told you so," she said and yawned.

We left her room quietly and went downstairs to the kitchen. The old cabbage was on the mend.

"Who wants coffee?" Ella said.

"I think I'll make us some iced tea, if that's okay?" I said, and filled the kettle with fresh water and put it on the stove.

"Humph," Ella said. "If you remember how. You been up there in that terrible New Jersey for too long!"

"Ella? New Jersey isn't terrible. It's gorgeous! Where're the tea bags? Still in here?"

She nodded. "What are you saying? You think I don't watch television?"

"Don't believe it. Those trashy television programs are how they control the population," Patti said.

"Really?" Ella said. "But isn't it too cold?"

Patti and I looked at each other and burst out laughing.

"You have *no* idea!" we said in stereo.

"Oh, Lordy!" Ella said and sat at the table. Actually, it was more like she collapsed onto a chair. "What are we going to make for supper?"

Patti and I looked at each other and said telepathically, Ella's pooped, too. And we decided we would cook.

"Ella? Why don't you go put your feet up? Patti and I got the rest of the meals today covered."

"You know what? I just might do that." A second or two later, she raised herself by leaning on the table with the heel of her hand and stood. "I'm gonna go shut my eyes for a few minutes. Y'all don't need my supervision."

"No worries," we said. "Get a good nap!"

Ella took the stairs and I looked at Patti when Ella was out of earshot and said quietly, "Holy hell. She gave us free reign in her kitchen. You know, they're starting to show some signs of aging."

"That's another reason I want to move back. They need us, Cate."

"I think you're right. And what the hell is the point of living someplace where nobody really loves you?"

"Well, I've got Mark, of course, but after this winter? I think he'd be thrilled to be here."

"You know what? I'm thrilled to be here, even if I don't have my life all worked out yet."

"You mean like having a shower?"

"Precisely. Anyway, let's go to that big Whole Foods and see what they've got."

After scouring and foraging like picky little animals in the woods for the best this and that we could find, we settled on a menu that did a fair job of showcasing our individual skills. Patti was going to prepare a risotto with a mélange of mushrooms—oyster, shiitake, and the hen o' the woods, finished with a truffle-perfumed olive oil and shavings of aged Parmigiano Reggiano. Her entrée was glazed, double-cut, organically raised pork chops, grilled with fresh rosemary and finished with a twenty-five-year-old balsamic vinegar. I was in charge of salad and dessert. I stood there in the produce aisle with a peach pie in my arms, trying to make a decision about the salad.

"What's the matter?" she said.

"I can't decide. Are two bags too little or are three bags too much?"

"We're not buying prunes here, you know." She grabbed two bags of prewashed mixed spring greens, threw them in the cart, and said, "Okay, we're going to make you the president of the slice-and-dice club. And I'm going to teach you how to make chops that will have John on his knees."

"I am your humble slave."

We brought home sandwiches and soup for lunch, which Ella and Aunt Daisy gobbled up. By five thirty, Aunt Daisy's and Ella's kitchen was crackling with warmth and delicious smells and Ella was shaking cosmos in the penguin. Aunt Daisy, still wearing a beret, was seated at the table chatting away. She was in fine spirits. Of course, Brian Williams would be on television any minute to tell us if the world was falling apart.

"Just a little one for me," I said.

"Why? Got a big head from last night?" Aunt Daisy said.

"No, I do not."

"Should I turn off the television and put on some music?" Ella asked.

"Do you have any Gershwin?" Patti asked.

"Have you lost your marbles?" Aunt Daisy said. "I have everything he ever recorded. Ella? Put on *Rhapsody in Blue*. I love that."

"Oh, Aunt Daisy, speaking of Gershwin, there's a leak in the Porgy House window. All that rain we had? It trashed the back of my piano and well, I guess we need a carpenter."

"Bring me my red leather address book from my desk and I'll give you his number," she said.

I got the book and handed it to her.

"Sit down," she said. "I want to talk to you."

I sat.

"I'm gonna talk and you're gonna listen."

"Okay," I thought, what have I done wrong?

"Ella and I have been doing a lot of thinking and talking about our future and we've made some decisions. You know that you and Patti are my only heirs so everything I have is going to y'all, split equally right down the middle. But here's the thing. I'm not dead yet. But I could've been if you and John hadn't been here."

"Oh, Aunt Daisy . . ."

"Hush, before I lose my train of thought."

"Sorry."

"Anyway, I want to retire. There are things in this world I want to see that I have never had the time to see. I want to see the pyramids and take a sail on the Nile. I want to go to Paris and learn the cancan. I want to see the Great Wall of China and go see every play on Broadway. I can't do those things and run my business. So if you're going to inherit it, you may as well learn about it now. I want you to take over as of today."

"Today?"

"Yes. And here's the rest of the deal. As of today, whatever the net earnings of the business are, you get half. If I die first, Ella stays here until she goes and whatever the business earns, Ella gets my half. When she dies, you and Patti own all the properties jointly but the earnings are yours because you're running the business. It's all spelled out in my will."

So there *was* a will. Patti and I were worried for no reason.

"I have retirement money and Social Security, too," Ella said and handed each one of us a cosmopolitan in a martini glass. "And I have excellent health care policies from the state."

"Well, I'm glad you do but can we not talk about dying, please?" I said.

"No, because we have to have this discussion at some point. So, cheers! Here's to Cate! Congratulations! Your future is secure!"

Patti put down her wooden spoon, with which she was stirring chicken stock into the risotto, and gave me a big hug.

"Don't you want to stay and help me manage Aunt Daisy's properties?"

"No, baby. I leave in the morning 'cause I've got cakes to bake. This is perfect for you, Cate. Congratulations! Aunt Daisy?" she said. "Here's to you!"

"Aunt Daisy! Thank you! Thank you so much!" I hugged her so hard I thought she might break and I kissed her face a dozen times. "I don't know what to say."

"Listen, this is the easiest money you'll ever earn. Most of my houses are rented by the same tenants over and over. I only open the office if I need to drum up business. Each house has its own file in my office in this house. I've got a kid from the College of Charleston who manages my Web site. Here's the list of all the people I use, been using them all for ages. Every third year, you paint. Sometimes every second year. Depends on the weather. Think you can handle it?"

"Yes, ma'am!"

"Good! Ella? Is the shaker empty? I'm a little parched."

Ella refilled our glasses, Aunt Daisy knocked hers back in one giant swallow, held it out for Ella to refill yet again, which she did, and Aunt Daisy took a lady sip.

"I'm gonna tell you something and I don't want you to ever forget it."

I nodded my head and waited.

"Every woman needs to have her *own* money."

"We all do!" Patti said.

"Aunt Daisy? I learned that lesson the hard way. Patti always said I needed a stash of FU money. And I had a little but not nearly what I needed."

"Yes, but that's in the past now. And you know what's really wonderful about you taking over?"

"What?"

"Now you'll have all the time in the world to write and you don't need a man to pay your bills."

"Thanks to you, Aunt Daisy. Only because of you."

CHAPTER TWENTY-NINE

Setting: Empty stage, soft light.
Director's Note: Show the silhouettes of Dorothy and DuBose on the back scrim. At the end remarks, Dorothy blows audience a kiss and stays onstage while the lights go down.

Act III
Scene 5

Dorothy: I am one of the luckiest women you will ever meet. I had so many spectacular opportunities and I am so grateful for having had each and every one of them. I actually lived my dream of having a life in the theater. I met and even knew many of the great creative minds of my day. I had the chance to help young playwrights find their voice and ultimately their wings. And most important, I was the mother of Jenifer Heyward and the very happy wife of Edwin DuBose Heyward. Oh, let's be honest, there were days I wanted to strangle him but there was never one minute that I regretted my decision to marry him.

Do I have any regrets? Only that I didn't meet DuBose sooner. And maybe that I was not born in Charleston, although I got here as quickly as I could.

My time with you is coming to an end. After all, it's late and DuBose is waiting for me in that big cocktail lounge in the sky. We still have our rituals, you know. These days we're drinking whatever heavenly thing that they're pouring and then we get together and sing. Not a bad way to pass eternity.

You all coming here tonight and listening so patiently marks the fulfillment of my dreams and I want to thank you for allowing me to tell you my story. Oh, there are endless anecdotal stories I could regale you with—bits of gossip about our friends, about us, but for me it is enough that you now know where DuBose fit in the scheme of things, just how very important he was to not only the Poetry Society of South Carolina and the Charleston Literary Renaissance but to also consider the bold risks he took to make his contribution to the collective social consciousness in matters of racial inequality.

Edwin DuBose Heyward was a great man. He was an intellectual decades ahead of his time. He literally had the sensitive soul of a poet, the gentlemanly manners of an aristocrat, and I cherished his love. Yes, I did.

Thank you for coming and good night.

Fade to Black

CHAPTER THIRTY

The Playwright

The Porgy House seemed lonely without Patti. If I had learned another thing it was that I was much happier surrounded by family. I had placed that recommended call to Jennet Alterman, who could not have been sweeter or more understanding. When I went to her office to tell her the whole story of Heather Parke, she did exactly what I had hoped she would. She took that worry away.

"I'll call my good friend, Susan Rosen. Big family attorney. Fabulous woman! She'll write her a letter that will give this Heather a religious conversion. Just give me her contact information."

I did and a letter went out the next week. Of course, I got the address from Patti, who got it from Mark. According to Patti, Mark wouldn't ever keep a secret like that from her again. Wish I'd been a fly on the wall for *that* conversation!

Having attended to yet another stinky detail of Addison's legacy, I knew I had to say something to Aunt Daisy.

So over supper one night that week I said, "Oh by the way, Aunt

Daisy. I had a lawyer write a letter to Heather Parke telling her she wasn't entitled to a dime and that if she harassed you ever again we'd have her locked up."

There was a pregnant pause in the conversation.

"Good! Thank you!"

"That's my girl," Ella said.

"I don't know why I ever worried about you, Cate. You seem to be managing life very well."

"Thank you! I'm just putting one foot in front of the other the way you taught me to."

Sara and Russ were thrilled to hear about Aunt Daisy's recovery and that I was taking over her business. And Sara was especially excited that I was attempting to write a play. We had talked last night for more than an hour.

She said, "I remember when I was a little girl you used to say that all the time, that you wanted to write."

"It's still true," I said.

"Remember all those silly plays we used to make up?"

"I sure do. There was a lot of laughing around the house in those days."

"Well, if making up stories makes you happy, maybe that's what you ought to be doing?"

Out of the mouths of babes, like they say.

So there I was, with my morning coffee, sitting on *the* chair at *the* desk allegedly used by the Heywards to write *Mamba's Daughters*, writing about the Heywards themselves. I decided to call my play *Folly Beach*. The subtitle would be *A One-Woman Show with Images*. The story Dorothy Heyward wanted me to tell, or so I thought, was about the deep love she felt for DuBose, which bloomed the first moment she met him and then became all-consuming. Okay, I thought, where to begin? Well, she's dead, I thought, so we have to bring her back to life so why not start in the cemetery? If anyone had a sense of humor, it was Dorothy Heyward and she would think it was a riot to rise from her grave, dust herself off, and set the record straight on a few things. Wait! Would she? Crap! Well, my lack of conviction was going to be a *huge* problem so I knew I'd better decide what it was I really thought and go with it. *Scene: St. Philips Cemetery, Charleston, South Carolina . . .*

I was on my way. The floodgates were officially open.

I wrote and wrote, the story gushing out of me in twists and turns like the white water of the Chattahoochee River. I laughed, loving the fact that I was helping Dorothy tell the world so many things they did not know about her, about DuBose, his mother, George Gershwin, and on and on. I was having the most exhilarating time of my life! I stopped for a moment and thought, people made money like this? Incredible!

I did not hear the knock on the door so when I looked up to see John in the doorway of my room I nearly screamed.

"Oh!" I jumped in surprise.

"Sorry. Oh, gosh, I'm so sorry. I've been knocking on the door for five minutes. Then you didn't answer your cell and I thought, oh please, don't let anything have happened to you so I just walked in."

"No! It's fine. I was just . . ."

"In the zone, Cate. That's what they call it when you're writing and you tune out the whole world. Let me see what you've got."

"What? Oh, no! I can't. It's just a draft!"

"I read drafts for a living. Remember?"

"Yeah, but let me just polish it up a bit."

"Oh, please. Come on. What do you think I'm going to do? Rewrite it?"

"No. You might, I don't know, laugh at me and think I'm stupid."

"Never. I would never laugh and I know how brilliant you are."

"Well, let me just try to read it through and spell-check it and then we'll see."

"How many pages have you got?"

"Twenty-two."

He whistled low and long.

"When did you start writing?"

"This morning. I'm waiting for the carpenter. Wait! What if he came and left?"

"Just call him. I'll tell you what. I'll go pull the back off of your piano like I said I would, you polish your pages, and then I'll read while you get dressed."

"What?" I looked down at my lap. I was still in my pajamas.

We lost it, laughing and laughing until we had tears rolling down our faces.

Then he said the magic words, "This is why I love you, Cate."

"You do?" Did I hear him correctly?

"Yeah, a lot, in fact."

"So, how come you never told me?"

"I thought you knew."

"I might faint."

He kissed my cheek. "You polish and I'm going to work on Cunningham."

Well, how was I supposed to concentrate on *anything* now besides the fact that John Risley just told me he loved me? My mind was spinning. What did it mean that John loved me? People love chocolate and opera and cars and a great movie or a song. Was it all the same? Of course not. But did it mean he wanted to marry me? No, you big crazy, I told myself. Or did he want to just keep going as we were? Well, I wasn't going to blow this historic moment by bringing any of my neurotic thoughts up to him. That was why women got called pushy and I wasn't going to wear *that* nasty label. *Oh,* I told myself, *just be happy, will you?* Breathe. Relax. Breathe some more.

I checked the spelling and grammar about ten times and I was ready to print.

"Hey, Cate?"

"Yeah?"

"Come here! You're gonna want to see this!"

I hit the print button and went out to the living room.

"Come around here," he said.

There, written in black ink on the inside of the back of my piano, were the signatures of George Gershwin and DuBose and Dorothy Heyward and underneath George's signature it read, *Folly Beach, June 1934.*

"Oh. My. God!"

"Do you realize what this means?" he said.

"Yeah, that either the one at the museum is a fake or Gershwin rented more than one piano?"

"Bingo. Is this another sign of karma or what? Plus, do you have any idea how much this thing could be worth?"

I shivered from head to toe. Karma.

"More than it was yesterday, that's for sure. I need a glass of water and I think I'm hungry. Do you want a sandwich or something?"

"It's almost three o'clock. I ate. You didn't eat?"

"No, I, well, I guess I was so preoccupied that I forgot."

"Wow, I may have created a monster, Igor."

"Oh, you're a riot," I said and smiled. I went to get a banana and thought, writing! What a great way to lose weight!

I picked up the twenty-two pages from the printer and gave them to John, who was still sitting on the floor, marveling at the fact that I owned a piano actually used and signed by Gershwin and the Heywards.

"I'm going to go change," I said.

"Isn't this incredible?"

"Yep."

Well, the discovery *was* phenomenal but I wasn't telling anyone about it except Patti and the kids and Aunt Daisy and Ella. It would be good for John's students to see it, because it would add more authenticity to the whole Porgy House story and bring it all to life. I wondered then if the museum's piano was signed as well. It didn't matter really. Mine *was*. What a piece of luck!

I was dressed and putting on some makeup and I heard John coming up the steps.

"Cate?"

"Yeah? It's terrible?"

"No, Cate. It's absolutely wonderful. I'm gonna put the curse on you now." He walked over and put his right hand on my shoulder. "God save you, you're a writer."

"Oh, John! You really think so? I'm so happy!"

"Just keep writing. I wouldn't change a word."

So I did.

February finally turned into March and flowers were in bloom everywhere you looked. John's wife, Lisa, passed away and John felt terrible.

"What did you tell them to do? I mean, did you make arrangements?"

"I told them to have her cremated and to send me the ashes."

"Oh, John. I'm sorry, baby."

"It's okay."

"So, what are you going to do with her ashes?"

"I don't know. I guess I'll keep them in the closet until I figure that out."

"Look, when you get them, we'll pick a nice windy day and maybe we'll go down to the beach across from the Morris Island Lighthouse and let her spirit fly. If you want, I can probably even find a willing member of the clergy to put a blessing on them?"

"You'd do that for me?"

"John? I'd do anything for you. You know that. I love you."

I did. I surely did.

And as threatened or promised, depending on your point of view, Aunt Daisy and Ella put on their vagabond shoes and started combing the globe. They sent me postcards from everywhere. I especially loved the ones from Egypt that were pictures of them riding on camels.

They spit! That was all Aunt Daisy wrote on the card. Classic Daisy McInerny.

And while they were away, I collected their mail, paid their bills, and took care of the dozen houses that were someday to be mine and Patti's. I hoped *that day* was never going to come.

By the middle of March, Alice was throwing up all the time but still gaining an alarming amount of weight. She cried all the time and Russ, who had become *poor Russ,* had his hands full. I walked the beach with Alice and tried to tell her that her feelings were normal. But I think all she *heard* was that her pregnancy wasn't special and that she wasn't the only woman in the world who ever had a baby.

"If she wants to sulk, let her sulk," Patti said.

"I don't think it's healthy, Patti, and it's not good for Russ, either."

"Then maybe you can find a nice way to remind her she has a husband who needs a healthy wife and a happy home?"

"Oh sure!" I laughed and said, "Tell you what. Since she's your niece-in-law, you have every right to have an opinion. So why don't *you* call her up and tell her that?"

"Are you kidding? I like my life. You think I want that little crank to come up here to New Jersey and kill me?"

"My poor son," I said.

"Truly. He carries a heavy cross. Say, how's your play going?"

"Oh, Patti, I am so nervous about this. I finished it. I mean, I stopped working on it because John said it was ready and that I was just whaling on a dead horse. Anyway, John *loves* it, and of course, I never could have written this without him."

"He helped you a lot, huh?"

"Well, *yeah*! He didn't actually write it, I did that, but he helped tighten it up, you know, he made suggestions."

"Well, good! You know what? It sounds like he's the Dorothy to your DuBose, you know, as writing partners?"

"Yeah, he sort of is! So then he wrote a letter and submitted it to the Office of Cultural Affairs, because he wants to produce it in a little black box theater at the College of Charleston."

"And he can't do it if they don't approve it?"

"I'm not sure how it all really works but if it's going to be advertised in all their printed materials it has to be accepted. So I'm waiting to hear if it's *worthy*."

"Worthy? God! What a scary word! I'd be a wreck, too. So when do you hear?"

"I guess when they make up their worthy minds."

"Ugh. Well, you call me *the second* you hear anything, okay?"

"Listen, if they say yes, you'll hear me screaming the whole way to Alpine. If they say no, you may as well take my number out of your speed dial."

"They're going to say yes, Cate. I can feel it in my bones."

"Wouldn't that be a dream?"

And it *was* but not the dream I expected. I was just coming back from the Next Stop Morocco, a house next to the Washout, where all the surfers went or I should say *hung out*. It was the last property Aunt Daisy acquired before she retired and hit the road. John's car was parked in my yard. I hopped out of the Subaru and there he stood with a bottle of champagne and the most incredulous expression I'd ever seen on his face.

"What's up? Did you *hear*? You *heard*! They said . . . *what*? *Tell me!*"

"You are one amazing woman," he said, shaking his head and smiling.

"*Why? Tell* me, you *stinker!*"

"So, I'm sitting in my office eating a tuna salad sandwich on whole wheat and the phone rings. It's not just some flunky calling me it's Ellen Dressler Moryl, the director of the entire Office of Cultural Affairs."

"*And?*"

"And she tells me who she is and all that, like I don't know, and then she says, *so, Professor Risley? How wed are you to producing this play* Folly Beach *at the college?* And I say, I think it's a fine first effort, don't you? Emerging voice and all that stuff. And she says, *Oh, yes, yes! But I happened to mention it to one of my colleagues from the Dock*

Street Theater and they just went crazy to put it up themselves! You see, the Dock Street is a little bit excitable when it comes to anything about DuBose and Dorothy . . ."

"Wait! Stop! Are you telling me that the *Dock Street Theater* wants to present my play?"

"Yes."

"For *real*?" I think I was squealing then.

"I'm still the director but, ma'am? You are the cat's ass! I *knew* you could write! I just *knew* it!"

He put the champagne down on the steps, grabbed my arms, and swung me around.

"They love it?"

"They *adore* it!"

My heart was pounding so hard I thought I had better sit down, so I sat on the bottom step.

"I am . . . I'm completely shocked! I don't even know what to say."

"Well, why don't we have a glass of champagne and plan our response."

"I think the answer is a big fat yes!"

"No kidding?"

"Stop! Listen, I'm drinking out of Dorothy's glasses tonight and if you tell I'll pinch you!"

"I'm not telling a soul."

I got up and unlocked the door. "I still don't have a porch light, you know."

"I'll go to Lowe's tomorrow."

"Talk's cheap," I said.

We drank the champagne and I called everyone I knew. There were screams of delight from South Carolina to California and of course, Patti was beside herself with a hefty case of glee.

"I'm making a giant cake of the Dock Street Theater for opening night and I'm baking it in Dorothy's oven."

I laughed and said, "Be my guest!"

"Oh, Cate, this is just *thrilling* news!" she said.

"Yeah, I'm pretty thrilled, like right down to my toes. I just can't believe it."

"What did Sara say?"

"She's quitting her job tonight, she's flying here as soon as she can pack, and we start rehearsals next week."

"She's playing Dorothy? Hoo, boy!"

"Look, she's John's problem to direct, not mine. But you know what? I think she'll do anything he tells her to. She's stubborn but she's not stupid. This is an enormous opportunity for her."

"For all of you, Cate. This is an incredible opportunity for all of you. Oh, I am so proud of you!"

"Thanks, Patti. I love you, you know."

"I know that."

"Yeah, but sometimes you can't say it enough."

That weekend, I picked Sara up at the airport.

"Mom!"

I was waiting for her in baggage claim and there she was, hurrying to me. One minute I was alone in the world and in the next I had my beautiful daughter's arms around my neck. I hugged her back as though I had not seen her in years.

"Do you have much luggage?"

"Um, Mom? I have everything that I could cram in three suitcases and ten more boxes coming at some point. My friends are sending them. Whew! I can't believe I'm here!"

"Me either. This is so incredibly wonderful."

"I've already memorized half of the lines, too."

"Oh, honey, that's great. We start rehearsals on Monday. Life's pretty surreal, isn't it?"

"I'll say. Dad kicks the bucket and *boom*! Meet Cate the Beach Bunny playwright!" She started to giggle like a schoolgirl and the music of her laughter was so infectious that people, milling around waiting for their bags, too, looked at us and smiled.

Beach Bunny?

It was only with the help of two stalwart skycaps that we were able to load her bags into my SUV. Each one was a hernia-maker in its own right. I pulled out of the parking spot, paid the toll, and left the airport.

"How're we going to get these terrible bags of mine in the house?"

"Aunt Daisy has an elevator."

"Oh, I thought I was staying at the Porgy House with you!"

"Aunt Daisy wanted you to stay in her house if you would, because she's in Greece and you know she worries about bandits all the time."

"Mom! Come on! I want to be with *you*."

"And the Porgy House has no shower . . ."

"No shower? So, like . . . how in the world do you wash your hair?"

"With considerable determination and about fifty different yoga poses. And it has no television, either."

"You're kidding, right?"

"Nope."

"So, what are *you* doing there? I mean, like what the hell, Mom. You're a creature-comfort kind of girl."

"When you see it, you might understand. It grows on you."

"Oh, wait. This is about John, isn't it? He sleeps over and you don't want me to hear you guys getting crazy."

I pulled the car over to the side of the road and said, "You listen to me and hear me good, young lady. *Yes,* it's because of John and you're right, I *don't* want you to hear your mother having sex. Happy? And guess what else? John Risley is the nicest, finest man I know and he makes me happier than anyone I have ever known in my entire life. Furthermore, the only reason you are here is because of *him*. *He* is the one who insisted on you playing Dorothy. Sight unseen, he wanted *you*."

"Mom . . ."

"I'm not finished. I also don't think it's a good idea for us to rehearse all day and then be together all night. You're twenty-five years old. When it gets dark, all adults should retreat to their own camps. You and I have a tremendous opportunity here, Sara. The world comes to

Piccolo Spoleto, scouts from every casting company on and off Broadway. Let's not blow it because you don't like the idea of your mother being in love with someone you don't know. Give this a chance, Sara. Now, if you don't think you can abide by my wishes, tell me right now and we'll go straight back to the airport and I'll buy you a ticket to Los Angeles. No hard feelings."

"Jeesch, Mom. Seems to me somebody else memorized *their* lines."

"What's it gonna be?"

"So when do I get to meet John?"

"Tonight. He's so excited to meet you he got a haircut."

"He did?"

"Yeah."

"That's pretty sweet."

We sat in silence for a few more minutes.

"Uh, Mom?"

"Yeah?"

"We can go now. Why don't we all try to be adults here and give your plan a chance? But if I get scared all by myself in that big house, can I come over?"

"On occasion. Not too often."

"Wow. He *must* be something."

"He is."

"Russ likes him. He said so."

"So does Alice."

"That's it! I'm not saying one *freaking* word. If Alice likes him he must be a god. That snippy thing doesn't like *anyone*."

"That snippy thing is so sick that I actually feel sorry for her. But between us? Her behind is as big as Texas."

"Oh my God! Really? When are we seeing them?"

"Tomorrow . . ."

We talked and gossiped like old friends the whole way out to Folly Beach. Once the boundaries were established, she took a deep breath and appeared to be acting her age. I hoped it would last. And when I told her that we had the piano Gershwin used in our possession she was absolutely astounded.

"Mom, that's like totally amazing!"

"I know."

I helped Sara get her bags into the house and gave her the key I had made for her. Fortunately, there was a guest room on the first floor—and it was a beautiful one—so we didn't have to push and pull those horrible bags of hers up the steps. I pulled back the curtains and there was the Atlantic Ocean, and Sara stood at the sliding glass doors with me, awestruck. There were millions of white caps and ripples and the ocean was rolling in its glistening cobalt expanse as far as the eye could see.

"Wow," Sara said.

"Yeah, that about sums it up," I said and smiled.

"Not a bad room, huh, Mom?" She threw herself on the queen-size bed and bounced, making a guttural noise that suggested exhaustion.

The room was a pale shade of apple green and the fabric on the curtains and headboard was a dusty tangerine and green wide plaid that was embroidered over the plaid with olive green vines and flowers a deeper shade of peach. I realize that sounds ungapatched and maybe even fachalata but it was really beautiful. Aunt Daisy's taste in fabrics was absolutely top-drawer.

"Not too shabby."

"You can come over and wash your hair any time you want."

"Thanks, honey. So get yourself settled and call me to let me know you're ready. John's picking me up at six so we'll be right over. Oh, and here's the key to Aunt Daisy's car, so you have wheels."

"Thanks. You're right, Mom, as usual. This is the perfect place for me to stay."

I gave her a kiss on the cheek. "See you in a bit," I said and left.

Dinner that night was just wonderful. We went to Oak Steakhouse on King Street. They gave us a table downstairs near the piano and as coincidence would have it once again, the pianist was playing Gershwin, but he also played a lot of Cole Porter, so I wasn't completely spooked.

But the most important thing was that John and Sara took one look at each other and nearly drowned in their mutual delight. All through a dinner of outstanding rib eyes, filets, and asparagus so fresh you could almost hear them growing, we talked about Dorothy and DuBose and that famous summer of 1934 when Gershwin stayed on Folly Beach for seven weeks.

"I think Dorothy thought he was a colossal pain in the derrière," I said. "There's a letter somewhere in her papers where she talks about Gershwin saying that there were so many alligators on Folly that they walked right up to his door, which of course is a wild exaggeration."

"Oh, I think old George was just rapturous about being here," John said.

"Rapturous?" Sara said, and giggled. "Twenty-five-cent word. Good one."

"No seriously, y'all, here comes George Gershwin, Mister Bon Vivant of New York and Hollywood, to a crazy little island surrounded by mosquito-infested marshes and there's not even a phone. What does he do? He takes off his shirt and goes around the town showing off his muscles and getting a tan. There's even a story about how he hired Abe Dumas . . ."

"From M. Dumas and Sons on King Street?" John said.

"Yep."

"Gee, even I didn't know that!" he said.

"Or maybe it was his brother or his son, but anyway he hired one of them to be his driver slash tour guide and there are plenty of stories there, too. Anyway, he was quite the character, way bigger than life, practically flamboyant, and I have no doubt that his bohemian shenanigans worked Dorothy's nerves."

"Why? I would think George Gershwin would be a blast?" Sara said.

"Well, I'm sure he was fun but remember he made the Heywards, who were arch-conservatives, to the outside world at least, wait for years until he got around to making the musical with them. Dorothy was struggling to live on DuBose's income and that was no easy task."

"Oh, I get it. Gershwin was rich and they knew it. And he probably knew they weren't and she thought he didn't mind stringing them along?" Sara said.

"My smart daughter," I said and blew her a kiss. "What Gershwin didn't know was that Dorothy was loaded, too."

"Wait, I don't get it. Why was she living on like bread and water when she had a lot of money? I saw those recipes of hers."

"Because she didn't want to emasculate DuBose with her trust fund," I said.

"Although," John said, "it should be pointed out that DuBose didn't mind dipping into Dorothy's resources to build a house for his mother."

"Listen, John. That could've been Dorothy's idea. Remember they were living with his mother, Janie, and she was some piece of work."

"What a story," Sara said.

"That story is the why of how we all came to be together tonight," I said.

We dropped Sara off at Aunt Daisy's and when she went to give me a good-night hug she whispered, "He's fabulous, Mom."

"I know," I said and smiled with relief.

John walked her inside to check for robbers and thieves and came back a few minutes later.

"She's a wonderful girl," he said. "She's going to make an incredible Dorothy Heyward. She even looks like her a little bit."

"Thanks! And I think you're right. She's tiny like Dorothy was. If she bobbed her hair like they did in the thirties she might be a dead ringer with the right makeup."

"Well, we can fit her with a wig and see," John said. "Anyway, I'm anxious to start rehearsals, aren't you?"

"I'm just anxious period," I said.

"I've got the cure for *that*," John said, and made a low-pitched growl that sounded like a leopard getting ready to pounce.

Men. So silly.

We arrived back at the Porgy House and I was still chuckling to myself.

"Want to have a nightcap?" I said.

"What do *you* think?" he said.

My anxiety was completely addressed and it magically dissolved before the night ended and I thought, whew, if Sara had been in the next room during this steamy episode, she'd spend the rest of her life in analysis.

Monday at ten Sara and I made our way to the Dock Street Theater.

"I fully expect the spirit of Emmett Robinson to open the door," I said, opening the door myself.

"Who's he?" Sara said.

"He was the most cherished artistic director of the Footlight Players and he was Alfred Hutty's best friend. His daughter is a new friend of mine." I told Sara how Jennet had helped me tell Heather Parke to get lost.

"Wow. I want to meet her."

"Oh, you will! I'll make sure you do."

We were meeting John with a lighting person, a sound engineer, a stage manager, and two assistants to see about props and costumes. The main stage was free so we decided we would begin there and just do a read-through to get used to the acoustics. Everyone trickled in and by ten thirty had introduced themselves to one another and we got started. A familiar face arrived with a cooler of drinks and sandwiches.

"Don't I know you?" I said.

"I'm Christi Geier. I think we met at the Red Drum."

"Oh, right! Well, how nice to see you again. Wow, you've got a job, your LSATs, and now this? That's a lot to juggle."

"Yeah, but you know what? I loved Professor Risley's playwrighting class so much, when he put out a call for volunteers, I jumped at it! Who wouldn't want to work on a play about the Heywards?"

"Actually, it's more about Dorothy."

"Oh, really? Have you read the script?"

"Yeah, about a thousand times. I wrote it."

"Oh! I didn't know you were a playwright."

"I didn't either. Well, now I am . . ." I could feel myself blushing.

"Oh my goodness. Congratulations!"

"Thanks! And that's my daughter . . ."

I sat in the audience in different places to see if I could hear Sara. Her young voice was so clear and carried so well, the only place I had a little trouble hearing her was the far corners of the house. John and the sound engineer decided to place several discreet and tiny wireless mikes on the floor stage left and right, which corrected that issue. Lists were made of props and costumes scene by scene and over the next three weeks, the props and costumes were found and approved or not and it looked like we were finally getting our proverbial act together.

At last, we got to dress rehearsal and it was almost flawless. Sara said, not to worry, she would be the reincarnation of Dorothy herself within twenty-four hours. The word was out that our play was a *must-see* and every single performance was sold out.

Aunt Daisy and Ella were home, for a change, Patti and Mark were flying in that afternoon. Alice and Russ were coming for an early dinner and we were all mighty excited. As soon as Patti and Mark checked into the Jolly Buddha, her favorite, we were all to gather with John at Aunt Daisy's and Ella's for moussaka and feta cheese salad and what other Greek delights Ella had taken a shine to on their trip. Patti apologized at least ten times for not making the cake. She'd had a wedding to bake for or she would have come down days ago. I told her it didn't matter one bit. There was no way I'd be able to swallow food. I just wanted to get to the theater and have the first performance of *Folly Beach* behind me.

"I've been stuffing grape leaves over here, Mom. Gross. When are you coming over?"

"I'll be there soon." I was just waiting for John to arrive. It was just three.

A few minutes later he knocked on the door.

"Hey," he said. "You look beautiful! Success must agree with you!"

I had on a new dress, something kind of silky and retro that I thought Dorothy might have worn.

"Oh, John! What a journey this has been. How can I ever thank you?"

"Oh, I know a few things . . ."

"Bad!" I said and then, "oh, John, I'm so nervous about tonight."

"Don't be. Sara's got this baby nailed. All you have to do is show up and collect tons of applause and bouquets with your daughter."

"And you, too, Mr. Director."

"I only had the slightest hand in this entire venture, ma'am," he said in what I think he thought was a Rhett Butler accent.

You see, this was one of the small peculiarities with theater people—they spoke in accents whenever they felt like it, leaving you to guess who they were imitating.

We went to Aunt Daisy's and stayed for only an hour. Sara was anxious, too, so we thanked everyone, kissed everyone, and they all told us to go break a leg. Happily, we arrived at the Dock Street unscathed and before we knew it, our eight o'clock curtain time was gaining on us. I went backstage to kiss Sara for luck. She turned to me in her dressing room, and with her wig, makeup, and period dress, she was almost Dorothy Heyward in the flesh. I was dumbfounded.

"Well, darling, I just came back here to say knock 'em dead."

"Thanks, Mom," she said.

"Need anything?"

"No. I've got it all covered. And Mom?"

"Hmmm?"

"Thanks for this, you know, this chance."

"My pleasure." My eyes started to tear. "Okay then, I'll be the wild one in the back row with Aunt Daisy and the gang."

The theater was filled and the lights were going down. The stage manager was calling *places* and a few minutes later the curtain rose. Sara climbed out of Dorothy Heyward's grave, brushed herself off, kissed her fingertips, and touched the headstone of DuBose right next to hers. Then she came down center stage and spoke.

"I married an actual renaissance man. Yes, I really did! The story I have to tell you is about the deep and abiding love we shared . . ."

Ninety minutes later the curtain fell, the audience was silent, and then, after what seemed like a year, there began the sound of thundering applause that grew so loud I started to cry. Sara took her bows, John his, and then they waved me up to the stage. People stood as I tried to make my way there without tripping or just falling out of my shoes and dissolving into a pool of relief. I couldn't believe how well it had gone but it was true. They cheered, they even whistled, and I joined Sara and John onstage. Somewhere in the back of the theater a small woman arose from her seat, a small woman who was the clone of Dorothy Kuhns Heyward. She smiled at us, we acknowledged her, she saluted us, and she vanished in front of our eyes. I caught John's and Sara's faces and their eyes were wide in surprise. But we should not have been surprised. After all, this was the Lowcountry, where impossible becomes possible every single day.

EPILOGUE

September 2010

"Hey, I got here as fast as I could!" John said. "How's Alice?"

"Screaming her brains out," I said. "Poor thing, she's waiting for the anesthesiologist to show up and give her an epidural. Poor Russ is in there, sweating. And she's two weeks early. She's probably scared to death."

"Is her mother on the way?"

"Maureen? Last I heard she was trying to get a flight," I said.

We were gathered in the lobby outside the emergency room where Alice was being admitted. They were going to move her up to labor and delivery as soon as they finished the paperwork.

"You want a bottle of water or something?" he said.

"Gosh, that would be great," I said, "it's only about a thousand degrees."

"Yeah, and it's not humid, either," he said. "I'll be right back."

It was so humid that when I took off my sunglasses, there was water under my eyes. Even the hair on my arms, which wasn't much more than light fuzz, was swollen and going in different directions. Never mind the hair on my head. It was a ponytail day, with gel.

Russ appeared from behind the swinging doors.

"Mom?"

"What's the matter?"

"I can't take it, Mom. She's calling me things I didn't even know she knew the names of!"

"*Get* back in there! This *instant*! All you have to do is *listen*! She's going *through* it! She's dealing with the pain the same way most women do! They scream and yell because it hurts like hell! Where's the anesthesiologist?"

"I'll go find out!"

"Good idea."

He disappeared again.

John came back with ice-cold water and I was glad to have it.

"There was a Russ-sighting."

"Oh, yeah? Is everything okay?"

I laughed and said, "Yeah. But it might be nice if the doctor would give her an epidural soon. Russ said she's calling him some very naughty names. I don't blame her."

"Yeah, you've been there."

"I called Addison every filthy thing under the sun. But then he *was* every filthy thing under the sun."

"Oh, did I tell you I heard from Manhattan Theater Club?"

"No! And?"

"They want to present *Folly Beach* in the spring!"

"With Sara?"

"With Sara, and you and me!"

"Wait, John! I have Aunt Daisy's business to see about. I can't go anywhere!"

"Yes, you can. It's only a two-week run and I already called Miss Daisy because I knew that was what you'd say. She's home that whole month and she'll cover for you."

"She will? Wonderful! So how many productions does that make?"

"Including San Francisco? Fourteen."

"Unbelievable."

"Yeah, so what are you writing about next?"

"You're kidding right?"

"No, ma'am! You've got to get back to the desk and write!"

"After the baby's born."

"Well, in most cases, that would be in a few hours."

"After they bring the baby home then."

"That could be as soon as tomorrow."

"After the baptism then."

"Do I detect a little reluctance on the part of America's newest playwright sensation to get back to business? Do you want to be known as a one-hit wonder?"

"No!" But what was I going to write about?

Russ reappeared. He looked haggard.

"We're going upstairs."

"Did she get her epidural?"

"No, the doctor said it was too late. She's nine and a half centimeters. But she's gonna be in room 516."

"What? You'd better get upstairs on the double, boy, or you're gonna miss the whole thing!"

Russ spun around and was gone. We took the elevator up to the fifth floor and waited. About an hour later Russ came and found us. He was smiling so proudly, just beaming really.

"She's a girl. You have a granddaughter, Mom. Her name is Daisy Ella and she's the most beautiful little girl in the whole entire world."

"Oh, Russ!" I threw my arms around him and hugged him with all my might. "Oh! I can't wait to meet her!"

"Congratulations, Russ!" John said and shook his hand soundly.

"Thanks!"

All summer long, Aunt Daisy and Ella had been planning nurseries for the baby. Ella was crocheting blankets and Aunt Daisy was shopping. They decorated an elaborate baby's room for Russ and Alice at their house but they made another even more elaborate one at their own house on Folly Beach. We could already see there was going to be a lot of bickering about to whom that baby really belonged.

"How's Alice?"

"Alice? She's thrilled. Tired but thrilled. Come say hello!"

We went in room 516 and there was Alice, propped up in bed with her hair brushed and wearing a fresh gown, holding beautiful little Daisy Ella Cooper in her arms. I looked at my granddaughter and wept. In fact, we all did.

A month later, as the temperature became bearable and the marsh grass began to turn brown, we had a lovely christening at the Catholic church on Folly Beach. Once again, Patti and Mark, who were to serve as godparents, were staying in the Jolly Buddha. Maureen was still staying with Russ and Alice as she had been since she arrived two days after the baby was born, which was driving Russ seriously crazy. And Sara, who was suddenly in demand for a role in this movie or that play could not be with us.

"I still don't understand why she didn't come," Alice said over dinner at Aunt Daisy's.

"Are you serious? Because she's reading for the second time for a leading role in a Julia Roberts film," John said. "As I understand it, she's the most likely candidate."

Alice's face turned beet-red. The corners of Patti's mouth turned up.

"You always said she had what it took, Cate. I'm just so happy for her," Patti said.

"You never stop believing in your kids, Patti. That's just what a parent does."

Well, later on we were to learn that Sara did indeed win the part.

"Mom? Julia Roberts is so cool."

"Do you call her Julia?"

"Yeah! She's like totally grounded and normal and I love her, but so does everybody . . ."

Sara gushed. I listened, happy to know she was at last getting that chance she wanted, to act in a grand arena. Movies. What could be more exciting for her? I still preferred theater, but I was so happy for my Sara.

Maybe it was a week later, or maybe it was two weeks, but I know it was sweater weather on the beach. I found one of Dorothy's recipes for something called Widow's Punch and thought, what the heck? John and I both qualified for that one. So I mixed up a batch, chilled it, and poured it into a thermos. We had plans to take a walk down to the far end of the beach that overlooks the Morris Island Lighthouse. He was bringing sandwiches and I had beverage duty. I put the thermos in a canvas tote bag and when he arrived I got in his car and off we went. We passed locals, surfers, and tourists and finally came to the place where we parked and walked the distance to the part of the beach we wanted to see. Once there, I spread a blanket on the soft sand and John sat down beside me.

"Want a glass of Widow's Punch?"

"What? You want turkey or ham?"

"Let's share half and half," I said. "Yeah, it's Dorothy's recipe."

"Hmmm. Well, I brought something else with me," he said and pulled out a pair of wire-cutters. He was going to cut my ring off and I was going to cut his.

"Finally!" I said and stuck out my palm. In one snip and a twist, the shackles of Addison Cooper were off. "Let me do yours."

And I did.

"What should we do with them?" he said, holding the broken rings in his hand.

I stood up and offered him my hand. We walked to the water's edge.

"I'll bet you ten bucks you can't throw them to the lighthouse," I said.

"Really?"

He did the windup for the pitch and threw them far out into the water, but not far enough. The same thing happened with the second one.

"Too bad," I said. "Ten dollars is a lot of money."

"Too bad," he said, "what a waste of two good rings."

"Why's that?"

"Because I'm thinking pretty soon we'll just have to buy two more."

"John Risley! Are you asking me to marry you?"

"I don't know. I was just thinking of making an honest woman of you. Really. That's all."

"Oh, you want to marry me for the sake of the neighbors? The bohemians out here on Folly Beach? You think they care? You're such a terrible liar."

"Nah, I guess I wanted to ask you to marry me because I really love you, Cate." He reached in his back pocket and pulled out a little satin sack. "Tricia Gustofson at Crogan's said you'd like this. What do you think?" He held up a perfectly gorgeous diamond ring, the center stone surrounded by so many little diamonds it was almost blinding in the afternoon sun.

"You're asking me to marry you?" I said, as he slipped the ring over my knuckle.

"What would you say if I did?"

"Well," I stepped in close to him and kissed one cheek. "I'd say they got married on Folly Beach," I said, and kissed his other cheek. "And then they moved into the Porgy House and lived happily ever after."

"Isn't that a coincidence? That's exactly what I'd say, too."

AUTHOR'S NOTE

I became interested in the Charleston Renaissance when SCETV Radio's finest personality, noted historian and friend to authors everywhere, Walter Edgar asked me if I had read *Three O'clock Dinner* by Josephine Pinckney. I had not and he loaned me a copy, which I read and enjoyed tremendously. It seemed so contemporary but in its day (1945) it must have been controversial, as it touched on some topics that were still taboo in 2011.

I couldn't forget the book or the writer's voice, and as fate would have it, I mentioned that to Faye Jenson, the executive director of the South Carolina Historical Society, where I have served on the board for a few years. She said that she thought I should come down and read the papers of Dorothy and DuBose Heyward and others. So last summer, the summer of 2010, I did, beginning with the Heywards. My first discovery was that DuBose was a high school dropout and that Dorothy was very well educated, having studied at Columbia University and Radcliffe College. Then I discovered the huge economic disparities between them. Dorothy was a wealthy woman and DuBose was comfortable at the time they met but he had grown up in poverty. I ran across a copy of her birth certificate, on which her name is "Dorothea"—my name—and letterhead that stated she lived on Fifth and Twelfth in Manhattan—my old address—and that she was a member of the Cosmopolitan Club, and so am I. I began to wonder if Dorothea/Dorothy wasn't trying to tell me something, and if so, what was she trying to say? I then discovered a letter from a friend to her, calling her "Dottie," which my friends and family have called me all of my life. Every time I turned around, it seemed I was bumping into another coincidence or similarity. Okay, I thought, there's a story here and I'm going to try and tell it. Who was Dorothy Heyward?

The most interesting and curious fact of all might be that because she survived DuBose by many years, what is in those boxes at the SCHS is there because it was what Dorothy wanted us to know. Every single letter from her to DuBose is absent. Perhaps *he* did not save her letters or perhaps *she* disposed of them. We will never know. But scores of letters from DuBose to her were carefully preserved. It appears that Dorothy wanted us to have a one-sided conversation with DuBose, not her. It is my opinion that Dorothy always wanted DuBose to be the celebrity, the icon, the one who was remembered and revered. She loved him that much.

It is a matter of historic fact that Dorothy herself adapted DuBose's book *Porgy* for the stage and that she also had a great hand in creating the adaptation of *Mamba's Daughters* for the stage, the two most successful works with DuBose Heyward's name attached to them. But she shied away from taking credit for herself and, in fact, spent her widowhood making sure that DuBose's name appeared in the credits of all of Gershwin's productions of *Porgy and Bess* so that his estate would receive the royalties that were due.

And, finally, while Dorothy Heyward seems to have gone to great lengths to disappear into history as "just a girl from Ohio who wanted a career on the other side of the footlights," the facts appear to be different to me. True, she was diminutive in the extreme, and the fact that she was from Ohio may have rendered her more easily dismissed by

DuBose's crowd, but Dorothy Kuhns Heyward was a powerhouse, who married into one of Charleston's most prestigious families and spent her life doing everything she could for the man she fiercely loved. Theirs may be the most powerful love story of the Charleston Literary Renaissance.

For those who want to learn more about the Charleston Literary Renaissance, I offer the following reading list:

Renaissance in Charleston: Art and Life in the Carolina Low Country, 1900–1940, James M. Hutchisson and Harlan Greene, editors

Mr. Skylark: John Bennett and the Charleston Renaissance, by Harlan Greene

DuBose Heyward: A Charleston Gentleman and the World of Porgy and Bess, by James M. Hutchisson

A DuBose Heyward Reader, James M. Hutchisson, editor

Folly Beach: A Brief History, by Gretchen Stringer-Robinson

The Morris Island Lighthouse: Charleston's Maritime Beacon, by Douglas W. Bostick

A Talent for Living: Josephine Pinckney and the Charleston Literary Tradition, by Barbara L. Bellows

The Devil and a Good Woman, Too: The Lives of Julia Peterkin, by Susan Millar Williams

For those who want to read the work of the writers of the Charleston Literary Renaissance, I offer the following reading list:

Sea-drinking Cities, poems by Josephine Pinckney

Three O'clock Dinner, by Josephine Pinckney

Mamba's Daughters: A Novel of Charleston, by DuBose Heyward

Porgy, by DuBose Heyward

Peter Ashley, by DuBose Heyward

Carolina Chansons, by Hervey Allen and DuBose Heyward

The Doctor to the Dead: Grotesque Legends and Folk Tales of Old Charleston, by John Bennett

Scarlet Sister Mary, by Julia Peterkin

Green Thursday, by Julia Peterkin

ACKNOWLEDGMENTS

I always say that many hands go into the making of a book, but this time the population is so very important that I want to try and thank each person for their contributions. Where to start? It would have to be with Harlan Greene of Charleston. I was introduced to Harlan by mutual friends and now I hope I can say that he is a friend of mine, too. First, he is the consummate gentleman and a brilliant one at that. And he is a fascinating writer and wonderful historian. I devoured his books, notated them to death, but when we got together and discovered our mutual interest in the Heywards, he opened his generous heart and told me what he knew about Dorothy and DuBose, about the whole literary scene in Charleston and indeed in America during the twenties and the thirties. I think I tortured him with questions, but he was always so gracious and patient with me and he encouraged me to keep digging for new truths. Harlan, I am deeply in your debt and very grateful. Next would be James M. Hutchisson of the Citadel, whose biography of DuBose Heyward kept me up at night as did his work on the Charleston Renaissance that he edited with Harlan Greene. Like Harlan, Jim also answered my countless questions and encouraged me to take literary license with my story, because, after all, I'm writing fiction. So, Professor Hutchisson, I thank you mightily for your time, good humor, and support. Without these two gentlemen, this book simply could not be.

Well, shoot me, but I just put age before beauty. Now I bow and scrape to Faye Jenson, the executive director of the South Carolina Historical Society, and her lovely assistant, Mary Jo Fairchild. I had such a wonderful time learning about the Heywards within the walls of the Fireproof Building that houses this venerable institution and again, this book would be so much less rich without the treasures I found and the ones you led me to within your archives. Many thanks for all your insights and thoughts and most especially for your incredible hospitality.

Also many sincere thanks to Harriet MacDougal Rigney of Charleston for all her remembrances, good ideas, and friendship. Most especially, thank you for the introduction to Kathy Glick of Folly Beach, proud owner of the Porgy House, the lynchpin of this story. And to Kathy Glick, huge thanks for allowing me inside the precious and adorable Porgy House and for telling me your stories. I loved meeting you, and your hand in this book is a very important one indeed. Admittedly, this story evolved into something entirely different from the pitch I gave to you, but that's normal in this crazy business.

Thanks also to Lisa Bowen Hamrick for helping me locate a copy of Dorothy Heyward's obituary and to two very helpful folks from the Charleston Museum for information on the piano used by Gershwin: J. Graham Long, curator of history, and Jenifer Scheetz, archivist. And special thanks once again to Rees Jones for his help with the golf clubs. To Peter McGee of Charleston, for his wonderful story about Oscar Wilde, I say many, many thanks to you, sir! And special thanks to John Zeigler of Charleston for the pleasure of his company and a delightful afternoon of remembering.

I'd like to recognize and thank the following residents of Folly Beach, who opened their doors to me five years ago when this story was in its infancy: Carl Beckman, Mary J. Rhodes, Gretchen Stringer-Robinson, and Marlene Estridge. And many thanks to Randy Robinson, chief building official of the Sullivans Island Building Department, for reminding me which way the sand blows; to Jennet Robinson Alterman for information on Piccolo Spoleto; and to Sue Tynan of Suty Designs for helping me take my notes in style.

To my agent and great friend, Larry Kirshbaum, the most charming and elegant gentleman in the whole darn city of New York, with my undying thanks for his excellent counsel, and to my wonderful editor, Carrie Feron, whose patience seems to know no bounds and for her priceless wisdom—both of you—look out the window toward the Garden State. Yes, that is me curtsying and blowing you so many kisses of gratitude.

And to the entire William Morrow and Avon team: Brian Murray, Michael Morrison, Liate Stehlik, Adrienne Di Pietro, Kristine Macrides, Tessa Woodward, Lynn Grady, Tavia Kowalchuk, Seale Ballenger, Ben Bruton, Greg Shutack, Shawn Nichols, Frank Albanese, Virginia Stanley, Jamie Brickhouse, Rachael Brennan, Josh Marwell, Michael Brennan, Carl Lennertz, Carla Parker, Donna Waikus, Rhonda Rose, Michael Morris, Michael Spradlin, Gabe Barillas, Deb Murphy, and last but most certainly not least, Brian Grogan: Thank you one and all for the miracles you perform and for your amazing, generous support. You still make me want to dance!

To Buzzy Porter, huge thanks for getting me so organized and for your loyal friendship of so many years. Don't know what I'd do with myself without you!

To Debbie Zammit, seems incredible but here we are again! Another year! Another year of tuna salad on Mondays, keeping me on track, catching my goobers, and making me look reasonably intelligent. I know, I owe you so big-time it's ridiculous, but isn't this publishing business more fun than Seventh Avenue? Love ya, girl!

To Ann Del Mastro, George Zur, and my cousin Charles Comar Blanchard: all the Franks love you for too many reasons to enumerate!

To booksellers across the land, and I mean every single one of you, I thank you from the bottom of my heart, especially Patty Morrison and Larry Morey of Barnes and Noble, Tom Warner and Vicky Crafton of Litchfield Books, Sally Brewster of Park Road Books, and once again, can we just hold the phone for Jacquie Lee of Books-A-Million? Jacquie, Jacquie! You are too much, hon! Love ya and love y'all!

And a special thanks to those whose names I grabbed from real life and used for characters. If you recognize yourself acting strangely or being peculiar, it is just me having a little fun with my friends, especially Cathy Mahon and John Risley.

To my family—Peter, William, and Victoria—I love y'all with all I've got. I'm so proud of you and so grateful for your understanding when deadlines and book tours roll around every year. As always, just for being who you are, my heart swells with gratitude and pride when I think of you and you are never far away from the forefront of my mind. Every woman should have my good fortune with their family. You fill my life with joy.

Finally, to my readers, to whom I owe the greatest debt of all. I am sending you the most sincere and profound thanks for reading my stories, for sending along so many nice e-mails, for yakking it up with me on Facebook, and for coming out to book signings. You are why I try to write a book each year. I hope Folly Beach will give you something new to think about and somewhere new to try. There's a lot of magic down here in the Lowcountry. Please, come see us and get some for yourself!

I love you all and thank you once again.

If you enjoyed
FOLLY BEACH,
then you'll love
LOWCOUNTRY SUMMER.
Turn the page for a peek! Available now.

Welcome Back to Tall Pines

IT IS A GENERALLY ACCEPTED fact that at some point during your birthday, you will reassess your life. When you are young, and by "young" I mean the sum of your years is under twenty, your whole life is still in front of you. Your un-jaundiced eyes are sunlit and wide. Your lungs rise and fall with breathless optimism. Whom will you marry? Who will you become? Will you be blessed with good children? Live in China? Climb Everest? Visit the Casbah? Sail the Amazon? Will the riches of the world find their way to your door? The details of your future life are still shrouded in the opaque mists of time's crystal ball and you, the anxious and impetuous young you, hopping from one foot to the other, cannot wait to get there.

But, darlin', when your years creep north of thirty, your assessing eye blinks, drifts to the past to scan your scorecard because your future is pretty much a foregone conclusion. Or is it? Surely by forty, you *should* know who you are and how well you are doing with your life. At least you hope you'll have life under control by then.

At least that's what I was thinking about on that Sunday afternoon, the fifteenth of April, 2007, when most of my family gathered at Tall Pines. They were there to toast the culmination of my forty-six years and wish me well as I embarked on my forty-seventh. None of us knew about the disasters to come that would change me and everyone around me forever.

Had I not learned a thing? Apparently not. It was God's grace that my mother, Miss Lavinia, was gone to glory or she would have slapped me silly while whispering in an even jasmine tone her deepest disappointment in my judgment. Mother had taught me better. She stopped any nonsense before it could gain steam. But where was she when I needed her? Gone. Yes, I still suffered over my mother's death for many reasons, not the least of which was that as soon as we were reunited in life, she slipped through my fingers and died. It was completely devastating and very, very unfair. And, how would you like to have the job of filling Lavinia Boswell Wimbley's shoes? You would not. Never mind she literally had hundreds of pairs, one size smaller than my foot.

I looked around. Rusty and my brother, Trip, still together after all these years despite all the interference, were in the living room and as always the heat between them was excruciating. I often wondered if what mischief they had with each other between the sheets was as provocative as their behavior in the company of others. As he handed her a plate of food, any fool could see his other hand traveling to her lap for a tickle. So silly.

I wondered what my mother's friends Miss Sweetie and Miss Nancy thought about them, not that Rusty or Trip would have been even slightly wounded for one second to learn that they had embarrassed their elders. They were oblivious. The old crows, knowing them, probably found the lovebirds' croon to be titillating. Why, they still fooled around in chat rooms for singles, pretending to be college coeds! They thought it was hilarious! I guess it's fair to say that out here in plantation country, your social life was really truly only ever going to be what you made of it. And available men of their age were almost all gone, meaning deceased. Any old coots who were still on the prowl wanted young girls, younger than me, something that made me feel uncomfortable.

And you might know, Trip was still campaigning for Frances Mae to sign new separation papers that she had no intention of signing. Perhaps it was the fact that Rusty and Trip could not marry that kept their fires burning. We always crave what we cannot possess, do we not?

And Millie and Mr. Jenkins? They had enough going on between them to produce smoldering embers in every fireplace at Tall Pines Plantation, but they would never admit it and we rarely caught a glimpse of it. They were old-school, discreet and modest. Ah, discretion! I admired them for those qualities, although discretion seemed to be difficult for me to embrace. Let's be honest. When a suitable man came into my life, Miss Lavinia's blood coursed through my veins like the fast train from Dijon to Saint-Tropez.

Speaking of "all aboard the TGV"? My current beau was a wonderful guy named Bobby Mack. Bobby was a little bit shorter than I am and sort of stocky. But he was a willing fellow who was passionate about everything, including me. There were many reasons why we were not likely to marry, but the main one was that he was an unreliable companion. Every weekend and holiday and even today was spent working. Bobby raised pastured Heirloom pork to the music of Chopin, but every time I turned around, he was throwing a pig pull for a hundred people or climbing on a truck to personally deliver a carcass to Daniel Boulud in New York. It was annoying. And the other reason was that he always smelled like traces of the literal pits—deeply smoky and a little greasy—an occupational hazard which could not be washed away by any soap yet produced on earth. But when we'd argue and I would decide it was time to say good-bye forever, he would show up at my door with five pounds of bacon. That was about all it took to sustain us for another month or so. I'm a fool for pork. And to be honest, I liked the way he smelled, but when we were around other people, I would see them sniffing.

My handsome son, Eric, now a freshman at the University of South Carolina, was there also. He had come home for the day with Trip and Frances Mae's oldest daughter, Amelia, who was a junior at the university, majoring in American history. Yes, it was true. Amelia, who had sprung from the fiery womb of Satan's favorite hellcat, had become lovelier to behold with each passing year. Except for her unfortunate hair, poor thing—that endless tangle of black strings was all twisted up on her head and held with combs and rubber bands. But her eyes were nice, bright blue like Trip's, with thick lashes. Millie and I often wondered why Amelia chose to major in American history. Maybe the poor dear thought that if she scoured our country's past with enough diligence, she could find a reasonable explanation for the piss-poor protoplasm of her mother's genetic code. Who knows? Thank God Amelia was more like Trip.

But my Eric? It's incredible to say this but all of his learning-style differences seemed to have practically disappeared or else he had developed such strong study skills and compensating skills from years of Rusty's tutelage that it seemed that way. In any case, he had blossomed under Trip's attention and my flawless mothering. Do I hear a groan from the peanut gallery? Okay, here's the truth. Between Millie, Rusty and me, Trip and Mr. Jenkins, Eric had enough parents for ten boys. And of course, when Miss Lavinia was alive she doted on her only grandson.

And Richard, my ex? Eric's father? That British slime of the earth with his postured accent? The not-such-a-genius psychotherapist/psychiatrist? His contact with all of us had dwindled to a bare minimum and that suited us just fine. Eric was already in college, practically grown, and the last decade of his life had played out with only Richard's slightest presence or interest. Richard's loss, not ours.

The university was under an hour's drive from Tall Pines, but to Amelia and Eric, it was light-years away. Freeing Amelia of her chaotic life in Walterboro and moving Eric away from the plantation had brought about all the changes in them you would expect as children finally come of age. Independence! They were learning how to inhabit the adult world and to draw their own conclusions about worldly matters. They stood taller, and without prompting, even self-corrected their student slouch from time to time. They were less rowdy and more considerate of others. I looked around to see my Eric leaning forward, listening in earnest to Miss Sweetie as she piffled on and on about my recent purchase of a portion of her strawberry business.

I think Miss Sweetie was happy about it. She had no children to inherit and she had always been like an aunt to me. We finally agreed after a lot of discussion that she should remain on as the spokesperson for the company, the president emeritus, traveling to state fairs and appearing on the Food Network as our ambassador, judging cakes, pies, tarts, and breads made with our jams, and salads made with our pickles, and giving small scholarships to worthy students. My job was to oversee the management of the business, which required very little time as it wasn't overly complicated and she already had great managers in place. We changed the name of the business to Sweetie's, much simpler all around than the confection formerly known as TBD-JOTP, The Best Damn Jelly On The Planet. She had wanted to retire, but I assured her that if she did, she would be as dead as Kelsey's cow in six months, whoever Kelsey was. Even Millie got in on the conversation that took place on the veranda last fall.

"What you gone do with yourself if you retire, Miss Sweetie? You gone dry-rot! That's what! Retire? That's some fool, 'eah?"

We giggled and it came to me that Miss Sweetie just wanted to be assured that she wouldn't be in the way and that her expertise was truly wanted and valued. Tears came to my eyes thinking of my mother then. Older people are terrified of outliving their usefulness and I would never let Miss Sweetie feel that way. Miss Sweetie was loving her new role and I was staying busy when I wanted to be.

My old career was packed up in boxes. After all, the Lowcountry didn't need another interior decorator, especially when the nearby population who actually *used* a decorator only did so every hundred years or so. We loved our threadbare Aubussons and Niens and petit point curtains about which we could brag Sherman had overlooked in his infamous march, attempting to burn the Carolinas all the way to hell. We cherished every nick and dent in our great-grandmother's four-poster bed and every hidden compartment in our great-grandfather's secretary. Ancient coin silver candelabras were irreplaceable; mint-julep cups were closely guarded. Napkin rings were still in use, even for kitchen meals. Okay, maybe not for kitchen meals, but you know what I mean when I say that we were trying to sustain a certain way of life. Besides all that, Eric was gone off to find his future and what was I supposed to do with myself? So it was me, strawberries, and the pig farmer. Until my birthday of that year.

We were enjoying each other's company and sharing a late afternoon buffet lunch. Millie had prepared chicken Pirlau, a salad of asparagus and orange wedges with avocado in a citrus vinaigrette, and, of course, steaming-hot biscuits so light they literally collapsed and melted in our mouths like a soufflé. Miss Nancy brought the dessert fresh from her oven. It was a hummingbird cake. The smells of sugar and spice taunted us like a whispering siren from its spot on the buffet. And Miss Sweetie made a strawberry trifle with whipped cream, my ultimate favorite.

There had always been something charmed about the personality of Mother's dining room. Food tasted better there. When we gave a party of any sort, the room seemed to sing with its own pleasure of playing hostess and I always half expected Mother to pop out from behind the curtains, announcing her own miraculous resurrection.

The day was warm and we were serving ourselves in the dining room and finding a place to sit in the living room. All the doors were open and spring was in full bloom.

I was telling Miss Sweetie, Miss Nancy, and the others about a dream I'd had last night.

"I was on the veranda and I can't remember what I was wearing but I think it was a dress, a long one, some gauzy combination of nightgown and beach cover-up. I'm not sure. Mother suddenly came out through the French doors and oh! She was radiant! Absolutely radiant! And, here's the thing, y'all! She looked to me to be about my own age."

"Your mother was one of the most beautiful women I have ever known," Miss Sweetie said, choking up. "Lord! I miss her so! It squeezes my heart every time I think about her!"

"Moi aussi!" said Miss Nancy. "There was no one like our Lavinia." She handed Miss Sweetie a tissue from the pocket of her expensive cardigan, French in origin, I had no doubt. "Take hold of yourself," she whispered to Sweetie.

"I'm perfectly fine," Sweetie whispered back, slightly insulted, taking the tissue and blotting the corners of her eyes.

"Boy, is that the truth," I said, glossing over Miss Sweetie's fragile emotions, hoping that telling the rest of the story would hold them in check. "Miss Lavinia was one of a kind! Anyway, Mother took me by the hand and the next thing I knew we were flying all over the Low-country. We flew over the Edisto, the Ashepoo, and the Combahee rivers and down to Charleston, over St. Michael's Church and the custom house. We were so excited looking at all the houses on South

Battery. Then we came down and walked along the seawall, arm in arm. And I think she said something like 'Look! Look at all the happiness!' Suddenly we were on Church Street or maybe it was Tradd, looking in the windows. Every living room was filled with pink and white balloons and people laughing, having fun."

"*What?* Mom?" All the color drained from Eric's face. "That is a very strange dream," he said.

"No, it isn't," I said. "I dream about my mother all the time."

"No, Mom, it's bizarre."

"Really? Tell me why, Dr. Jung. Are you going to interpret my dream for us like your daddy used to do?" I was just teasing my adorable boy and reached out to ruffle his carefully combed mop of strategically placed locks that nearly covered his eyes. "Hey, are you okay?"

"No, uh, where's Amelia?"

"I'm right here," she said, walking across the rug and eating at the same time, a habit I detested. "Aunt Caroline, this is the best meal I've had in ages! I sure hope you're enjoying your birth—".

I forgave her on the spot.

"Amelia!"

"What, Eric? What's the matter with you?"

"Uh, we forgot something in the car. Be right back." Eric put his plate on the table and took Amelia's arm. "Come on."

"Right!" Amelia said. "OMG! How stupid are we?"

Amelia shook her head and they hurried from the room.

"What in the world?" Miss Sweetie said.

"Who knows?" Miss Nancy said.

"Humph," said Millie. "I got my own suspicions."

Millie knew about things before they came to pass, which could be useful, worrisome, or highly irritating.

"Kids!" I said. "Anyway, I kept thinking she was trying to tell me something."

"Maybe she was telling you to have some more fun," Miss Nancy said. "All work and no play? Should be the other way around once in a while. *N'est-ce pas?* That's why I'm off for France! What was she wearing?"

"Bon voyage!" said Miss Sweetie, still slightly bent out of shape.

"I think she was—no, wait . . . I can't remember!"

My back was to the door but I could see the sudden changes in Miss Nancy's expression and then Miss Sweetie's, and there was never a woman who could shoot her eyebrows to the stratosphere so quickly or grin as widely as Millie Smoak.

"What?" I said.

"Turn around," they said together.

There in the doorway to the outside stood Eric and Amelia holding bouquets of balloons. Pink and white. I nearly fainted. Miss Sweetie sank into a club chair with her hand over her mouth and Miss Nancy patted her on the arm. They both had tears in their eyes.

Rusty said, "Is this a joke?" She rubbed her arms as though she'd caught a sudden chill.

"No, darlin', it's just a little birthday greeting from our mother," Trip said, and chuckled.

"It was my idea but I don't know where the idea came from," Amelia said. "You never said anything about liking balloons before."

"Well, I adore them!" I said, and took the ribbons into my hand. "I really do!"

"Yeah," Eric said. "Amelia asked me what to buy you for a gift and I said you didn't need anything. So she said what about balloons?"

"It's so perfect, you just don't know!" I said, gave them a kiss on their cheeks, and turned to Millie. She was giggling like a schoolgirl and I joined her in a burst of laughter. Then I looked around the room at my slack-jawed gathering. "Oh, come on! You know Mother! Isn't this the grandest feat?"

"Freaky," Eric said.

"Completely weird," Rusty said.

"For once I agree with her," Amelia said, and hooked her thumb in Rusty's direction.

"Thanks," Rusty said.

"Well, I think it's completely wonderful," Miss Sweetie said. "Completely wonderful."

"I think so, too . . . is that the kitchen doorbell?" I said.

"I think that door is locked up," Millie said.

"Finally!" Trip said. "Probably my dear estranged wife with my daughters . . ."

I saw Amelia cut her eye at Rusty in disgust as though Rusty were the living embodiment of Hester Primm. I was glad Rusty had missed it because I didn't want there to be trouble and why insult her? Like most people, bad manners made me uneasy.

"I'll see about it," Mr. Jenkins said, making his way toward the dining room.

It buzzed and buzzed with such persistence that Millie and I and then Trip followed. What we found was a horror show. There in the doorway was off-the-wagon Frances Mae, gathered upright by the muscular arms of Matthew Strickland, the sheriff of Colleton County. On his other side stood Chloe, crying like a baby. Her forehead was cut and there was blood all over her. She was entirely disheveled, and Frances Mae, for once in her slovenly, drunken, miserable life, appeared to be penitent—that is, if her silence could be translated into regret.

"Oh Lord!" Millie cried, and hurried to the sink to wet a clean dishcloth.

"Daddy! Oh, Daddy!" Chloe had begun great gulping sobs. She was traveling toward hysteria and I didn't blame her. Who wouldn't be hysterical?

What had Frances Mae done now?

Trip swooped up his pudgy seven-year-old Chloe and sat her on the kitchen counter like a rag doll. Millie moved in and gently applied pressure to the wound, handing Trip a second cloth to wipe the rest of the blood away.

"It's all right, baby," she said to Chloe in the sweetest voice she had. "It's just a little bitty cut. You're not even gonna need stitches."

"Head wounds bleed a lot. Should I bring this one into the kitchen?" Matthew Strickland said, bringing our attention back to my low-life sister-in-law.

"Good grief!" I said. "Well? Let's see if you can park old Hollow Leg at the table. I'll make some coffee." I reached into the refrigerator for the coffee and into the cabinet for a filter.

Matthew poured Frances Mae into a chair and she put her head down on her folded arms and appeared to pass out. I began filling the coffeepot with water.

"It's all right now, sweetheart," Trip said to Chloe, and then asked, "So, what happened, Matthew?"

"I saw her Expedition swerving a little going down Highway 17, so I followed her. I knew it was Frances Mae because of the bumper stickers. So I figured she was liquored up. Then, no surprise, she turned on Parker's Ferry and I kept on behind her. When she went to turn into Tall Pines, she bounced off the gate and then slid into the ditch. So I picked them both up and brought them to you."

"Nice," I said, and flipped the switch on the coffeemaker. "God in heaven, Matthew, and that's a prayer of thanksgiving. What in the world would we do without you?"

"Well, you might be spending some more time in the courthouse. That's for sure." Matthew smiled at me and I remembered what it was like to fool around with him not so long ago. God, he was hot. Probably inappropriate for me, but white-hot, honey. By the look in his eyes I could see that he was still interested. I blushed. Okay, I didn't blush. I twitched in the South.

"Frances Mae?" Trip shook her shoulder. His voice was filled with disgust. "Frances Mae?" There was no response. The fumes coming from her were powerful enough to cure a string of bass. "She's as drunk as a goat. Out cold."

"Obviously," I said.

"The SUV is still in the ditch," Matthew said. "Fender's messed up."

"I'll call a tow truck directly," Mr. Jenkins said, and opened the cabinet where we kept the phone book. "Won't be the first time. Won't be the last."

"Jenkins?" Millie said. "Don't you be scratching they mad place!"

"Humph," Mr. Jenkins said. "My age? Say what I please."

At that precise moment, Eric and Amelia appeared at the kitchen door.

"Do you want us to light the candles on your cake, Mom?"

"Yeah, Eric's eating all the icing around the edges with his finger, Aunt Caroline."

"Gross, Eric!"

"You do it, too, Mom!" he said.

"Mother would never do something so vile, son," I said with a wink, and handed him a pack of matches from the drawer.

"Yeah, right," he said, and then he added, "Hey! What happened here?"

"Aunt Frances Mae wasn't feeling very well and she accidentally ran off the road into a ditch," I said, without missing a beat. After all, we had become accustomed to spinning this sort of *situation* into some reasonable explanation over the past few years.

"Mom!" Amelia called out.

Frances Mae raised her head and opened her eyes. "Yewr sisters are li'l bitches. Woulna drive Chloe," she said, and once again, her head went down and her lights went out.

She referred to her other daughters—my namesake Caroline, known as Linnie, and Isabelle, called Belle, as in southern, and she was anything but.

"Holy shit!"

"Eric!"

"Sorry! But she's baked!"

"In the parlance of the young people? Duh," I said, and gave Chloe a kiss on the hand. Poor thing. "Tell Miss Sweetie and Miss Nancy I'll be right out. The Wimbleys were never ones to let a *situation* ruin a party."

"A party?" Matthew said.

"Another birthday," I said, and put the back of my hand over my forehead, feigning the next step to a swoon.

"Well, I should be moving on, then," he said.

"Heavens no!" I said, and took him by the hand. "Come have a slice of cake!"

Matthew smiled. "Well, thanks! Don't mind if I do."

His entire six-foot-two frame just radiated testosterone. What was I thinking? Hmm, maybe he'd like to play with the birthday girl later on? I know, shame on me.

"Tell Rusty I've got my hands full here," Trip said.

"Oh, now. You go on out and sing for your sister's cake," Millie said, attaching a Band-Aid to Chloe's forehead. "Mr. Jenkins and I have this all under control."

"I want cake!" Chloe whimpered. "Can I please?"

"Of course! Just wash your hands and skedaddle!" Millie smiled and helped Chloe jump to the floor.

The candles were lit and everyone sang, wishing me a happy

birthday. Happy birthday? My pig-farmer boyfriend was in absentia, the county sheriff was the current cause of some very naughty thoughts, my drunk sister-in-law was passed out at my kitchen table, and my dead mother had sent me balloons. What else could a girl want?

Books by
Dorothea Benton Frank

FULL OF GRACE
ISBN 978-0-06-137453-1 (paperback)

THE LAND OF MANGO SUNSETS
A Novel
ISBN 978-0-06-171570-9 (paperback)

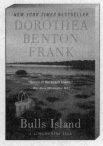

BULLS ISLAND
ISBN 978-0-06-207322-8 (paperback)

RETURN TO SULLIVANS ISLAND
A Novel
ISBN 978-0-06-198833-2 (paperback)

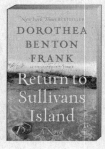

LOWCOUNTRY SUMMER
ISBN 978-0-06-202073-4 (paperback)

FOLLY BEACH
ISBN 978-0-06-211173-9 (paperback)

Visit www.DotFrank.com and find Dottie on Facebook!